W9-CBL-090

PRAISE FOR MELANIE DOBSON

The Winter Rose

"Melanie Dobson is a master at time-slip stories, and *The Winter Rose* is no exception. With skillful prose, impeccable research, heart-tugging characters, and a plot full of intrigue, Dobson keeps readers turning pages until the very end."

JODY HEDLUND, author of the Bride Ships series

"*The Winter Rose* is a blossom of hope in a broken and hurting world. From the snowy Pyrénées to the lush forests of Oregon, from the scars of war to the solace of family, Melanie Dobson weaves a story of how God can transform the pain of the past into a loving plan for the future. This book will remain in your heart long after you turn the final page."

STEPHANIE LANDSEM, author of *In a Far-Off Land*

"A magnificent novel set in the midst of WWII in France with ripples that continue to the present day. Dobson's beautiful descriptions, well-drawn characters, and deep insights pull the reader into this story and won't let go until long after the last page. Altogether brilliant and breathtaking."

LIZ TOLSMA, bestselling author of *A Picture of Hope*

The Curator's Daughter

"Fans of Kristy Cambron and Rachel Hauck will devour this split-time tale with two equally strong story lines."

LIBRARY JOURNAL

"Drawing from historical events and modern-day issues, Dobson creates a story that transcends the years and combines multiple themes—resilience, faith, and forgiveness—and is filled with vivid historical details and emotional twists. . . . A great book for fans of WWII inspirational stories."

HISTORICAL NOVELS REVIEW

"Melanie Dobson is a master. With great insight into racism in the past and in the present, the novel brings up deep questions about what risks we would take to stand up for what's right. Exceptional research shines on each page, but the intertwined stories of Hanna, Lilly, and Ember are what kept me flipping those pages. A gem of a novel."

SARAH SUNDIN, bestselling and Carol Award–winning author of *When Twilight Breaks* and the Sunrise at Normandy series

"A haunting, totally immersive novel."

CHRIS FABRY, bestselling author of *Under a Cloudless Sky*

"Intriguing, multilayered, and suspenseful, *The Curator's Daughter* winds through generations like the labyrinth it portrays. . . . I started this book late one morning and could not put it down. Melanie Dobson's historical research alone is astounding, but the story is also brilliant and masterfully told. Readers of time-split fiction will love this."

CATHY GOHLKE, Christy Award–winning author of *Night Bird Calling* and *The Medallion*

"An unforgettable saga. . . . Melanie Dobson transports readers to Nuremberg, Germany, during World War II, telling what might seem at first a familiar tale of the Nazi regime, yet leaving us with a new, deeper understanding of the legacy of evil left in its wake decades later. The history at the heart of this story should never be forgotten."

MICHELLE SHOCKLEE, author of *Under the Tulip Tree*

Memories of Glass

"*Memories of Glass* is a remarkable, multilayered novel that weaves stories of friendship and faith in wartime Holland together with a modern-day orphanage in Africa. Memorable characters portray the complexity of human relationships and reveal the lasting consequences of our choices, whether cowardly or courageous, and the mysteries kept me turning pages, leaving me with much to ponder."

LYNN AUSTIN, bestselling author of *If I Were You* and *Legacy of Mercy*

"Like colored shards in sunlight, Melanie Dobson once again shines her light of truth in this elegantly complex and gripping tale of the hidden terrors of the Netherlands during WWII. *Memories of Glass* is a remarkable story and one that will linger in the hearts of readers long after the last page."

KATE BRESLIN, bestselling author of *For Such a Time*

"Breathtaking, heartbreaking, and ultimately uplifting, *Memories of Glass* shows the beauty of helping others, the ugliness of people helping only themselves, and the destructive power of secrets through the generations. Melanie Dobson's memorable characters and fine eye for detail bring the danger of the Netherlands under Nazi occupation to life. This novel will stay with you."

SARAH SUNDIN, award-winning, bestselling author of *The Sky Above Us*

"Heart-wrenching history combines with gripping characters and Melanie Dobson's gorgeous writing to create a tale you won't be able to put down—and won't want to. *Memories of Glass* is an amazing, intricately woven story of finding light in the least likely of places."

ROSEANNA M. WHITE, bestselling author of the Shadows over England series

Hidden Among the Stars

"This exciting tale will please fans of time-jump inspirational fiction."

PUBLISHERS WEEKLY

"A romantic tale of castles, lost dreams, and hidden treasures wrapped inside a captivating and suspenseful mystery complete with an unpredictable, unforeseen, and unexpected ending. Not a book to miss!"

MIDWEST BOOK REVIEWS

"*Hidden Among the Stars* is a glorious treasure hunt, uniting past and present with each delightful revelation. It's must-read historical fiction that left me pondering well-crafted twists for days."

MESU ANDREWS, award-winning author of *Isaiah's Daughter*

Catching the Wind

"Dobson creates a labyrinth of intrigue, expertly weaving a World War II drama with a present-day mystery to create an unforgettable story. This is a must-read for fans of historical time-slip fiction."

PUBLISHERS WEEKLY, starred review

"Dobson skillfully interweaves three separate lives as she joins the past and present in an uplifting tale of courage, love, and enduring hope."

LIBRARY JOURNAL

"A beautiful and captivating novel with compelling characters, intriguing mystery, and true friendship. The story slips flawlessly between present day and WWII, the author's sense of timing and place contributing to the reader's urge to devour the book in one sitting yet simultaneously savor its poignancy."

ROMANTIC TIMES

"Readers will delight in this story that illustrates how the past can change the present."

LISA WINGATE, national bestselling author of *Before We Were Yours*

THE WINTER ROSE

a novel

THE WINTER ROSE

MELANIE DOBSON

Tyndale House Publishers
Carol Stream, Illinois

Visit Tyndale online at tyndale.com.

Visit Melanie Dobson's website at melaniedobson.com.

Tyndale and Tyndale's quill logo are registered trademarks of Tyndale House Ministries.

The Winter Rose

Cover designed by Faceout Studio, Amanda Hudson

Interior designed by Dean H. Renninger

Edited by Kathryn S. Olson

Published in association with the literary agency of Natasha Kern Literary Agency, Inc., P.O. Box 1069, White Salmon, WA 98672.

For information about special discounts for bulk purchases, please contact Tyndale House Publishers at csresponse@tyndale.com, or call 1-855-277-9400.

Library of Congress Cataloging-in-Publication Data

A catalog record for this book is available from the Library of Congress.

ISBN 978-1-4964-4421-9 (HC)

ISBN 978-1-4964-4422-6 (SC)

Printed in the United States of America

28 27 26 25 24 23 22
7 6 5 4 3 2 1

ANN MENKE

My beautiful friend and storyteller.

I love your heart for God's grace

and your passion for restoration and all things French.

PLEA FROM GURS, FRANCE

We, far from our native forest
Lost in a foreign land
Are tender young trees that a woodman
Uprooted with violent hand.
Surely there must be another;
Somewhere on this earth
To plant in a friendlier climate
Our roots as they seek a new birth.

Alive are the delicate fibers
In every tender shoot;
Which need but the hand of a gardener
To help them take new root.
Richly would we reward him
His toil and ardent care.
Resplendent foliage render—
In return for his being there.

In the spreading shade of our branches
Would all mankind rejoice;
And from our limbs heavy-laden
Pluck fruits of the finest choice.
Where are you, gentle gardener?
From the north blows a wind of hate,
Take us into your keeping
Before it is too late.

WRITTEN BY REFUGEE CHILDREN
INTERNED DURING WORLD WAR II

Chapter One

SAINT-LIZIER, FRANCE
SEPTEMBER 1943

Sunlight broke through the mist like a spotlight in Hollywood, the crimson globe guiding Grace Tonquin and the twelve children in her care. It was only minutes now before they'd be tucked away in the cathedral of Saint-Lizier, hidden from the light.

Red sky in the morning—

Grace tried to shake off the sailor's warning as she led the children beside a moss-cloaked wall, the jagged stones along this passage blocking out the embers of dawn. The cobbles were slippery under her oxfords, her toes blistered, but she couldn't stop now. Americans had been recalled home, but she couldn't leave until all the Jewish children had been hidden or evacuated from France.

Élias, the oldest boy, carried a younger child named Louis in one arm even as he lifted his sister, Marguerite, over a puddle, the smell of rain drifting across their shadowed path with the autumn leaves.

Grace had spent her childhood summers hiding from lights and the crowds that oohed and aahed as if she were a celebrity. But the crowds never really saw her. The daughter of Ruby Tonquin, that's who they saw, not a timid child who wanted to lock herself into a closet at the Beverly Wilshire Hotel. A strange girl who preferred exploring the beaches along Santa Monica rather than perusing the shops. The only person in California, it seemed, who didn't worship Ruby.

Marguerite turned around, and her eyes swelled like the sun. Grace leaned down, pressing her finger against her lips. The quiet, she'd explained to all the children, was their ally until they reached the cathedral. Silence, their shield.

The oldest girl in their group was fifteen, and she turned a corner ahead of them. All the children followed Suzel like ducklings in their drab winter coats, small knapsacks weighing down their hands, the padding of *espadrilles*—woven shoes—against stone. It was much too warm for the heavy coats, but they would need them soon when snow fell in the nearby mountains.

"Muet comme une carpe," Grace whispered.

As mute as a carp.

Two of the kids bumped into each other, giggling in spite of her mandate in both French and English for silence. They didn't understand, couldn't possibly understand, what was at stake.

She couldn't even comprehend it all, but she'd heard rumors of what was happening outside Vichy France. That violence was bleeding over into the few zones still considered free for Jewish children. She had to get these children out of France, to a safe place, before the Nazis found them.

She'd also heard rumors of the Allies gaining ground in the war against Germany, heard reports from Charles de Gaulle, a French general who had secured himself up in London, but all she saw on the ground were the French police and Nazi officers who seemed to hate anyone Jewish, no matter what age. When the war was finally over, she prayed the children would be safe, but until then, she and her coworkers who remained in France continued to help.

Ahead was the cathedral, its medieval bell tower crowning the sky, the stone walls a fortress. A place of great comfort, she thought. A sanctuary like the farmhouse where she and the children had stayed last, sleeping most of the day before resuming their night travels. These children had been walking for two nights now, relocating from the orphanage in a village called Aspet. The weariness had crept into their bones, sores pocking their feet, but they couldn't stop. Soon, Roland Mercier had said, they would hide together in a château until he secured passage for these kids over the Pyrénées mountains, into Spain and then Portugal.

The stillness of these morning hours was a blessing, but it was almost too quiet, she thought. No bark of a dog or rattle of the dairyman's wagon. Even the breeze that rustled up the alley felt like a desert wind, as if they were the only ones who dared enter this river town.

She shook her head, trying to shake off her premonition. The cathedral was the only safe place in this village to hide her wards. A few more steps, then they would hide until night fell.

A paper fluttered down the narrow street, dancing across the cobblestones until it landed at her feet. *Avis Aux Israelites*, it read. Another notice to the "undesirables," as they were called, asking them to present themselves to the authorities.

How she hated these notices. The constant reminder that the government—a body of men who'd sworn to protect—was after her children.

She kicked the paper toward the gutter. They had to find refuge for these kids in Spain before the French police or the winter storms found them.

Marguerite reached for her hand, and Grace paused, bending down again to look into her eyes. "What is it?"

"I have to use the toilet," Marguerite whispered.

"We're almost there." Less than a block now.

"I can't wait." The threat of tears, the enemy from within, capped the urgency in Marguerite's voice. Clothing was something they could clean, but on these quiet streets, tears from a nine-year-old could be the death of them.

A prayer, as natural as the breath on her lips, slipped out, and she listened for any sound. All was quiet except the sway of branches in the breeze.

She must stop for Marguerite. To protect every child in her care.

Élias handed the boy to Suzel and moved back toward his sister, both hands secured casually in his pocket. A tourist, it seemed, on a stroll through this ancient town. His tan overcoat, the relaxed posture, all of it was inspired by his favorite cartoon character, the Belgian reporter and adventurer named Tintin. While he might have seemed indifferent, Élias's brown eyes were as fierce as a lion's. He was ready to pounce if necessary, protect those he loved.

At thirteen, Élias could be hotheaded, but he was always reliable. She could trust him to help Suzel escort the other kids into the cathedral.

"Snowy," he whispered to his sister, the nickname he'd swiped from Tintin. "Are you hurt?"

"She needs the toilet," Grace said.

"Blistering barnacles." Élias, it seemed, had memorized everything from the comic including the many gibes of Captain Haddock, Tintin's best friend.

"Get the others to the church while I help her."

Élias hesitated, his face turning toward the convent. "I will keep watch for you."

"No," Grace said, urging him forward so he and the others would be safe. "Tell the sisters we will be there soon."

Élias kissed Marguerite's cheek before stepping back in place as the rear guard. A home—that's what she wanted for all these children. But not today. Right now, they needed only the basics—food, water, and a few hours of sleep.

Sunlight sparked across the sky, the fiery red fading away.

"We must hurry," she whispered to Marguerite as they ducked under an archway, rushing back to a courtyard behind a row of shops, a place away from the wind. Grace wanted to plug her nose at the stench from those who'd already used the grass as a latrine, but she clutched her rucksack to the side instead as she helped Marguerite remove her heavy coat, counting as the girl relieved herself in a corner.

Each second marked another step as her wards shuffled away. Another breath of life as they swam along, quiet as fish.

Marguerite, like all the others, had much practice in caring for herself. More than a year ago she'd fled with her mother and brother from their home near Paris, ultimately relocating to an internment camp called Gurs, located west of here. Grace only knew a bit of her and Élias's story, but it was enough to know they could persevere. Resiliency, that's what this war, the animosity around them, had given these children. Each one had endured more than any adult Grace had known in America. They'd already seen much in their escape from the Nazis, and now they were running again.

When would they finally be free from the fear that someone might steal them away? She prayed the running would end when the children crossed over the jagged mountains that fortified Southern France, into the somewhat-neutral country of Spain. Once she met up with Roland, her coworker who would lead them partway up the mountains, she'd return to Camp de Gurs to help any other kids who needed to leave France.

More light flickered across the sky, making it impossible for their convoy to hide. Daylight was as dangerous as the noise.

"Come along." Grace's finger shook as she pointed toward the exit. They had to rush into the cathedral before the sisters locked the gate.

Marguerite pulled up her tights, slipped her arms into her coat, not bothering to button it before she retrieved her knapsack. They hurried back through the narrow corridor, but before they stepped into the street, Marguerite threw her hand in front of Grace, stopping her.

"La cigarette," she whispered.

Another gust of wind, and Grace smelled the acrid smoke. Only a whiff, but it burned her nose, her throat. Cigarettes meant someone other than the nuns was near.

They must reach the cathedral before the town awakened. Before whoever was smoking the cigarette knew an American Quaker woman and a French Jewish girl had stumbled into their world.

She must move now for the sake of Marguerite and all the children.

"One," Grace whispered, the count of English numbers familiar to her ward. "Two."

But three seconds didn't seem nearly long enough. Not when they didn't know who was outside.

Her heels planted in the cobblestones, her legs paralyzed in full rebellion as the numbers extended in her head. Six, seven, then eight, piling up like the beans she'd used to teach the children arithmetic.

When she finally tugged on Marguerite's hand, a pair of strong arms wrapped themselves around her waist, pulling her back from the street.

She swallowed her screams lest they shatter the silence, struggling instead against the hold.

"Grace—" The man's voice was low, strong, like the breaking of this new day.

It took a moment before she realized he knew her name.

Marguerite recognized him first, releasing Grace's hand to cling to his trouser leg, and her fear began to subside, the struggle draining away, the man still holding her waist. His face was obscured by the shadows, but when he said her name again, she knew Roland had found them.

"You are safe now." He relaxed his hold to pick up Marguerite. "But you have to leave Saint-Lizier."

"We've just arrived—"

"Vite," he said. "There's no time to spare."

She moved toward the street. "I have to round up the children."

"Oh, Colibri . . ."

Hummingbird. A name he'd chosen when they first started working together in the labor camps. For all of her flittering, she supposed.

Why was he holding her back now when they should run?

An automobile rumbled over the cobblestones, then she saw two men with royal-blue uniforms and shiny black boots march into the street, their brass buttons glimmering in the morning light.

"We're too late," Roland said.

Each policeman held a gun as if her children might fight back, and she stepped into the street, crisp leaves stirring over her shoes. A war was being fought across Europe—why must the police focus on hunting down the country's children? They hadn't committed a crime. Not like the Nazis who'd taken over Northern France.

She'd talk to the French officers like she'd done a few months ago on the train, tell them that these children were under the protection of the Vichy government. They couldn't take her children away.

"Grace." Roland jerked her into the alley. "You can't help them right now."

"I will speak to the police!"

"And they will shoot you. What would that do to the children?"

"They won't—"

"They will," he insisted. "You and Marguerite must run the opposite direction. Follow the river south."

But she wouldn't cower. She would fight with her words instead of guns, no matter how terrified she was.

Grace shook off his arm, the wind whipping hair into her face, ready to face the police, but then she heard another rumble, this one like thunder. A canvas-covered truck pulled in front of the children, a half-dozen soldiers piling out, red armbands stretched around their brown uniform sleeves.

When had the Nazis arrived in Saint-Lizier?

"Dear God—" The plea fell from her lips, begging for mercy for them all.

The men began pushing her children into the truck, silence replaced with sobbing, and she wanted to scream. Stop all this madness with rational words.

She turned to Roland. "I can't just stand here."

"If you leave in that truck—" he nodded at Marguerite—"the Nazis will surely find her."

Grace sank against the wall of cold stones. "Take her to a safe place. Please . . ."

Back in Aspet, Roland had mapped this route through the hills for her and the children since they could no longer travel by train. He could find someone to care for Marguerite until Grace returned.

"I must go." He rattled off directions to a church outside town where they could hide. "Wait for me there."

"I can't do this."

He tilted her chin up in the cup of his hand. "You must fly, Grace. For one more day."

One more day. That was the mantra she'd lived by for months now. She could endure, with God's help, for twenty-four hours, no matter how each minute broke her heart.

"God be with you," he said, kissing her cheek.

Then he was gone. Off to help someone else in these morning hours.

Marguerite buried her head in the folds of Grace's wool skirt so she didn't have to watch her brother being taken away. How could she leave this girl behind to rescue the others?

Almost everything in France felt impossible.

The soldiers took the tallest child first—Suzel—forcing her into the truck. Grace wanted to bury her head as well, the scene too much to bear, but looking away, ignoring their pain—she must watch, even in their pain, *especially* in their pain, lest she abandon them again.

She couldn't see their faces from this place, only a shadow of their forms, but she prayed for each child as they were pushed inside.

"Protect them," she whispered. "Help them know Your love."

Grace brushed back Marguerite's hair, the girl's tears soaking her coat. "I'm sorry."

Marguerite glanced up before burying her head again. "The colors hurt my eyes."

Grace saw no color now except the daffodil petals of dawn, defying the sorrow in her heart. If only she could paint the sky black again, wash the light away. Instead she watched these men from the shadows round up her children. And she could do nothing to stop them.

One of the sisters was taken from the cathedral. And then the remaining children were loaded into the truck. Ten she counted before a German closed the gate. Not eleven.

Had she miscounted?

She scanned the plaza but didn't see anyone else.

As the trucks rolled away, Grace closed her eyes, leaning her head against the stone wall. The children she was supposed to care for, fight for, were gone. She'd failed those entrusted to her.

Marguerite strung the rucksack straps over her shoulders, ready to move.

She had one girl left beside her. One who needed a place to hide.

She wouldn't fail this time.

Grace checked the area again, searching for the eleventh child, but the stony passage and plaza had been scared into silence.

As she and Marguerite rushed out of Saint-Lizier, toward the covering of pine hills in the distance, the question haunted her.

How would she ever be able to free these children now?

CHAPTER TWO

Yamhill County, Oregon
September 2003

Conifer branches bobbed in the wind, raining needles across Addie Hoult's rental car. She switched on her wiper blades and instantly realized her mistake. Between the cloud cover and haze and sappy wiper fluid smearing the glass—how would she ever find the Tonquin cottage if she couldn't see the road?

Rain she'd been expecting in Oregon, but the water variety, not a downpour of pine.

Gravel crunched under the Civic's tires, the sound like kernels exploding in hot oil. She'd give just about anything right now for a bowl of freshly popped corn, slathered in butter. A frosty Coca-Cola in a real glass. Blackberries on a scoop of homemade ice cream.

On the long flight between Chattanooga and Portland, she'd eaten spaghetti from an aluminum tray. Then she drove an hour west from the airport until she reached the small town of Newberg, rich in history, she'd read, from Quaker pioneers. Home to both President Hoover and pinot noir. In this county, she hoped to find a family member to help her dear friend Charlie. *Papa C*, the girls at Sale Creek called him. The man who'd stepped in as a father a decade ago when Addie had none.

Now Charlie had a disease called myelodysplastic syndrome—MDS. His bone marrow was failing. His body, in essence, had stopped producing red blood cells. A drug called danazol was keeping him alive, along with regular transfusions and prednisone, but without an infusion of healthy stem cells, this man who'd saved her life might die before the end of the year.

Charlie's doctor had tried unsuccessfully to find what they called an HLA match in their database. He needed a bone marrow transplant from a sibling, preferably, or a niece or nephew. A blood relative under the age of sixty to save his life.

The doctor had agreed to test anyone Addie could find. A family member willing to donate a part of themselves to someone they might never have met. Or barely remembered.

Addie had veered off from civilization in Newberg, onto a dim back road that curved through a valley. A few lights twinkled in the hills at first, but the forest around her grew dense when she turned onto a narrow lane. And the lights disappeared.

She should have stopped for food in town, but between the travel and time difference—back in Tennessee it was two in the morning—all she'd wanted was a bed. The rental agent had assured her that the cabinets in the cottage were stocked, and at the moment, Addie wasn't the least bit picky. She'd heat up a can of soup or something and then sleep for a solid eight hours before she resumed her search.

Stopping the car again, Addie reached for the directions she'd printed before leaving home. After a mile on this county road, the agent had told her, she'd reach Laurel Ridge. There she was supposed to turn right.

According to her odometer, more than a mile had passed now, and she'd yet to find a connecting road. Switching her beams to high, she scanned ahead. She couldn't see much beyond the trees and a barn, but this valley was supposed to be tucked back between farms and forest and vineyards that attracted thousands of tourists each fall.

Her foot on the gas pedal, she crawled forward again, searching the bramble below boughs of pine for a place to turn. Around a bend, two miles up the road, she finally saw a street sign.

L—el Ri—

That's all she could read between the drapery of vine, but it was close enough.

A quick scan of the narrow road, and she turned right. A wall of leaves rose on both sides and over the top, circling her car like a wreath. Laurel, she assumed, although she didn't have any idea what laurel looked like.

Anything could hide in those branches.

Blackberries. Bunnies. Bigfoot.

Lists, however random, usually brought some sort of order to her scattered brain, helping her make sense of the world. When she was a girl, she used to spend hours piecing together misfit Tetris blocks on her Nintendo, creating order from chaos. In a strange way, the structure steadied her when her home was anything but steady.

As an adult, she relied on her own rule of three, patterns of words to calm the racing in her mind. But this list with its nod to Bigfoot did little to comfort her tonight. She hit the button for the automatic locks, as if this legend of a creature might try to hop into her car for a ride.

The road climbed between the trees, and even with cool air pouring through the vents, the tight walls made her sweat. Surely the road would break out onto a ridge soon. Maybe even a view of the lake if the starlight cut through the clouds.

Her car shook as if Sasquatch himself had stomped on the gravel, the entire ridge trembling, and she braced herself. A gust, that's all it was, sweeping leaves over the hill, but still she stopped the car, waiting for the wind—and her heart—to calm.

Tara Dawson, the rental agent, said the cottage was only a half mile up, but the woman's directions had already missed their mark. She'd give it another mile and then head back to Newberg. Hopefully the hotel she'd passed would have an unoccupied room.

Flipping open her mobile phone, Addie scanned the screen, searching for the climb of gray bars, but it seemed no phone service was to be had on Laurel Ridge. Tara had warned her of that possibility, but she hadn't been concerned until a weather delay scrambled her plans to arrive here long before dark.

She was supposed to call Emma Tonquin when she reached the house, but a late-night call would startle Charlie—Emma's husband. She didn't want to put her friend in the awkward position of having to explain why Addie was in Oregon. Emma wanted to tell him after Addie found one of his relatives.

She would give Emma an update in the morning, then she'd begin to search. Someone around here, she hoped, would remember the family who built Tonquin Lake.

Laurel Ridge Road ended abruptly, leaving her with two branches of lane, one shooting out to her left, the other right. Frustrated, she reviewed Tara's directions, but there was no mention of a fork in the road. The rental car office had supplied her with an Oregon map, but its neat lines didn't spread beyond the main roads.

Tara had said to turn right at the last crossroads, then Addie would see the house straight ahead. Once she was on the ridge, the woman said, the cottage would be easy to find. *Easy peasy*—those were her specific words.

But nothing seemed easy out here.

Ferns grew along both roads, their fronds covered in dust. The left path looked slightly more groomed, so she veered left this time. Seconds later Addie drove under a tunnel built of bramble and pine. Potential headlines shot through her mind as she crept forward, all of them centered around a woman lost in the Pacific Northwest. But she was almost to the cottage. Only fear would stop her, and she refused to succumb.

Another bend, and the trees began to clear. Stopping the car, she turned off the headlights. Once her eyes adjusted, maybe she could see the lake in the distance and, alongside it, the cottage where she was supposed to spend the next week searching for the Tonquins.

Slowly she began to focus in the faint starlight on another cropping of trees across the ridge, some of the tallest ones she'd ever seen. And then she saw something else. A tower cresting the pines.

Her heart pounding, the headlights rekindled, she began driving again until she reached what appeared to be a rutted driveway, overrun with grass. As she moved up the drive, her jaw dropped at the sight of an old Victorian manor, both lovely and creepy in this light, with peeling red paint and worn white trim along the porch and roof. A house that didn't look anything like the pictures Tara had sent.

The rental agent, she decided, should be fired. So far, the woman hadn't gotten anything right.

Addie wished she was back in Chattanooga. Wished that Charlie was well enough so he and Emma could travel to Oregon together to look for his family.

The house appeared to be completely surrounded by trees and thicket, some of the branches brushing against the windows. Ahead was a gate linking a picket fence around the property, and beyond it was a small yard and porch. The key was tucked away under a flowerpot, the rental agent had said, hidden on the front stoop. Easy to find.

Just like the house.

She should have packed a flashlight—would have if she'd known a jungle awaited her—but the car's headlights would have to do.

Tentatively she stepped outside in her jeans and REI sandals, willing her heart to slow its rapid beat as she walked toward the gate. This was ludicrous really. Tara said it was a comfortable cottage. Small. Quaint. And the most important part, it was overlooking Tonquin Lake.

Charming—that's how Tara had described it. Even if the charm had faded on the exterior, perhaps it had been retained inside. The flip of a switch, and it was probably a lovely, well-groomed place.

Light would change everything.

Addie lifted the gate's latch to retrieve the key, holding her ground in a confidence rooted from years scaring off men in her mom's apartment, unwilling to yield to their demands. Typically they were too distracted to bother her, but she'd learned early how to tell if one of them posed a threat. A solid knee to the midsection worked well, followed by a fortress built from a dresser and chairs to block her door.

The wind stilled on the other side of the gate, inside a cocoon of trees, even as rain—the liquid variety—began falling on her head. The gate opened about a foot before catching, and she scooted through it, shivering as she studied the house. Part of her was drawn to this place while another inwardly vocal part was horrified at entering alone, day or night.

As she took another step forward, Addie gasped, her heart almost springing out of her chest.

A flutter of wings in the shadows.

A bat. An owl. A giant moth.

Some sort of creature flew across her path, and she was done. Not even the familiar patterns in her lists would calm the chaos.

Backing up through the gate, she didn't bother to close it.

The house would have to wait until morning.

Chapter Three

Grace rocked Marguerite inside a drafty loft until the girl finally slept. Then she leaned back against the knobby wall as light stole through the open windows and chinks between stone. They hadn't made it to the church, but she prayed this dilapidated barn, set back from the road, would keep them safe until darkness fell again.

Love is like death, a French worker once told her. The pain of it felt like death this morning. Roland, she prayed, would find the other children. Negotiate their release and return them to her.

Most of their team—Les Secours Quakers, they were called—had gone home to America or the United Kingdom, but a handful continued to partner with Roland and their other French friends to help children still interned at the horrific Camp de Gurs. The adults knew quite well that they might not survive the war, but they still risked everything to rescue these kids, wanting them to know, deep in their hearts, the love of God.

While Roland had spent years in England after graduating from Oriel College at Oxford, he had grown up in this southern region of France—now called Vichy—and seemed to have endless connections in these hills. He knew innately who to trust and who they must avoid, where to find food and when they must hide.

Straw scratched her legs between her long skirt and the socks she wore with her oxfords—one of the many things she'd taken for granted even through the Great Depression. After leaving her mother's lair in Hollywood, she'd had all she needed on her grandparents' dairy farm, centered in a peaceful community of Quakers.

The sweet smell of hay, the familiar stench of manure, reminded her of their farm in Oregon. Of the years spent with Grandpa and Grams Tonquin after they'd rescued her, enfolding her into their arms and lives. Saving her, really, by introducing her to the boundless love of God and the simplicity of their faith. And then they'd encouraged her to help others.

But how could she continue to help when the Germans and French were collaborating to apprehend her children?

She'd started walking three days ago with twelve boys and girls, all of them sad but willing to leave the farmhouse where they'd lived for almost a year. The children's faces ticked slowly through her mind, the color of their eyes, the scars on their knees and chins. She knew their favorite foods. Which toys they liked best. How to cheer them up when they ached for their families.

While she and the other aid workers had partnered with the Vichy government in the first two years of the war, officials were no longer helping them shelter the children. Most of their parents had already been deported, transported east to what the regime was calling *centres d'hébergement*—lodging centers—but no one believed they were simply lodging the Jewish people. Before they left, each parent had given the Quakers permission to escort their child, if necessary, to a relative living outside France.

She closed her eyes, praying for Élias and Suzel and each child by name. Praying that someone would rescue them like God had rescued her. That they would each experience His boundless love.

A goat bleated outside the barn, and she tucked Marguerite close beside her in bedcoverings made from their coats. If a farmer entered, her story was ready. An American woman—that much was accurate—and the wife of a Frenchman. She and her daughter were refugees who'd gotten lost on their way to visit family in Saint-Lizier.

Marguerite's star was no longer stitched on her coat, the red *Juive* erased from her identity card, the rest of her paperwork sewn into her clothing. But the only light this girl needed was the one deep inside her, a God-given light to love others. Help instead of harm.

Marguerite and Élias's father was an Aryan man, a doctor who'd been respected in Paris. She didn't know much of his story, but their mother—Madame Dupont—said he'd sold his soul to the devil.

Madame Dupont was a Jewish woman who'd been born in Paris. After the Nazis took over Northern France, she and her children, like so many others, had been promised a safe haven in the southern villages and countryside, a place the Nazis would never occupy. One more lie of this regime. The Germans marched right into Vichy in November of last year. No place in the entirety of France was safe now from the Nazis or French collaborators.

The local police sent Madame Dupont and her three children to the internment camp in Gurs, once used for the Spanish refugees. A desolate place where organizations like the American Friends Service Committee—AFSC—helped provide sustenance for the children until Americans were no longer welcome in France. Then they'd changed their name to Les Secours Quakers.

When the camp first opened, some of the children had been released to live in homes with Grace and the other Quaker men and women who offered assistance, but the Nazis had begun recalling these children so they could deport families together. While some of the parents wanted their children returned, Madame Dupont had begged Grace to take her two older kids out of France.

How could she tell someone like Madame Dupont, if the woman survived the Nazi camps, that she'd lost her son?

Grace pulled her arms close to her chest, trying to clear this impossible question from her mind. She and Marguerite must spend their daylight hours sleeping if they were going to travel again tonight. Roland was expecting them at the church south of here, and after four years of partnering together, providing for hundreds of Jewish children and then helping dozens of them leave France, Grace had never failed him. And he had never failed her.

A year, that's how long she had volunteered to be in this country. She'd arrived in 1938 after one of her Quaker professors discovered that Ruby had insisted her only child know how to speak French. Her professor suggested she spend a year in Southern France, helping care for thousands of Spanish children who had climbed across the Pyrénées to escape the violence during and then after the Spanish Civil War.

But then everything flipped. Instead of a year overseas, she'd been here almost five years. After they'd helped the Spanish children flee, the French began sending their own citizens, entire Jewish families, to the same camps that once hosted refugees.

Grace stayed with a small team to care for the French kids and help them, if possible, make the opposite journey back over the mountains, into a sympathetic Spanish town since the country was now divided between support for the Allies and Axis powers.

Opening her eyes again, Grace rechecked both exits. The closed door in the loft—one used to toss hay into wagons below—and the door near the ladder they'd climbed. It was partially open, just like she had found it.

Through an open window, she could see the slopes of a vineyard, the tangle of vines rising up a hill crowned with golden leaves, snowy mountains in the distance. The Pyrénées were another formidable adversary, a rampart of forested hills bolstering its peaks. It was an arduous journey in warm weather, but with winter approaching, the crossing could be just as fierce as their German and French opponents.

Her work stopped in the foothills, turning back to transport more children from Gurs, while Roland would hand their current charges off to a *passeur* further up the mountain who would guide them safely through Spain, to the AFSC office in Portugal.

Without the use of a train or automobile, with the winter blowing in and new laws stifling their work, it was becoming harder each day to do what was right in this increasingly evil world.

Protect them, she prayed silently.

She couldn't bear to lose Roland or the children.

A gust of wind swept over the hay, laden with the scent of apples and oleander. Sleep tugged on her like a mother who knew what was best for her child, but like most children, she warred within herself to stay vigilant. Still she'd never be able to escort Marguerite to safety or return for the other children if she didn't get some rest.

"One thing have I desired of the Lord, that will I seek after; that I may dwell in the house of the Lord all the days of my life . . ."

The words from Psalm 27 settled over her like a blanket in this drafty barn. She had no place consistent to dwell right now, no home on this continent, but her heart dwelled in the place of the Lord, like David the poet in this psalm fleeing from his enemies, a shepherd who wanted to protect his sheep. The house of the Lord, a shelter over her heart, was where she wanted to be.

Sleep swallowed her slowly, and she awoke hours later as darkness was beginning to fall, her stomach an alarm, the smell of woodsmoke replacing the fermented apples. Someone was cooking dinner perhaps. Fresh bread, she liked to think. Maybe *gratins dauphinois* with a nice *coq au vin*—chicken stew simmered in red wine.

Her stomach growled even louder, reminding her that she hadn't eaten in . . . she couldn't remember exactly how long it had been. The days bled together, the food she'd consumed along the way hardly enough to be classified as a meal.

The children's faces paraded again through her mind, and she felt herself being swallowed by sorrow this time instead of sleep. She prayed they had food. That God, in His mercy, would send Roland or someone else to help them.

Right now, she had to focus on escorting the girl who'd cocooned into a ball beside her, hay sticking out of her fallen braids, to a safe place.

"Marguerite," she whispered.

When she didn't stir, Grace nudged her, then froze when she heard another sound. A whistle.

The barn door creaked open below, and a man stepped inside. Was he searching for them? Many were patrolling the villages and farmlands alike in Southern France. La Milice. Gendarmerie. The German military police.

Grace pressed herself back against the wall, hoping the brown tweed in her skirt, the honey blonde of her hair, would blend in with the hay. She wished, just like she had as a child, that she could disappear.

Marguerite inched up beside her, whispering, "He's a kind man."

Grace didn't respond, embracing the quiet once again. Kind or not, if he was a supporter of Philippe Pétain, the leader of Vichy, they were sunk. It was difficult enough in France to trust someone she knew. Impossible to trust a stranger.

The man's head arched back even as Grace tried to fold herself into the hay, pulling Marguerite with her. The man caught her eye though, holding it for just a moment, his whistle fading. He was an elderly man, about the age of her grandfather before he passed away.

Had he fought against Germany in the First World War? If so, he might have some compassion on them.

The man disappeared as quickly as he arrived, and Grace eyed the open door where he'd stood. "How can you tell he's kind?"

Marguerite shrugged, as she always did after she called out someone's character. And she was always right by Grace's account. It was a mystery how she could tell if someone was trustworthy.

But even so, they needed to leave. No matter how seemingly kind, the man might return with others.

"We must hurry."

"He won't harm us," Marguerite said.

Grace shook her head. "We don't know that."

Marguerite studied Grace's face before speaking again. "I know."

Grace brushed the hay off her blouse and skirt before reaching for her coat. This in-between felt impossible at times. The not knowing what lay ahead. The smallest of decisions, a simple turn left or right, to trust or not to trust, could change everything for the two of them.

She reached for her rucksack, praying for direction like she did with almost every breath. "Even if he is kind, we can't rely on his hospitality any longer."

"Where are we going tonight?"

"To a safe place." Roland had told her to follow the road outside south. At the foot of the mountains was the basement of another church, in the tiny *ville* of Artix.

But she couldn't tell Marguerite the destination. If the police asked questions of any of her children, none of them knew where they were stopping next. Or that they were about to climb over the Pyrénées.

The door began to creak open again, much sooner than she expected, and she tugged Marguerite to the other side of the loft so they couldn't see over the edge.

"Thought you might be hungry," the man called out in French. "I'll leave something for you by the door."

She held her breath, not daring to make a sound.

"I'm preparing to load up some hay tomorrow," he continued. "I'm going to set up a ladder tonight, lean it outside the loft so it's ready for the morning."

She glanced over at the wooden door, a bolt securing it.

"Some of our neighbors aren't very accommodating to strangers. You'll want to avoid leaving through the main floor."

Grace didn't move, but she replied quietly, "God bless you."

"Bon vent!" he said before stepping back outside.

Grace climbed down the stairs first and found two bowls of chunky soup made with squash and ham alongside two baguettes and a thermos filled with black chicory. They finished the hot soup quickly and Grace tucked the baguettes in her knapsack, grateful for the sustenance, but she was even more thankful for the man's generosity. Many people were afraid to offer the simplest of kindnesses these days. This dinner would fuel them for the long night ahead.

Before she opened the upper door, to climb down the ladder, the main door opened again. She couldn't see the entrance, but Marguerite glanced back over her shoulder in the dim light. And her eyes grew wide.

Grace placed her hand on Marguerite's arm, a reminder to stay silent, and she felt the girl tremble.

Heels clipped across the wooden floor below and then the door opened again, the visitor stepping out of the barn.

They waited in the stillness for several minutes before Marguerite spoke. "We must hurry."

"Was it the farmer?" Grace asked.

"No, it was a woman. And she's not kind."

"How do you know these things?"

"Because she's red," Marguerite said, a quiet confidence woven through her voice. "You can never trust red."

Grace slid back the bolt from the loft door, felt the ladder against the wall.

She didn't understand how a woman could be red, but this was no time to debate. She and Marguerite must continue their journey—for one more night.

Chapter Four

A newborn moon was cradled in the sky, guiding Grace and Marguerite along a stone wall. Sleepwalking, it felt like, as they listened for the bark of a dog or crack of a branch against heels.

They were following Roland's directions, searching for the church to rest until a *passeur* arrived to transport Marguerite—and hopefully all the children—over the mountains. But at the first hint of a *rafle*, she and Marguerite would hide their rucksacks and pretend to be lost. They'd been on a mushroom hunt in the woods, they would say, so afraid of missing curfew, they'd dropped their basket filled with *chanterelles*, *bolets*, and *morilles*, losing them in the darkness as they ran home.

She'd distracted the police before, when it was just her and four children on the train. Her story was simple, her stutter pronounced to distract them from her accent as she explained slowly that they were on a school outing. Acting skills Grace had inherited from her mother. Skills she despised but used whenever necessary to protect the children.

The last time she'd delivered a convoy of children to a safe house, they'd taken a train car from the city of Pamiers. The policeman who'd checked their identity cards had been so distracted, probably more interested in searching for downed Allied airmen or French fugitives who'd deviated from their so-called duty to fight, that she'd never even had to speak.

Trains were no longer a safe place for her wards. Officials had begun asking what happened to the kids who were supposed to be reuniting with their parents. *Regroupement familial*, they called it. A joyful reunion to keep families together.

Sadly, those who'd been regrouped quickly discovered it was a ruse as children were deported east with their parents.

Disgusting, all of it.

As they drew close to the village, Grace scanned the buildings on the perimeter, the cemetery that lined the edge of the churchyard and the door to the basement. Her head high, as if she hadn't a care, Grace led Marguerite between the gravestones, ducking under a low roof before she dropped the girl's hand to open the door, breathing a prayer of thanks when she found it unlocked. The small windows were blacked out with curtains, so she flicked on her flashlight . . . and froze when she saw someone sitting at the table.

Then relief flooded over her when she realized it was Roland. His dark hair was combed neatly back as if he were meeting her for croissants and coffee, but his clothing—a dirt-smudged pair of overalls and worn cap—was filthy.

She rushed toward him, glancing across the room as if the children might be hiding in the shadows.

"Did you find them?" she begged.

Roland rolled up a ratty sleeve and checked the gold-faced watch he'd purchased in London before the war. "We'll talk about it later."

"I need to know—"

"We can't stay here," he said before nodding back toward the door.

"But we're supposed to rest . . ." The sun would be rising again soon, the light their enemy.

He shook his head. "We've been compromised."

She reached for her bag and Marguerite's hand before following Roland back out of the church and into the dark forest. Marguerite didn't complain once, not even a whimper.

It was far from normal for any age, this hiking through the trees at night, but nothing was normal for her. She'd already seen much evil, much loss, in her nine years. Her father had left them in Paris, and her mother had been transported east with Marguerite's baby brother. Now Élias, her older brother, had disappeared as well.

So much grief, yet Marguerite marched onward like a soldier who'd grown numb in war. Grace wished that she could gift her with a few carefree hours to simply dream. That she could lift the burden off her shoulders and carry it for her.

There'd be no returning to the camp at Gurs or locating her mother now. Once parents gave permission to send their children out of France, the kids would find new homes with relatives in another country.

When Grace was a child, the only way she'd been able to resolve the confusion in her head was by diving into Tonquin Lake, pumping her arms and legs like a frog until she reached the other side. She didn't have any cousins—she'd learned much later in life that Ruby's birth had been considered a miracle—but her grandparents had an open invitation for the farmhand children to play in the lake with her, as long as they passed Grandpa's strict swim test. If they couldn't swim, Grandpa Tonquin taught them.

Then she and her friends would dig newts out of the mud and transfer them to an aquarium that she kept on the back porch, rescuing them from grass snakes, herons, and fish. While other girls seemed to be afraid of squirmy creatures, she'd always been intrigued by living things.

If only she could dive back into her family's lake right now, swim until her thoughts cleared, then rescue Marguerite and the others.

Sunlight began to settle in the mist between pines, and Grace tried to calm her fears. Light was something she usually prized, the great revealer of truth inside and out, its ability to warm and heal, but they must hide the truth now. God's light was among them, but evil still ran rampant in this part of the world. Depravity. When humans extinguished the light within, choosing darkness instead of walking alongside their Creator, they actively worked to destroy all that God had created.

The promise of heaven pressed her forward. God would welcome her home in His perfect timing; she had only to trust Him.

When Roland stopped, she and Marguerite folded themselves into the arms of a conifer tree. For a moment, in the theater of her mind, she was ten and her mother was planning a visit for Christmas. Grams had decorated a tree even though Quakers didn't celebrate this holiday. A terrible fight ensued on Christmas Eve between her grandmother and Ruby, and Grace had wished she could stay hidden behind the Christmas tree, under the shingles of pine, forever and ever. Amen.

But she'd had to crawl out eventually—after Ruby slammed the front door on the farmhouse—and face the problems in her family.

Roland took several steps, scanning a road ahead. Then he motioned them forward.

"The light," she whispered, as if he couldn't see the glow of dawn. The light that she loved, that she'd embraced her entire life, could do more harm than good.

"Grace—" He cupped her chin in his hand, inching her face up to meet his gaze. "It will be all right."

He didn't know this, of course. None of them could predict what might happen next in their world of uncertainty. But still she nodded, trusting him like she'd trusted her grandparents. As long as he spoke the truth, she would indeed be fine.

Two horses stood on the other side of the trees, hooked onto a wagon that carried eight oak barrels, blanketed by mist. A man in denim overalls climbed off the bench, whiskers shadowing his ruddy chin, a bandanna tied neatly around his neck. Instead of acknowledging them, he eyed Roland briefly, then stuck his hands in his pockets and walked away.

Roland glanced up at the single lane that ran like a brook through the trees. Then he looked down at Marguerite. "You ready for an adventure?"

She shook her head. "I've already had an adventure."

"We have to go a little farther." He opened the lid to one of the barrels, nodding at Marguerite. "Although instead of walking, you will have a special seat in here . . . and a meal waiting for you on the other end."

Grace scanned the eight barrels, listening. They had all sorts of ways to transport children—parcels, they were often called to throw off those who wanted to harm them. Was it possible they were hidden in the other barrels? She prayed that Roland had brought eight with him.

She leaned down so Marguerite could see her eyes. "Monsieur Roland will take the best care of us."

"I want Élias!"

"I'm sorry, *chérie*," he said.

Tears poured down her cheeks. "My brother . . ."

"I know," Grace replied. "We will look for him."

Roland scanned the lane again and then the misty field beyond. "Time to make haste," he said. "You must stay as quiet as a carp, Marguerite, until I reopen the lid."

She wiped away her tears as Roland tucked a blanket into the bottom of the barrel. Then he lifted Marguerite inside, covering her with the lid. A small hole, barely noticeable, pierced through the oak.

Walls, Grace thought, were all these children knew. The invisible walls in their homes and communities, set apart with the Star of David. The barbed wire around their internment camp. The formidable wall ahead between them and Spain.

Roland reached for Grace's hand. "Are you ready, my wife?"

"As ready as possible." The familiar tremor raced through her skin when she took his offered hand. They'd played this game before of husband and wife, she holding his hand on trains, at checkpoints, pretending they were parents. Sometimes she wondered . . .

War was not the time for foolish dreams.

A smile pressed on her lips. "I don't think I will fit into a barrel."

He patted the bench, his cap tilted, chestnut-colored bangs falling over his eyes. "You can ride here beside me."

After he helped her up, he tucked both rucksacks behind the bench, hiding them under a woolen blanket. Whistling softly, he stepped up into the driver's seat and winked at her. Only Roland could make light of this situation, as if they really were preparing to bottle their vineyard's wine.

He lifted the reins, clicked his tongue, and the horses followed the narrow lane through the forest and then fields that had been harvested on both sides, morning light crowning the mist. The countryside reminded her of the hills and farmland back home, the place where she'd felt safe as a child.

Peace flooded her with the memories. Her friends, the Quakers who'd worked alongside her across France, had come from a long line of those who had stood up for religious freedom with their founder, George Fox. All the way back to England in the seventeenth century until Parliament passed the Act of Toleration so Quakers could freely worship God.

Friends of Jesus, they called themselves. Children of Light.

In the book of John, Jesus said that anyone who did what He commanded was His friend. That's what she wanted more than anything with her life. To have Him as the dearest of friends and in turn, follow the command of her heart to help as many children as possible escape evil in this world.

"Did you find the other children?" she asked Roland again as he turned onto another lane, traveling toward a forested hill to their south.

"Not yet."

Her hands trembled. "Why aren't you looking for them?"

"Others are searching," he said, scanning the road. "My job is to find shelter for you and Marguerite."

Her stomach tumbled in despair, but Roland knew things that she did not. Sometimes he was privy to information and sometimes he just *knew*. Like Marguerite, he seemed to have a sixth sense for danger.

"Whoa," he called to the horses, and they slowed.

A man dressed in a gray-blue uniform stepped out onto the road. A collaborator.

It was almost as if Roland had been expecting him.

"Bonjour." Roland tipped his cap to the militiaman. Or men. A second guard, wearing the same uniform along with a blue beret, stepped up to the bench and asked for his papers.

They didn't ask for hers, but she had them ready, tucked inside her coat pocket if needed. An American and a French version.

"Where are you going?" the bereted militiaman asked.

Grace tucked both hands under her skirt so they wouldn't see them shaking.

"Making a delivery to Saint-Girons," Roland explained. "My wife and I."

The man eyed Roland's dirty overalls and cap. "Why aren't you on the front lines?"

Roland pointed to his leg. "An altercation with a tank ended my time in Morocco. I was sent home to manage my family's farm so the soldiers stationed here can eat."

Grace's gaze was settled on the road before them as she quoted Psalm 27 in her heart. *"The Lord is my light and my salvation; whom shall I fear? the Lord is the strength of my life; of whom shall I be afraid?"*

Not these men, even the one who was staring at her while the other reviewed Roland's papers. She wasn't supposed to be afraid of them. Even though they were forced to live in the midst of evil, she prayed God would have mercy on her ward.

"You see anyone else on the road?" the man asked as he thumbed through Roland's papers.

"Not this morning. As dormant as the dew out here."

The militiaman handed back the papers. "We've had reports of strangers in the area."

"I'm always watching for strangers. Wouldn't want any disturbance at my vineyard."

When she glanced over again, she saw the dreaded curiosity in the man's eyes, the same puzzling look moviegoers back home gave her when they caught a glimpse of Ruby. Not the perfectly rolled black hair—Grace's was more like windswept sand that she fought to control—but the same mahogany-brown eyes, narrow cheeks, lips shaped like a heart.

"You look familiar," he said. "Are you from—?"

She opened her mouth, prepared to deter his curiosity in her best French, stuttering to cover the accent, but Roland spoke instead. "You gentlemen must be thirsty."

He tapped on the barrel right behind her, holding her gaze for the briefest of moments, long enough to know that she must heed his words.

The man dropped his inquiry as he studied the barrels. "Everyone is thirsty these days."

"A bit of wine might warm your bones."

"Indeed."

"Why don't you give these fine men a taste of our fare, *chérie*?" he said to Grace before turning back to the guards. "We grow the best grapes in the entire valley."

Both men produced a canteen in record time, dumping out the previous contents.

Grace stared down at the barrel, at the metal rings wound tightly around oak to secure the lid. Roland had popped off the top of Marguerite's barrel, but when she tried to open this one, it didn't budge.

"Actually." Roland reached behind the bench and pulled a leather case onto his lap, unsnapping the latches. "I keep the best of my wine here."

While he uncorked one of the bottles, the men held out their canteens like they were the finest of wineglasses. Then Roland filled them like a skilled sommelier.

"And now we will bid you both a good day." Roland handed Grace the bottle. "We must conduct our business and return home before curfew."

The militiamen nodded, engrossed now in their canteens, and Roland leaned casually against the bench, prompting the horses on.

The mist began to rise as they rounded another bend. The cool air comforted her, but the warm walls of the barrel were wrapped tightly around Marguerite. She must be terrified.

After the guards were out of sight, she turned around and spoke softly. "Are you okay, Marguerite?"

The return answer was equally as quiet. "Yes."

"It's not much longer now," she said, trying to encourage her even though she had no idea the length of their journey. Then she glanced at Roland. "Is there wine in any of these barrels?"

"Not a drop."

"So I almost opened an empty container . . ."

"I wouldn't have let you open it."

She studied his face, his gaze focused on the road. "You didn't want them to see my face. That's why you had me turn."

"I didn't like the way he was looking at you."

Jealous, that's how he sounded, but she wasn't about to tease him, not when he was protecting her. They'd worked as colleagues for years, but Roland didn't know her movie star mother graced the covers of magazines in France as well as back home. It was safer this way, a shelter of her own making, hiding behind her fear that he, like many before him, would only care about her as a link to her mom.

Often she wondered, hoped in her heart, that Roland might care for her as more than Ruby's daughter or a Quaker coworker. But even if he did, he would refrain from saying anything in the midst of this turmoil. Love would only complicate their mission to save as many children as possible from deportation . . . and probably break both of their hearts.

"You are a good man, Roland."

He shook his head. "Not good enough."

If only she could take his hand, tell him that she saw barrels filled with goodness inside him, overflowing to those like her who were privileged to know him.

"Dew isn't really dormant," she said instead.

He shrugged.

"It's life-giving to plants, quietly sustaining them."

"You learn that in college?"

She nodded. "Biology."

"You are going to make an excellent nurse, Grace."

"If I ever return to school—"

"You will, one day. And you're going to save many more lives."

Right now, all she wanted was to save the life of the girl in this wagon and the eleven others who'd been stolen from her.

"Who is looking for the children?" she asked.

"I can't tell you that."

Prayer she believed in with all her heart, but she wanted power as well to do something. Save the children on her own. But she was here as a servant, to bring her five loaves and fish to the table and pray God would multiply them.

She didn't understand, nor would she ever, why God didn't rescue everyone in this life, but it was her job, her grandfather had often reminded her, to be faithful in caring for those God gave to her.

The wagon hit a bump, and Marguerite cried out. Grace began singing, just loud enough for the girl to hear, a song she'd heard at a French Reformed church. A song about following Christ through the darkness and storms, following Him through roadblocks and battlefields and evil lurking in these hills.

Soon Roland joined in. She'd never heard him sing, but the richness of his voice, the strength that carried across the fields, made God's presence feel even closer.

Where he was taking her and Marguerite, she didn't know, but he was a devout man of God. They would walk through these valleys, shoulder the storms together.

No matter the consequence, they would do their best to follow God wherever He led. And in the following, pray that His will would be done.

As long as they could keep singing, she thought, they would overcome.

CHAPTER FIVE

A tapping sound woke Addie, and she blinked several times, startled awake in the morning light. A middle-aged woman was knocking on the window, her ginger hair falling across her chin as she peered in the car.

Addie turned the key and rolled down the window. "Are you Tara Dawson?"

"That's me." The woman's hair draped back over her shoulders as she stood, long strands that angled down into a wedge. "I was up half the night, worried sick that you might get lost back here."

She'd been awake much of the night as well, talking to the baby that grew inside her as if he or she could hear every word. But no matter how uncomfortable the car seat, she wasn't about to open her door again in the dark and the downpour. In the few hours that she'd slept, she dreamed about Bigfoot circling her car. While not many things scared her, she had zero desire to confront a mythical creature in the midnight hours, even in a nightmare.

"Did you call me?" Addie asked.

Tara shook her head. "I figured you would call if you needed something."

Addie held up her phone. "No coverage out here."

"The cottage has a phone."

Addie nodded toward the rickety gate in front of them, the house beyond. "Is that the rental cottage?"

"Heavens, no." Tara pushed her glasses back up her nose. "I messed up the directions, didn't I?"

A massive understatement, Addie thought. "I had trouble following them."

"Half the time, I can't follow my own directions." Tara sighed as if she'd been wronged. "Half this, half that. Half should be my middle name."

Addie stared at the woman, dumbfounded.

"It's impossible to find anything out here in the dark if you're not familiar with the roads. Cow paths, really, from the old dairy farm." Tara eyed Addie's rental car. "Did you sleep in that?"

"There wasn't anywhere else for me to go." Addie took a sip from her water bottle. "I was afraid I'd get even more lost trying to find my way back to Newberg."

"There's truth in that." Tara wrung her hands together. "Terrible is how I feel right now. About the size of a mouse. Or a spider. Half a spider."

"I could do without a mouse or spider." Addie studied the house again in the light. The wide front porch wrapped around the side, the edge tilting slightly like it was a spooky fun house, but it didn't look nearly as frightening as it had in the dark.

"Nothing small about my mistake." Tara rocked on her heels. "Let's get you to a much nicer place."

Addie opened the door and stretched her legs before climbing out. "Whose home is this?"

The rental agent glanced at the old house. "An actress from years past used to live here. Enormously famous. Had her very own star on the sidewalk down in Cali."

Adrenaline pumped through her. "Ruby Tonquin?"

Tara turned back quickly, surprise flashing under her glasses. "You've heard of Ruby?"

"Her and Grace."

"Most people don't even know that Ruby had a daughter. Most people don't know anything . . ." She rattled a chain of keys at her side. "How exactly did you hear about Ruby's family?"

Addie decided to hold on to the little she knew about Charlie's story until she learned more about Tara Dawson. "I'm a fan of old movies."

"Quite the fan, I must say. Ruby always tried to . . ." Tara's voice faded away again as if she was keeping information close to her as well.

"Do you know what happened to the Tonquin family?" Addie asked, studying a broken window on the second floor.

"They moved away ages and ages ago. Ancient history now," she said. "I sure hope you didn't rent the cottage for stargazing."

"Only those in the Milky Way."

"You'll see plenty then." Tara pointed at the Audi she'd parked at the end of the drive. "A good breakfast in town, that's what you need right now. My treat."

No way was she driving back to Newberg with a woman who'd deemed herself something between a mouse and spider. Besides she needed a couple more hours of sleep first, a hot shower, and a cup of decaf to feel human again. Then she'd begin to search for Charlie's family.

"I just want to find the cottage."

"The cottage it is then," Tara said. "I'll take you right there."

She sure hoped the woman wouldn't take her halfway.

While Tara walked to her car, Addie took another sip of water before climbing back into the Civic and reversing it down the long drive.

If the Tonquins had left Oregon, where had they gone? The idea for this trip had sparked last week in Emma's living room while Charlie slept nearby. Before they married, Emma said, Charlie had traveled to Oregon to visit his family, but his parents had both passed away. He hadn't wanted to speak anymore about the Tonquins. Almost as if his life began the moment he'd stepped off the train in Chattanooga.

Emma had respected his decision to keep his family history private . . . until now. She'd searched through his things until she found a yellow-tinted picture of him as a teenager, his hair a wild mess, standing by a girl a few years younger whose hair was wrapped up in a kerchief. The two of them were huddled together by the boughs of a willow tree, Charlie with a plate, it looked like, in his hand.

Handwritten in cursive on the back was *The Tonquin Children, 1946*.

Charlie and his sister.

Perhaps his sister or her kids were still alive. Or the Tonquins had other children who had children.

Time wasn't on their side. Addie had already searched online and in the Chattanooga library to find information about Charlie's family, but all she'd uncovered were stories about Ruby Tonquin with several mentions of her daughter, Grace. Nothing about a son named Charlie.

Still she hoped that Grace was Charlie's sister. Ruby his mother.

Addie couldn't find a single Tonquin listed in the entire state of Oregon, but when she found Tonquin Lake to the west of Portland, a lake that looked a whole lot like the one in Charlie's picture, and a rental cottage right beside it, Emma bought her an airplane ticket.

Addie suspected that Emma also sent her to Oregon because she thought Addie needed healing as much as Charlie but she never let on. Either way, Addie would do everything possible to find a donor for him this week.

As she pulled her car behind Tara, her cell phone rang, and she opened it to see a single bar sprouting on the screen. Emma's number blinked below it.

"How is he?" Addie asked as she followed Tara back toward the crossroads.

"He's resting," Emma replied. "I was getting worried about you."

"It was much too late to call last night. I didn't want to wake him."

"You can call me at any hour," Emma said.

"Thank you."

Charlie and Emma had practically parented Addie since she was seventeen. She didn't want to worry Emma with her lack of both cell service and accommodations.

"I'm praying for you," Emma said.

"I'm glad," she replied. "We're going to find his family."

No matter where they had gone.

She rounded a bend, tunneling under the canopy of leaves, and her service disappeared before Emma sent her love. But she knew that both Charlie and Emma loved her. And she loved them back.

A tear slid down her cheek, and she wiped it away. She wasn't going to let Charlie go without a fight.

The crossroads was ahead, the one at the top of Laurel Ridge that had thrown her off last night. At least, she thought it was the same place. Everything looked different in the morning light. The creepy vibes were gone, scrubbed away by sunshine and a brilliant-blue sky, the leaves polished by last night's wind and rain.

After two more turns, none of which she remembered from Tara's directions, they arrived in another clearing. And she could finally see Tonquin Lake centered in the valley below, a vineyard sweeping up the hill on the other side, the fronds of a willow tree draped over the water.

She'd found the place, it seemed, where Charlie once lived.

Tara honked her horn several times, pointing out the left side of her car as if Addie might miss the view.

Charlie had talked often about the beauty and resilience of a willow. In fact, over the years, he'd collected a whole gallery of weeping willow photographs and paintings for his office. A constant reminder, he'd said, of strength in the midst of the sorrow. Bending without breaking.

Willows. Weeping. Widows.

She shook her head to erase the last word from her list, but tears flooded down her cheeks now, impossible to contain.

"A tree that shoulders pain," Charlie had said. He'd planted a willow more than thirty years ago in Tennessee, beside the creek on his property. She'd taken refuge under it many times. Especially after . . .

She quickly wiped her tears and followed Tara down into the valley, to a white cottage that overlooked the water and a circle of pine.

One more day—Charlie said that often. One more day to hold their lives up to the light.

She only had to push through the hours in front of her, not think about tomorrow or even yesterday. Today was already set before her, he liked to say. The table prepared.

And she would show up again. Find his sister as quickly as possible and return to Tennessee.

Chapter Six

The abandoned château reminded Grace of a chivalrous musketeer from the French Revolution, battle worn but ready to wield its weapon against anyone who threatened its occupants. The gray stone walls, she hoped, would protect her and Marguerite until they were able to secure passage for Marguerite.

Grace breathed in the morning air on the back patio, pretending that the tangled thorns and bramble were blooming with flowers. She almost heard the flutes and violins from years past, the fragrance of jasmine and rose wafting through the windows, delighting guests inside who danced the lively gavotte across the parquet floor.

A garden meant life. A bit of Eden where they'd be safe.

No one, Roland hoped, would bother them here.

Closing her eyes, Grace leaned back against a step and imagined this place full of children like the home where she'd first worked in France. Kids playing hide-and-seek in the hedges or the overgrown vineyard beyond the stone wall. Kids seated around long tables between flower beds, eating their afternoon snack, oblivious to the cruelty in camps like Gurs.

How she missed them all.

In the distance, between a crack in the crumbling wall, she could see the treacherous mountains that separated France and Spain. The French Jews from freedom.

A length of valley stretched out beyond the château, and fierce clouds hovered over the Pyrénées. Soon the snow would come, barricading the children's path to freedom until spring. They needed to leave before it became impassable.

Other children from the Quaker-run homes had escaped by using smugglers' routes between the peaks. It was an arduous journey, at least four days of hiking until the border crossing, but the children were strong well beyond their years. And they were determined to survive.

Until Roland found a guide for Marguerite across the mountains, the three of them would wait in this vacant space once owned by aristocrats, he'd explained, who'd summered inside its walls. One of their descendants, a shepherd woman named Hélène, now lived in a cottage nearby. Last night, she'd welcomed them with a meal and a promise of more supplies soon.

With the peeling walls and lack of anything modern, no one had lived inside the château, Grace guessed, for at least a hundred years. How Roland had found it tucked back in these wooded hills was a mystery, but it was a beautiful, formidable waiting place.

Once Roland arranged passage for Marguerite—for all twelve children into Spain—Grace would travel back to Gurs to escort any others who remained in hiding. Then, when the war was finished, when the Nazis finally left France, she would return to live with her grandmother in Oregon.

She took another sip of the water she'd retrieved from an outdoor well. While she'd yet to see Roland this morning, she'd heard his wireless off the main hall. He'd been nursing it since they'd arrived, listening and perhaps transmitting information, searching for Suzel and Élias and the others.

If the Nazis released these children, if the Spanish guards let them cross the border, perhaps Marguerite could meet her brother in Lisbon. Then they could secure passage together to their waiting uncle in New York.

A tear streamed down her cheek, and Grace quickly brushed it away. All the emotions bubbling inside her, the anger and sorrow, the open wounds lingering just below the surface, would have to wait until after the war. Later she would grieve, but for now she must be strong for herself and the children.

The back door opened and Roland stepped onto the patio, his bangs sticking up on one side as if he'd just crawled out of bed.

"Thought you might want some coffee." He sat on the stoop beside her, holding out a cup. "Wish I could offer you milk and sugar."

"I will savor every bit of this." She took a long sip, the bitterness a welcome jolt to her tired limbs. "Any news about the other children?"

"I believe they're still near Saint-Lizier."

Her heart quickened. "What have you heard?"

"Enough to give me hope."

"We'll need to secure passage for Marguerite with the next convoy," she said. "The AFSC office in Lisbon will help her."

"The convoy doesn't leave for another week, but you should be safe until then."

"*We'll* be safe," she said, expanding the pronoun to include him. She could not do this alone.

He didn't seem to notice the correction. "The French have no interest in the ghosts back here and the Germans don't know this place exists."

"What ghosts?" she asked.

"Most locals are firmly in de Galle's camp, but the ghosts are legends to keep people away since the château is also a stop for Allied airmen on their way out of France."

"The Allies are close to taking Europe, aren't they?"

"That's what de Galle says, but the Germans have a very different story. They believe they are firmly winning this war."

"If the Nazis win, we're sunk."

He reached for her hand, and she savored the press of his skin against hers. "We are not going to let them sink us."

"No, we aren't." She nodded at the white-capped peaks spiking into the sky. "Marguerite is a strong girl, but I don't know how she will make it across."

"She'll surprise us with her strength."

"I pray so." She sipped the coffee. "Once Marguerite and the others are safe, I will return to Aspet."

"Grace—" His gaze wandered toward the mountains again before looking back at her. Cashmere, she thought, his eyes the softest of browns.

"What is it?"

"Will you wait for me?" The gentleness in his eyes hardened like plaster, as if she might shatter him with her answer.

"You're leaving?"

"Not for long, just to find the children. If I don't return . . ." He glanced at the mountains again. "You need to leave here when I send word, before the snow begins in the mountains."

Her heart clutched. What would she do if she lost him? She couldn't bear to think about it.

"You have to come back, Roland."

"I don't know what the future holds." His gaze lowered to the garden. "You need to live your life, Grace. Return to school in Oregon. Become a nurse."

"But you just asked me to wait," she said, confused at the switchbacks when Roland usually spoke the plain truth.

"I'm asking because—"

The door opened again, and Marguerite stepped outside in a flannel nightgown, her cheeks bruised from the barrel, a cut swollen across her pale hand. Instead of complaining, she sat down on the stoop between Roland and Grace, watching a bumblebee as it circled the forlorn plants, searching for nectar among the debris.

In what sense had Roland been asking her to wait? How she wished he'd speak plainly of a future with her. Wished he'd begun to care for her as she had for him. But she couldn't inquire about his request with Marguerite sandwiched between them.

Nor would she ask later. Falling in love during war was dangerous. Roland knew this as well as she did. Love could jeopardize the children in their care. They had to stay focused solely on their mission until this war was done. Then he could finish asking.

Grace kissed the girl's cheek. "A good morning to you."

Marguerite's gaze remained on the bee. "It's hungry."

"Not for long." Roland tossed a stone into the garden. "It will move to the orchards soon. Probably torment the sheep."

Grace shook her head. "Bees don't torment sheep."

He gave her a curious look. "Your family have sheep on the farm?"

"A few. It's the botflies, not the bees, that are the problem. They climb up the sheep's nose and—"

Marguerite waved her hands. "Stop!"

"The important question is—" Roland smiled at Marguerite—"are you hungry?"

She nodded. "Very."

Grace was incredibly happy to hear that word. A child willing to eat was one choosing to live.

The three of them slipped back into the crumbling château. The corridor led to a grand staircase, the banister now splintered on the floor, and to a ballroom lined with formerly upholstered chairs, their fabric long foraged by mice. Strips of brittle paper draped off the walls, and marble chunks from the fireplace had fallen to the ground.

Stacked in the corner of the room were a number of cans and several paintbrushes. Before the war, perhaps, someone had started to renovate the place. She'd never enjoyed living in the palace-like hotels that attracted her mother, but she appreciated seeing beauty created from ashes, bringing things back to life. If someone decided to try another renovation, after the war, this would be an elegant place.

Next door was the kitchen with copper pots hanging over a second fireplace and a rusty pump standing by the wooden sink. While the pump no longer worked, a bucket of fresh water had been filled from the outdoor well.

She held up her cup and took the last sip. "Where exactly did you make this coffee?"

"On a fire out back," Roland said.

She put the cup in the sink. "Very resourceful of you."

He dug out a small linen bag from his coat pocket. "I will leave the rest of the beans for you."

She shook her head. As much as she appreciated it, he would need coffee more than her. "You must take them with you."

Still he put the bag in a cupboard alongside several wooden bowls, one filled with apples that he'd brought in the barrels, another with potatoes and turnips. Several glass containers stood beside these bowls with flour and honey, and on the floor was a burlap bag with chickpeas.

"Hélène will leave fresh vegetables and perhaps even some meat by the front door," he said. "There are mushrooms in the forest for you to forage. Do you know which ones to pick?"

"I know enough."

"Avoid the ones that are veiled around the bottom and any with green and yellow on the top."

She rubbed the shiver from her arms. "Death caps."

"Exactly." He leaned back against the old oven, patting it. "Neither the stove nor the fireplaces work, but there's plenty of wood on the pile. You think you can cook over a fire?"

She laughed. "I spent most of my life on a farm, Roland. As long as we have food to prepare, we won't go hungry."

"Hélène will make sure you have enough."

Grace salvaged through another cupboard and found several eggs along with a slab of butter. Then she grabbed a wooden spoon. "I will bake some sort of campfire cake before you leave, so you can eat and so you no longer have to worry about my cooking skills."

"I'm not worried—"

"You're good at lying to everyone except me."

He grinned, the hair that he'd pushed back falling over one of his eyes. "I never like lying to you, *chérie*."

She flicked the hair away from his eyes with the end of the spoon. "I need to give you a haircut before you leave."

"But I hide behind this mop."

"Just because you can't see the Nazis doesn't mean they can't see you."

After he returned to the wireless, Marguerite helped her mix the flour and honey, the eggs and water, in a buttered Dutch oven. Then she sliced up several apples to add to the top before securing the pan to a metal arm that swung over the fire.

A bush rustled beside them, and Marguerite jumped. "What is that?"

"A rabbit, I'm sure."

"Élias would catch it for dinner."

Grace had been much better at caring for the farm animals than preparing them for a meal, but she would provide as much sustenance for Marguerite as possible, especially meat. The girl would need it when it came time to climb the mountains.

"If you catch it, I will figure out a way to cook it."

The breakfast cake was a lumpy mess, but the three of them enjoyed it together on this autumn morning. Then Grace helped Roland gather his things, hiding the wireless in one of the barrels. When he wasn't looking, she slipped the contraband bag of coffee beans beside his radio.

He retrieved the horses from their hitching post near a stream and harnessed them to the wagon. Grace and Marguerite climbed up on the bench and rode with him down the narrow drive until they reached the iron gate.

Roland rested his hand on hers for the slightest of moments, long enough for the familiar embers to warm her. "You will be fine."

"I am praying for you," Grace said. "Every hour of the day."

He leaned down and kissed her cheek. "And I am praying for both of you."

"I will miss you," she said, her heart warring inside her again. Why couldn't she stop these blustery emotions that blew like a storm? This aching that didn't want to let him go.

"Soon, Colibri."

He kissed Marguerite's cheek next, then tipped his cap to both of them before lifting his reins. "I will send word."

She and Marguerite stood at the end of the overgrown lane, behind the iron gate, waving until they could no longer see his wagon. And it felt as if he'd taken a piece of her heart with him.

What if he didn't return?

She couldn't linger on the answer to that question. Every day she asked God to blind their enemy, but she knew not His plans. She had to continue helping the children here, no matter what happened, until the war ended . . . or the Nazis took her away too.

"Monsieur Roland is blue," Marguerite said.

Grace glanced down at her. "I'm blue too."

"No, you're not." Marguerite studied her. "You're yellow."

Grace loved this girl, but she didn't always understand her and the colors that seemed to swirl in her mind. "Is yellow a good color?"

Marguerite shrugged, looking back between the wrought iron scrollwork on the gate.

They stood there for a long time, almost as if Roland might reappear.

But he didn't come back to her.

CHAPTER SEVEN

From the cottage's wooden porch, Addie watched two mallards paddle across the water. A wall of pine trees guarded most of Tonquin Lake, but the willow tree stood proudly on its own.

She studied the copy of Charlie's photograph on her lap. The boy and girl looked like they were standing right at the edge of this lake, and the girl, her hair in braids, was clinging to his arm.

Addie had to find this girl.

She'd been known to break down a wall or two in her life, many of those torn down in anger during her early years. Then Charlie had helped her break down the unhealthy walls she'd built to keep anyone, good or bad, out of her life.

But this time she would break down the wall of secrets for Charlie's sake. Demolish it in love.

Kirsten's number flickered on Addie's cell phone, and she quickly answered her friend's call. "I'm currently in the middle of nowhere, so I might lose you."

"You'll never lose me." Words spoken lightly, yet both women knew well the weight of their meaning.

"I'm glad of it."

Soul sisters, she and Kirsten called themselves. Even though they came from very different places, God had knitted their hearts together seven years ago when Addie joined Knoxville Christian Church as the wife of their pastor. Addie had just turned twenty-two, a recent graduate of Bible college, and she knew little about the inner workings of an actual church. Kirsten had grown up in the Christian community and was an expert on almost everything that Addie needed to learn about being a pastor's wife.

"Have you started looking for Charlie's sister?" Kirsten asked.

"Emma mandated that I'm supposed to rest today." The Newberg library was closed on Sundays anyway, but she didn't want to rest.

"I adore that woman."

"Me too, but I'm not as excited about this Sabbath as Emma. I haven't spent an entire day alone in . . ." *Three months,* she thought. *Since the day after Peter disappeared.*

"Are you okay?"

"Yes," she said, twisting the wedding band on her finger. "I haven't been alone since June."

"You're not alone, Addie."

"I haven't felt God's presence in a long time, if that's what you mean."

"But He's still there, just like Baby Hoult, even though you can't feel her yet . . . and me, of course. Just a phone call away."

Addie placed a hand on her still-flat middle. "Thank you."

"When are you coming back?"

"Saturday, at the latest. If the librarian can help me find someone from the Tonquin family before then, I'll catch an early flight back to Tennessee."

"I sure miss you," Kirsten said. "If you were staying longer, I'd take next week off work and join you."

"The children at the academy need you more."

"I have a perfectly good substitute—"

"We will get together when I come home."

"Knoxville or Sale Creek?" her friend asked.

"Sale Creek for now." The only place that felt like home.

After she disconnected the call, several other ducks joined the mallards and a goose, all of them bobbing their heads into the water. Eating lunch, she supposed, since it was almost one.

She'd slept much longer than she anticipated, the cottage bed so warm, comfortable, that she hadn't wanted to leave it. Even after the fitful night in the car, she should have managed to get up hours ago but some days the simple act of lifting her head took a Herculean amount of strength. Those days when it felt like an anvil was crushing her chest, she couldn't seem to breathe.

Once she managed to get up, the anvil heaved away, the day's light offered hope. It took time to heal, that's what the counselor had said, and everyone's clock was different. Maybe it would take a lifetime for her to shake off the anvil and soak in the light.

Her eyes closing, she leaned the chair back against the cedar siding, listening to the chatter of birds. Growing up in a city apartment, with the neighbors shouting and all the honking and the constant buzz of TV, she'd never realized that birds really sang until a judge gave her the option of juvenile detention or moving into the Sale Creek Home for Girls.

Twelve years had passed, but she still remembered waking up that first morning as a seventeen-year-old at the girls' home, wondering what strange song was coming from the radio. When she realized the noise was outside, she'd thrown her pillow at the window, making her roommate laugh, the bird undeterred.

It was the first tremor in a long series of shocks.

That same morning, the birds caroling like it was Christmas Eve, Emma announced that all the girls would be piling into vans to attend church. Addie had never been inside a church building, not even for the obligatory Easter service. While she'd pretended to hate the thought, wearing her defiance like armor, she'd been curious for much of her life about what went on inside the brick and stained glass. A friend in junior high told her that they sacrificed animals in church buildings, and she'd wondered where it was done and why, but her mother never allowed her to step into a church to find out.

Her mother was one of the most devout believers in God she'd ever known. Except God, she'd decided, was the enemy.

Addie checked the time on her phone. Charlie and Emma would be preparing to leave for the evening service. When he wasn't in the hospital, Charlie refused to miss a single Sunday—morning or night—of worship. He was rooted in his community, rooted in the Word of God.

Charlie and Emma had helped root her in the same place. A place that she'd thought would be indestructible, even when the fierce winds blew.

The revival of her heart was one of the reasons Addie had wanted to work in a church, helping to root others in their faith. She'd met Peter when he spoke at the Bible college she was attending, and they'd married after her graduation. As a young pastor's wife, she'd supported him with her entire being, taught every week at the youth group, mastered a peanut butter cookie that became a potluck hit, shared her husband with parishioners who called him at all hours—some with emergencies and others, not so much.

Peter liked his role as a pastor. After several years of marriage, she began to think he might like it a little too much. Charlie had always directed the people in his care back to God, but Peter became quite good at playing God.

Still they had a good marriage, it seemed, for a few years. Then all she'd thought was true, all that she'd nourished in their relationship, was swept away.

Peter, in the clarity of hindsight, had become her god too.

Standing quickly, Addie knocked over the patio chair, leaving it on the ground. No matter what Emma thought, staying alone in this cottage was not a good option, but neither was driving around. She had a much better map now, thanks to the one she'd found in a drawer. Still she didn't want to get lost.

This was why she rarely left Tennessee. She and Peter had traveled to Mexico for their honeymoon, but when they returned, she moved into his home a couple hours north of Chattanooga, near Knoxville Christian Church. Peter had been a full decade older than her, one of six children. His family was from Boston and her parents both died before her sixteenth birthday, so she and Peter spent most of their holidays with Charlie and Emma.

Early on, Charlie had seen the pride that ultimately led to Peter's demise. He'd advised her, warned her even, not to marry him. But he still welcomed Peter in his home as Addie's husband. Not once had he condemned her for this choice, and she would love Charlie forever for that gift.

She couldn't bear to lose both him and her husband in the same year.

While she longed to know what God would have her do now, without Peter and his vision for their church and family, her future was unclear, any whispering of instruction muted in her ears. Waiting, it seemed, was what He had for her.

She tied the laces of her hiking shoes, wrapped her favorite scarf around her neck, and headed out the front door. Even though September was just beginning, she could already feel the chill of autumn in the air. In spite of the rain shower last night, no humidity lingered like it would back east.

A slender trail snaked around the lake, between the trees and water, taking her away from the willow. As pretty as this place was, an idyllic vacation spot, she preferred to surround herself with Charlie and Emma and the girls at Sale Creek.

She wouldn't be alive today without Emma and Charlie and the love of those who'd dedicated themselves to partnering with God for a miracle. Charlie and Emma were both in their seventies. Someone would need to take their place eventually . . . but not yet. More than a thousand girls like her had graduated from the program outside Chattanooga, and many more needed Charlie with his compassion and drive, a gentleman who loved them like a father.

He and Emma had been married for thirty-five years, and while they had no biological children, most of the women who'd graduated from Sale Creek thought of him as their dad. It would be a travesty to shut the doors even for a season when so many young women needed the stability, the soul recovery, there.

Addie ground her heel into the bank, her heart churning as she refocused on the beauty around her.

The lakeside path had been well cared for, the weeds cleared from the dirt, but both sides of the path were carpeted with an assortment of plants—tall grasses and thorned blackberry bushes and a chorus of cattails standing tall with their furry caps.

Choir. Cats. Caps.

A neat lineup in her mind.

Strung across the waterside was a brightly colored vine with red berries and the prettiest purple flowers she'd ever seen, each petal orbiting around the sunlike center of their universe. The vibrancy of this one plant, all the colors, mesmerized her for a moment, and she wondered at its name.

On the other side of the vine was a worn dock. After testing a plank, she stepped out, the platform sinking until she was just a few inches above the water. Almost as if she was walking on the surface. A breeze rippled across the water, the aroma of pine spreading through the valley.

Across the lake, on a hill beyond the pine trees, was a vineyard. To its left she could see another cluster of pines and then a white turret, the same one she saw last night. Ruby Tonquin's house, according to the rental agent who got about half her information right.

Had Ruby's children grown up in that house with her? If so, was any information about Charlie's sister still there? Something small that could direct Addie to her.

People didn't just disappear. At least not without some sort of trail.

A narrow path led up the ridge, and she began to climb slowly, glancing back over her shoulder to make sure she didn't lose sight of the cottage or lake. It wouldn't pay to get lost again, especially with Tara being the only local who knew she was here.

The gravel road stretched across the ridge, and she followed it back to the overgrown driveway. In hindsight, she wasn't certain how the Civic fit through the narrow drive between the trees.

The two red-painted stories on Ruby's house and turret towered over the nearby trees, its white trim coated in moss. While the window on the second floor was completely shattered, from rocks being thrown perhaps, the glass on the first floor was still intact and draped with a faded cherry-red-and-white fabric to match the exterior paint.

Why hadn't someone renovated this place? A house that once overlooked the lake, at least from the second floor, would surely have sold for a significant price. Nature had overtaken much of it now, obstructing the view from any window except the turret, but surely someone could breathe life back into this place with a hammer and a fresh coat of paint.

After unlatching the front gate, she slipped inside the weed-ridden front yard to see if the interior was still habitable. A stone walkway led up to the front porch, and she jumped from one stone to the next as if she were playing hopscotch.

No signs had been posted to deter trespassers, and she wondered for a brief moment if someone still lived there. Only the rarest of persons—the most desperate, she supposed—would choose to live in such a broken home.

A deep breath, and she scanned the mash-up of oak and pine trees in the front. No winged creatures appeared to buzz her again, so she tested the wooden planks on the porch, like she'd done with the dock, before stepping up.

She knocked once on the front door and waited before checking the knob. Locked.

Turning right, she rounded the side porch and then stopped suddenly, surprised to see an immaculate garden behind the house. Flowers blossomed on the sloped edge of the ridge, a line of trees beyond it, and she stepped off the porch to wander down a bluestone walkway, so different from the front of the house. A masterpiece of beauty, painted with bold strokes and terraced in two levels. The house might be in shambles, but someone had been taking excellent care of the flowers.

The centerpiece was a white fountain with a woman holding up a torch, the water springing from sculpted flames and splashing back down into a small pool. The walkway ended at the fountain, and three mowed paths fanned out between the formal hedges and flower gardens.

Mesmerized, Addie strolled through the pruned flower beds, inhaling the fragrance.

Lilacs. Lilies. Lavender.

The words ticked slowly in her head, a host of purple blossoms stringing through them like ivy, calming her mind. The spring blossoms in this garden were long gone now, but the roses shone like gems on a crown. Peach blossoms tinted with magenta. Silvery blues and the darkest of red. Rose wine.

At the far end of the garden was a curved pergola wrapped around two manicured hedges. Addie smiled as she ran her hand over one of the hedges. An artist, she decided, must have designed it.

If Ruby had left here long ago—who was continuing to tend this beautiful place?

This garden, carefully tilled and tended, could overshadow the pain in one's life. Forget, for just one glimmer of a moment, and bask in the beauty. In the light, Charlie would say, of the eternal.

She rounded the edge of the flower gardens and stepped back onto the porch. The back door was locked like the front, but the curtains on this side of the house were tied back. Circling her hands like a porthole, she gazed through the glass.

Inside was an old-fashioned dining room, complete with two worn velvet sofas and a long table. The furniture was intriguing, but it was the far wall that captured her attention. A mural was painted across it, a marvelous work with Swiss-like mountains and a château and a group of people who—

Addie cupped her hands closer to her eyes to block the light, squinting for a better look. The people on the mural were all dressed differently, some more modern, others clothed in alpine attire like they were preparing to climb the mountains.

She couldn't see the faces, but the colors around each person were brilliant like those she'd seen in the rose garden, a variety of them crowning each head and draping like silk down the sides of their bodies. An aura of sorts.

She'd never seen anything like it before.

Was Ruby an artist, or had she hired someone to match the colors in the garden?

Addie inched across the picture window, scanning the mural until she reached the far end of the house. The porch ended here, the yard on this side filled with weeds like the front. As if someone only cared about the garden.

Something shuffled behind her, and she spun, scanning the hedges and flowers until her gaze stopped on the row of trees near the end. Perhaps it was only a bird, flitting between the branches, like the one that startled her long ago at Sale Creek.

Still she had a feeling she was being watched. A feeling she'd relied on heavily in her younger years.

Moving back around the house, Addie stepped off the porch and hurried back to the trail. Stirring up ghosts, in her experience, never did any good. She needed to stay focused on the future, finding out where the Tonquin family went, not concern herself with Ruby's house or land.

Whatever ghosts remained here wouldn't want to be disturbed.

CHAPTER EIGHT

Who was the girl looking in Ruby's windows? She was pretty enough with light-brown hair tied up behind her head, a pink scarf around her neck, but much too curious for her own good. For anyone's good.

The house was Ruby's, and it was his job to keep it safe until Ruby returned. No one should be smearing the glass.

The girl had already spent last night outside as if she owned the place, and only Caleb was allowed to visit, the boy who came on Saturdays to help him work in the garden.

Ruby had never liked flowers much. Men used to send her dozens upon dozens of them, but she only liked the ones he would bring home. Grace had planted this garden, and he had pruned and planted and cared for it so one day Ruby would have plenty of flowers to enjoy.

Finally the girl with the pink scarf left, and he cleaned the back window with a rag, checked the lock. The damage was minimal, but he would have to be more vigilant.

No one except Caleb was allowed inside. Not those curious kids who came up from town in the night hours. None of the people who arrived in their fancy cars as if they might be able to buy the place. Not the girl who had been nosing around here last night and today.

He didn't want any of them near Ruby's home.

A tuck of the rag into his pocket, and he ducked under an overhang of tree branches, to an A-frame built with wood from the Tonquin land. He'd renovated it over the years. Added a monocular to the loft and trimmed the upper branches between his foxhole-of-a-hut and Ruby's place. Not enough so anyone would see the hut, but with his scope, he had a clear view of the house. No one, day or night, visited without him knowing it. And they all left without knowing he was there.

The door bumped against a tree trunk when he unlatched it, a gust tilting one of his pictures. He quickly straightened the frame before looking into Ruby's eyes, like he always did when he came home. And he told her that everything was okay.

This stranger wouldn't bother her home again.

Chapter Nine

FRANCE

The attic window, a cushion of pillows on the dormer seat, became Grace's sanctuary in the evenings. Below she could see fragments of the driveway between trees, and she watched it closely as the sun began to fade behind the mountains, waiting for Roland to return.

An entire week had gone by since he'd left the château. A week with no word about the lost children or a guide to take Marguerite over the mountains.

The front gate was covered with leaves along the lane, too far for her to see. Hélène had warned her not to revisit the front gate, and they'd established firm boundaries around the château. The well on one side, the stream on the other.

Most adults near here, Hélène had said, feared the ghosts, but children weren't nearly as intimidated by the supernatural stories. A child, she feared, would spread the word, and not even the ghost stories would keep away mercenaries who profited from turning in their Jewish neighbors.

Marguerite kept herself entertained these days with the paint cans collected in the kitchen. Hélène said the girl could do whatever she wanted with the paint, so Marguerite blocked off the door into the ballroom with a sheet, spending most of her daylight hours inside, promising to surprise Grace soon with her work.

While Marguerite painted, Grace had spent hours in the garden, weeding and pruning so that after a long winter's rest the flowers would bloom again come spring. Not that she would see them—she'd be traveling home the moment the war ended—but she would imagine it in her mind's eye for many years to come.

She'd pulled ragweed and a creeping ivy out of the patch, the very act giving life to her and, she hoped, the edible lamb's-quarters and purslane and nettles that remained grounded. Ripping out what would bring death to the beauty here while keeping the plants they could eat if necessary.

Those years on the dairy farm had prepared her for this journey like nothing else could have done. And her earlier years in Hollywood too, if she was honest, had given her exactly what she needed.

At an early age, she'd become an expert at fading into the background, even disappearing when necessary. She'd spent hours watching her mother charm men at the parties Ruby loved. Men of all ages would scatter like chickens when her mother walked into the room, scratching up bits of feed served on fancy plates, fetching colorful drinks topped with cherries and lime. Then they'd return like proud roosters, ready to impress the hen with their bounty, and Ruby always lauded them for their gifts.

Sometimes they brought her jewelry and other extravagant gifts that ended up in the hotel drawers. Even though she was extravagant with her words, Ruby wasn't really impressed by these gifts or the men who gave them.

Grace had vowed never to use these same skills to manipulate others for her own good, but she would do what she must to protect the children.

"Miss Grace?"

She turned around, startled to see Marguerite. "What is it?"

"Would you like to see what I've painted?"

"Very much." She eyed the darkening sky again, only a halo of pink light shimmering now above the peaks. They'd have to hurry if she was to see anything tonight.

As rain began to fall, splattering the window, Marguerite grabbed her hand. They stepped around a pile of dirt and debris that had fallen through a crack in the roof, then Grace followed her down the servants' stairs and through the corridor, past the former library and the kitchen. The curtain hiding Marguerite's work still hung across the entry into the crumbling walls of a room where ladies and lords once danced and dined.

The girl pulled back the curtain as if a theater production was about to begin. Grace closed her eyes, letting Marguerite lead her inside, and when she opened them again, even with the dwindling light, her mouth dropped open in wonder.

The interior wall had been stripped and cleaned and transformed into a mural with a series of pictures in chocolate brown and copper, a sky blue and sunflower yellow and evergreen. The expedition began with a bell tower, it seemed, the creation much like that of Claude Monet with swirls of color in the sky.

"It's the church," Marguerite said, pointing to the image on their left.

A path, painted with green-and-brown circles and a blue river mist, led from Saint-Lizier to a flecked stone barn and then into a forest, the trees bending over to create a tunnel.

Grace touched her fingers to the dry paint. "You have a gift, Marguerite."

The girl crossed her arms, disappearing into herself. "It's just what I see."

"They are extraordinary." Her fingers followed the path to her right.

"It's so Élias can see where we've been. So he will know—"

Grace stopped at an inky-black portion, a pinhole of light near the top. "Is this the barrel?"

She nodded.

"It's remarkable," Grace said. "I'm glad you are sharing these."

Marguerite lifted her brush from a pail of water and wiped it on a towel. "I have to get the pictures out of my head."

Grace pointed at a line of small pots and cans along the wall. "Where did you get all these colors?"

"Hélène dyed them with her herbs and some plants that she found in the woods."

Marguerite moved a footstool so Grace could continue trailing down the wall. Next along the journey was the gray exterior of the château and a long stripe with two people at the end. A man and woman beside a wagon.

"It's you and Monsieur Roland," Marguerite explained.

Both faces were a blur of cream-colored paint, the blotting of a young artist except—Grace leaned closer and examined the bright yellow blending into her sandy-blonde hair. And the blue in Roland's.

"Yellow and blue." She looked back at the girl. "What do the colors mean?"

Marguerite shook her head. "They're not exactly right."

"It doesn't have to be right," she said. "I'd just like to know."

Marguerite pointed to Roland. "He's sad."

"That's true. We're both blue."

The girl shook her head again, indicating the gold color. "Yours is love."

Grace shivered at that single word, exposing everything in her heart. "Sadness and love."

Marguerite looked at the cans. "I've run out of paint," she said, sadness of her own creeping in.

"What else do you want to paint?"

"The mountains and the trees, but I need more colors."

"God has given you a gift," Grace said. "Using whatever colors you have."

She envied those who shone light into the darkness of this world, transforming it with their talents. Those with the voices of angels to sing, the wisdom of words like King David to write, the perception to paint like Marguerite.

A shadow swept across the floor, darkness drawing a curtain over this room for the night.

"We must go upstairs before we can't see at all." It was dangerous to lose one's sight in this place with the missing banister and broken floor pieces and glass shards.

Hand in hand, they moved toward the curved staircase, hugging the wall so neither would fall. She counted as they climbed, hopping over the missing steps.

Partway up the staircase she heard a noise from below. Or perhaps through a broken window. A voice, it seemed.

Then all was quiet.

Voices, she feared, were beginning to talk in her head until Marguerite whispered. "Did you hear that?"

"The voice?"

Marguerite squeezed her hand. "I don't know what color it is."

She counted more rapidly now as they rushed up the steps, into the bedroom they shared at the back of the house, near the servants' staircase. The window was still intact, covered by a black curtain.

There were four cots in this room and another four in the connecting one. Cots used, she'd been told, for those escaping this regime. Perhaps they would be receiving guests soon. Tonight even.

If so, she prayed they would be friendly.

Marguerite retrieved a candle, and Grace lit it with the matches in her pocket. Then she checked to make certain the dark curtains covered the rain-soaked glass.

"The Lord is my shepherd; I shall not want."

She began quoting the psalm about God comforting them in the darkest of valleys.

Another voice outside, a shuffle from the hallway, and she opened the closet door for them to hide.

"Ghosts," Marguerite whispered as Grace blew out their candle.

Did the Nazis know they were in the château? If so, who had given them away?

"Miss Grace." The name slipped into the closet and echoed between the narrow walls.

The murmur of children followed the call of her name. This wasn't an enemy or fugitive airman. Nor was it a ghost . . .

It was the children. *Her children.*

Her heart soaring, Grace pushed open the door and glanced at a ring of tired faces, each one smudged with dirt, their noses running. The most beautiful faces she'd ever seen.

She counted them quickly—Suzel and Élias and Louis and all the others. Eleven of them. Even the child who hadn't been taken by the Nazis in Saint-Lizier was here.

But not the tall man who'd left to find them. The one whose casual smile and fearless gaze disarmed their enemy.

Opening her arms, she gathered them under her wings, covering them like she hadn't been able to before. Even with her hope, her many prayers, she hadn't really thought she would see them again.

But somehow Roland had found them. Somehow he'd brought them here.

Looking up, she saw Hélène, tears captured in creases around the older woman's eyes. Marguerite stood beside her, staring at Élias as if he'd just walked out of the pages of a picture book. Or a grave.

"Snowy," he said softly, holding out his hand. Then he put both arms around his sister, pulling her to his chest.

Grace was relieved for both of them. More than almost anything in this world, they needed each other.

"Where is Roland?" she asked Élias.

"He left us hours ago."

The joy in her heart started to siphon away; she could feel the drain of it in her toes. "What do you mean, he left you?"

"He escorted us to a road and told Suzel and me how to find the château."

Her chest seemed to knit itself together, pressing against her lungs, and she struggled to catch her breath. These children were in her care again, the grief at this loss replaced with joy. Yet without Roland, fear threatened to smother her joy.

She reached down to help one of the younger children out of her damp coat.

This was why she could not allow her heart to wander in the midst of a war. Love made her lose focus, cast their entire mission into a blurry haze when time was short for all of them.

She stepped toward Suzel and smoothed back the dark strands that had escaped from her braid. "Where did the Nazis take you?"

"To a jail in Saint-Girons. They put us together in one cell and left us with the French police."

She shivered at the thought of her kids imprisoned. "You took good care of everyone."

The young woman rubbed her arms, warding off the chill from the night air. "There was little that I could do."

Getting these children, as many children as possible, across the mountains was all that mattered now. While she was relieved that they were healthy enough to travel here, a quick glance showed ruddy noses, sunken cheeks. And a palpable fear. What these children must have seen, experienced, while imprisoned must have been horrific.

"Where are your knapsacks?" she asked Suzel.

"The guard took them."

She carried their identity cards in her knapsack, their other papers stitched in their clothing, but they had no extra clothes beyond the coats or blankets wrapped around them. The Nazis had taken their families and stripped them of everything they needed to survive. A bit of God, she'd been taught, could be found in every man, but she was hard-pressed to find a glimmer of light in those who implemented this cruelty.

She helped another child untie her *espadrilles*, hanging the fabric shoes up to dry. "How did you get out of the jail?"

Suzel answered. "Roland and Élias found us."

When Grace turned toward Élias, he shrugged, his eyes focused on a cracked floorboard. Then she realized that he still had his pack.

He was the eleventh child, the one who had gone free, but instead of hiding, he'd returned for his companions.

Did Roland know that Élias hadn't been captured? Part of her wanted to wring his neck—for not telling her that Élias was free, for letting this boy assist him on a mission that might have killed them both—but Roland often saw strength in those whom others might see as weak. He'd seen a man where Grace saw a boy.

She wrapped Élias in her arms. While she wasn't old enough to be the mother of a thirteen-year-old, she felt like one in that moment, proud of him for standing up against this great enemy and negotiating the children's release.

"You did this," she said in awe, scanning him from head to the toe that was sticking out of his shoe.

"I couldn't let the Nazis send them away."

She shook her head, trying to clear it. "Did Roland tell you where he went?"

Élias dug into his coat pocket and removed a crumpled piece of paper. "He said to give you this."

She read the note quickly.

I have work to do before I return, but I will find you, after the children fly.

At the bottom, he had drawn a hummingbird.

Her face grew warm. Perhaps the conflict in his heart was as great as hers.

The children couldn't know the details about their mountain journey ahead, but she had to prepare them with food and rest. Neither the mountains nor the Nazis would have compassion on them if they were too worn to climb.

One of the children huddled in the corner, the four-year-old boy named Louis. He was shaking so hard that he couldn't unbutton his coat. Grace helped him remove it, and his threadbare shirt billowed over his frame like an oversize tent. No wonder he was shaking. His body had nothing left to insulate him from the chill.

It would take months, years even, for these children to recover body, mind, and soul.

Marguerite wrapped a homespun blanket around Louis, and when the boy scooted away, Grace turned back to Élias. "You are a courageous young man." Selfless, like she wanted to be. "How did you get them out of jail?"

He shook his head. "I don't want to talk about it."

She wanted to know every detail about their rescue, but she wouldn't push him to talk until he was ready. Perhaps he would tell her in the morning.

"How long has it been since you ate?"

He shrugged. "We found apples along the road."

"Come along," she said. "Let's get all of you some food and then you can sleep on the cots."

The children continued to whisper as if the Nazis might be in the next room, and it was probably wise of them. None of them knew exactly when their enemy might appear.

Hélène sliced a loaf of brown bread in the kitchen, working by a kerosene light. Grace scooped up a pound of chickpeas and added them to those she was already soaking in a pot of water. Tomorrow she'd make soup with the beans and fresh carrots that Hélène had provided.

"Thank you for doing this," Grace said.

"I took care of the other children." Hélène patted each slice with white butter, churned from sheep's milk. "When they were staying here."

Grace lowered the pot. "What children?"

"Those my nephew brought to me."

"Your nephew . . ." As soon as the words rolled from her lips, Grace understood. That's how Roland knew about the château.

Once again, he was trying to guard a secret. Protect them all.

"Did Roland live near here before the war?"

"He grew up in the village, before he went to college in Oxford. Then he returned from England to help me with the Spanish children flooding over the mountains."

"And now you help him," Grace said as she buttered bread with Hélène.

"I will do anything I can to help those trying to escape this regime."

"The children can't stay here for long."

Hélène put down the knife, her voice sad. "Where else would they go now?"

Grace's hand trembled as she buttered the last piece. She couldn't focus on what might happen. Only on what God had provided them.

This blessing of food for the children. Protein and proper nutrition to prepare them for the treacherous hike ahead. "Hopefully Roland will send a guide soon."

"When it is safe, he will make sure you find your way across."

"I'm not leaving France," Grace explained. "Only the children."

Hélène lifted one of the trays, and Grace joined her with the other. Some of her wards ate rapidly; others picked at their bread until Grace insisted they eat. They must keep up their strength, she explained.

Sleep came quickly to the children, but Grace lay awake for hours. Helping them find freedom was what she wanted, the reason God had brought her here. How she longed to hear His voice tonight, louder than all the others in her head. Louder than the fears that plagued her.

She could hear the soft breathing around the room, the stirring in the dreams. None of them knew when the Nazis would appear, searching for Jews to meet their quota, but Roland had told her to wait, and she would have to trust his lead.

When it was time, the children would leave together.

This time, not a single child would be left behind.

CHAPTER TEN

Addie waited outside the Newberg schoolhouse-turned-library until a young librarian, her dark hair braided neatly in cornrows, opened the front door. Growing up in a rough neighborhood, Addie had learned more about reading people than books, but she would research today until she found a trail back to Charlie's family. A short trail, she prayed, to find a donor.

"How can I help you?"

Addie regained her focus to look at the woman across the reference desk. Late twenties maybe. Same as Addie.

"I'm trying to find information about the Tonquin family," Addie explained. "They used to live near here."

The lady gave her a curious look. "Are you writing a story?"

"No—"

"Usually people who ask about the Tonquins are working on a documentary about Hollywood or something."

She'd read a biography about Ruby on the plane, but it was more scandal than substance. The writer didn't even mention that Ruby had children, but Addie had already found the information about Grace online. "This is more personal."

The woman blinked. "Are you a relative?"

"I'm trying to find out what happened to Ruby's children," she said.

"She only had one daughter, and Grace left here a long time ago."

"What about her son?"

The woman busied herself with rearranging a pile of books. "I don't know anything about a son."

"Do you know where Grace went?"

The woman shrugged. "Some say she went into hiding after her mom was killed."

Addie flinched. She'd read about the possibility of murder in the biography, but according to that author, no one had ever found her body. "Who do you think killed Ruby?"

"No idea," the librarian said. "Some of the locals think she ran away instead. Or was kidnapped by an admirer. She had lots of them, you know."

"I don't really know much about her."

The librarian stood. "We have the clippings about Ruby and Grace all bundled up in a folder. I'll get it for you."

Addie found a seat near the reference desk, watching people file through the front door. Perhaps she would find the information about the Tonquin family today and then head home. Emma and Charlie had said she could live in their guest cabin for as long as she needed, helping out with chores and spending time with the girls. Not forever, she thought, but she was grateful for a nest to land.

The materials inside the thick folder were mostly a collection of magazine articles about Ruby, a silent movie star who became queen of the silver screen when motion pictures found their voice.

Inside was a feature from *Glamour of Hollywood* in 1939 and one from *Vogue*. Ruby Tonquin had certainly been a glamorous woman, photographed with many of the leading actors of the time—Clark Gable, Spencer Tracy, Cary Grant. In one photograph, at the annual film festival in Venice, her shiny black hair was cut and rolled just below her shoulders, her lips thick with gloss, dramatic dark eyes seeming to capture the camera instead of the camera catching them.

Addie wouldn't describe her as beautiful. More like a witch with a gleaming apple in hand. A temptress, waiting for someone to bite.

It was an image, perhaps, cultivated for her audience. No photographs had been snapped by paparazzi while she was out walking her dog or taking her children to school. Each accompanying story was as coiffed as the woman's hair, perfectly brushed, rolled, and sprayed.

What was Ruby like off the pages?

She was here to find information about what happened to the woman's children, not Ruby, but she was still intrigued. Several of the articles from the 1920s displayed pictures of Ruby with her young daughter, cuddled up next to her on a love seat, but Grace looked more like a pet than a toddler—a cat or dog miserable in their cage.

She pulled out her photograph of Charlie and his sister. The pieces wouldn't seem to fit, no matter how she twisted and turned them. The girl in this picture, taken in 1946, was much too young to be Grace.

Perhaps Charlie had two sisters.

He'd traveled from Oregon to Tennessee when he was seventeen, the same age as Addie when she arrived at Sale Creek. The future, Charlie once told her, mattered to him much more than the past.

Forgetting the past, looking forward to what lies ahead. He'd quoted that verse often from Philippians. His focus, he liked to say, was on the next bend, but in order for him to embrace the future now, they had to look back.

Addie flipped through two more articles. Why didn't any of them talk about Ruby's son? Charlie was seventy-three now, born in 1930, but none of the stories from the 1930s mentioned him.

Charlie never talked about Ruby or Grace, at least to Addie. If only Emma would ask him again about his family, find out what he remembered about his sister, it would make her search much easier. But Emma was worried that he would tell them to quit searching, and neither she nor Emma wanted to quit.

Next was an article, torn and smudged, in an entertainment magazine called *Photoplay* from 1946, a year after World War II ended. Between advertisements for Pond's skin cream, Royal Crown Cola, and Parisian face powders was a feature story about Ruby, starting with her birth on her parents' dairy farm.

A photograph accompanied the story, a picture of a farmhouse near Tonquin Lake. Ruby had arrived in Hollywood in 1917, on the eve of her eighteenth birthday, and over the next two decades, she starred in almost twenty movies, winning an Academy Award before her star dimmed. It wasn't a slow fade. After her last two movies tanked, Ruby's departure was like a shooting star that burned across the sky.

The next article was from a local newspaper, written in the spring of 1947. It talked about the completion of Ruby's house in the hills north of Newberg, a design that would rival a Hollywood mansion. *Château sur la Colline*, she'd called it, a nod to her obsession with all things French. The castle on the hill.

Addie creased her finger over the edge of the story and skimmed through the article. The writer didn't even mention Ruby's family.

Several other articles followed, much different in tone. Ruby, it seemed, had stepped completely out of the spotlight with a final house party near the end of the 1940s. Murder, one article mentioned. Others simply said she disappeared.

Had her family hidden the cause of her death from the media? Charlie would have been in his late teens when she died. Had he and his sister already left Oregon? If so, where had Grace gone?

Addie understood well why the family wouldn't want to speak with a reporter about the loss of a loved one. Today it was difficult to suppress such news, but then, it seemed, people were more respectful of privacy. Audiences didn't lay claim to knowing all the details about their favorite celebrities.

But surely someone in the Tonquin family knew what happened.

The last party at Ruby's castle-like home was in 1947, according to *Photoplay*, hosted by her and her son.

Addie leaned back against the chair, calculating the numbers in her head. It was the same year that Charlie arrived in Chattanooga. Did something frighten him back then? Frighten the whole family perhaps.

The cause of Ruby's death wasn't relevant to keeping Charlie alive today, but still she wondered what made him leave.

At the bottom of the folder was a stack of papers bound by commercial-size staples, the cover typed in a courier font. A research paper by a student at George Fox College in Newberg, written in 1960. Instead of focusing on Ruby, this man—Jonathan Lange—spent twenty pages writing about Grace.

Gold—that's what it felt like she'd found. The answer, she hoped, to finding Grace or her children.

She edged her finger across the top, the paper crisp as if no one had bothered with Ruby's daughter. Then she opened the cover and began to read the story of a baby girl born in Hollywood in 1918.

The year after her birth, Grace—along with 500 million people around the world—contracted the Spanish flu, and the senior Tonquins brought their granddaughter back to Newberg. According to the paper, Grace visited Hollywood multiple times to see her mother, sometimes staying for months, but she always returned to her grandparents' home.

After high school, Grace attended Pacific College, later renamed George Fox College and then George Fox University. Her second year, she relocated to France to help children escaping the Spanish Civil War, then she stayed to help French children during World War II. In 1943, Grace was imprisoned after attempting to transport a group of children into Spain.

Addie turned the page quickly, hoping that Jonathan Lange had recorded what happened to Grace after the war. And then more information about Charlie and another sister and perhaps even the reason Charlie left Oregon.

She had just begun to read the next page when her phone vibrated.

"Charlie was asking about you," Emma said after Addie slipped out the door.

She sat on a bench. "Did you tell him where I went?"

"I had no choice."

Neither of them wanted to raise his hopes or frustrate him in their search, but Emma would never lie to her husband.

"What did he say?"

"He wants to talk to you."

Addie took a deep breath. "Okay."

A shuffle in the background. The handing off of Emma's telephone.

"Adeline." Her full name, what he'd called her from the day she'd arrived at Sale Creek. "You didn't say goodbye."

"We didn't want you to know where I went," she said. "Didn't want to get your hopes up."

"My hope is in the Lord alone."

"If we can find a donor match in your family, the marrow could save your life." A 25 percent chance, the doctor had said, that a sibling would be a fit. Lower for a niece or nephew, but she refused to give up hope in that possibility.

A long moment before he spoke again. "Is Tonquin Lake still there?"

"It is."

"And the willow tree?"

"It's here too."

"Strong in the midst of its tears. Just like you, Adeline. It will help you shoulder the pain."

But she didn't want to talk about her pain.

"Did you find Grace?" he asked quietly.

"Not yet. I'm at the library right now, searching for information about where she went."

"Grace had to leave Oregon." His voice rattled with grief. "She had no choice."

"What happened, Charlie?"

"I did something terrible. Something that . . ."

She leaned back against the bench, smoothing her hand over her stomach. "Perhaps it's not too late to make amends."

"This time I'm afraid it is."

"You say that God's always in the business of redemption."

"And I believe it to be true, except sometimes that redemption takes place in the next life."

She looked up the side street, at a mother pushing a stroller, a boy chasing after his dog. "I want it for you now."

"You are a piece of that redemption," he said. "God rescued both of us when we were drowning and set us on higher ground."

She didn't say it but most days she felt as if she were still drowning.

"What happened here?" she asked again. She didn't want to agitate him, but it would help her understand why he wasn't as compelled as she and Emma were to save his life. Almost as if he wanted to continue serving penance for something that happened long ago.

"I don't remember all of it."

"You remember enough to tell me." He had always been straightforward with her. Strong when she felt shaky, hiding behind a mask of animosity in those early years.

Somehow he'd seen through her mask, just as she could see through his now. Whatever happened here must have wounded him deeply.

It had been more than fifty years since he'd arrived in Chattanooga. More than fifty years since he'd left this behind.

"Was Grace your only sister?" she asked.

"Adeline—"

"Or did you have other family?"

"The rest of my family wouldn't want anything to do with me."

"You might have nieces or nephews . . ." She was pushing too hard, like she often did, but she wasn't ready to let him go yet.

"I only want you to come home," he said, his voice tired. "I can't change the past, but I can choose who I want to be with in these last days on earth. You and Emma are my family now."

"But we can't give you the bone marrow you need."

"Neither can my family."

She tried to piece it together, a neat list in her head, but nothing seemed to fit.

"Grace wasn't my sister," he finally said.

Emma had gotten her away from Tennessee, given her time to think through the past three months on her own, but she couldn't help Charlie if he didn't have any blood relatives here. "Then who was she?"

"Grace stepped in as my mother after I lost mine. Let me borrow the Tonquin name."

A key piece finally slipped together in her mind. "Grace returned to Oregon after the war . . ."

"Please come home, Adeline."

"We need to find a relative for you. Your sister might still be here—"

"There's no one left for me there," he said. "You are loved, Adeline. By our God and me and Emma and a host of others. Don't you forget that."

"I won't." She rocked back on the seat. "Why won't you tell us what happened to your family?"

"Maybe . . ." His voice broke with the word, and she knew that she'd pushed too hard, but he had pushed her long ago when she hadn't wanted to live another day. Once she found his family . . . perhaps he would tell her then why he'd boarded a train alone to Chattanooga so long ago. "Grace was nothing but good to me."

"What would you say to her, if she's still alive?"

He paused. "That I'm sorry."

"If I find her, I will tell her for you."

"Come home," he said one more time.

She heard a clunking sound in the background, the passing of the torch back to Emma. She could almost see the woman slipping out onto their back porch to continue the conversation. "I'm worried, Addie."

"Me too."

"He's a strong man, but his heart is easily wounded. He wants you back here."

A group of preschoolers paraded by her bench, all of them clinging to a single jump rope in their trek to the library. "He said he did something terrible . . ."

"He won't talk about it," Emma said. "It's been like this ever since I met him. He's an open book about everything until you ask a question about his childhood. Then he talks about his time playing on the lake, memories on the farm, but he won't talk about his family. If you find his sister and she rejects him—I fear it won't be the MDS that kills him."

"I only want to help, whatever that looks like."

"Search a few more days and see if you can find his sister or another sibling." Emma took a deep breath. "He may be ready to go home, but I'm not ready for him to leave."

The older woman's voice broke, and Addie wished she could hug this sweet woman who brought life to all those around her. Who'd loved Addie well. "It's a gift, what you're trying to do for him."

"I pray so," Emma said. "And I'm praying for you. Every moment."

Addie moved back into the library.

"Where did you go?" she whispered before losing herself in Grace's story.

Chapter Eleven

Élias followed Grace up the hill behind the château, a moss-cloaked bed of leaves and logs sheltered by the trees. He was in charge of the knife while she carried a large wicker basket for their bounty.

They'd pick mushrooms until their basket was full, then they would boil chestnuts and thistle and fry these mushrooms with Hélène's butter to make a stew. Their stomachs would be blessedly full this evening on something other than turnips and chickpeas, the only remaining supplies from Roland's cache.

The children were recovering from malnourishment and exhaustion and the flea bites that had left welts on their legs and feet. Soon, she hoped, the children would be in Spain and the authorities across the border would let them stay, before the supply of forest food disappeared for the winter.

For almost a week now, they'd waited for the *passeur* to arrive, and with each passing day, each hour, fear rooted deeper inside her.

She was as much a refugee as the children now, unwelcome in this occupied land.

Last night, Roland had wandered back into her dreams, offering his hand, and she'd held it to her heart, never wanting to let go of him again.

How she missed that man who'd grown to be her anchor in this storm. Who fought for peace for all of them. In those night hours, when her resolve slipped away, she desperately wanted to be with him.

"Here's one." Élias pointed his pocketknife at a wavy beige mushroom buried in pine needles.

Kneeling beside him, Grace flipped over the cap and saw the mustard-yellow stem, bright-yellow pores, no cape around the stem. A *bolet*. This one would be safe to eat.

Élias opened his knife and sliced off the stem.

A glint of bronze caught the sunlight, and she saw the swastika embedded in metal.

"Where did you get that knife?"

He folded it back up and stuffed it into the pocket of his overcoat. "Near the jail in Saint-Girons."

They circled around a crop of mushrooms she didn't recognize, then Élias pointed at a pale-green mushroom with his blade.

Grace pushed the cap back with her stick. "See that?"

"It looks like the other ones."

"Not this part." She pointed out the white curtain draped around the stalk. "A skirted mushroom like this can be deadly."

He took a step away, shaking his hands, his eyelashes flittering with concern.

"I'm told they taste good when they're cooked, but one this size will kill an adult." She glanced toward the château. "Or multiple children."

"Chickpeas are just fine with me."

She smiled. "We'll find plenty of good mushrooms among the bad."

But he didn't look convinced. At thirteen, it seemed almost everyone and everything was against him. He'd had to survive in a world that already sent away his mother and baby brother. Where an entire army of adults were conspiring to take his life.

But he still had Marguerite, and she adored him. A long life was what she wanted for both of them. One that defied all those who were trying to steal it away, where they could discern well between the good and the bad.

They continued their walk through the old pine trees that played host to these mushrooms, no rush this afternoon as she'd left the capable Suzel in charge.

"What do you think of your sister's paintings?" she asked.

"They remind me of home."

"I hope that's a good memory."

His gaze seemed to wander away, back to Paris. "She and my mother painted together since Marguerite was old enough to hold a brush."

"I've never seen anyone paint such interesting colors for hair. Perhaps your mother showed her . . ."

He shook his head. "It's not hair. Marguerite paints that way because she sees a sort of cloud around people, depending on how they feel."

Grace stopped. "What do you mean?"

"They are green or yellow or blue. All different colors. Red is the worst."

Her eyebrows pressed together. She knew a lot about nature from her years on the farm, the science behind how the world worked, but she'd never heard of anyone seeing someone's emotions in color.

"She can tell if someone is afraid or cruel or angry," Élias said.

Or in love, she thought, her face flushing warm.

"That's an incredible gift."

He shrugged. "She doesn't think so. *Maman* saw colors in letters and numbers, so it's normal to her."

Grace scanned the forest and soaked in the shades of green and brown, the bits of mist that hung in the distance, the muted blue above. Color she took for granted.

"They call it *la synesthésie*," he said. "*Maman* and Marguerite see the world different than most people."

What would it be like to see emotions in color? The internment camp at Gurs must have been a crush of cruel colors against a backdrop of gray. Overwhelming to see all those hard emotions in a crowd, but especially the fear and shame, the anger and hatred, all of it together in one place with little hope or joy.

It was like Marguerite could peer inside an individual. See the color of their soul.

"Élias—"

He cut the base of another mushroom. One that was safe to eat.

"How did you and Roland get the children out?"

She'd asked him several times over the past week, but he hadn't wanted to talk about it.

He added the mushroom to her basket, then slowly folded the knife. "The police didn't think they'd try to escape, so they only had one guard on watch."

"Did you go into the jail?" she asked.

He didn't meet her eye. "I found the uniform of a Hitler Youth. Nobody cared much about a messenger boy."

Still she didn't understand how he could free ten children. "How did you distract the guard?"

"I didn't distract." His brown eyes lit. "I charmed him."

"You are just like Roland."

"Roland said I was more like you."

When she laughed, his smile chiseled into something like strength, a glimpse of the man he was becoming. Her respect for Élias continued to grow. Instead of running away to save his life, cowering with fear like so many adults would have done, he had charged forward to help the others.

She smiled. "I'm proud of you."

"There's nothing to be—"

She stopped him. "You are braver than most adults I know. You're certainly braver than me."

"Blistering barnacles," he muttered like he was Captain Haddock, his focus back on the forest floor, scanning for more mushrooms. His instinct now was to feed the children he had rescued. Just like Roland, who wanted no accolades for his heroism, only assurance that those in his care were safe.

Élias deftly swiped his blade through another stem, and she added the giant brown mushroom—this one called a *cèpe*—to the pile.

"Like *The Pirates of Penzance*," he said, holding up the blade.

"What do you know of pirates?"

"From *The Adventures of Tintin* and . . ." He lowered the knife. "My mother talked of going to the Savoy Theatre one day to see it."

"That's far from home."

He nodded slowly. "London was where she wanted all of us to live."

"I'm very sorry about your mother."

Élias turned to look back up the path as if he could see the château on the other side of the cropping of oak trees. "Marguerite looks just like her."

"Then you must look like your father."

"I will never be like my father!" Fury sparked in his eyes, twin blazes raging on ice.

She bit her bottom lip, frustrated at her insensitivity. Once, at the home in Aspet, another boy had called Monsieur Dupont a traitor. The accusation resulted in a punch and subsequent black eye.

It broke her heart to see how the Nazis divided families. Turned children against their parents with a display of force. No child liked to see the weakness of their mother or father. The shame that cloaked them when their parents couldn't stand strong. When one of them sold information to their enemy for gain.

Her hand rested on his shoulder until his gaze, both angry and scared, found hers. "I pray you will be exactly who God made you to be."

A fierce love, more of a fiery orange than yellow, stirred within her. Warm and soothing like a campfire on the coldest of nights.

She loved this boy and his sister. Loved them like they were her own children, though she'd never envisioned herself as a mom. The fear that plagued her, had plagued her for most of her twenty-five years, was that she'd fail like Ruby at mothering a child.

Élias and Marguerite had already been cut away from the roots of their family. If only she could sweep both of them into her basket and take them home to Oregon. Her grandmother could help care for them, like she'd done with Grace.

She turned away from Élias to stop her wandering heart. He and Marguerite had an uncle waiting to reunite with them in New York. Her own sadness wouldn't get in their way.

Maybe tonight would be the night that Roland returned with an escort to Spain. He'd be whistling, she could almost hear it now, as he strolled into the house. Then he'd wink at her before all the children surrounded him, thrilled that he was back.

The children appreciated her, but they adored Roland. Everyone loved that man.

Familiar longing simmered inside her, the richness stirring in her heart. She breathed deep of the wilderness, soaked in the laying down of autumn to the winter frost, waiting to begin anew in spring. Hope abiding in the most dormant of places.

A sound echoed through the trees, but it wasn't whistling. Someone was calling her name.

Élias turned around, and the two of them rushed toward the château.

It was Hélène who shouted for her, and Grace's heart began to pound when she saw the woman's wide eyes. Grace stomped out the gently stoked embers inside her as she prepared for another wildfire.

"What is it?" Grace begged.

"You must leave right away."

She glanced over at Élias, wondering if he was afraid, but his face only hardened.

"A company of Germans are in the village, and a friend heard them speaking about the château. They will be here soon, I fear."

For a moment she couldn't breathe, her lungs stopped by the memory of the truck in Saint-Lizier, taking her children away. The escape from the prison must have bruised the ego of the local gendarmerie. Everyone was probably talking about the Jewish children who'd duped them.

Did they know a thirteen-year-old boy had led the charge? They wouldn't be so careless the second time.

"How many of them?" Grace asked.

"At least ten on motorcycles."

Élias sprinted into the château.

"Go quickly," Hélène told her. "I will gather food while you gather the children."

A hundred thoughts swarmed like the botflies back home, paralyzing her. Not even the familiar count of three worked.

Hélène pushed her forward. "Get the children."

The older woman ignited her lungs and legs alike. Grace ran to the well first, and she didn't need to say a word. The children were always on guard. Always ready to flee when the enemy crouched again in their backyard. Suzel and the other girls dropped their buckets and raced back to the château. They would run together and hide. She wouldn't leave any of them behind.

Élias was already upstairs, collecting Marguerite and her rucksack. The others wrapped their few supplies in woolen blankets. It would be much easier to slip away in the forest if they could wait until nightfall. Only two more hours.

Eleven of the twelve children crowded into the ballroom, silently awaiting her command in their woven *espadrilles* and threadbare coats. How would they ever make it across the mountains dressed like this, without a *passeur*? But they had to try. If the Nazis found them here, they would shoot each one on the spot.

Roland, she prayed, would meet them on the way.

Élias rushed into the hall. "A motorcycle is coming up the lane."

She heard the rumble of engines outside. Several motorcycles, it seemed. The children started to shake, tears streaming down cheeks, but none of them cried out. Silence, they'd learned, was the only way to survive.

Her legs froze again. She'd traveled to France to care for refugees who needed food and medical care. No one had prepared her on how to escape men trained to hunt, except perhaps Ruby. Her mother never let a man intimidate her. Nor did she wait for anyone, male or female, to act as her guide.

Grace couldn't let her own fears stop her from saving these kids. No matter how fragile her wards, no matter how scared she was to face the mountains, they had no choice.

"We'll leave through the back." She turned around to thank Hélène, but the woman was already gone. Hiding in a safe place, Grace hoped, so the Nazis wouldn't find anyone.

The children shuffled toward the back door in rapid fire, the enemy on their heels again. None of them wanted to return to jail.

"Quietly," she whispered as each one walked outside, following Élias into the forest until only Louis remained.

"I don't want to go," he said. A rash had crept across his thin face, the little hair he had left clumped to his head. Grace didn't know his story—a coworker had met with his parents in Gurs—but after they crossed the mountains, he was supposed to live with a relative in Palestine. Just a few more days, and he would be free.

Louis fought against her when she picked him up, but she wouldn't leave him here, no matter how hard he struggled. One day he'd understand why she had to steal him away.

Hélène was waiting for them in the forest with a rucksack and a large basket filled with food, a black kerchief hiding her silver hair. "I will walk with you until you reach the mountains."

"The Nazis will kill you if they catch us," Grace said.

"And they'll kill me if I stay."

Behind them, the château's windows lit with lanterns, the glow burning through the trees. It wouldn't be long before they found the cots. Their little convoy would probably have a half hour lead if the Nazis decided to chase them.

However she hoped the soldiers wouldn't want to muddy their boots by traipsing across the slippery, mushroom-covered floor at night. That should buy them a few more hours, until the Nazis set out at first light.

As she divided the children into partners, a million stars began lighting the sky, staining it purple. When she lifted Louis again, he struggled against her, not wanting to be carried, but he also refused to walk alongside. Until all the children were safe, she tried to explain, he had no choice.

Hélène buttoned the top of her cloak and volunteered to take the lead with Élias since she knew the forest. Grace and Louis would guard the rear to make sure they didn't lose anyone in the dark.

"One, two . . . ," she began to count and then stopped herself. "If we're separated, keep walking toward the mountains. Hélène and I will find you in the morning."

"Three," Élias shouted from the front.

Louis kicked her side again, and they followed the others toward the Pyrénées.

CHAPTER TWELVE

He watched the girl through the brass binoculars he'd used in Vietnam. Before Lyndon Johnson sent him home. She stepped out of the cottage in the valley, the pink scarf wrapped around her neck again as if she hadn't a care.

Three days—that's how long this girl had been here. Would she never leave?

Pinky, he was going to call her. Like Pinky Tuscadero from *Happy Days*, the girl who always wore a pink scarf in her hair. Who never left well enough alone.

He clutched the binoculars tighter as Pinky turned toward the hill. Next week, when Tara dropped off her bag of treats, he'd ask how long the girl planned to stay in the cottage. If he could catch her before she ran.

Tara didn't like him much; she'd told him so quite clearly ten years ago when she'd started managing this property for her father. And that was perfectly fine with him. He didn't care much for her either but welcomed the fudge and cookies she left on his stoop. Never knocking on his door unless she wanted to remind him to leave her rental guests alone.

In exchange for the supply of sweets and a bottle of whiskey or two, he was supposed to stay on the hill while her guests played on the lake. This arrangement suited him well. He had plenty to keep him busy, watching over the forest and garden and all of Ruby's things.

Hundreds of people had stayed in the old Lange cottage since Tara's family began renting it out. They were like annoying gnats, buzzing around in circles for a week or two. He only made an appearance if they stomped up to Ruby's house, smudged her windows with their dirty fingers. And he'd do it again if Pinky paid another visit.

Instead of continuing his direction, the girl walked down the slope and stopped by the willow tree.

As long as she stayed down there, she'd do no harm to him or the house. Still he wouldn't let down his guard.

He swallowed the drink that fueled him day and night. Until it didn't. Then he would sleep for a day or two. Or four.

But he refused to let his body fail him now. He would keep vigilant. Protect Ruby's things.

When the girl disappeared underneath the tree, he lowered the binoculars.

He couldn't see her anymore, but she was there, waiting for him to sleep. Watching him, perhaps, from behind the leaves.

Someone else was walking below, at the far edge of the lake. Probably Caleb, making his rounds again, keeping track of Grace's land.

Or it could be the enemy, tracking him through the jungle.

Lifting his binoculars, he focused on the newcomer, but it wasn't the boy walking this time.

Turning, he looked back at the willow. Pinky was still hiding under the leaves.

He wouldn't let her get the best of him.

CHAPTER THIRTEEN

Addie collapsed on the grassy bank, drawn to this willow tree like a moth to light. She leaned back against the trunk, a hobbit hole under draping branches and a palisade of cattails that barricaded her from the water's edge.

Emma had called this morning to say Charlie had a nightmare, tossing and fighting against the darkness, but when he woke, he couldn't remember his dream. Something deep within him was trying to claw its way back out, and Addie had begun to wonder if it was more important for him to find out what happened to his family than restore the damaged marrow in his bones.

Wind rustled through the valley, the mint-scented leaves twirling like ribbons around her. Then the limbs bowed and rose in a dance, worshiping their Maker.

Bent but not broken. That's what Charlie always said. The pliant willow branches were attached to the strength, the deep roots, of the trunk.

To her left, creeping under the wall of willow leaves, were vines filled with red berries and purple-starred flowers. To her right several ducks swam in a stagnant pool dammed by felled logs.

She wanted to sit in this place, for hours even, to bask in its beauty and strength. So the tree could help shoulder the pain.

Trees. Twigs. Tears.

Gilded leaves spilled into the lake, stirring up ripples that traveled away in the breeze. The entire lake, she thought, might be made from tears.

She brushed away her own tears and stepped over to the lakeside, swiping her fingers through cold water, adding the grief from her heart to years of sorrow.

She had wanted the elegant beauty and strength of a weeping willow, not the sadness. She'd wanted to live the fairy tale, the happily ever after many women seemed to take for granted. She wanted to gift this baby growing inside her with a father and a mother. A family. What she'd wanted for herself when she was a girl.

I'll take care of you.

The whispered words empowered her. A declaration in humility and grace. She would bow like the willow, ask God for strength to parent her baby alone. He loved this child growing inside her, even more than she did. With His help, she would mother well.

She tossed one of the star flowers into the water and watched it sail away. This was the place where Charlie had stood in the old picture, and she could imagine him diving into the lake, paddling across the water, laughing with his sister.

Whatever happened here must have broken his heart as well, but they needed to exhume the past, no matter how painful. If his sister or another sibling was still alive, if they had children, they could save his life.

Yesterday she'd exhausted the collection of materials at the Newberg Public Library, reading every word about Ruby and Grace. And she found another missing piece to Charlie's story.

He'd said that Grace had stepped in as his mother, letting him borrow the Tonquin name, and according to the report, two French children had lived with Grace after the war. The thesis didn't record their names—for privacy reasons, the author said—but she felt certain these children were Charlie and his sister. The Tonquins in the photograph. Grace's adopted kids instead of Ruby's children.

Charlie might have other relatives living in France, but even if she searched the records, even if Charlie knew where he'd been born, it would be too late to find a donor.

According to Jonathan Lange, the author of the thesis, the Tonquin family left Yamhill County in 1947, after they lost their farmhouse to a fire. Jonathan Lange had grown up on this land and lived here for the first twenty five years of his life. The Lange family, he'd written, continued to care for Tonquin Lake and the surrounding property long after the Tonquins were gone.

Addie settled back against the tree, the slender leaves swaying around her. Charlie had rescued her more than a decade ago, even though she hadn't wanted rescuing at the time. How she wanted him to meet this child whom he already considered grand. Wanted healing for both the blood that ran through him and the brokenness of his past.

Was it right to keep searching even when he didn't want to know what happened to his family? She certainly hadn't wanted help when he rescued her. She'd stonewalled for a long time, but in the end, he had given her the gift of life. Just like she wanted to do now for him.

Her flight didn't leave for four days. Even if she didn't find Charlie's sister, if she found out what happened to the Tonquin family, perhaps there was healing still to be had.

A dog barked behind her, and she jumped up, bracing herself when the creature broke through the branches. The blue heeler stopped in front of Addie, eyeing her as if surprised to find company under this tree. The animal wore tags, but no way was she going to try and read them.

"Wallace!" a girl shouted from outside the covering of willow.

Addie wiped her hand over her face again, clearing away the tears. "You'd better go, Wallace."

But the dog didn't budge.

"I don't need you to fetch me," Addie said as if she could reason with the animal, but the dog just stared back.

"Good grief, Wallace." The owner carved out a doorway between the leaves and ducked under the canopy. "What are you—?"

Addie lifted her hand to wave at the college-age girl, followed by a shrug of her shoulders, an apology of sorts, as if she'd lured the dog under the tree.

"I'm so sorry," the young woman said, waving her hands. "I didn't know anyone was here."

Addie glanced at the dog sniffing the perimeter of water. "It seems I'm intruding on Wallace's space."

"He thinks the whole world is his space!"

"Funny name he has."

"My brother named him after the warrior in *Braveheart*." The girl plopped down on the grass as if she belonged here, crossing her fuzzy boots before leaning against the tree. Her jeans were fashionably splattered with paint, her short black hair spiked in different angles. She wore two silver beads in one earlobe, none in the other. "I'm Reese."

Addie saw in this girl one of the many who'd come to Sale Creek. A girl trying to figure out her place in the world as a tumultuous wave of expectations swept her into adulthood whether or not she was ready to swim.

"My name's Addie Hoult. I'm staying in the lake cottage."

Reese glanced over her left shoulder. "No one stays in that cottage for long. The old man scares them away."

Addie eyed her curiously. "What old man?"

"My uncle," she said. "He's harmless, really. Just doesn't like visitors."

"I haven't seen anyone."

"Nor will you unless he wants to be seen."

She wondered if Reese was trying to scare her. "I'm only here for a few more days."

Reese glanced down and saw Addie's wedding band. "Is your husband with you?"

"No." *He's at the bottom of Watauga Lake.* That's what she almost said. Plunging sixty feet over a cliff. "He wasn't able to come."

"Are you on vacation?"

"More of a research trip. I'm trying to find Grace Tonquin and her children."

Reese looked back at the lake. "That family has been gone forever."

"Do you know where any of them went?"

"No clue, but they still own most of this land. Just talking about it makes people edgy around here."

"Someone must know where they've gone."

"The Dawsons probably do, but they won't talk about it. They want to buy this land like a horde of others."

One of the ducks began climbing up the bank, and Wallace chased it away, swimming out into the water as if to remind all those with webbed feet that the shore was his space.

"Where do you live?" Addie asked.

"I'm from Seattle, but I'm staying with my brother for a few weeks to help him prepare for the grape harvest." She pointed across the lake, at the slope of vineyard and the house above that looked like it was made of glass. "My parents will be coming soon."

"You must have the best view in the whole valley."

Reese grinned. "The whole state, I think. We can even see Mount Hood on a clear day."

The dog hopped back onto the bank, and Reese groaned as he rained water over both of them. "Sorry about that."

"No worries. I needed another shower."

Reese smiled. "I'm afraid you won't find much about the Tonquins here. The only thing left, really, is that old house on the hill."

"Ruby's place?"

"That's what people like to call it, but her daughter actually owned the property. Still owns it, I guess. My brother will be up there this afternoon if you want to ask him."

Wallace's ears perked, and he turned to the left, hearing something beyond the branches.

Reese reached for his collar. "Don't even think about it."

But it seemed that he'd already thought. Seconds later, the dog tore away from her grasp and was gone, the curtain of leaves rising and then falling behind him.

"Nice to meet you," Reese shouted as she raced toward the leaves. "Wallace!"

And Addie was alone again.

Chapter Fourteen

"He's not going to make it." Hélène pressed her cheek against Louis's face in the fading light. His body dangled from her arms like an icicle, fragile and still, waiting to either melt or shatter. Even with the roar of the waterfall nearby, the spray of river water on his skin, he didn't shiver.

Grace and Élias had taken turns with Hélène, carrying this fragile boy through the woods and then up the pass, but for the past half mile or so, Hélène had refused to let go. After traveling for two nights, Grace worried Hélène wasn't going to make it across the final mountain in their path either, with or without Louis.

Reaching forward, Grace felt Louis's head. His skin burned against her touch, but he was still alive.

Should they turn back now from the Spanish border? The hope of freedom for all twelve children.

Her hands fell to her side, defeated. Every child here should be rescued, no matter how hard Louis fought against her. She'd made a promise to herself that none of them would be left behind.

Then again, if they turned around now, escape would be impossible if their enemy had been tracking them. She'd be offering up all their lives to the Nazis.

Should she sacrifice eleven children to care for the one? Or should she find shelter for Louis and Hélène, leaving the others to follow Élias and Suzel south?

It was an impossible choice.

Her stomach rolled even as she tried to clear her mind. On nights like this, she wished she could sail back to her bedroom in Oregon, pull the covers over her head, and hide from the evil in this world.

The river lapped against the shore, the other children waiting beside her, even as her mind shifted again. This time to Saint-Lizier, tucked back in the courtyard with Marguerite, watching the soldiers corral her children into a truck as if they were cattle. Then Roland stepping into the darkness, telling her what she must do.

If only he would appear again at the base of this mountain. Lead the others so she could help Louis and Hélène.

But this time she was on her own.

In His presence.

That's what David—when he was a shepherd—said in the Psalms. Even today, no matter what happened, God was with them.

Her feet began sinking into the mud along the riverbank even as her chest straightened. She would have to carry Louis across the river. Up and over the mountain if she must. Élias and the older children could help Hélène.

"I will carry him." She held out her hands, but Hélène shook her head.

"If you take him any farther, he will die in your arms."

Slowly Grace lowered her arms. "What are we to do?"

Hopeless, it seemed, and she desperately needed a thread of hope to continue.

"I will find a place for him." Hélène rocked Louis as if he might wake. "There are farmers, good people, across these hills. They will care for both of us."

Grace considered her words, the children all waiting for her to respond. She could insist on abandoning their plans, taking all the children back down the mountain with Hélène. Or Grace could go alone with Louis. Perhaps Hélène would be able to continue without the boy in her arms.

"Roland will find me," Hélène insisted. "And eventually he will find you too."

But the Nazis, she feared, would track them down first.

"You and Louis must come with us." Grace glanced at the foam swirling in the dark river before them. "We will find a way together."

"Across the water is a shepherd's path," Hélène said. "Follow it up the hill until you reach a meadow. Beyond it is another forest and to your left, tucked in the gray rocks, is a cave. The shepherds age their cheese inside. They won't mind if you eat what they've stored."

Grace nodded. They'd finished their remaining food two days ago, while they'd rested in a stone hovel that seemed to blend in with the other stones on their path. They would need sustenance to finish their climb.

"From there, it's straight over the mountain into Spain," Hélène said. "I will pray the soldiers on the other side will be kind."

Strength siphoned out of her. "I can't leave you, Hélène."

The older woman kissed her on the cheek. "We're out of options."

And she was right. Even if it split her heart again, what was left of it, she had to escort the remaining children over this mountain. Louis and Hélène—she would have to place both of them in God's hands.

A dog barked nearby, and her heart raced. They must hurry.

Grace brushed her hand over Louis's head. "The enemy will not defeat you."

This precious boy would live, she prayed, and love with his whole heart. Then she prayed for all of them, that in life, in death even, the Lord would be their light and strength.

If they didn't fear death—what was there left to fear?

"I'll go with them," Élias volunteered, but Hélène had already disappeared, blending with the trees.

Élias turned to her. "You shouldn't have let her go alone."

"I didn't have a choice." At least her friend knew who could be trusted in these hills. Where to find help. Grace and her wards must continue on.

The other children waited in silence, eyeing the stormy river that divided their path. A snake, she thought, all scaly and gray in the starlight, waiting to take them down.

Even if Élias was angry at her, even if she was just as scared as the children, she must remain strong for their sake. No matter the cold, the loss, they all needed to ford this river tonight and follow the trail worn by both shepherds and their sheep.

"Take off your shoes," Grace instructed, and the children removed them in spite of the cold. Their *espadrilles* were mere wafers now anyway, offering little protection to their feet, but the fabric soles would still help them climb. When they reached Spain, Grace would buy them new shoes. "Follow the rocks across," she instructed. "Like a game of *marelle*."

Hopping along the rocks instead of sketching them with chalk.

She untied her shoes and strung them over her shoulder with her rucksack. Then she lifted one of the younger children—a girl named Alice—so she wouldn't be swept away as they hopscotched across.

Suzel cried out when the icy water rushed over her feet and Grace wanted to cry as well. A brief memory rushed by with the current, helping her grandpa milk the cows, the bucket sloshing in her frozen hands, taking care not to spill a drop.

Even as the river rushed cold, the rocks slick under her feet, she wouldn't drop Alice or her rucksack or the dream of getting them all to a safe place. Two more days, three at the most, and they would cross the border.

She placed Alice on the opposite bank before returning to help the other children. Élias carried Marguerite across, then helped retrieve two others who might fall in the current.

The shock of the cold revived them as they dried off their feet on the grass. Once they slid back into the flimsy *espadrilles*, they took the hand of their partner and continued to climb. She couldn't afford an injury tonight or losing one of the children in the starlight that hid itself often behind the boughs of sky.

Finally they reached a plateau, a grazing meadow for sheep. Even with the dangers in the forest, she preferred it to the open spaces. Anyone could shine a lantern across a meadow like this and see her wards.

"Hurry now," she whispered, and they lifted their blankets and bags, running to the forest on the other side.

"We need something to eat," Suzel said after they ducked back under a covering of trees.

"The cave should be near." Grace scanned the woods. "We'll eat inside."

The cheese along with some chestnuts or mushrooms or winter greens. Whatever she could gather at first light.

"I will find you food." A man stepped out from behind a tree trunk, a middle-aged Frenchman in a *bure* shepherd's cape and beret. One of the girls gasped, several children scattering to hide.

Grace's heart leapt, but she didn't run.

"I don't have money," Grace said, her voice strong. At least, none that she would give him. The bills in the toe of her shoe were to bribe the Spanish guards.

"I'm a *passeur*." He eyed the remaining children, the stink from his clothing ripe as Limburger. "I have just completed a trip with . . . I don't suppose it would be wise to say."

They could use a guide, that much was certain, but she'd just told this man that she had no money. No reputable *passeur* would work for free.

"This path is no good." He nodded to the narrow trail she'd intended to follow. "A unit of Nazis are camped out at the top like it's a holiday."

The shiver that shot up her spine wasn't from the cold air.

"You must follow that path." He pointed to her right, away from the cave and the purported group of Nazis.

Someone took her hand and squeezed it, so hard that she felt as if it might shatter in the cold.

Marguerite stood beside her, relentless in her grip. Could she see the colors of a person's heart in the dark? Red was the color, Élias had said, that she didn't trust.

"Are you—?" Grace searched for a way to ask the girl without betraying her gift. "Are your hands red from the cold?"

Marguerite's voice was soft, barely a whisper above the breeze. "Very."

This was not a good man before them. He—and perhaps others—meant to harm her children.

Marguerite was on one side of her, and Élias stepped up to the other.

"We don't need your help," Grace said to the guide. No matter what he said, they wouldn't follow his lead.

"I will return with food," the man replied, "within the hour."

"We don't want your food either."

"They know me around here as a friend." He eyed the children as if he were counting heads. "You have no reason to fear."

But fear, in this case, would work in their favor.

"You must leave us alone," Grace said, but he shook his head, ignoring her words.

"You need me to take care of you."

The man stomped back into the trees, and she surveyed the rocky path in front of them. Did he know about the cave? Even if he didn't, he could follow them up the path until they stopped.

But if they bypassed the cave, continued up the mountain, she'd lose several children to exhaustion. Then they'd surely be caught.

Perhaps she could deter this man before he returned. So her children could rest in the daylight hours before continuing their journey.

"The cave is on the left," she whispered to Élias, pointing up the path. "Hide the children inside."

"Where are you going?" he asked.

"To find that man."

She knew he was about to protest, say that he must go with her into the woods.

"Please, Élias," she begged. "This time I need you to stay with them."

He called the children softly, gathering them together like a shepherd would his sheep.

Frozen leaves crunched under her oxfords as she hiked back through the forest, but her attempt to follow the man, it turned out, was as futile as trying not to crush the leaves. She began to worry that she'd lose her way in these trees.

Light had begun to swell over the mountain, dancing along clusters of mist as if trying to illuminate anything hidden inside. She didn't see the man again but stopped walking when she heard voices. Several men were talking about her and the children, in broken German and French. And Marguerite was right—this man who'd purported to help them burned red.

"I will bring others this evening," he said. "At least ten more."

More.

Had he already found Hélène and Louis?

She couldn't think about it now. Couldn't imagine Roland's aunt, a true heroine, or Louis gone.

One of the Germans asked how this man was certain, and she

could hear the smirk in his reply. He could smell them, he said. The Jews always stank.

Her heart bled as if he'd stabbed her with a knife. Take away the livelihood of her friends, their schools, their food, their beds, and their baths—what did the Nazis expect? And yet her children continued to fight for survival without a single comfort. From the rancor of mud they emerged, cut deeply and ready to be polished.

The man negotiated a deal as if he were smuggling horses or sheep across the border. A French traitor, a blackhearted mercenary, giving up these kids for a few hundred francs. Instead of smuggling them across the border, he was ensuring that they'd never make it to Spain.

Half now, he bargained, half later. She could almost hear the coins—blood money—clanking as he deposited them in his pocket. Anger burned within her. Raw at the injustice of it. And she could smell the stench that festered under his skin.

How dare he betray these kids?

The children were hiding, the traitor told the others. Soon he would lead the Nazis to them, after their morning meal. They were collateral for him now, necessary for the down payment. He knew about the cave, she was certain of it. And he'd corner them inside.

Every limb in her body ached as she wove back through the trees, her mind as depleted as her strength, but she couldn't give in to the fatigue. Wouldn't allow these men to harm another child.

If she woke the children now, dragged them away, this man, she suspected, would follow them up the path. They would have to go off the trail, find another way over the mountain. Their heavenly Shepherd, she prayed again, would guide their every step.

The light flooded back into the corridor of the cave, and she found the children, most of them curled up together between the rocks for warmth, asleep on the lumpy floor among cages of cheese. Cloth wrappers doubled as linen cases over their rock pillows.

Marguerite was still awake, shivering as she sat on a flat boulder.

The temperature between these rock walls was still warmer than the forest, but these children might never feel warm again. She was cold herself, hungry. Beyond exhausted. She couldn't imagine how tired the children must be.

Still they would have to leave right away.

She counted heads swiftly, twice. Someone was missing.

"Where's Élias?" she asked Marguerite.

"He left soon after you."

Her heart should have plunged again in worry, but she felt nothing. All emotion, it seemed, had surged down the mountain, drowned in the river when Hélène and Louis turned back. Even the thought of the Nazis taking them, her fear, her anger, had drained away.

She collapsed on the ground, barely able to move, and yet—

"We have to keep walking," she told the girl.

"None of us can move," Marguerite said. "Not until we sleep."

And she couldn't take them away from this place, corral their tired bodies up the hill, until Élias returned.

She leaned her head back on the cold wall, the dim light disappearing when she closed her eyes, exhaustion pulling her deeper into the darkness. She couldn't sleep now . . .

"Miss Grace." Élias stood before her, opening the rucksack in his hands. "I found a bag filled with sugar cubes." Sustenance for a desperate climber.

"We will carry it with us," she said, pushing away from the wall, her mind sinking like her feet had done on the riverbank. "We have to leave here right away."

"Where were you?" Marguerite asked her brother.

"I followed the man who stopped us," he said casually. "But he was only a shepherd, staying in a hut nearby."

Marguerite didn't leap up to hug him. Instead she curled her legs to her chest.

What was the color of lying? One day, she'd ask. Marguerite could see it, she was certain, in her brother.

Élias slipped off his overcoat and draped it over his sister. Then Grace nodded toward the entrance, and Élias followed her away from the others.

"We must leave right now," she repeated.

"We can't go outside," he said, his gaze on the emerging rays of dawn.

"They are coming to arrest us."

Élias shook his head. "The man told one of the Nazis to meet him along the trail. He said he would deliver the goods."

As if her children were cargo for these men to buy and sell. Like the sheep that roamed these hills.

"How do you know?"

He turned to face her. "I heard them talking nearby."

"So we must go now—"

"The Nazis don't know this path," he whispered. "He didn't tell them about the cave."

She thought back to their conversation, and Élias was right. That information he'd kept for his own good.

How many others had he betrayed here?

"If he tells them about the cave, they no longer need him," Élias continued. "He's only paid when he brings them Jews."

"He'll find a way to betray us," she said. "They already paid him half."

Élias shook his head, his face grim. "He will never speak of it again."

She shivered. "What did you do?"

"Only what must be done."

Her hollow stomach rolled again. The soldiers, the adult men, had been called to fight, but this boy, any boy, shouldn't be hurting another. Neither should men, in her opinion, unless they were fighting the evils of Nazism. He'd taken the man's life, she suspected, before he took theirs.

She'd never tell her Quaker grandmother about her changing views on war, lest it break her heart, but she'd begun to think that the weapons she hated might be necessary to subdue the evil in this world.

"Why did you lie to your sister?" she asked.

"Sometimes," he said slowly, "you must protect the ones you love from the truth."

She wouldn't debate that with him, at least not here.

"The sugar cubes?"

"They were in his pack."

"We'll save them for tomorrow."

"Look," Élias whispered.

Snowflakes fell outside the entrance, blending with the crystal leaves. How would they make it to Spain now?

"We must sleep," Grace said, directing him back into the cave.

He looked as if he might argue, but he sank down on the floor near his sister. And Grace pulled her knees up to her chest, wondering at it all.

This wasn't a comic strip, she wanted to tell Élias, nor was he the heroic Tintin. He—all of these children—should only be pretending to escape like she'd done as a child, hiding from friends in a game, not from adults who wanted to kill them.

This was no game, but if God used the character of Tintin to give Élias the courage he needed to prevail, then so be it. She prayed he would always use this courage for good.

She found a place on the packed dirt, her scarf as a pillow, and folded her arms like a mummy inside her coat. And she dreamed of snowy passes and mounds of chestnuts and a shepherd who called her name.

CHAPTER FIFTEEN

Addie began climbing Laurel Ridge, hoping to find Reese's brother in the garden beside Ruby Tonquin's house. She understood why the family might want to protect their privacy, but Charlie was a Tonquin. Even if he and his sister were adopted, they were still family. While her own family might have failed, families were supposed to help each other heal.

Sometimes it took a long time for wounds to mend, she knew that well, but if the family could forgive whatever happened long ago, if they could embrace the honorable man that Charlie had become, they might be able to stop this loss together.

She glanced at her phone and the bars flickered between one and two. Back in Knoxville, Kirsten would be wrapping up her day at school.

"Are you on your way home?" Addie asked when her friend answered.

"Almost," Kirsten said. "But I'm alone at the moment. You doing okay?"

"I could use some prayer."

"You've got it."

"Thank you." Addie paused on the hillside so she didn't lose the connection. "I only have one bar and I'm afraid it's not going to last."

"It's good to hear your voice. I miss you."

"I miss you too." While she hadn't returned to Knoxville since Peter's death, she missed her friend and the whole church community.

"Any luck finding Charlie's family?" Kirsten asked.

"Nothing significant. It seems they've disappeared."

"I wish Charlie would just tell you his story."

She glanced back down at the willow tree. "I tried to talk to him yesterday, but he won't tell me anything about his sister or his parents. It's like he doesn't want the transplant."

"I used to ask my grandmother about our family, but she refused to talk about them," Kirsten said. "Looking back, it was almost like she wanted to protect me from the truth."

"Charlie doesn't have to protect me."

"Maybe he's scared of it."

"Maybe." A bald eagle circled the lake before disappearing into the trees. "He asked me to come back to Tennessee."

An engine hummed in the background as Kirsten started her car. "Are you coming back before Saturday?"

"I don't think so. Emma asked me to keep looking."

"It sounds like he doesn't want you and Emma to find the truth."

"Whatever happened, it won't change my love for him."

"I know," Kirsten said before changing the subject. "How's baby?"

"Reminding me regularly that I'm not alone."

"Good girl." The phone cut out and then she heard Kirsten's voice again. "That's exactly what I told her to do."

"We don't know it's a she—"

But the trusty bar of service vanished, leaving her and baby on their own again.

Some days she wished she could fly away from this world like the eagle, soar above the haunting despair. She'd carried this load for three months now. Peter had wronged her, had wronged the entire church, but she couldn't let the anger, the hurt, swallow her. Especially now.

She didn't understand all that had happened this spring, but she knew in her heart that God never left her side. One day, she prayed, she and baby would soar.

The warmth of the sun drenched her skin as her feet carved their own path up the gravel road. The turret, like a beacon, rose above the trees, and she kept her eyes on the tower until she was standing in front of Ruby's house.

Something about this place cried out to tell its story. As if Ruby's star, long burned away, might illuminate what happened to all the Tonquins.

When she didn't see Reese's brother, she opened the front gate and basked in the beauty of the garden, its colors blending together like the intricate detail on a butterfly's wings, as if the mosaic of flowers and trimmed hedges might take flight. And her own heart began to steady.

A secret garden, she thought. A masterpiece hidden far above town. She wouldn't disturb any of the beauty, only savor the fruit of someone else's labor. Think about something other than the shambles of her life.

"You're trespassing." Something moved in the trees to her left, and she jumped as a man stepped onto the lower terrace of the garden. Black T-shirt and jeans, a blue bandanna tied around his neck, he held a rake in one hand like a scepter, a handful of weeds in the other. A beard shadowed his jawline, and his charcoal hair was cropped close to his head.

This was his kingdom, it seemed.

"Wasn't trying to." At least not this time. "You must be Reese's brother."

Or was he the old man that Reese had warned her about? He was in his early thirties, she thought, but Reese probably considered anyone over twenty as old.

A bark, then a flash of black and gray across the garden. Wallace came bounding toward her like they were the best of friends, and she scratched him behind the ears.

The man propped his rake up against the porch railing. "It seems my dog already knows you."

"Wallace and I are old friends."

The man studied her. "He's generally a good judge of character, even among trespassers."

"It's not trespassing if you've been invited."

One of his eyebrows slid up. "Who invited you?"

"If you're Reese's brother, she said I might find you here."

He scrutinized her to determine, it seemed, whether she was a criminal or simply curious. When Wallace didn't leave her side, his suspicion melted away. "How exactly do you know my sister and my dog?"

"I met them under the willow tree this morning."

"You must be renting the cottage from Tara."

She nodded. "I'm Addie, from Tennessee."

He wiped his hand on his jeans and then offered it to her. "My name's Caleb."

She shook it quickly.

"And you've already met Wallace."

"It would be hard to forget him." She looked back at the creature with his tongue hanging out, a patchwork of black and gray rubbing against her leg. "He doesn't seem to be much of a warrior."

"He may be small, but he has a fierce bark." The animal moved over to Caleb, who began scratching this wagging warrior of a dog under his neck. "Here's hoping that he might have growled or something if you'd been a real intruder."

"He certainly startled me," she said, throwing Caleb a verbal bone. It would do no good to insult the man's dog.

A goose landed in the garden, but Wallace didn't even chase after it.

Caleb sighed. "He's really not a very good guard dog, is he?"

"I bet he'd take me and that goose down in a second if we threatened you."

"I wouldn't count on it." The man picked up a stick and tossed it, but Wallace didn't budge. "He's not your normal kind of dog."

And she suspected the man in front of her wasn't the normal kind of master.

Wallace wagged his tail like he wanted nothing more in this world than to be with Caleb. Until the goose drew closer. Then Wallace finally barked, scaring it away.

"So he's a warrior after all . . ."

"He just wants to play." Caleb smiled. "Are you here for vacation?"

"I'm looking for information about someone who used to live on Tonquin Lake. Reese thought you might be able to help."

"Ah." He looked disappointed. "Ruby?"

"No, I want to find out what happened to her daughter."

The disappointment was quickly replaced by a flash of surprise across his face. "Grace?"

Her heart beat faster. "You know about her?"

"Only a little."

"What about a boy named Charlie?"

He shook his lead. "The Tonquin family left here long before I was born."

"Do you know where any of them went?"

He looked away. "No idea. My family has been trying to find them for years."

She searched for the right words to shape her plea. "Charlie is a friend, and he is going to need a bone marrow transplant soon or . . ."

She couldn't bear to say the words, the conclusion to a story she didn't want to end.

Caleb tossed another stick toward the garden, and Wallace raced after it. "Is your friend related to Grace?"

"He came from France, I think, after World War II."

"A lot of refugee children lived here after the war."

"But Charlie took the Tonquin name."

"I'm sorry—"

"He had at least one sister."

"I'm afraid I can't help you," Caleb said.

She sighed. "No one wants to help."

"It's not that I don't want to help." He picked up his rake again. "But unfortunately for all of us, the Tonquin family doesn't want to be found."

Was he lying to her, like Peter had done? "I need to find a relative for Charlie. If you are related to him, you could save his life."

"If I was related to him, I would do whatever I could to help him."

"I pray every day for a miracle," she said. "That God will restore whatever was broken here."

He blinked, seemingly surprised at her mention of prayer. "I will pray that with you."

She glanced back at the house. "The mural inside—"

He flinched. "Why were you in the house?"

"I wasn't," she said, flustered. "I looked through the back window."

He leaned on his rake. "The building is private property."

"Who painted the mural?"

"A local artist," he finally said.

"I don't need to know the whole story about the Tonquins. I just want to help Charlie."

He looked at the trees. "You'd better go now."

Addie scanned the forest but didn't see anyone. Was he trying to protect the legacy of the Tonquin family or was he trying to protect something—someone—else?

CHAPTER SIXTEEN

"She's gone," Caleb called into the forest.

Still he stood behind a pine tree, a stick in his hands, watching the front gate to see if the Pinky girl might appear again.

"Are you there?"

He shuffled forward into the garden, the shaky stick wielded ahead of him to ward off an enemy.

A rake clutched in one hand, Caleb clapped him on the shoulder with the other. "You okay?"

The stick drummed against the ground in his trembling hands, his head spinning like an eggbeater. Pinky had startled him, and he didn't like to be startled. Plain courtesy, that's all he asked for. Like this boy who always knocked on the door of his hut, even if he was asleep.

But the girl kept showing up without warning to scope out the place. He could smell danger, and she reeked of it. No courtesy or care for Ruby's property. She acted as if she owned the house. As if she might take it away.

Why did people keep trying to take away this land?

He had to stand guard, but his body was failing him. Curse the bane of aging. Curse every person who tried to bring Ruby down. Even with the years he'd collected like raindrops in a bucket, he could still outrun men half his age. Outsmart them.

No woman, especially Pinky, was going to have the best of him.

"Are you okay?" the boy asked again.

A stupid question. One he didn't have to answer.

Caleb kept talking. "She isn't going to hurt you."

"No one's going to hurt me." The stick slipped out of his hands, and he reached down to retrieve it. He must stop the shaking.

"And she isn't going to harm the house. She's only curious."

"Curiosity killed the cat."

The boy shook his head. "She's not a cat."

"Lots of things can kill a cat."

Caleb sighed like he was disappointed, but he didn't know yet what a woman like this could do. Her curiosity could ruin them all.

"Do you need anything?" Caleb asked.

He shook his head.

"I'll check on the house again before I go."

While he appreciated the food Caleb left on his doorstep, he didn't like that the boy was in charge of Ruby's house. And neither did Tara.

That was the only thing he and Tara could agree on.

Caleb pointed his rake toward the house. "If the woman shows up again, you have to leave her alone."

"I won't hurt her, if that's what you're saying."

"Don't talk to her or scare her or bang those pans like you do when the kids come up from town."

The rattle of those pans, their clang when he struck them together, always made the children run.

"She's trying to get into the house," he said.

"You keep the kids out of the garden." The boy staked the handle of his rake into the ground as if it were a flag, marking the territory for both of them. "I'll take care of her."

He rubbed his hands together to fight off the tremors. Every few months, he gave the boy a gift to reciprocate for the weekly ration of food. A bottle of pine vodka unearthed from the cool soil behind his hut, the jars hidden like soldiers in the trenches, prepared to fight.

This green drink, taste of earth and wind and trees, had kept him alive since Vietnam and he desperately needed a sip now to make this shaking subside.

Caleb reached for his dog's collar and snapped on a leash before repeating his words. "You have to leave her alone."

"I won't make a promise that I can't keep."

The boy sighed. "Nothing you can do will bring Ruby back, no matter how well you guard this place."

"You don't know that."

The boy shook his head again. "She and Grace are gone."

But the boy was wrong.

He didn't care a lick about Grace, but one day Ruby would return. She'd promised him.

Chapter Seventeen

"Where will we sleep?" Suzel asked as she carried Alice up the mountain, their coats dusted with snow. After walking all night, the younger girl's legs had failed her.

"I don't know," Grace said, the words stinging her ears. The path had blown away with the drifts of snow, impossible to follow now even with the whisper of sunrise on the horizon.

She wanted to lead well, love well. And she wanted to be honest with all of them, even when the truth hurt.

But what if Élias was right? What if she needed to lie to those she loved in order to protect them? To give them hope.

The remaining children, she'd determined, would arrive in Spain together, all eleven of them. But they couldn't survive much longer in the wilderness, not with this autumn snow.

The children were an eerie quiet. Some of them, she feared, wouldn't last the night, but they were still together. Stopping now would end all their lives.

Once she found a guide to take them to Lisbon, she would return back over the mountain to help other children, but she couldn't think about that now. Grace gently squeezed the hands of a boy and girl who clung to her. While she could no longer carry a child in her arms, she could help lift their burden. Let them know they weren't alone.

"Look!" Marguerite marveled at the shavings of copper-colored petals in the snow.

"A winter rose," Grace said. Like the ones her grandmother had cultivated at home. *Hearty*, that's what Grams called them. Simple and strong and radiating beauty long after the other flowers had succumbed to the winter months.

Nearby were the dark tones of a burgundy rose. Then a defiant white one rimmed with blue. A treasure trove in this rugged place, wild with hope, blossoming through the snow and stone.

Élias scrambled up another rock wall like a billy goat, taking the lead, and the others followed as Grace helped each child find their footing.

After their rest in the cave, they had clambered over a stony mountaintop, then down into a valley where they'd found an abandoned shepherd's hut sloped into an A-shape to keep snow from collapsing the roof. The walls had kept out the wind, the snow, and they'd all hung their wet clothing from the rafters to dry, eating the cognac-soaked candies that Élias had found as their meal.

But that was two nights ago . . . or was it three?

A fire this morning would be lovely, but the smoke—if they found a place to build a fire—would be a beacon for their enemy. She and the children must continue to blend in with the snow and hope the Nazis weren't keen about summiting the Pyrénées. They couldn't stop walking until they found shelter anyway, the dangers of falling asleep in the snow an equal threat.

She prayed again as they trudged up another mountain, all the children scattered in front of her as they neared the Spanish border.

Where was Roland this morning? Her mind wandered with the fatigue, her heart longing for the children's home in Aspet, Roland by her side, a steaming hot cup of chocolate with him and all their wards.

Was he in prison? Or had he been transported to one of the camps? Perhaps he'd found his aunt and gone into hiding with one of his many friends in Southern France. A woman even, one who loved him. One whom he might love.

Had he ever loved Grace, as she'd loved him? Perhaps she would never know for certain, but her heart was his.

Her thoughts swirled with the wind that rippled her coat and scarf, burned her face, but the rocks didn't shiver. Nor did they bend when she stepped on them. If only her mind could be as unmovable, as steady, as these stones.

She prayed Roland would find his way out of any prison. That she would meet him back at the home in France.

Ahead was a corridor between stone walls, and she squeezed through it last. At the top of the mountain were her children, all eleven of them, lined up in a queue. Two men dressed in long gray coats watched over them, one wielding a rifle. Frenchmen, she feared, guarding the border.

Her heart sank until she heard one of them speak.

"Who are you?" the armed guard demanded. In Spanish.

She almost dropped to her knees, to kiss the patchwork of land that divided the Nazi kingdom from their Spanish neighbors. To praise God for bringing them across the pass.

"I am Grace Tonquin." She said the words in Spanish, like she'd done so many times with the children who'd traveled the opposite direction. "From the United States."

The man lowered his gun, a glimpse of curiosity skipping between her and the kids. "You know Spanish?"

"Un poco."

He waved toward the snow-splattered Spanish rocks below. "We must get you off this mountain."

It was an invitation she'd readily accept, but even as the words left his mouth, his gaze wandered to the path behind them as if he was straddling a line.

"Please," she begged. "I have money to pay for our passage."

Enough, she hoped, to convince the authorities to let them stay.

He motioned for her to move south. "This is no place to talk of money."

She wouldn't argue.

"How long have we been in Spain?" she asked as she followed the children down the rocky terrain.

He pointed his gun back at the stone wall, the immovable barrier in their path. The line between Fascism and freedom. "About five minutes."

She breathed a prayer of thankfulness in that moment for the rocky gateway into this new land.

Their trail-worn group descended into a village with about ten stone houses that seemed to tumble in on themselves, most of the windows shuttered, the roofs covered in snow.

"Where are you taking us?" she asked.

"To *la cárcel.*"

In France, perhaps, the prison camps had become normal for people of all ages, but when had Spain decided to follow suit? Instead of the familiar plunge into fear, it seemed her heart had frozen over, too numb to be afraid.

Élias leapt up beside her, the boy who was really a man now, trying to care for all of them. "We are not criminals!" he spat, his hands balled into fists.

She reached for his shoulder before he threw a punch, turning him back toward his sister. If they thought he was old enough to fight, they might return him to the French guards at the border for a reward.

"Why would you take children to jail?" she asked.

The guard lowered his voice, speaking only to her. "It will be warm there. And you will have food."

If he allowed them to go free, they wouldn't last another day without food or shelter, but this promise of warmth, even in jail, urged her forward.

"We will follow you," she agreed as if he'd given her a choice.

The village jail was much different than the internment camp at Gurs. Housed in someone's home, it seemed, and crowded with cots, a roaring fireplace at one end of the room to fight their chill. The border guard made good on his word for food and warmth—bowls of hot soup were delivered along with warm cider and a loaf of bread.

After they'd devoured the food, the children undressed to their underclothing and crawled under blankets. Grace strung their wet clothing on pegs along the wall and over the edge of cots, anyplace where they might dry. Several of the children coughed, and she hoped they might be able to linger in the warmth of this makeshift prison for several days.

"This is a fine mess."

Grace swirled to find Élias standing behind her, dressed in his undershirt and trousers, his blistered feet bare, his toes a bright red.

"At least it's a warm one," she said.

"Are they going to send us back?"

"Let's think only about tonight," she said. "Tomorrow and its challenges will come soon enough."

"I can't help thinking about tomorrow."

How she loved this boy. His honesty and boldness and vivid imagination. His fierce love for his sister and willingness to fight for all of them. She'd wanted to run away on the mountain path, but he had been like David, the shepherd boy who'd stood his ground, taken down Goliath with a single stone. Stopped the informer from taking these children away.

As he grew into a man, reined in the fire of his fists with the power of words, she hoped he would continue to fight for others. After everything they'd been through—these months, years, would shape him and the other children for the rest of their lives.

"Thank you for standing up for us, Élias."

His nod was quick, embarrassed by her praise.

"I pray you will always fight for those who need a brother." She directed him toward a cot. "For now, you must sleep."

"So must you," he said as if he were her equal.

And he was her equal, exceeding her even in strength. As long as they stayed united, with the breath of life pumping through their lungs, they could overcome almost anything.

"Roland gave me these." He pulled out two letters, wrapped in cloth, from beneath his undershirt. "One is for you. The other is for the magistrate."

Her hand trembled, the offered letter clasped between her fingers. "Why didn't you give this to me before?"

Roland's instructions could have helped bring Louis and Hélène safely over the mountains.

Or did Roland have another plan? Perhaps he had wanted her to meet him in France so he could escort them across. Had he been waiting someplace for her? She couldn't bear to think that she might have missed him.

"He told me to give it to you when we reached Spain."

Élias walked toward the door and opened it, speaking to the guard outside.

She didn't hear what Élias was saying, everything within her focused on the letter. Words from Roland she'd longed to hear. Words, she prayed, that would tell her where to meet him when she returned to France.

Some of the writing was smeared, the envelope damp, but she could read enough.

Dearest Grace,

If you are reading this, you and Élias have both made it to Spain. Not once did I doubt you would do everything possible to rescue the children. The light, I knew, would guide your way.

You cannot return to France. They will arrest you, and I could not bear it. You have done everything possible here. Now you need to find homes for those you've led and return to the safety of your Oregon.

One day you will fly again.

One day soon, I pray, we will fly together, for I have loved you with all my heart.

As long as I have wings, I will find you. After this war is won.

He'd signed his name at the bottom, such a common thing, and yet she studied it as if the letters might fly away.

Roland loved her, with all his heart, he said. Loved her enough to protect her from his feelings lest she'd stay in France to wait for him. Loved her enough to give her wings to fly away.

He had never intended to return to the château. He'd wanted her to escort the children on her own instead of hiring a *passeur*. Leave France before it was too late.

And he'd known she would never leave France as long as she could return to Aspet to help other kids.

Closing her eyes, she leaned back against the rugged stone wall and saw Roland's handsome face, his strong hand in hers, the two of them wandering through the vineyards in France. What would he say when she told him that she hadn't been able to take all the children with her? That she'd had to leave Roland's aunt and Louis behind?

Her heart began to fracture like the border between France and Spain, an almost-impossible mountain to cross between them. And yet, perhaps one day they would both be able to climb their sides of the mountain, reunite at the top. One day . . .

"Mademoiselle?"

Her eyes flickered open and she saw a man, pasty and thin like *fideo*, his mustache curled up at the ends. The magistrate, she assumed.

He held the letter that Élias had delivered in one hand, a cigarette in the other, his voice brisk as he spoke in French. "Why did you travel to France?"

Not Spain—to France, five years ago.

She remembered, of course, but it had been a long time since anyone had asked why she'd left her grandparents' farm in Oregon. Why she had spent weeks traveling on a train and then a ship across the Atlantic to the port in Bordeaux.

"To help refugees," she replied.

He searched her face. "Our refugees?"

She nodded slowly, wondering if he'd stood with the Nationalists or Republicans during the Spanish Civil War. This whole country, she suspected, was tired of the fighting.

"French or Spanish or German, it matters not to me. I came to help those who needed it." Like the Spanish woman who had brought them soup.

He lowered the letter. "This, I thank you for."

Élias slipped back into the room when the magistrate left and stretched out on a cot near his sister. Grace didn't know what to make of the conversation, but her mind was too weary to process it. The children were safely across the border, that's all that mattered, and Roland's letter was in her hand. Now she could rest.

She slept through the remaining day and night, and when she finally awoke, another woman was serving them stew.

They didn't stay long in Spain. The magistrate secured her and the children railway tickets to the refugee mecca of Lisbon along with a letter of recommendation for the proper paperwork lest they find themselves jailed like many refugees in conditions much less friendly for children. The train swept them away from the Pyrénées, to the Moorish ramparts and pastel-washed buildings on the Portuguese coast. Salty air mixed with the smell of seaweed, tobacco, and cheap cologne.

A woman named Dorothy Thumwood took charge at Lisbon's assistance office for the AFSC, obtaining a round of new shoes. Then Dorothy secured affidavits in lieu of passports for the children who didn't have their documents.

Nine of the kids, including Suzel, had relatives waiting for them in Palestine. Suzel was old enough to accompany the younger ones on the ship, so Grace kissed each child on their cheeks twice, knowing she'd never see them again, and prayed a blessing over all of them, that God's light would lead the heart of each one.

"You are a hero," she told Suzel before the girl stepped onto the gangplank. "Don't let anyone ever tell you differently."

Suzel stood a little taller, a new rucksack strung over her shoulder.

"I want to be a nurse," Suzel said. "Like you."

"I'm not a nurse yet." Two more years of school left, if the college in Oregon would still have her. "You might become a nurse before me."

Grace stood alongside Élias, Marguerite, and Dorothy to watch the ship leave the harbor, its deck filled with men and women seeking refuge in a Jewish state. A country to call home.

These children who had been in her care for so long were on their own now. She'd miss them terribly, but they would live, every one of them. They had faced a mountain together and pushed over it. For the rest of their lives, she hoped, they would continue scaling the mountains in their paths.

Next she'd escort Élias and Marguerite through Ellis Island, to their uncle's house in New York. Then she would return home.

Home.

It seemed like a lifetime since she'd said goodbye to her grandmother in Oregon.

Instead of a boat, she boarded a seaplane with Élias and Marguerite. Élias had read *Tintin in America* as they waited in Lisbon, declaring himself an expert now on both flying boats and mobsters in the strange country across the sea.

"Snowy." Élias tousled his sister's hair, clearly excited by their new adventure. "Our troubles aren't over, by any means."

"They're over for the moment," Grace said.

Marguerite pushed him away. "He's quoting Tintin again."

Élias crossed his arms. "Tintin would fly this winged boat and land it too."

"On the fumes of fuel," Marguerite said as if she'd heard this a hundred times.

Grace clung to the edge of the upholstered seat in their compartment, but neither of the children were disturbed by the rattle of metal wings as their flying ship defied gravity over Portugal.

"We'll count the waves," Marguerite said. "Like they're beans."

Grace agreed, counting the waves and the boats and then the clouds. A few more hours now, and they'd be safe from the threat of prison and guards returning them to France and tin birds that might fall into the sea.

"What's going to happen to us in America?" Marguerite asked once the plane settled above the clouds.

"Your uncle will care for you." Even as she spoke, Grace felt the pang of loss. Their uncle would adopt both Élias and Marguerite, she hoped, welcome them into his family, but she would miss them.

"I want to be with *Maman*," Marguerite said.

"You can't," Élias explained, his eyes still on the window. "*Maman* and Papa are gone."

Marguerite's eyes welled with tears as if it hadn't occurred to her that she would never see their parents again.

"But what if Uncle Henri doesn't want us?" Marguerite asked.

"I will find you a home," Grace promised. "And one day you can return to France, after the Nazis are gone."

Élias shook his head. "I'm never going back."

She set the black purse Dorothy had given her on her lap, resting her hands on the knobbed silver lock. Inside was the letter from Roland, words she would treasure for the rest of her life.

Élias might never go back to France, but one day she would return.

If Roland couldn't find her, she would find him.

CHAPTER EIGHTEEN

"You're Jonathan Lange's son." Addie stood at Caleb's doorstep, her hands clenched as if she might throw a punch.

"Guilty," he said, lifting both of his arms. "Is that a crime?"

"Your father wrote his master's thesis on Grace Tonquin's life."

"That's definitely not a crime."

She pushed up her sleeves, flushed from the walk and her frustration. "You should have told me you were related."

Something flickered through his eyes. Surprise, perhaps, that she'd discovered the truth. "You never asked."

"I told you that I needed to find Grace!"

He leaned back against the doorpost. "You told me you needed to find a relative for Charlie."

"But you should have—" Addie crossed her arms, facing off as she contemplated his words. She'd spent her morning reviewing records in the McMinnville courthouse, talking to the clerk. They had no record of adoption papers for Charlie or any other Tonquin children.

"The Tonquin family still owns this property." The deed, she'd found in the county records.

"Most of it," he said. "They sold part of the land to my family years ago. We rent the other portion, with conditions."

"All I want is to ask them a few questions. Or you can ask for me."

"Who was your informant?" Caleb asked.

"A clerk in McMinnville." One who enjoyed sharing what she knew about Caleb and his return to revive the vineyard on the property where his father was born.

"She knew about Grace?"

"I don't think so, but she knew an awful lot about you."

He looked away. "I doubt that."

The woman's eyes had lit up like a Christmas tree when Addie told her where she was staying.

"She said your family lived here after World War II."

"Plenty of people from around here know about my family. My grandpa was injured in the war, and he and my grandma lived on the Tonquin property with dozens of refugees while he recovered."

"It's a good thing," she said slowly. "To help those who don't have a home."

"Especially good to help a German family when everyone else turned them away. My grandparents weren't Nazis—my grandpa fought with the Americans—but between his German heritage and his injury, no one would hire him." Caleb waved his hand. "My grandparents ended up living and working here for the rest of their lives."

She sorted through the overgrown intersection of the Lange and Tonquin families in her head. "Did you live with your grandparents?"

"No, my dad and mom moved us up to Seattle when I was in grade school, but I moved back here after my grandparents passed away." He inched the door open. "Would you like to come inside?"

She hesitated by the step, still wary.

"Reese is on the patio," he said. "You're welcome to join us for dinner. We're grilling out."

Her stomach rumbled at the mention of food, the baby agreeing wholeheartedly with the invitation. But she still wasn't ready to acquiesce.

"Will you or your dad call the Tonquins for me?" she asked.

"Neither of us can contact their family. We don't know where they went."

"Someone must know."

"I own this house, but I rent the vineyard and the rest of the property through a manager. If she knows where the Tonquins are, she won't tell me. I've wanted to buy the land around Tonquin Lake for years, but she says her client won't sell."

"Tara Dawson?"

"That's her. She manages the logistics, and I care for Ruby's house and the vineyard."

"But she must know something. She rents out the cottage—"

"She forwards our annual rent as well, but she says that she doesn't know who receives it."

"That sounds suspect."

He shrugged. "Nothing I can do about it."

Wallace wandered up beside her, knocking his head against her leg so she'd pet him, but Addie wouldn't be deterred.

"I'll speak to Tara then."

"Good luck." He held the door open again. "Why don't you come in?"

She leaned down, petting Wallace on the head, and then followed both dog and master inside.

Ahead was a rustic wood coffee table and two khaki-colored couches, but the focal point of the room was the expanse of windows that overlooked the vineyard and pine scarf warming the banks of Tonquin Lake.

She stepped toward the glass wall but stopped when she saw an antique armoire with a dozen motifs of sea creatures and animals and a solitary nun, her hands folded in prayer.

She'd never seen anything like it.

"This is beautiful." Addie brushed her hands over a carving of Neptune and his fierce trident.

Caleb grinned like she'd awarded him a medal. "It's one of my favorite pieces."

She traced her fingers between the prongs of the trident, amazed at the precision of the work. Under it was the figure of a woman riding a swift horse, a sword and shield clutched in her hands, a winged helmet on her head.

Addie pointed at the woman. "Who is she?"

"A Valkyrie."

"I've never heard of that."

"It's a woman in Norse mythology," he explained, his gaze focused on the maiden. "She could either help a warrior or send him into battle to die."

"That's terrifying." Sending a man to his death.

"The one who is gifted to help can also hurt those they love."

And she thought of her mother, a glimpse from years ago when Addie had been sick. She'd lifted Addie's head to spoon some sort of medicine, sweetened with the sharp tang of orange, into her mouth. Love, that's what she had shown in the briefest of moments, before her mother had destroyed her own life.

Addie blinked, clearing her mind. Mythology, in her youth, had been the mystery of a happy family.

"Where did you get this piece?" she asked.

He leaned his shoulder against the stone fireplace. "It was carved by craftsmen on the peninsula of Brittany, four hundred years ago. Back in the days when Louis XIII ruled."

A helmeted warrior stood in the panel to the right of Neptune while a royal lion's head seemed to roar on the left. An eclectic troupe staged on walnut.

She looked back at him. "You didn't answer my question."

"Which one?"

"About where you got this."

He smiled. "You ask a lot of questions."

"So?" she asked, crossing her arms.

"I restore furniture in my spare time," he said. "Scrape off layers and layers of toxic lacquer to reveal the grain underneath."

"Like a treasure hunt."

"Exactly. After all the scraping, I usually find the unique character of a piece. Most of the furniture I sell, but . . ." Caleb tapped his hand on the lion's wild mane, the hair of the animal piercing the edges of the panel. "I couldn't let this one go."

She heard the longing in his voice, the connection.

"Every nick in its grain, every dent, tells a story," he said. "I like to embrace the nicks and put them on display to show the beauty in every scratch. The uniqueness. People pay extra for the stories."

Her story had so many nicks and scratches no one would ever appreciate the beauty in them. But when she was younger, she had determined to take those scraps, all the wounds, and mold them into something beautiful. Nothing extraordinary like these engravings, but a collage in her mind to share with her son or daughter.

Every nick, every gash, was a chapter in her life, not the ending of her story.

"I'd like to know the history of this piece," she said, studying the armoire again, searching for the smallest gashes.

"It's been on quite a journey," he said, but still he didn't tell her where he'd found it.

"Addie!"

Turning, she saw Reese swinging a metal spatula as if it were a flag. "Did you bring your husband?"

Addie buried her left hand into Wallace's fur, hiding the finger she'd once proudly displayed. Then she was ashamed of her shame.

Both Reese and Caleb were looking at her, but she didn't owe either of them an explanation. This wound had slashed right through the grain of trust and love, gouging her heart.

She turned back to the windows, the vineyard that swept down like a magic carpet to the lake. "I don't know how you manage to do any work with a view like this."

"It's my favorite part of the house." He slid open a door and motioned them out to the wide porch. Under a covered section to the right were cushioned chairs and a fire table, and on the left was a grill with smoke clouding the open sky.

She hadn't eaten a decent meal since she'd arrived in Oregon.

"Hope you like shish kebabs," Caleb said, taking the spatula from his sister. "With steak and a whole lot of veggies."

Her stomach rumbled. "I could eat an entire cow on my own."

He smiled again. "Then you've come to the right place."

While he worked the grill, she looked back at Reese. "Did you have school today?"

"No more education for me." She added a ceramic plate to the table. "I tried a year at art school, but the artist in me rebelled."

Caleb circled the spatula. "College stifles her creativity."

"College stifles everyone's creativity," Reese said with a roll of her eyes.

"What was stifling about it?" Addie asked, sliding onto a bench.

"The deadlines and all the teachers assigning me projects that I didn't want to do. I want to paint, not sketch with pencils."

Back in middle school, Addie's art teacher had told her that in order to be successful, she had to start with the basics. That she must draw the lines first and then slowly color them in until she'd filled her canvas. And she remembered wishing that real life worked in the

same way. That she could color between the lines instead of letting someone else color them for her.

The teacher was one of several who inspired Addie to continue on when she wanted to quit. Who knew with every missed parent conference, every day that Addie arrived at school without money or any semblance of lunch, that things were not well at home.

"Reese sees a million colors in life and embraces every one."

The younger woman seemed to glow as if her brother could offer her no greater compliment.

He joined them at the table, holding up a bottle of pinot noir. "This comes from the grapes growing right below us."

Growing. Grapes. Gratitude.

She placed a hand over her midsection. He wouldn't know that she was expecting. "Just water for me this evening."

Reese handed her a pitcher and Addie filled her glass while Caleb transferred the grilled food onto a platter. "You mind if we ask God to bless our meal?"

"Please do."

Caleb prayed for their food and their company like Charlie always did. Then Reese pulled both meat and vegetables off her skewer and proceeded to pick out the steak, piling the meat on her brother's plate.

"Do you always help with the harvest?" Addie asked her.

She grinned. "I come down for the harvest and whenever my parents need a break."

"Do you have other family to help?"

Reese groaned. "Our uncle should help but—"

Addie caught the look that passed between brother and sister. A warning of sorts.

Reese tapped her long nails on her glass. "Apparently I'm not allowed to say another word."

"And now that we've bored you with our family—" Caleb said.

"I'm not bored." Addie took a bite of the tender beef. It was cooked perfectly with just a hint of pink in the middle.

"We want to hear about your friend who needs a transplant."

Her gaze fell back onto the water. "Charlie lived here when he was younger and then he seemed to lose touch with his family when he moved to Tennessee. Now he's sick with a blood cancer called myelodysplastic syndrome, and he won't survive much longer without healthy bone marrow. His sister, I'd hoped, could help him find a donor."

"I called my dad this morning and asked about Charlie, but he doesn't remember him."

Disappointment reared again inside her. "It would have been right after World War II."

"Hundreds of people stayed on the Tonquin land," Caleb continued. "Refugees like my family who were trying to start over."

She could see Charlie here with all the refugee children, throwing rocks with them into the lake. "He had a sister, and I'm hoping to find her or her children."

"Our uncle might remember them," Caleb said. "He's lived here for almost sixty years."

Her heart beat faster. "I would love to meet him."

"No, you wouldn't . . ."

Caleb leaned toward his sister. "I thought you weren't saying another word."

Reese stuck out her tongue. "Word."

"Tell you what." Caleb took a sip of wine. "I'm not going to tell you where I got the armoire—"

Addie nodded. He didn't owe her anything either.

"When we're done eating, my sister and I will show you."

Reese shook her head. "I'm not going anywhere near that place."

"What place?" Addie asked.

She followed Caleb's gaze across the vineyard, to the other side of the lake, the house whose turret spiked proudly through the trees.

"We're also trying to find out what happened to the Tonquin family," Caleb said.

"You're trying to find out." Reese pointed her fork at him. "I'm trying to stay out of his way."

"Whose way?" Addie asked, confused.

"My uncle. He can be as mean as—"

"A bear." Caleb shot another look across the table. This one silenced his sister.

Addie crossed her arms. "I'm not fond of bears."

"A teddy bear," Caleb replied. "He won't hurt you."

Caleb glanced around again. "We only have an hour or so left until the sun goes down."

Reese waved them on. "I'll take care of the dishes."

Caleb and Addie crossed the ridge together, to the purported castle on the hill.

Chapter Nineteen

YAMHILL COUNTY, OREGON
DECEMBER 1945

Freshly picked holly and Douglas fir transformed the sitting room into a wonderland. Grace's grandmother was gone—she'd passed away the same week that Grace had crossed into Spain—but the farmhouse was full again this Christmas Eve.

Almost two years had passed since Grace had landed in New York with Marguerite and Élias. No uncle was to be found in New York, so the three of them traveled across the country via train, the children taking the Tonquin surname so they could find freedom in this new country as a family.

Grace traveled back to France often in her mind. To the struggle but also the simplicity of those years, a singular purpose to rescue the children from an enemy instead of trying to live alongside one.

For two years ago, after Hollywood stopped calling, her mother decided to move home.

"You wicked child." Ruby slapped Marguerite's arm as the girl, now eleven, rearranged the porcelain figurines in their Nativity scene.

"Leave her alone!" Élias leapt to his feet from the davenport, his hands balled into fists.

Grace stepped swiftly between them. "What's wrong?"

"She stole baby Jesus!" One gloved hand was on Ruby's hip, the other preparing to slap Marguerite again.

"Since when do you have a problem with stealing?" Élias asked, no fear of this woman after facing off Nazis and gendarmes alike. Élias and her mother were like flint and steel. When rubbed together, they sparked into a blaze.

Ruby's eyes narrowed, her own anger flaring until her face matched the bright color of her name. "I don't have to answer to you or anyone."

Grace scooted Marguerite away from the Nativity on the bureau, shifting the girl behind her. "Marguerite and I will talk in the kitchen."

Élias's jaw looked as if it might crack into pieces. She was proud of him for holding back those fists clenched at his sides. For swallowing his words.

She nodded toward the front door. "Can you do the milking on your own?"

Instead of answering, Élias grabbed his coat from a peg and pulled on rubber boots before stomping outside. The barn, in all its disrepair, was a refuge for him when Ruby was here.

Her mother began straightening the shepherds and angels, the donkeys and camels and parents who were missing a child. And Grace flashed back to that Christmas long ago when she was a girl, hiding under the tree to avoid the verbal bullets hurling between her mother and grandparents.

Quakers didn't celebrate Christmas—her grandparents remembered the birth of Jesus every day of the year—but they had wanted to do something special for both their daughter and granddaughter, like Grace wanted for Élias and Marguerite. A few presents under the fir tree. A pot of vichyssoise on the stove. Carrots for Gui, the donkey of Père Noël, left in their shoes.

The darkness that had shrouded them during the war also inspired them to remember Jesus' life with candlelight and song. With joy as they prepared to bring in a New Year free of fighting with Germany.

For Christmas, Grace only wanted things to be well for all—and between all—of them.

Marguerite trailed Grace to the kitchen, following her like she'd done across Southern France. Their lives were no longer in danger, thank God, but they'd found little freedom or peace with Ruby living in the house.

Even though her mother had taken up residence at the old farmhouse, Ruby spoke incessantly about returning to Hollywood. One day, she assured them, her star would shine again on the screen.

Grace wished Ruby would slide into her fancy roadster and drive south—they all did—but she'd decided to build an extravagant house above them instead. While Grams had left the land to Grace, she'd told her daughter long ago that she could build on the Tonquin property if she ever decided to come home. Grace wanted to honor this agreement just like she wanted to honor her mother.

The holiday soup simmered beside her and Marguerite, and from the sitting room, "I'll Be Home for Christmas" began playing on the radio. Grace shut the kitchen door, separating them from Ruby's never-ending scrutiny.

Soon Ruby would be living in her own place, pretending that she was still a movie star. Then Grace and Marguerite and Élias could be a family.

Grace knelt beside Marguerite, sadness still plaguing the girl's eyes from all the loss.

"Did you steal Jesus?" Grace asked.

Marguerite shook her head even as her gaze fell to the ground.

Grace suspected that if she could see Marguerite's colors, the girl's braids would be crowned with green. The color, Marguerite later told her, that had shadowed Élias into the cave after he'd detained the informer.

"We need to return Jesus to the manger," she tried to explain. "So He will be safe with His mother and the angels."

Marguerite's lips pressed together in a stubborn line, staring now at a stained-glass tree propped against the kitchen window.

Grace loved to care for children, clothe and feed them, but she was struggling to parent. Even so, she'd never wanted to leave Élias and Marguerite in New York.

When they'd searched for the street address in Manhattan, they quickly discovered that it didn't exist. The letter from a man named Henri—their mother's only brother—was forged.

She didn't blame Madame Dupont one bit for this deception. Without the letter, a relative waiting to welcome them, the AFSC would never have allowed Grace to escort the Dupont children away from their mother in Gurs.

If she was honest with herself, she was relieved that no uncle had been found. She loved both Élias and Marguerite like they were her own kids. Would do almost anything to ensure their safety in this land of opportunity for people from around the world.

Somehow they—all of them together—would live their lives in a way to honor those who had died under the wicked Nazi regime.

Grace crossed her arms, trying to be stern. Even though she had no respect for Ruby's theatrics, her mother was still right. She could not allow this lie to slip past or more would fester. She had to learn how to mother well, like Grams had done with her. Lock Marguerite in her room, even, until she was willing to be truthful.

"I am very disappointed in you for stealing this valuable piece."

The girl's long braids bobbed across her shoulders when she shook her head. "I didn't steal anything."

How did one explain the importance of truth to a child who'd had to deceive in order to survive? To lie in order to live. But Marguerite had to learn this lesson now. "Stealing is what you call taking something that isn't yours."

"But I was only hiding Jesus," she said. "Not stealing Him."

Grace eyed the girl curiously, struggling to understand. "Why would you need to hide Jesus?"

A tear trickled down the girl's cheek, tumbling onto her braid. "So the bad men won't steal Him away."

The truth settled slowly over Grace. The terrible fear in those words. She stretched out her arms and Marguerite folded into them.

Jesus, the Jewish child. A refugee in a strange land. Marguerite didn't want this baby to be taken away, deported to a foreign camp like her younger brother.

Grace looked her in the eye. "It must make God very happy to know how much you love His Son."

The girl stood as silent as one of the boulders on the trail, tears clinging to her eyelashes. If she wanted, Marguerite could hide Mary and Joseph and every figurine.

"You are a courageous young woman to care for Him like that," Grace said gently.

"My teacher said that Jesus cared for me."

"Yes, He does," she agreed. "Very much. We can celebrate His birth, no matter where He is."

When the girl nodded, Grace wanted to shut herself in her bedroom. Why was she so quick to judge when Marguerite had never tried to deceive her? And Ruby didn't care about anyone except herself.

She kissed the top of Marguerite's head and told her to stay out of Ruby's way until Grace could speak with her. Not that her mother would understand, but Ruby would have to be okay with a missing Jesus. This house was Grace's, bequeathed to her by her grandmother.

She would share it for as long as Ruby needed a place to sleep, if her mother would choose kindness instead of condemnation. Treat the children with grace.

The first of March—that's when Ruby's house on the hill was supposed to be finished. Grace and the children could make it sixty-six days. Then they'd take a deep breath and live as a family, however misshapen it might be.

Marguerite had learned English at school over the past two years and spent every free hour in the basement, filling canvas after canvas with color. While Élias still struggled to find his place, at fifteen years old he had become the man of their little family, chopping wood, caring for the cows, fixing whatever was broken. Ruby wasn't fond of either child, mostly because they didn't wilt in admiration whenever she walked into the room. But Grace was immensely proud of their hard work and creativity and independence mixed with compassion.

She stirred the soup, then leaned back against the curved slope on the refrigerator and stared out at the lake. So many memories were packed into this house. The entire property.

How she missed her grandparents. They'd never been able to control Ruby, but they'd been strong enough to draw firm boundaries after she'd left, healthy perimeters around her relationship with them and Grace.

Now Grace had to learn to set up these boundaries on her own.

Several snowflakes fell, and she smiled at this rare treat, her memories flittering to the other children who'd traveled over the snowy Pyrénées. Often she wondered about them and all those from Camp de Gurs who'd stolen her heart. The hundreds who had been fed through Les Secours Quakers. Hélène and little Louis.

She wished she knew what happened to all of them.

Roland . . . she didn't allow herself to think of him often lest she slip into an abyss. Spiral really, down into the darkness.

How could he have survived in Nazi-ridden France? They'd known the concentration camps in the east were bad, but the crimes committed there—she never imagined back in 1943 how horrific they were. The news was still reporting on the deaths, the torture, that the regime had subjected on those they feared.

Her mind began to slide again, collecting fragments of grief and fear, lingering doubts and questions, along the way. But for the sake of Marguerite and Élias, she needed to stay present. They would celebrate this holiday together. Celebrate the Jewish refugee who could rescue them all.

Snowflakes began clinging to the pine branches, a rare occurrence in this valley. Whenever it did snow, she would remember those she had lost in Europe. And she would celebrate their lives, remembering the God who wants to save.

"Grace!" Élias called from the front room, and she raced out of the kitchen. What had her mother done now?

She stopped by the bureau, staring at the thin rail of a man beside Élias, wrapped in a threadbare coat like so many refugees. A smile played on his lips, warming his eyes in the cold. A stranger, she thought, like so many she'd seen in Europe. Someone else who needed a meal and a bed. He could stay in the barn, if needed, to shelter him from the snow.

"Colibri," the man whispered, and her mouth dropped open. Catching flies, that's what Grams would have said. A swarm of them.

He said the word again, a little louder, and her heart leapt. It was the man who'd accompanied her across the hills and valleys, the man who had protected her from the Nazis and instilled in her the confidence needed to escort their kids across the Pyrénées.

Hummingbirds, he'd once told her, always returned home.

He stepped forward, and when he spoke again, he called her Grace.

In that word she heard a question. Two questions.

Would she welcome him into her home?

And would she welcome him into her heart?

She hadn't thought Roland would return to her. Not even on the nights when she tucked his letter under her pillow and prayed he would find her, prayed that someone would care for him like he'd cared for her. She'd thought she lost him forever in the aftermath of war.

But he'd come, just like he had promised. The years didn't matter. Two or twenty. She'd wait fifty years, if she must, to be with him.

Words escaped her as she fell into his arms, losing herself like she'd dreamed of a thousand times.

"Who is this?" Ruby asked from the hallway, her evening gown twinkling in the Christmas lights.

Grace took a step back but not away, shielding him like she'd done with Marguerite to protect this hero of a man from someone who craved the attention of every man in her presence.

But Ruby wasn't looking at Roland. Her eyes were on the boy standing beside him, curls of wet hair pasted to his scalp. A ward, it seemed, in Roland's care.

The child looked bewildered, staring beyond them, at the white lights that Grace had strung around the windows and tree.

"You remember Louis?" Roland asked.

A gasp escaped from her lips, gratefulness pouring out. "You found him . . ."

The boy she thought lost to the Nazis. Six years old now instead of four.

"Tante Hélène found me after the liberation," Roland explained. "She hid with Louis and several others for the duration of the war. The AFSC sent inquiries to the address of his family in Palestine, but they couldn't locate a relative there or one left in France. My aunt and I hoped he might thrive here."

Grace opened her arms to hug the boy, but Louis didn't come to her. Instead his gaze traveled from the lights to the shiny necklace that Ruby wore.

"Joli," he said. Pretty.

And her mother, who loved everything French, was just as enchanted with him.

Grace and Roland talked late in the tree-lit sitting room, after bowls of creamy vichyssoise and freshly baked bread and cups of spicy wassail. Even Ruby was subdued as Roland told them the Christmas story in French, then English. As he spoke, Marguerite retrieved baby Jesus from her room, replacing the figure in the manger.

After Ruby left in her roadster and the children fell asleep, Louis on the floor between twin beds, Roland and Grace sat on the davenport. When he reached out his arm, Grace nestled into his chest as if it were a place for her wings to finally rest after all the miles.

He kissed the top of her head, his skin smelling like cinnamon and soap. "I wish I had something more for you."

"This is the best Christmas present I could ever receive." Knowing that he loved her as much as she loved him.

"I've spent the past two years trying to return to you."

"Where did you go?" she asked. "After I left France."

"To Camp Le Vernet."

She jolted up. "The camp of fear . . ."

"The SS arrested me near Saint-Girons and escorted me there."

She shivered. "Until liberation?"

"No." He breathed deeply as if he could cleanse the memory with the scent of pine. "They transferred me to Dachau in 1944."

Her heart plunged, no words to console. What he must have seen there, what he must have experienced, she wished she could hide this man she loved from all of it.

He pulled her close again, and she sank deeper into his chest, this time tumbling into a place she never wanted to leave.

"I do have one gift," he said, digging into his pocket.

She leaned back against the sofa, her heart trembling at the thought of what it might be.

"Merry Christmas." Roland retrieved a ring woven with silver and sprinkled with tiny diamonds that glistened like ice. "It was my grandmother's."

She'd chosen simplicity for her life as a Quaker, but there was nothing simple about this ring or the man before her. Nothing simple about a movie star mother or three French children who now packed her home. Still God could make something beautiful, she felt certain, out of all these strands.

"I can't have children," Roland said. "The Nazis . . ."

Grace hushed him with her finger. "We already have a houseful of them."

He gently slid the ring on her finger. "One more day."

In that moment, she gave him the gift of her heart. And a lifetime of days, she prayed, as a family.

CHAPTER TWENTY

"It's me," Caleb called as they neared Ruby's house, Wallace at their heels.

Addie glanced both directions on the gravel road and across the chain-link fence, but she didn't see anyone in the trees. "Who are you talking to?"

"My uncle." Caleb whistled at the edge of the forest. "Louis keeps watch over the house."

She shivered. Had his uncle been watching her that night she'd spent in her car? Perhaps the creature outside her window hadn't been a dream.

They rounded the curve and strung along the fence was the vine with red berries and purple blossoms, yellow stars shooting out of each flower.

Bramble. Berries. Blossoms.

That list summed up Oregon in her mind. Gems tangled with thorns.

She pointed at one of the flowers. "Do you know what this is?"

"A problem weed." He tossed a stick and Wallace ran ahead on the road to retrieve it. "At least, most people call it a problem. The vine is actually a stowaway from Europe."

She glanced across the twilight-splashed ridge. "It seems like people and plants alike found refuge on this farm."

"I suppose so," he said. "The vines can take over, but they also give shelter to a number of animals around here. More like a partner than a problem."

"What's the real name of it?"

"Scarletberry, poisonberry, or bittersweet nightshade, all depends who you ask." He ran his fingers over the arrow-shaped leaves. "I guess I don't have to tell you not to eat it. The blackberries are fair game though. You can eat those until your stomach hurts."

This time she smiled. "I already have."

He picked one of the purple flowers and held it up to the light. The petals turned a sky blue, the center shining like the sun. "Even if they are poisonous, they're much too pretty to kill."

He threw the stick for Wallace again, and she liked how this man saw fierce warriors in friendly dogs. Beauty in what others called a problem.

"Your dad's thesis said that Grace was in Europe during World War II."

Caleb opened the front gate. "Dad has always been interested in the Quakers' work in France."

"I can't imagine what they must have experienced." She stepped through the gate, watching for the man who guarded Ruby's house. "Are you certain this is safe?"

One of his eyebrows slid up. "When have you ever been guaranteed safety?"

"No guarantee, I suppose, but one shouldn't walk directly into danger either."

"My uncle won't hurt you, if that's what you're worried about." He handed her a flashlight. "I can't make any promises about the roof, but it's held up since 1946."

"I'll take my chances."

"Then I will tell Louis we're here."

She sat on the front step, arms wrapped around her knees as he walked through the formal garden and disappeared into the trees. Hopefully his uncle would lay down anything that hurt his relationship with Charlie to help him now.

Then again, it was easy to tell someone else they must forgive the past, much harder to do so herself.

Peter's face flashed into her mind as she waited, his winsome smile that welcomed every newcomer into church. The way he'd loved wholly at times and then withdrew that love, at least from her, near the end, ripping her up inside, wondering what happened to the man she'd married.

Three months had passed since he'd kissed her lips and pulled away from their home. An emergency, he'd said, to help a parishioner. Time, on some days, that spanned an eternity. Other days it seemed like just a blink, a single piece of sand on a seashore of days. Forever and a single moment since her husband had left her late that night for a woman he'd met online.

And then he was gone. According to the police, both Peter and his companion died on impact when his car hit Watauga Lake.

For six months, Addie found out later, they'd been having an affair, and still she wondered what she'd done to fail him. With the thorns in her past, it might be impossible for any man to love her as his wife.

Her fingers lingered on her abdomen. While she was grateful for God's outpouring of love on her thirsty soul, she'd longed for a husband on this earth who would love her and their child . . .

"With God's help," she whispered to the baby growing inside her, "I am going to love you well."

She would be different than her parents. Different than Peter. Different than what she'd seen modeled on the television screen. She'd love her baby and the girls at Sale Creek and whoever else needed it.

Caleb stepped back out of the trees and crossed the lawn. "Unfortunately, my uncle isn't in the mood to talk."

"What does his mood have to do with it?"

"I have to tread carefully," Caleb said. "He doesn't like to talk about the past."

She stood up beside him. "Does he know what happened to Charlie's sister?"

"I'll ask him again later."

"How much later?" she begged.

"I'm sorry, Addie. I can't force him to talk if he doesn't want to share his story."

"It could save Charlie's life . . ."

Caleb unlocked the front door. "I don't think that matters to him."

She followed him into the Victorian home, and evening light filtered through the front room when he pushed aside the curtains. "Ruby wanted to bring Hollywood with her when she moved to Oregon."

And Ruby had carried a bit of Tinseltown north with the plush red carpets and shiny molding, a pair of faded velvet sofas with bejeweled lampshades on both ends, glass beads dangling from each one. All that was needed were tumblers filled with vodka, the click of heels, ice clinking when someone raised a toast.

Not that she knew about these things, but she'd seen plenty on TV in her younger years. Drama always followed the velvet and beads.

"Most of the furniture is still here, but I rescued the Louis XIII armoire from the dining room." He directed her back into the hall,

the Oriental runner as faded as the sofas. "The walnut was lacquered in black and the drawers were filled with sketches."

The dining room housed the mural Addie had seen from outside with its lofty cathedral and dark forest and chain of children strung together like the paper cutouts she'd created in elementary school, holding hands along their journey.

"Each person is a different color," she said with reverence to the artist's imagination—a bright aura above each head perfectly brushed and blended like the painting of a master. "I've never seen anything like it."

The line of children wound through an old European street and then a field of flowers, to the foot of a mountain. The children on this wall, they were all together and yet each one was unique. But the last child was only partially finished, the mountain undone. The artist had stopped before he or she had completed the work.

Caleb pointed at a boy and girl in the middle. "Look closely."

On the elbow of the boy was a letter *E*, painted orange, and hidden in the blue and yellow skirt of the girl was an *M*, the same colors that swept like an emerging storm over her head.

"Reese found the letters."

"An unfinished story," Addie said.

"But not completely undone." He pulled out the drawer to a bureau and removed a small stack of papers. "These were in the armoire."

The top sketch was a drawing in colored pencil of a château behind an iron gate, a range of lofty mountains in the background. Then a river with snow on its banks. A cluster of homes clinging to a mountain. And last, a willow tree, very much like the one on Tonquin Lake. Veiled between the branches was a woman instead of a child, beckoning the others forward.

"Are they escaping with Grace?" she asked, mesmerized by the details.

"I believe so."

She turned toward the window. "Charlie planted a willow tree on the bank of Sale Creek when he and Emma started the girls' home."

"This must have been a good place for him to grow up," Caleb said as he slid the sketches back into the drawer. "Everything was a grand adventure for my dad here when he was a child."

"Now you want to buy all of the Tonquin property . . ."

Caleb looked out the window at a hummingbird that flitted near the porch, feeding on a raspberry bush. "Eventually, if the owner decides to sell. Right now, there is a provision for our rent." He hesitated. "It's complicated."

"Because of your uncle?"

"Louis needs to be here, more than anyone else, but Tara wants him gone."

"Reese said he scares away renters."

"Louis doesn't want anyone on this land except family, and if Dawson Management buys the property, they'll build a housing development around the lake."

She glanced out the window again. "Louis is the provision . . ."

He pointed toward the carpeted steps. "You want to see upstairs? There's a view of the whole valley from the tower."

"I'd love to."

As they crossed the hallway, she peeked into the doorways of four bedrooms, all of them elaborately decorated. All but the one with a broken window neat and clean, the entire house a time capsule from fifty years past.

"Did Ruby die in this house?" she asked tentatively, remembering what the librarian had said. She'd searched through their collection but couldn't find a single newspaper or magazine that reported on the murder of this Hollywood star.

"No one knows what happened to Ruby, but each new generation makes it their mission to get inside the house. See Ruby's ghost, I suppose."

"So your uncle watches over it for your family."

"For himself. He can stay here as long as he helps care for the place, but he . . . Some days he doesn't remember that Ruby is gone."

"Why would someone kill Ruby?" Addie asked as they neared the end of the hall.

"A million reasons, I suppose. My grandma said locals didn't like her much."

"And your grandmother never mentioned Charlie or his sister?"

Caleb shook his head. "She spent most of her life focused on raising her kids and watching over Louis. The dairy farm closed in the 1980s, but my grandparents lived in that cottage where you're staying to keep an eye on Louis until they passed away."

"Then you took over for your grandparents?"

"My dad came down on the weekends from Seattle to check on him until I was able to buy the property above the vineyard."

She looked up at the man in front of her, at his dark hair and gray T-shirt and jeans, a confident strength in his eyes. "It seems like your family must have remembered something about him . . ."

Caleb opened the last door on the hall, this one hiding a staircase. "Has Charlie asked you to find his family?"

"No," she said slowly. "But I want to give him the gift of life."

What Charlie had given to her, but she couldn't explain that to the man in front of her. He wouldn't understand.

"How old is he?" Caleb asked.

"Seventy-three, and he has many years left in this world."

"Has he made his peace with God?"

"He's devoted his life to serving Him."

"Then perhaps you have to make your peace with God too."

She flinched at the words, startled. Had he done his own research on her story?

"What do you mean?"

"Perhaps God has something else in store for Charlie's legacy."

The word made her cringe. "I'm here about his life, not his legacy."

She stepped across the hallway to study a gallery of paintings on the wall, impressionistic work portraying the gardens and streets of Paris. She'd yet to see a family picture or portrait. Almost as if this were a movie set, designed to impress on the surface, nothing warm or personal underneath the trimmings.

Much like the place where she'd grown up. No expensive art adorned the walls of their apartment, but neither did they have personal pictures or family heirlooms or anything that suggested a home. Only a showplace for her mother's guests.

Was Ruby like her mother, always craving the attention of people outside their home? Strangers? If so, Grace probably ran to France.

Did Ruby provoke Charlie to run as well?

"On earth as it is in heaven." That's what Jesus prayed. Why couldn't some heartaches mend in this life, like they would in heaven? God could heal Charlie's heart and his body here.

And He could heal hers.

Caleb motioned toward the circular staircase, and she climbed the steps behind him. From the tower, she could see the lake and cottage, the lights of Newberg beginning to glow in the distance and the roof of an A-frame in the trees.

When she looked straight down in the dim light, she saw a man standing at the edge of the forest.

Louis, she suspected, had the answers she needed.

Chapter Twenty-One

JULY 1946

A giant blackberry plunked into Grace's wooden bucket, and she turned quickly to see Roland and Élias standing behind her with buckets in their hands, galoshes up to their knees, the two of them flanking Cocoa, their shepherd dog.

Her leading men, she called them. A handsome pair who were inseparable as they worked farm and land, both of them bearing wounds from the war but healing, it seemed, together.

Roland dropped the bucket and a picnic basket before lifting her off the ground, planting a kiss on both cheeks and then her lips. She giggled like a schoolgirl. How she loved this man who'd swept back into her life last year and married her in the small meetinghouse he'd built on their property. Loved how he cared for her and the children.

A groan rumbled from the lips of Élias—Charlie, now that he'd been able to obtain his driver's license. *Free man*, the name meant in

French, although Roland had explained it was slang for "foolish" in England.

Charlie didn't care. The new name sounded American to him, and he was tired of being set apart as different when he wanted to be like the other boys in his school.

"Would you two stop it?" Charlie said.

But Roland continued twirling her around like she was a pinwheel, and she laughed even harder. Then he lowered her to the ground and lifted his bucket as a sword. "We've come to defend you ladies."

Marguerite rolled her eyes, a purple ring fresh around her mouth, juice staining every finger, a messenger bag filled with art supplies banging her hip. She lifted one finger freshly snagged by thorns. "Defend us from the blackberries?"

"From the creatures of the deep."

Grace glanced at the lake, her hand over her heart as if she were the leading lady. "You've come just in time."

"He wants lake creatures," Charlie said, stepping up beside his sister. "I want berries."

The four of them cleaned off the prickly bushes beside the water, half the berries going to their buckets, the other half deposited straight into their mouths. Grace knew she'd cling to the memory of these summer months, the long sunny days. Nothing would ever steal away their sweetness, staining a ring around her mind like the berries had done on their lips, capturing every thought.

These people, her family. The enemy of this world had tried to kill them all. She didn't know why they survived when so many others died, nor did she understand exactly what she needed to do with this life she'd been given, but God had brought the four of them together, that much was clear. In this moment, on a warm summer evening, she embraced the sheer joy of it. Strength for whatever tomorrow might bring.

Marguerite's and Grace's buckets filled first, and they helped the men collect as many berries as their buckets would hold.

Blackberry jam. Blackberry pie. Blackberry cordial. Blackberries with vanilla ice cream made from their dairy's sweet cream.

The possibilities were endless.

Roland unfolded a blanket that he'd tucked between the handles of the picnic basket and swooshed it in the air. The breeze rippled through the wool, unfurling as it fell neatly on the grass, sending a flurry of dandelion to mix with the cottony willow seeds that floated through the air.

"Did you bring lemonade?" Marguerite asked as the shower of seeds rained down.

Roland tilted back the hamper lid and pulled out a jar. Thick lemon slices swam in the sugar water. The sweeter, the better—that was Marguerite's mantra—and he was more than pleased to accommodate her request. While he poured lemonade, the others gathered round the feast of sausages and crusty bread that Roland had baked. Crumbled Roquefort-like cheese in a salad of fresh greens.

They didn't sneak away often, just the four of them. Soon after Roland arrived from France, Ruby moved into her new home, and the Quaker community elders asked Grace and Roland to open the farm to immigrants who needed a place to live and work until they found a new home in town.

Three generations of Tonquins had poured themselves into this lake and property, and now it was their turn to continue building a place for their family and others to find sustenance and peace. Roland and Charlie had worked with their guests to build small homes with A-shaped roofs, like the ones in the mountains of France, along the lake and in the forest.

The adults and older children helped with the farm and tended the grapevines that Roland brought as cuttings from his family's vineyard. They fed the sheep and chickens, milked cows, made soft

Camembert cheese. This land, so far from the influences of the world, was full of life.

Her grandparents would have been thrilled to see the community toiling together to bring wholeness and healing to their farm, the land used to glorify their Creator.

"A picture please." Grace lifted the camera that Roland had packed in the hamper and focused the lens on the children, the willow tree behind them, wanting to capture this moment forever.

The shutter clicked twice, then Marguerite slipped her sketchbook out of the messenger bag and sat by herself on the dock, painting whatever caught her eye in watercolors, her mind off in another world. Back in France, perhaps, with her mother.

Roland pulled a tin pan out from the hamper and tossed it toward the water. Charlie launched off the blanket, his lanky legs delivering him right to the edge. Then he stumbled into the lake as he caught it, seconds passing before he rose again from the mud like a monster, the disk over his head, a triumphant grin across his face.

This boy, their son, was almost a man. The lawyer they'd met with in Newberg said they weren't able to formally adopt him or his sister, but paperwork didn't matter anymore. Charlie Tonquin, he'd decided, was his name. A member of the growing Tonquin family. He and Roland and Marguerite had all embraced the British surname.

She couldn't replace Madame Dupont, but Grace was determined to mother him and Marguerite well. After Roland's injuries at Dachau, they would never be able to birth children, but a host of children lived here now with the refugee families, and she hoped more would follow. Children born from their hearts.

Charlie tossed the pie pan back, and Roland chased it the opposite direction. Two boys, really, who didn't want to grow up.

Roland pretended to tackle her, and she laughed with him.

"Do I look like a pan?" she asked.

"You were much harder to catch . . . more like a plane."

"And I was quite exhausted by all the running. Over the hills, across the river . . ."

He took her hand. "All the way to America."

His skin was ruddy and calloused from the farmwork, and she traced the tip of a scar on his wrist that he kept hidden under long sleeves, no matter how hot it was in the barn. To him this mark brought shame, but to her it was a badge of honor. The Nazis had tried to break him and yet he lay on this blanket beside her, a man devoted to protecting all of them from evil.

"I'm glad you came, Roland."

"Truly?"

"With all my heart."

In the richness of his love, he'd given his life willingly to offer her freedom, thinking he would never see her again, and now here they were, a second chance.

"I'm going in." Charlie stripped off his shirt as he raced back toward the water.

This time he didn't stop at the bank. A swift dive and he swam across the lake like she'd done often as a girl. Nothing scared Charlie. Nor did anything ever stop him. God would use him and his tenacity, she felt certain, just as God would use Marguerite and her paints.

He popped his head out of the water, waved at them, and then dove back under.

"His energy knows no bounds," Roland said, collapsing back on the blanket, his hands propped as a pillow behind his head.

"Like someone else I know." She snuggled into the valley between his arm and chest, a place where her head fit perfectly night after night. Nothing could ever take this moment from her.

He pulled her closer to his chest, her body fitted at his side. "Not as much energy these days."

"You are a fighter, Roland, in the best sense of the word. Don't ever forget that."

Even though he didn't believe her, he kissed the top of her head, but she knew it was true. Roland fought for those he loved. Her and everyone in his care. He would do anything to protect his family.

Charlie hopped up on the dock to sit beside his sister, poking her side as she tried to paint, probably dripping all over her paper. It gave her hope, this simple teasing, that perhaps the darkness that settled over him at times would one day blow away.

Still she worried.

"Something is plaguing him," Grace said.

"We are all haunted by what we saw during the war. What we had to do." Roland's voice rolled like a wave caught onshore, traveling alone over a drift of sand. "He has experienced more sadness in sixteen years than most adults will in a lifetime."

A heron dipped its long neck into the lake, catching a fish, and its steel-colored feathers, the pointed beak, reminded her of a Nazi with a sword. Or a knife.

The knife that Charlie had brought with him across the mountains flashed through her mind. The knife, she suspected, he used to eliminate the man who wanted to capture her wards.

"What happened back in Saint-Girons?" she asked softly. "When he helped you rescue the children . . ."

She'd wanted to ask Roland for months, but their relationship had been too new, fragile, as they'd tried to rebuild under the probing eye of her mother and the pressure of parenting two kids.

Roland paused, seeming to choose his words carefully. He never wanted to talk about the war or its aftermath, but this she wanted to know, for both her and Charlie.

"The French police weren't very motivated to keep the children. The jailkeeper left the front door unlocked. Made it easy for us."

"None of it was easy," she said, knowing there must be more to the story for both him and Charlie. She wanted to bear this burden with him, but she wouldn't demand that he tell her when he so desperately wanted to protect her mind as well as her body.

"I had to kill men to save others," he said slowly. "Like I was God, the judge and then the executioner of those who were trying to hurt others. But even worse, when I got to Dachau, I saw those monsters with their big guns and cowardly souls drag women away, children even, to the gas chambers. And I couldn't do anything to stop them. I was powerless, Grace. A coward like the others . . ."

This man, who'd devoted his life to rescuing, had been ripped apart on the inside. Not being able to save those at the camp—it went against every cell in his being.

His voice was quiet now, as if the trees might betray him. "They stole my courage."

He hadn't lost his desire to protect—she felt it every day—but the concentration camp had dulled his senses. He hesitated now, afraid of himself at times, that he might hurt someone else in his passion to defend.

A stirring of gravel under tires, and she turned to watch a Streamliner, as shiny and polished as her mother's silver, cruise past. The sedan was chauffeured by a starstruck man named Paul who kept up Ruby's house and made her meals and escorted her around town. Ruby had no lack of visitors, but she still managed to keep her eye on Grace.

Sometimes Grace wondered if her mother hated her because Grandpa and Grams had stepped in as parents when Ruby discovered she was averse to motherhood. And because Grace never adored her like the crowds in Hollywood.

In the back seat, his nose pressed against the window, Grace saw Louis, seven years old now, watching the older children play. When he'd first arrived in Oregon, she and Roland tried to fold him into their family, like the two older kids, but the bustling in their home, the necessary farm chores and animals, frustrated him. He fought against her like he'd done back in France.

When Ruby invited him to stay for a week, Louis settled into her big house, refusing to leave. Then Ruby hired another attorney and made her guardianship official.

Grace tried to fight the guardianship, afraid for the boy, but Ruby promised the judge that she would care well for him. On paper, at least, Ruby appeared to be a better option. Her only child was grown, and she had the finances to provide a nicer home and education than Grace and Roland ever could.

After Louis moved up the hill, Grace invited him on their family outings, but he didn't like playing in the dirt. Instead he seemed quite content living with Ruby. An admirer in training, Grace thought, dwarfed by the sun.

The government hadn't allowed Ruby to adopt Louis, just as Grace and Roland were unable to adopt the Dupont kids, but she embraced her role as his foster mother and legal guardian. And her friends oohed and aahed over the boy as if he were a souvenir like her fancy armoire from France.

Grace understood quite well what it felt like to be on display, but unlike Grace, Louis seemed to enjoy the attention.

Ruby watched them as the driver slowed the car, like Grace and family were the ones on the silver screen. Her mother never visited nor did she invite them up to her home, but she was always watching them, waiting for her daughter to fail.

Grace sighed. "Why must she keep checking on us?"

Roland twirled her hair, ignoring the automobile. "She's just being nosy."

"She could at least say hello or something. It's strange that she never stops."

"The whole situation is strange."

Roland had grown up with a family who embraced normalcy.

Until the war, they'd stuck together like a cluster of Mercier-grown grapes.

The sedan circled at the end of the road and headed back their way.

Grace sighed. "It's like a parade."

"Let's give her something to remember then."

Her husband leaned over and kissed her, blocking the view with his arms.

The sound of rolling gravel faded away behind her, but still . . .

Grace didn't like her mother's intrusion at all.

Chapter Twenty-Two

JULY 1947

Ruby shot through the back door of the farmhouse like a torpedo. But instead of exploding, shaking the entire house, she waved a white envelope addressed to Grace.

Ruby dropped the letter on the breakfast table as Louis trailed into the house behind her. "This came to *Château sur la Colline*."

Grace glanced at the return address from London. *Urgent* stamped in red below.

She didn't want to touch it, afraid at the news it might contain. And she was also concerned—why had Ruby taken it upon herself to deliver this personally instead of returning it for the postman to carry down the hill?

"Aren't you going to open it?" Ruby eyed the envelope as if she'd been blessed with X-ray vision to see the contents inside.

"Later." Grace took a ham out of the oven for Charlie's seventeenth birthday celebration. "It must be something for Roland."

"The envelope's addressed to you." Ruby glanced at the doorway into the living room. "Where is Roland?"

"Probably the barn," she said even though it was more likely to find him in the small studio he'd built out back, installing lights for Marguerite. The girl spent every free hour in there, spilling color out on canvas.

Ruby hiked up a penciled eyebrow, her cherry-glazed lips out of place in this plain kitchen. "I was already in the barn."

"So you brought me this letter in order to see my husband?"

Ruby's eyes narrowed. "I brought you the letter because it belongs to you. And I want to ask Roland a favor."

Grace eyed the date on the postmark. It was mailed more than two months ago. "How long have you had this?"

When Ruby shrugged, Grace wondered if it had been days or weeks even. The envelope was her mother's ticket to visit the farmhouse. Spend time with the man Grace had married after her mother's male guests returned home.

"There you are." Ruby's voice turned sickly sweet. When she smiled at Roland, a hammer in hand as he stood in the doorway, an icy anger froze inside Grace. Her mother could have any number of men who called, sporting their pin-striped suits and fancy cars and cigars, but not this one.

Roland placed the hammer on the kitchen counter, Marguerite close behind him, and took Grace's hand, his eyes warming the chill, their fingers entwined. This man was hers.

"How can I help you, Ruby?" he asked.

"I have a leak in my kitchen faucet."

"Then we'll call for a plumber. Mr. Lange, I'm told, can fix about anything."

"I don't like that man."

Grace covered her mouth when she coughed, certain that Mr. Lange was not fond of Ruby either.

"He will do much better work than I ever could," Roland explained.

But it wasn't about the work; even he knew that now.

"I don't trust him. It's like he's just waiting to steal something when I turn around."

Grace bristled. "That's ridicu—"

Roland squeezed her hand, quieting Grace before she said something she would regret, the same way he'd done when they had been stopped by the militiamen in France. No good would come from her accusations, even if they were true.

"Ruby, you don't want me stomping around your pretty home," Roland said. "I'm certain to break something."

Tears spilled from her mother's eyes. "The least you can do is check on it."

Louis reached for Ruby's hand like Roland had done with Grace, but she swatted him away. "Not now, Louis."

"But—"

"Not now."

Grace followed the boy's gaze to the kitchen window and then gasped. Orange flickered like a matchstick beyond the lake, crowning a grove of trees.

Ruby shrieked at the sight, her acting skills taking off like the Pan Am Clipper over Lisbon. The rattling sound of her voice ascended until Marguerite crowded into the kitchen with them, her smock smattered with paint.

Had her mother set a fire to get Roland's attention? That was Grace's first thought, but she batted it away. Surely Ruby wouldn't do anything to harm her castle.

Grace opened the back door and retrieved a pair of mud boots and a wool sweater stored under the covered patio.

Roland pulled on his boots. "You and Marguerite stay here."

"I'm going with you."

"Please, Grace." The desperation in his eyes shattered her heart, reminding her that the strength of this man would shatter if something wounded her.

She turned to Marguerite. "Go get Charlie."

The girl shook her head. "He never came home from school."

She groaned. Charlie had been disappearing more often these days to spend time with Kirk, a boy about two years older than him. A boy who seemed to cause more harm than good.

She kept telling herself not to be concerned. All young men stumbled their way through these years. While she didn't know about Kirk, Charlie was going to make it to the other side.

"I'll find him," she said. "So he can help you."

Roland kissed her cheek. "Call the fire department first. I suspect we'll need their ladders."

Ruby headed out behind him, Louis's hand clutched in hers. Grace couldn't imagine the drama that would ensue in the forest. Her husband wouldn't do anything to return Ruby's advances, that much she was certain of, but her theatrics might put him in danger.

"Louis should stay here," Grace said, her eyes on the boy.

"He's coming with me."

"Louis—"

The boy shook his head. "She needs me."

"Please, Ruby." But her mother had turned her back, leading the boy up to the woods.

Right now Grace had to focus on fighting this fire. Shoving the letter into her pocket, she called the fire marshal, then hurried with Marguerite and their dogs to the meetinghouse. Roland had installed a bell in its tower for such a time as this.

As the dogs waited inside the white-planked room, she and Marguerite climbed the tower. The warning bell echoed across the valley, and she watched several men run out of the cottages below. Only about ten families remained on the Tonquin land and many of the residents worked in town, but everyone nearby would hear the bell, see the flames. Hopefully Charlie would join them soon.

With smoke settling over the lake, sirens screaming as fire engines rushed onto their land, she and Marguerite hurried down from the tower hand in hand.

When they returned home, the girl escaped into her studio, a private place to shut out any fear. The dogs weren't supposed to be inside the house, but for this evening, Grace broke her own rule. Instead of using the davenport, she sat on the carpet, three dogs plopping down beside her, their fur pressed into her sides. As she waited for Roland, her hands trembling, she pulled the urgent letter from her pocket. The seam was wrinkled like someone had steamed it open and glued it back together.

Had her mother read it first?

The handwriting was in French, then translated into English so no one could mistake the content. She read it only once before dropping it to the floor, wondering at all that happened in the past three years since she'd arrived from France. At this family she and Roland had created out of the rubble of war.

She'd known this season as the Tonquin family might not last, but she had hoped in the depths of her heart that *foster* would be replaced with adoption one day. That the four of them could live peacefully together until the children launched out on their own.

Cocoa snuggled in close, and Grace dug her hand into his fur.

"Wait on the Lord: be of good courage, and he shall strengthen thine heart . . ."

The words from this psalm of courage washed over her. She must wait first, even when it was hard. Then He would give her strength.

The men worked for hours, soaking all the trees around the fire so the embers wouldn't rekindle during the night. When Roland finally returned, well after midnight, she was still on the floor, the letter on her lap, Charlie's birthday ham ruined on the stove.

"The fire is out," Roland said.

"How did it start?"

"The fire marshal thinks someone doused the area with alcohol and lit a match. They'll have to investigate."

The investigation, she suspected, might lead them up to the newly minted castle on the hill.

She looked at the door. "Where's Louis?"

"He and Ruby went back to their house."

"And Charlie—"

"I don't know," he said. "I thought he'd telephone."

"I haven't talked to him since he left this morning. He knew we had a birthday dinner planned."

"He's trying to find his way to becoming a man." Roland nodded toward the envelope on the floor. "What's in your letter?"

"Oh, Roland . . ."

The tears came in a tidal wave, grief pouring out at last. He wrapped his arm around her and she sank into his chest.

"What is it, my love?"

"Later." She tucked the envelope back into her pocket. "We'll talk about it in the morning."

He nodded quickly, trusting her even when he shouldn't, weary to the bone.

The two of them waited in silence, watching the God-lit stars over the lake.

Waiting together for Charlie to come home.

CHAPTER TWENTY-THREE

Pockets of fire topped the lake like candles, Addie thought, lighting this dark world. Sometimes it felt unbearably dark in her life, but God was there. How else could she explain starlight firing the darkness? Blossoms on poisonous berries.

A baby growing in her womb.

Blossoms. Babies. Blessings.

"You are a blessing," she whispered as she waited for a return call from Tara Dawson, the cordless phone on the table beside her. Rocking back on the patio chair, her hand on her stomach, she sang softly to this baby who would never know its father. Girl or boy, she didn't know which. Nor would she find out until the moment baby was born . . . if he or she was born.

She was fully prepared to miscarry like she'd done with her first two pregnancies. Better, she thought, to be ready for another loss than lose herself in the hope of becoming a mom.

Still, in spite of all that had happened these past three months, baby was still alive and fully formed now, according to her maternity book, with hands and feet and tiny toes—just not a daddy waiting to welcome him or her into the world.

When she was younger, Addie had promised herself that one day she'd give her children a father who would be kind to them. Proud of them.

Was it possible this time, in the midst of the grief, her shame, that she might carry this little one to term? A single mom now, like the woman who had birthed Addie almost thirty years ago.

She rocked again, a breeze sweeping pine branches across the edge of the porch, brushing over a collection of rocks that someone, a child perhaps, had lined up like boxcars on a train.

The rocks transported her back to Sale Creek, to the years she'd shared a cabin at the home for girls, learning how to do life in a much different way than in her early years. A shift in both heart and mind as she paddled in the tributary of the Tennessee River, wishing back then that the current would take her away.

And yet she had chosen to live because Charlie and Emma and others at Sale Creek told her that her life was worth living. That God had created her for a purpose.

She'd thought that purpose was to help pastor a church, and she'd poured herself into caring for Peter and developing relationships with the young people at Knoxville Christian Church. She didn't know what was next for her life except to help Emma and Charlie. Perhaps that was what God had intended for her, at least in this season. To help save Charlie's life so he could continue championing the girls who lived at Sale Creek.

There had been tremendous purpose for Charlie's life and there would be purpose in his death, she felt confident of that. One day, Charlie would have to go—Caleb didn't have to remind her of that reality—but it wasn't time yet.

Closing her eyes, she thought of those months more than ten years ago when she'd first arrived at the girls' home, at the anger, hatred even, that she'd spattered like lava on anyone who tried to befriend her, an eruption burning anyone in her path. Yet she never was able to empty herself of the anger. The magma continued bubbling inside her, replenishing those empty spaces until Charlie had found her on the riverbank, fuming on a rock where the river trimmed into a creek. He sat on the grass beside her, a cloth bag in his hands, and she'd refused to look at him even as she told him why she didn't need to be here. Why he and the judge were holding her against her will.

Why neither of them could possibly understand.

"You're right, Adeline," he'd said. "Only you can understand what you've been through. No one wants to hold you against your will. We want you to master your will so you can be in control of yourself."

Those words had sunk into her, easing the burn. If she could somehow control her will, cool the embers that swayed her, perhaps she could leave.

At the time, she'd never wanted to see Sale Creek again. At the time, she hadn't even wanted to see the dawn of the next day.

"I've brought you a gift." Charlie opened the bag, and she tried to pretend that she didn't care what was inside. But curiosity reigned as she leaned in, wondering what he'd brought to the river.

She rolled her eyes. "They're stones."

It was stupid to carry around a bag of rocks, and he knew it. Was he trying to mock her? She wasn't going to let him or anyone else manipulate her.

"Not just any stone." He carefully picked one out of the bag and rolled it between his palms as if it contained some sort of magic. Then he held it up to the light.

"This is a wrong," he said.

She'd studied the rock, the silvery glitter on its gray-and-red face. "What's wrong with it?"

"Nothing's wrong with it." He tossed the stone into the river. "It is a wrong."

"You're full of—"

He shook the bag. "This is a whole collection of wrongs."

She stared at him, thinking he must be on the verge of mad. "That makes no sense."

"Every time someone wrongs us, we have two choices. We can collect them—" he held up the bag as if he were about six years old, ready for show-and-tell—"and carry them around for the rest of our lives. With the weight of this, we wouldn't be able to go far in life, but whenever we'd like, we can take out a wrong and mull over it until we're ready for a fight."

And that's exactly how she'd felt at seventeen, like she was carrying around a battery of wrongs. So many people had treated her poorly, cruelly even. She'd thought of herself as a warrior with armor of steel to protect her from further pain, but perhaps the armor was one of the reasons that she sat on this bank, unable to move.

"Or?" she asked.

He glanced over like he didn't understand.

"You said we have two choices." She sighed. "We can either collect these wrongs or . . ."

"We can throw them away." He lifted another rock over his head and flung it into the mouth of the creek, the stone disappearing under the surface. A watery grave for wrongs.

He handed her a rock, and she finally threw it. Haphazardly at first, slipping through the surface, sinking. Then he held out the bag and she dug both hands into it, cramming as many stones as possible between her fingers.

She stared at all these wrongs, weighing her down.

Charlie moved up beside her. "God can take them away, Adeline. Every single hurt. Every fear."

Would God really take all those wrongs if she tossed them in the river?

I'm not afraid—that's what she wanted to say. But the truth was, she was terrified. Hurt and scared.

Still, she didn't want to heave around a bag of wrongs. She wanted to live a life free of what other people had done.

"Throw them away," Charlie said again.

Addie didn't toss the entire handful together. She'd tossed them one at a time, each one a different memory. What her mother had said about Addie's life, the laughter of her so-called friends when they thought she wasn't listening. What the judge said about her future.

Charlie had stepped toward the water, but he didn't walk away. After she emptied the bag, Addie picked up the rock where she'd been sitting and rolled it off the bank, her scream of triumph piercing the air when it splashed—sank—into the creek.

Then she turned to see if the man behind her was concerned. If she'd gone too far. Surely he'd send her away now that he'd seen the lava flow out of her mouth and hands.

But Charlie's grin radiated back instead. "Well done, Adeline."

She'd looked down at the river and then the creek, all of the rocks submerged.

In that moment, she had felt lighter than she'd felt in her entire life. As if she could walk across the water. Fly, even. Charlie hadn't redeemed her, but God had used him to resurrect her life.

"You don't have to carry those wrongs anymore," Charlie said.

She'd returned to the river often in the following years. Sometimes by herself, a bag of rocks in hand. Sometimes with a new arrival at Sale Creek. A young girl who carried a heavy load with her as well.

Caleb had questioned why she wanted Charlie to live instead of releasing him to the next life. Because she loved him and Emma, dearly, but it was more than just her love, her selfishness, even, to keep Charlie in this world. Emma didn't want to direct Sale Creek

Home for Girls alone, and without Charlie's vision, his heart and passion to share their story, Addie feared the home would have to close.

Her cell phone rang, startling her. The present—not the past with its bag emptied of rocks—was where she needed to be.

"How's it going over there?" Tara asked when Addie answered the call.

"The cottage is beautiful."

"Nothing broken?"

A pine bough brushed over the rocks again, and she fingered the needles. "Nothing inside."

"Fabulous news then. Your voicemail was rather cryptic."

Addie glanced up at the stars. "I was hoping you might be able to connect me with the Tonquin family."

Tara sighed. "I don't know where they live. I do all my transactions with an attorney in London."

Addie pressed her feet into the porch, stopping the chair. "London?"

"Can't give you the man's name. Privacy and all that. It's a mess of red tape whenever I have a question."

"Your client allows you to use their cottage for a vacation rental?"

"They do," Tara said, "in lieu of management fees. It works for all of us."

"Half and half."

Tara laughed. "Something like that."

"Could you ask this attorney if he knows what happened to the Tonquin children?"

"Sorry, my friend, I can't rock the boat."

A loud splash, in her mind alone, but she could almost hear the boat tip over. Benefactors, that's what the Tonquin children would be. If Tara wanted the land, like Caleb claimed, she wouldn't want anyone communicating with a relative.

Then again, neither would Caleb.

But Addie wasn't done yet. "What do you know about Louis Lange?"

Long pause and then a huff. "Is he bothering you?"

"No—"

"He promised he'd leave my guests alone."

"Caleb said he isn't dangerous."

A stony silence met her ear. She'd said too much.

Tara clicked her tongue. "I didn't realize you were friends with the Lange family."

"New acquaintances."

"Checkout is at eleven. I have new guests booked for Saturday night."

"I don't want this land," Addie said, but the woman had already hung up.

She'd speak with Louis in the morning. Then she'd go home.

CHAPTER TWENTY-FOUR

Where was the girl going? Louis trained his binoculars on Pinky as she skimmed alongside Tonquin Lake before disappearing into the trees.

Nothing but trouble. That's what she'd been. Worse than a hundred kids who tromped up to this place. Worse than—

He shook his head as he lowered the binoculars.

Nothing was worse than the night of that fire . . .

Trembling, he lifted his binoculars again to fight the memory, searching the hillside. If only he could see the girl under the canopy of trees, but nothing moved except a heron searching for breakfast.

Caleb had already taken Pinky into the house. What was he supposed to do if she kept invading his space?

She should stay at the cottage. Or go back to her home, wherever that was, and leave him and this house alone.

A noise behind him, and he jumped, turning to see a fawn tangled in the wire fence. He moved quickly to her side, wishing he had pliers.

"You'll be all right," Louis said softly, his hand on the fawn's head.

The animal flailed, pulling the wire tighter in panic, until he covered her eyes with his shirt. Then she stopped struggling. He carefully inched the wire down her leg and removed the piece that snared her head. When he removed the blindfold, the fawn bolted off, back into the forest. Toward her mother, he hoped. Someone who would keep the enemy away.

He turned back from the ridge, retreating into his A-frame to stretch out on the bench that he'd carved from a downed pine. Here he could drink his vodka, calm the demons in his mind, forget about an enemy who trapped baby deer.

He'd closed his eyes, for just a moment, when something tapped on the glass. Jumping, he reached for his M16, his heart pounding, but it wasn't there.

Who had taken his rifle?

The Vietcong were at his door and . . .

His mind cleared, his hand clasped over his chest. It was the girl with the pink scarf outside the window, not the muzzle of a gun, staring back at him.

Was she trying to give him a heart attack? She might kill him if he weren't careful. Or get herself killed.

The door inched open, and he shrank back into the corner, the eaves a barricade. The enemy was in his camp, and he'd forgotten to secure the sandbags.

Careless. He pounded his fist on his chest. How could he have been so careless?

Pinky walked inside as if she owned the place, no regard for him or his property. He didn't walk into her cottage and demand answers as to why she was snooping around Ruby's castle. She wasn't allowed in his home either.

What was wrong with him? He was a soldier, an infantryman. He cowered to no one, especially not a woman. He could take her out with one punch, land her on the floor for breaking into his hut. Tara had said not to bother her guests, but what was he supposed to do when this guest kept bothering him? Trespassing. He'd call the police if he had a telephone, report her for this crime. They'd haul her and her pink scarf off to jail.

He watched her from the shadows, his fists trembling. He'd hit plenty of men over the years, clobbered several at Ruby's house when he was a kid, but he'd never hit a girl.

Could he hit this one? Just enough to scare her.

Scaring people was what he did best.

He stepped out of the shadows, his fist ready, when he saw the curve under her white shirt.

A baby.

He stood in front of her now, facing off. She should be terrified. He hadn't cut his hair in years. Or shaved. And while he sometimes swam in the lake, in lieu of a bath, he hadn't done that since she arrived.

Why wasn't she afraid?

"Hello," she said as if he'd invited her into his space. "My name's Addie."

He didn't care one whit about who she was. Only why she was here.

"A friend of mine used to live on this property," she said. "I'm trying to find his sister."

He eyed her closely, watching to see if she flinched, wondering who she might have known. He and Ruby were the only ones who'd ever lived in the castle.

Unless she meant the old farmhouse. Everyone who'd lived there left after the fire.

The girl didn't flinch. Instead her gaze fell to a stack of papers that he'd collected over the years, a tower of them on a tree stump that he'd cleaned and polished for a table.

She lifted the top paper, skimming the type. "What is this?"

He snatched it from her. "My business."

Still she didn't listen. She picked up another set of papers and began to thumb through them, her eyes widening.

Why wasn't she afraid?

"These are about Grace."

This time he didn't steal the papers back. How did she know Grace?

"They are about a lot of people," he said.

The next piece was a report from the AFSC. Words he'd memorized a long time ago. It was about the state of France during the war. The men and women who'd been in what was supposed to be the free zone—the unoccupied half of the country. The thousands upon thousands of children—babies even—who'd been starved and abandoned.

No one should ever steal a child's food. Hell to pay for anyone who stole a meal from a kid.

He didn't stop her now. She was determined, and she'd called his bluff. He wouldn't hurt her over a stack of papers even if these reports meant everything to him, the very trunk on which the branches of his life had grown.

He'd read them many times over the years. The names of Quaker men and women from around the world who'd gone to Southern France to help the refugees. Men and women who distributed food and clothing at the camps. Who had decided, at times, life or death for their wards.

Some of these Quakers had been sent to camps themselves for their service. Others had returned home. Others, like Grace, had left sick children behind who needed care.

Among the papers were pleas for more supplies, more medicine, shoes for children who had none. For governments to wake up and send food.

Why hadn't people cared? He had rescued every child he could in Vietnam. Carried them through jungles, across rice paddies, onto a helicopter once when he refused to leave a baby behind for the Vietcong.

Among these reports were the names of children the Quakers had transported from Europe, his name included. He'd tried to find clues for his own family, many years ago, thinking he might still have a family who wanted him. But his mother had died from typhoid fever. And his father had . . .

His arms began to shake again as he collapsed onto a chair, watching this girl traipse through parts of his story.

If he had siblings, aunts, or uncles, he didn't know. No one had recovered their names.

All he'd had was Ruby.

He braced himself when Pinky sat on his bench and began reading paper after paper. Searching for something.

This was his business. His things. His life story recorded on these pages.

Finally she rested the papers before looking back up at him, her lips poised to ask a question, but he had his own questions for her.

"Who is your friend?" he finally asked.

She glanced out the picture window, searching the trees as if they held the answer. "Charlie Tonquin," she said. "Do you remember him?"

His legs shook as if she'd shot him, waiting for him to fall. As if she was about to leave him for dead.

When he was much younger, Grace and Roland had invited him to spend time with their family. Told him that he had a brother in Charlie. But Charlie hadn't been a good man. He'd tried to destroy Louis and Ruby and the whole Tonquin family.

He'd never wanted another brother. Not Jonathan Lange when the Lange family adopted him. Not even his fellow soldiers in Nam.

She looked back at him. "I think Charlie used to live near Tonquin Lake."

"I know where he used to live."

Her eyes grew wide, a fresh light breaking through the sadness. "Did you know his sister?"

He watched her closely, to see if she was trying to trick him. After what happened, no one talked about Charlie or Marguerite. The family had tried to cover it up, and then most everyone who lived around here, those like him who remembered, had scattered.

Except the Langes. They'd stayed here long after Ruby and the other refugee families were gone.

Addie held up a paper and turned it toward him. A paper from the AFSC office in Lisbon granting Grace a temporary guardianship. The names on it, he knew. Élias and Marguerite Dupont.

Grace had loved those two as her own. Like Ruby had done with him.

"*E* is for Élias," Addie whispered, tracing her finger across the page. "Was that Charlie's name in France?"

He didn't answer.

"And Marguerite," the girl said softly. "*E* and *M*. That must have been his sister. Why did you save these papers?"

"They are important."

She looked out the window again, and he clutched his hands together, trying to make the trembling stop.

"Are you cold?" she asked.

He dug his gloved hands deep into his pockets.

She studied him for a moment and then looked down at Charlie's paper and back up again, as if she'd found something she'd been searching for.

"Why did Charlie leave Oregon?" she asked.

"Because he killed someone."

The look on her face, like he'd launched a grenade. He had no clock, no need of one, but he could hear the seconds ticking by in his head as he waited for it to explode.

"Ruby?" she whispered.

"This isn't your house," he spat. "Not your business. You barge in here and—"

"I never had a father," she said, "didn't even know mine. Charlie is like a father to me."

Louis lifted his hands and rubbed them together. "You're much too young to be his daughter."

"A grandfather, then."

"So he's still alive . . ." He'd never wanted to hurt anyone as much as he'd wanted to hurt Charlie Tonquin. The boy had everything, and he'd thrown it all away.

"I suspect, at one time, he was good to you too," she said as if she could convince him of this lie.

Could she read the hatred in his mind?

Ruby used to invite readers of minds to her castle, a novelty for her guests. They came up from Hollywood to escape from the lights, they'd said, and for the country air. An excursion to the farm. As long as they paid proper respect, Ruby would invite almost anyone from California to her games.

None of those people liked her. They fawned appropriately, extravagantly at times, but he heard their whispering behind closed doors, their laughter when she couldn't hear, mocking the decor, her dress. All while they ate her food and slept in her rooms.

She's using you.

That's what one of the guests had told him.

He shook his head. Ruby had loved him like he was her son. She'd never been mean to him when he was young. Not until that one night so long ago. A guest had forced himself into Ruby's room during the night hours, that's what Louis thought, and this man tried to hurt her.

Louis threatened him with a baseball bat, but the man had ripped it out of his hand. Laughed at him right in front of Ruby until tears filled his ugly eyes. Called him King Kong. Then the ugly man had looked over at Ruby, all tucked away in her bed, and she'd laughed too.

Louis had come to defend her, and she had laughed at him.

That man wouldn't laugh now. Neither of them would.

"Do you know where Marguerite went?"

The ground knotted under his toes, vines snagging his ankles, sweat blinding his eyes. And all around him, the stench of dead animals and dirty soldiers and flaming napalm.

Then a gunshot, coming from the woods.

Where was his rifle?

He ducked under the trees, eyes on a hole in the ground, the camouflaged entrance to one of the tunnels. The Vietcong—the *Charlie*—hid between jungle vines, ants among men.

Another gunshot and the soldier beside him went down.

They were coming for him now, swarming like fire ants, their rifles aimed at his head. Another soldier tripped, an explosion, the wire grenade stealing his life.

He should retreat. Hide. But he couldn't take his eyes off the boot of his friend.

No one should have to die like that.

No one.

"Louis?"

His feet moved without his consent, fleeing from the enemy until they snagged on a branch. He fell into a ditch of stagnant water, a cloud of malaria-infected mosquitoes around his head. He scanned the swarm for the pythons and kraits that could take down a man as quickly as a grenade.

A shuffle of leaves above him. They were coming closer . . .

"It's just a branch," someone said. "It keeps hitting the glass."

A girl—she was speaking to him. In English.

How did an American girl get in the jungle?

He blinked, focusing back on the slanted wood frame above his head, the rattling window.

"Just a branch," she said again. "From the pine trees."

Of course it was just a branch. What did she think it was?

The girl was at his kitchenette, filling a cup with water.

"Vodka," he said, his shaky finger pointed at the shelf with the dust-covered bottles.

She handed him the water, and he gulped it.

"Vodka," he repeated, wanting her to reach it so he didn't drop the bottle, like he'd done last time. "Please."

She crossed her arms. "Where did you go?"

He swore. It was none of her business, not that she really cared. All she wanted to know about was Charlie Tonquin when an entire group of Charlies were searching for him in his waking hours and his sleep.

He didn't have to tell her or anyone else about Vietnam. None of them would understand.

Addie stepped toward the door. "I'll be right back."

Good riddance.

He shoved a chair in front of the door and then looked back at the papers that had intrigued her, glancing at the top one.

It was his birth certificate, the original from Riom where he'd been born. After Grace left him behind in France, she'd taken his birth certificate to America.

Louis Blanc, that had been his name before Louis Lange. Stark white in a sea of color. And yet he was a direct descendant of a king—that's what Ruby told anyone who wanted to hear.

Bring me my vodka.

That's also what Ruby liked to say.

He moved the chair again, from the front door to the kitchenette. Above the sink was a shelf where the boy had stored his drink. Only four bottles remained, lined up like soldiers prepared to march at his command. He guarded them like a general, unwilling to sacrifice one unless the enemy attacked.

He took down a bottle and ripped off the cork stopper. A long swig as he propped his hand against the wooden shelf. The memories of Vietnam drowned, but ones from his childhood emerged in their place.

Bring me my vodka.

He took another swig.

How he'd hated those words as he grew older, like he was a servant when he'd wanted to be a son. But he always did Ruby's bidding. Always . . .

He teetered on the chair and reached out, stopping himself before he fell.

The shelf slid to the right, the bottles sliding with it. One at a time they fell like bombs dropped from a Huey, blasting when they hit the wood floor, spraying shards into the air.

He stared at the damage below, clutching the bottle to his chest.

Bring me my vodka.

He took another swig as he lowered himself on the chair.

Ruby would demand he bring her liquor.

Then she'd always share a bit of it with him.

Chapter Twenty-Five

"What are you doing?" Grace propped the door open with her hip as she glanced around the abandoned hut. Cigarette butts were scattered across the floor, a magazine partially hidden under a couch, two teenage boys sitting cross-legged on the wood floor.

Fire and ice, that's how Roland described Charlie and Kirk. Charlie a simmering red. Kirk a cool blue. Her son transformed into a different person whenever they were together, the fiery red ablaze.

Charlie shoved the magazine under the sofa with his heel. "We're studying."

"You've become quite devoted to your homework."

Kirk snickered, and she wanted to punt the kid back to his house. Then she'd send Roland to puncture the tires of his prized Harley-Davidson so he couldn't cruise onto their property, his radio blaring, taking Charlie off to the coast to surf when her son was supposed to be doing schoolwork or helping Roland on the farm.

She and Roland had talked about banning Kirk from their land, but with three refugee families still living here, it was impossible to manage who visited whom.

The hut was hidden back in the trees near Ruby's house. Her mother hadn't liked having strangers so close to her home, but the space was needed for their growing community, back when they'd hosted almost a hundred refugees. No one lived in this hut anymore. Some of the kids used it as a playhouse, but these two, at seventeen and nineteen, weren't playing.

One of the cigarette butts was still glowing, and she stomped it out with her heel. "You're going to start a . . ."

Her voice faded as she studied the boys, their long legs spread out on the dirty floor, neither of them caring that she'd found them and their filth.

Was it possible they'd started the fire last month? Charlie had returned home in the middle of the night, his birthday long forgotten. They'd never found out where he'd been or who sparked the flames.

A memory flickered in her mind. More than twenty years ago, her mother and a host of so-called friends had hidden behind a curtain of smoke, in a fancy room of long tapestries and laughter broken only by the guzzle of liquid tumbling into glass. How Grace had hated the laughter as she concealed herself under a staircase with someone's cat asleep on her lap, afraid of who might find her.

Then her mother had emerged through the screen of smoke, waving a red cigarette holder like a wand. Someone started banging on the piano, the guests gulping their contraband and laughing as Ruby, who could barely stand, dragged Grace from her hiding place and tried to jive with her daughter.

The party ended with a knock on the front door by LA's finest. Alcohol, she'd learned that day, made people do stupid things. Things they often regretted come morning.

The police called Grace's grandparents, and her grandpa drove Grace up to Oregon for the last time.

"I'm a miserable wretch," Charlie said from his dazed state on the floor, but she didn't laugh this time at his imitation. Instead she picked up a bottle from the table. Benzedrine sulfate—the tablets Ruby took like aspirin for alertness, she said, but Grace suspected it was more about keeping her weight down and her energy high, especially when she was trying to impress the few guests who continued traveling north.

If only Ruby would embrace the truth of who God made her as much as she embraced the lies.

Grace dropped the pill bottle into her pocket. "I'll return these."

Charlie shrugged as he rolled up his baggy Levi's, his feet bare on this spring afternoon. The tan overcoat inspired by Tintin was long gone, replaced with a plain white shirt and a burgundy cap.

Some days, it seemed, the torment from the war had tracked him across the Atlantic, and she wished more than anything that she could help him chase away the shadows.

Now, with the letter from London, everything was about to change again.

Grace glanced at the fireplace and the small refrigerator and sink on the far wall. In the back was a bedroom and bath, the loft overhead meant to house children. The hut could house another family, but the community elders didn't need their help anymore. She'd rather they tear down this place than let the boys smoke in here and pop Ruby's pills like they were gumdrops. And scheme—she knew they were planning something.

These days, this boy who'd once been her greatest advocate, who'd helped her and others escape the killing in France, seemed to embrace evil. And it terrified her.

They'd escaped it once, but he—they all—needed deliverance from evil once again.

Grace held up the history book she'd found back home on Charlie's desk. "You said you were studying for your history test."

He waved his hand. "I already know that stuff."

She almost said Tintin didn't count, but he would argue about the educational value of Tintin and his travels.

She wasn't here to embarrass him. She was here to rescue him again. Except this time he wasn't running away from the Nazis. He wasn't even backing away from the sin that she feared would entangle him, kill him even, if he didn't flee.

"It's time to go, Charlie." She opened the door a few inches wider. "You two will have to visit later."

"With all due respect, Miz Tonquin." Kirk took a long drag on his cigarette. "He don't have to answer to you."

"I'm afraid we have a much different definition of respect."

"Guess we don't have to pretend then." He tossed the cigarette butt on the wooden floor and ground it with the heel of his boot. "Charlie and I are going to my house."

She crossed her arms, not about to give in to the demands of this boy-man. An outlaw, that's what Roland called him, as if they had motorcycle clubs roaming the back roads of Oregon.

"Charlie is coming home with me," she said.

Kirk jumped to his feet and stood beside her, almost a foot taller and as wide as the doorframe. "Not today, Miz T."

Grace didn't move from her post. Five years ago, she'd been negotiating with officers on a French train. Kirk could say what he wanted; Charlie wasn't walking out this door with him.

His gaze planted on her, a nail against wood, Kirk opened the front window. Then Charlie dangled one leg over the sill and dropped to the ground, Kirk following him. They raced toward the dusty motorcycle parked on the narrow path through the woods.

What was she supposed to do now? She was too small to tackle him—he'd overpower her in a second—and the farmhouse was too far away to fetch Roland.

"Grace?" Ruby called through the trees. The last person she wanted to see right now.

Her mother stepped out from behind the curtain of pine, onto the stage dressed in a satin house robe and heels, eyeing the boys. "Where are you going?"

When Charlie climbed onto the motorcycle behind Kirk, Ruby stepped in front of them, her heels sinking into the mud, her hands thrust in front of her like a stop sign as Kirk pumped the kick-starter with his heel.

"This insolence must be stopped." Ruby was looking at Charlie, but her words were directed toward Grace.

"And what do you suggest that I do?"

"Show him who's in charge."

Charlie had respected Grace for more than five years, loved her in recent years as if she really were a mother to both him and his sister. She'd never before had to wield a scepter.

"Charlie—"

He looked straight at her, but she didn't recognize the hatred darting from those handsome eyes. The vehemence in lieu of courage or even concern. How exactly was she supposed to show a seventeen-year-old boy who'd once fought to survive that she was in charge?

She couldn't convince him anymore that he was about to destroy his life. That was Roland's role. At least Charlie still respected him.

"I'm not going home," he said. "Not now or tomorrow or ever. You're not my mom."

And he was right. She hadn't birthed him, hadn't even been able to adopt him. "You're my ward until you're eighteen."

At least until his French mom crossed the sea.

He snickered, the pills or something else, she guessed, driving his words. "The police ain't gonna make me go home."

Her stomach knotted, everything within her wanting to untangle the cords that bound him.

"Please, Charlie." A beggar, not the boss, but she didn't care. She would get on her knees if necessary, lay prostrate even, if he would come home with her.

Kirk kicked the lever again to ignite the engine, and Charlie grasped the back of the seat. The rumble shook everything within her.

He didn't look back when Kirk drove them away. Not even a goodbye.

She'd chosen Charlie as a son when she brought him into her home, promised to care for him as if he were her own, but he hadn't chosen her.

Grace handed the half-empty bottle of medication back to her mother, and Ruby shook her head as if Grace had failed.

"Louis would never do that," Ruby said, and Grace felt like a child again, cowering under the stairs.

This moment was pivotal, but she had no idea what was next.

CHAPTER TWENTY-SIX

"Up you go," Caleb said as he lifted Louis to his feet.

The older man leaned on Caleb like he was a cane, wobbling as he tried to stand, glass sprinkled around his boots. Remnants of a promise no bottle could keep.

"I'll help you." Addie stepped forward, one arm outstretched, but Louis pushed her away. She stumbled back, almost tripping over the glass. Caleb couldn't catch her, not without dropping Louis, but his shoulder helped break her fall.

With her hand braced on the counter, her legs steady again, she saw nothing but kindness in Caleb's eyes. Compassion for his uncle and for her. Because she hadn't understood.

Louis had fought in Vietnam—Caleb told her on the way down the hill. He'd been in combat, seen his comrades suffer horrific deaths as they were forced to choose in a moment's notice whether someone was an enemy or a friend. One wrong step, one wrong choice, and Louis would have been dead too.

No wonder he was afraid.

The man hobbled forward, Caleb in perfect sync as if he'd done this many times.

"They'll kill you, boy." His eyes were wide-open, his lips frozen in shock between his ratty beard.

Caleb shook his head. "No one is going to kill either of us today."

"The Charlie will kill you . . ." Louis's voice drifted off as they rounded the fireplace, back to a bedroom, she assumed.

Addie glanced at the puddles of vodka, the shards scattered on the rug, pieces as broken as the man who lived here. But the rest of the hut was neat with a wooden bench by the picture window, several crates and a tree stump for a table. Old magazines were stacked on the floor underneath a walled shrine, of sorts, for Ruby Tonquin with studio pictures and awards and magazine covers. A strand of red lights had been strung over the gallery, and below it, each frame was dusted, the glass clean.

This was his private space, and once again, she'd pushed too hard. Driven someone else to their breaking point.

Why hadn't she stopped when he began to fail?

She never should have come here in the first place. And she should have walked away the moment he told her to leave, long before she'd taken off running up to Caleb's house for help.

In a small closet, among pots and bird feed and bags of potatoes, she found a broom and dustpan. As she waited for Caleb, she collected the glass shards and piled them into a cardboard box that doubled as a garbage can, Wallace watching her from the other side of the window.

Caleb had been so gentle with the man, unlike her, barging into his private world to find information about the Tonquins. At first, she'd thought he had a heart attack when he collapsed on the floor, until she realized that his mind had gone someplace else.

Vietnam, she knew now, back in 1968. The bloodiest year, Caleb said, of the war.

The floor was clean when Caleb stepped back into the small living space. He stopped to straighten a crooked frame, a black-and-white portrait of Ruby.

"I'm sorry," she said. "He was here with me at first, and then he was gone."

Caleb sat down on the bench, elbows on his legs. "Vietnam haunts him wherever he goes."

Both Louis and Charlie, two boys who'd escaped from the Nazis long ago, were now fighting unseen battles. Brothers, in a sense. "I can't imagine what he must have seen."

Caleb scanned the soot-stained fireplace. "Louis renovated this place after Vietnam. My dad said he was always good at building things."

"Louis said he knew Charlie."

And Marguerite. Now that she had a name for Charlie's sister . . . surely she could find her or her family.

"Did my uncle tell you why Charlie left Oregon?"

"He said Charlie killed someone." She moved to the window. "But I think he was talking about the Vietcong."

Caleb rubbed his chin, the shadow of a beard shaved away this morning. "I'm afraid someone died on this property in the 1940s."

But she couldn't bear to think about Charlie taking a life. "I just want to find Marguerite."

He studied her for another moment, as if he was making a decision. "Louis will be asleep for a few hours."

She glanced at Wallace again on the other side of the glass. "I'll head back to the cottage."

"There's something else that you might want to see first . . ."

"What is it?"

"A gravestone," he said, "back in the trees."

Chapter Twenty-Seven

How she hated the shouting. The two men she loved more than life itself as matador and bull—Charlie charging with words, Roland distracting with his cape.

Neither wanted to kill the other—that's what she told herself. One just wanted to rear and roar around the arena of their home, completely untamed. The other wanted to subdue the rage.

After a week of living with Kirk, Charlie had returned early this morning to get his things. She stood outside Charlie's bedroom now as Roland tried to reason with him. Remind him of their love. Ask him to stay.

"Your mother saved you," Roland said. "So you could live."

"She's not my mother."

Something banged inside Charlie's room as he stuffed clothing into a duffel bag, and Grace braced herself against the wall of the narrow hallway, the words wounding her anew. She hadn't birthed Charlie, but she'd loved him as much as she could love any child.

What had happened to make him hate her so? She'd wanted nothing but good things for him and Marguerite. The thought of his French mother returning, of having to give him up, was hard enough, but this rejection was almost more than she could bear.

Roland tried again. "Grace saved you—"

"I never asked her to save me."

"And now you are throwing it all away."

"You don't know what I want," he shouted.

"You were made for something big, Charlie. God has—"

Charlie spat. She could hear it in the hall. "God has done nothing for me."

Had she been wrong to bring him over the mountains with her, into this strange new land? Perhaps God had meant for him to stay in France. Not to die—she could never imagine that—but to help others in Europe instead of traveling to a new continent where he had stumbled with the language, with the people, never quite fitting in.

Her insides clenched, sick at the thought. All she'd wanted was to help. Had she taken a wrong step as she'd tried to follow God's lead?

She wanted to rush into the room behind Roland, stop the fight, but she was like the red muleta hanging from the matador's stick. The bull, she feared, would charge straight back out the door if she unfurled herself.

Instead she sank onto the carpet, her heart torn as the voices dulled to a grumble on the other side of the wall. Her eyes closed, she could see the light—Marguerite's colors—swirling with the fight. Red, orange, bolts of yellow. A blaze of them.

"The Lord is my light and my salvation; whom shall I fear?"

How they needed the light of their Lord to rescue them all.

She would write Madame Dupont tonight and invite her to Oregon. Perhaps Charlie would listen to her. Or perhaps he would be happier living with her in London.

But Marguerite . . .

Unlike Charlie, his sister had thrived on the Tonquin farm. She loved the animals and gardens and the studio Roland had built. Spent hours in that cottage, swirling together flowers and trees and animals like the ones they'd welcomed as pets in their home. Even Ruby recognized her talent. Marguerite had escaped to her dining room this morning to work on a mural Ruby had commissioned to impress her dwindling set of friends.

The telephone rang, and Grace hurried to the kitchen to answer it.

The voice on the other end, her mother, was as agitated as Charlie. "I need Roland right now."

"He's in the middle of—"

"Right now, Grace."

She bristled. "Not without a good reason."

"Look out your window."

Grace turned to look out the glass, at her mother's house perched like an eagle's nest on the hill. She gasped when she saw another fire ablaze on the branches of pine. Two fires in a month's time.

"Is that good enough for you?" Ruby spat. "I know for sure that your boy started it this time."

"Charlie!" The receiver dangled beside the door when she shouted, her eyes on the fire. "What did you do?"

The men crowded into the kitchen beside her, a breath of silence as they stared up the hill.

"It was just a joke," Charlie said, his voice dull, gray even like the ash. "A silly prank."

"You thought it would be funny to start another fire?"

"She deserves it."

"It's time for you to find your way in this world, Charlie." Her husband pulled on his coat, his hand reaching for the door. "Away from here."

Then Roland was gone. She watched him from the window,

running up the hill. While so many people ran away from trouble, he always seemed to run toward it.

She turned back to the boy who had stolen her heart almost six years ago, the one she no longer knew. His eyes were wild like an animal caged, sweeping right past her.

"Charlie—"

"He doesn't want me here."

She glanced back up at the hill, but Roland had already disappeared into the trees. The fire that licked their forest would be no match for the fire blazing inside him.

"You should help him put out the fire," she said. "You could work together again."

Like they'd done when they freed the children, milked the cows, pounded nails into boards to build a community.

She waited for one of Haddock's phrases.

I'm terribly sorry. It's unpardonable. I'm a miserable wretch for what I've done.

All he needed to do was ask for help, and she'd pardon him in a heartbeat.

Instead his brown eyes narrowed. "Kirk started it."

But in that same heartbeat, she didn't believe Kirk had started the fire alone.

Charlie stomped out of the kitchen, the front door slamming. Away from the questions. Away from the fire.

Away from her.

And a new blaze ignited inside her, one sparked by fear.

She loved this young man with all of her heart, but he no longer wanted her love. He no longer wanted to be a part of their family.

This boy she loved—

How could she love him well even as she feared he might hurt her or Roland or . . . ?

She couldn't bear to think about Marguerite.

CHAPTER TWENTY-EIGHT

A copse of evergreens circled the gravestone, a mossy slab of granite engraved with a Bible verse in lieu of a name.

"One thing have I desired of the Lord, that will I seek after; that I may dwell in the house of the Lord all the days of my life . . ."

"Psalm 27," Caleb said. "I looked it up."

"Do you think it's Ruby's grave?" she asked, brushing her hand over the year inscribed below the verse. Someone, it seemed, had been buried here in 1947.

"No idea."

"Or Marguerite . . ." Her voice trailed off. "It's hard to know when to pursue something and when to leave it alone."

Wallace wound the leash around Caleb's legs, and he unsnapped the leash. "Like asking Tara to contact the attorney who forwards our rent."

Addie sighed. "I spoke with her yesterday. Did she call you the moment I hung up?"

"Probably. She thinks I hired you to find the Tonquins."

"Then she doesn't know that I'm a lousy detective."

"It's hard enough to find someone who doesn't mind being found," he said. "Almost impossible to find someone who's hiding."

"You think Marguerite is hiding?"

"I don't know anything about her, but Grace seems to be."

All the pieces were here, but she still couldn't fit them together.

She ran her hand over the arch of the headstone. "Does Louis know who is buried here?"

"Direct questions don't get very far with him."

"Apparently not with Tara either." She scanned the epitaph again. "Why did you decide to show me this?"

"You shouldn't have barged into my uncle's home like that."

"I know." The man in the hut nearby, the one more than two thousand miles away in Tennessee, both of them were still carrying wounds from the past. Even though she wanted answers, she shouldn't have intruded on his space.

"But you care about the people in your life, and I admire that," Caleb said. "I wish I had more answers for you, but I only have questions."

"Charlie is the one withholding the information we need." She was frustrated at Tara and the others, but the reality was Charlie might be the only one left who could tell them what happened.

"It seems he's content with the family he's collected in Tennessee."

"Any of us would donate bone marrow if we were a match."

"I've no doubt that you would be first in line," he said. "You keep asking about my family and the Tonquins, but what about your family?"

She shrugged. "Not much to say about them."

"Did you grow up in Tennessee?"

"Chattanooga." Wallace stepped up beside her, and she scratched him behind his ears. "The man who fathered me died when I was two, and then my mom passed away when I was a teenager. I made some bad decisions when I was seventeen and ended up with Emma and Charlie at their home for girls."

His eyebrows arched. "A refugee."

"Of sorts, I suppose. Took a few years for me to figure out how to do life with a family. I would have left there except it was Sale Creek or probation. When I was nineteen, I received a scholarship at a Bible college, so I headed off . . ."

She turned away from the grave, and they hiked back toward Laurel Ridge.

"Reese thinks you're married."

"I was married." She twisted the gold ring on her hand. "My husband died in June."

"I'm sorry."

"He didn't make the best of choices either."

"You want to talk about it?"

She'd loved her husband, but it hadn't been enough. She hadn't been enough. While she'd thrown the wounds from her childhood into Sale Creek, the shame of this failed marriage, the humiliation, the twisted grief, had canvased her heart.

She didn't want to talk about Peter with him or anyone else.

The cell phone rang in her pocket, and she pulled it out.

"It's Charlie's wife," she said before stepping back into a shelter of pine to answer the call. "How is he?"

"Not well," Emma replied.

Her heart sank deeper into its fortress, trying to arm her emotions, but she couldn't stop the tears. "I'm close to finding his sister. Another day or two. Then maybe we'll have a match."

"Addie—"

Whatever Emma was about to say, she didn't want to hear it.

"Please, Emma," she begged as if this woman could single-handedly stop the disease from ravaging Charlie's body. As if she could make it all go away.

"He's back in the hospital in Atlanta," Emma said. "And he wants to see you."

"I can talk to him on the telephone."

"He's trying to fight, Addie, but the doctors don't know how much longer it will be."

"I'll be there as soon as I can."

Chapter Twenty-Nine

Grace dipped her toes into the lake water like she used to do as a girl. The first child in the Lange family, a baby named Jonathan, was in the stroller behind her, secured on the bank while she cared for him, the warmth of summer luring him to sleep. It's what they all needed in this season—a little one to snuggle and laugh and eventually swim in Tonquin Lake with the older kids.

Mrs. Lange was spending the day unpacking boxes to move into their newly built cottage after Mr. Lange had agreed to join Roland full-time as their farm manager. All the other refugees were gone now, but she was pleased to have the Lange family remain. Mr. Lange had battled the fires with Roland, and he'd faithfully cared for their livestock and buildings and Roland's prized grapes. Mrs. Lange had been a kind friend to her as well, helping with the gardens before she'd birthed her son.

As Grace trailed her toes through the cool water, the threads of wake lapped gently against the small dock that her grandpa had built twenty years ago for her and her friends. It had been one of her favorite places as a child, her own world far from the lights of Hollywood. When chores were done, she'd swim and sing and pretend that she was exploring the whole world under the safety of these pine trees.

After years of heartache and fear, of always having to be suspect of those around them, she'd wanted Charlie and Marguerite and Louis to have a safe place where they could be as carefree as she'd been after years spent in the throes of California.

Charlie hadn't returned home in the past week since he'd piled his stuff on a truck and relocated to Kirk's house. All three children had brought an immense load to Oregon, burdens she couldn't carry for them. They'd been hunted when they were young and sometimes it still felt like they were prey, running when no one was chasing them.

Except demons. They'd been chasing Charlie until, it seemed, he was cornered. And she was scared for him. She'd seen what those demons could do when someone didn't fight back.

What would happen to Charlie if he didn't break free? She could feed him if he returned home, give him a place to sleep, pray for freedom for his heart and mind, but she couldn't force him out of the cell where he'd locked himself. Nor could she force him to fight the demons like he'd fought the traitor in France. He had to desire freedom more than the chains.

Love, she feared, meant giving him up, giving him back to God, even as she prayed every day for him, for the rest of her life.

Since Charlie left home, Marguerite had lost herself in her art, a place that stilled her heart and mind, beauty pouring out on her canvas. This morning, Marguerite was up at Ruby's house again, working on the dining room mural. She and Ruby had started bonding over their discussions of the masters as if Ruby knew something about painting.

Somedays it felt like her mother was trying to steal Marguerite's affections, and she hated the jealousy that festered inside her when she should be grateful that Ruby had taken both Louis and now Marguerite under her wing. Charlie would never succumb to Ruby's charms, but that didn't make Grace feel better. Charlie had already succumbed to something else.

She wanted the best for everyone. Truly.

Inside her pocket was the crumpled letter from London and she pulled it out again to stare at the shaky handwriting. She knew the words by heart, but each time she read them, they seared her.

Dear Madame Tonquin,

I have learned from the AFSC office in Paris that you escorted two of my children, Élias and Marguerite, from Lisbon to the United States. I am forever grateful to you and the entire network of Quakers for rescuing them.

As you must realize by now, my brother does not live in New York. He was killed, like my parents, in one of the Nazi camps. I do not know about my husband's family, but to my knowledge, I am the only adult in our family who survived the war.

I am searching now for the whereabouts of my son and daughter and hope to receive a visa soon to travel to the United States and bring them back to my new home in London.

In the meantime, I would be grateful for a reply with their whereabouts. I am anxious, as you might imagine, to reconcile.

Sincerely,
Madame Dupont

Grace stuffed the envelope back into her front pocket and raced her toes through the water again. The poor woman must be worried sick over the state of her children. More than a month had passed since Grace had received the letter, and she'd yet to tell anyone, not even Roland, about it. Instead she'd hidden the letter inside her aluminum cooker, trying to process a future without the Tonquin kids.

It was wrong, she knew, to withhold this information from Madame Dupont and Roland. Probably wrong, as well, to withhold it from Charlie and Marguerite. But what would it do to the turmoil inside them when they realized their mother was still alive? That she wanted to take them back to Europe, like Ruby had taken Grace to Hollywood when she didn't want to go.

She shook her head. This wasn't about her and her sordid childhood. Madame Dupont would provide a safe home, but another change, she feared, would crush Charlie and Marguerite. And crush her.

If she was willing to be honest with herself, she didn't want to lose the children, *her* children, as she'd come to think of them. Her heart was fully wrapped up, no matter what Charlie did.

Tears flowed down her cheeks like the water flowing around her toes. It was selfish to weigh her emotions alongside those of someone like Madame Dupont who'd lost almost everyone dear to her in this war. She had no choice but to write back Madame Dupont, tell her to come the moment she received a visa, but how could she say goodbye to Charlie and Marguerite? She'd thought they would be a family forever.

"Mom?"

Turning, she saw Marguerite on the shore, gently rocking Jonathan in the stroller. She'd been so young when she lost her baby brother. Had she helped her mother care for him in Gurs?

Marguerite rushed forward. "What's wrong?"

"Just remembering." Grace wiped her tears away. "Are you already done painting?"

Marguerite slipped off her sandals and sat on the edge of the dock, trailing her feet through the water like Grace, soaking the hem of her trousers. "Ruby needed a break."

"What exactly did she do to warrant a break?"

"Helped make sandwiches since Paul is out for the day."

Grace smiled. "Did she really help you?"

Marguerite returned her smile. "She told me what she wanted on hers. Fried mushrooms and Roland's cheese."

Wild mushrooms, one of her mother's favorite foods. Grams had taught them both which ones to pick in the forest and which ones to avoid.

"Did Paul collect the mushrooms?"

Marguerite shrugged as she lifted her toes, the lake water sprinkling back down.

"I'd avoid eating any mushrooms that Ruby collects for herself."

Marguerite's brown curls had turned into soft waves in the past three years, her hair resting gently on her shoulders, her brown eyes golden in the light. She had a dot of teal paint on one cheek, a stripe of yellow running up her arm, but she didn't care the least what anyone thought about the veneer of paint on her skin.

Would the same demons that haunted Charlie haunt her as well? Grace prayed that Marguerite would embrace the light instead of the darkness. That her colors would always be bright. That she'd never lose her ability to see what others could not.

"You are very kind to Ruby," Grace said.

"The painting helps on those days when she is feeling orange." Not the ruby red of danger or betrayal, but an amalgam of good and evil. Love and hatred.

Marguerite couldn't always match the emotion to a color, but this time Grace asked, "Do you know what orange means?"

"Hurt on the inside, I think."

"Ah." Grace rarely thought about her mother as hurt, more like someone who hurt others. "What about the days she isn't orange?"

"The painting doesn't help much on those days."

"She has other colors . . ."

"A dark purple," Marguerite said. "And sometimes green."

Those colors Grace recognized. Anger and guilt cast deeply into a soul. Lies that had rooted themselves.

Marguerite ran her toes again through the water. "Why did she name you Grace?"

"I don't know."

"Seems like she may have been searching for a bit of grace for herself."

How little she knew the woman who had birthed her. Asking about the past would only deepen the purple, the rage, but perhaps, at least in her early years, her mother had wanted something to soothe the anger inside her. Grace couldn't give her what she was searching for—nor could Louis—but she hoped Ruby would find peace one day in God's grace.

Worry flooded over her again. If Charlie continued on a similar path, it would only damage his relationship with the people he was supposed to love.

"Do you miss Charlie?"

"I miss him," Marguerite said, "but I'm not very fond of him right now."

That she understood. "He'll grow out of it."

Marguerite stared at her.

"You see green . . ."

"A storm of it." Marguerite brushed back a fallen strand of Grace's hair. "You shouldn't lie."

"I pray he'll grow out of it."

"Me too." Marguerite lifted her legs out of the lake and bundled them between her arms. "What happened to him?"

Nazi Germany happened to him . . . and the evil raging in France.

Grace pulled the girl close to her. She didn't need to see color to know Marguerite's wounds ran deep. "He's trying to find his way."

"I hope he'll find it soon."

"Me too."

"Where are you in the mural?" Grace asked.

"The château is next and then the mountains."

"I'm glad you remember it all."

"I'll never forget those places. What happened . . ."

"That's good, Marguerite. You need to tell others, in your own way."

The baby whimpered behind them, like a cricket in the grass.

Marguerite popped up. "I'll get him."

Grace watched this sweet girl, on the eve of her teenage years, as she lifted the Langes' son from the stroller and cradled him to her chest. She'd make a remarkable mother one day, sensing, just by the color, what her child needed.

As Marguerite danced with Jonathan along the shore, singing softly to comfort his cries, Grace fingered the letter in her pocket. How would she ever be able to say goodbye?

Still, it was wrong to keep Marguerite from her mother. Wrong to keep the truth from Madame Dupont, no matter what it did to her own heart.

She'd talk to Roland this afternoon and then she'd write a letter.

She'd make right her wrongs.

CHAPTER THIRTY

Emma opened her arms when Addie walked into the room at Northside Hospital in Atlanta, and Addie fell straight into them.

"He will be so happy to see you," Emma said, her red-framed glasses pushed back over graying hair as she waited in a chair beside her husband. Only a week had passed since Addie left for Oregon, but it looked like Emma had aged years.

Charlie was asleep in the hospital bed, unaware that Addie had flown in a day earlier than scheduled. His gray hair was combed back over his head, almost down to his neck, and he wore blue-and-white flannel pajamas. One of his feet had traveled outside the blanket, and she saw the black woolen socks that he always wore. The aftermath of frostbite, he once told her, meant his feet were never warm.

And yet, even with the buzz of a machine beside him, another transfusion pumping life into his veins, a gentle stillness had settled in this room, an unexplainable cloud of comfort to quench the fear.

Prayer. Passion. Peace.

The man encompassed all of those things.

While she knew the promises for redemption in the next world—promises she believed—she wanted healing for him in this life too. Healing that ran deeper than bone marrow or blood.

Addie sat down in a chair beside Emma. "How is he?"

"Failing quickly, I'm afraid. The steroids are no longer working."

Addie's back slammed against her chair as she listened to Charlie's breath, every inhale a reminder that life still filled his lungs. She'd hoped for better news when she arrived.

"But he will be thrilled to see you!"

"Can the doctors still do a transplant?" she asked.

Emma shook her head. "There's no match in the database."

A breeze wafted through the window screen, settling over her. Even if they located his family, the odds of finding a match in time were against them.

"I'm not saying goodbye to him yet." Tears came again, from where she didn't know as it seemed the well of them would have dried up months ago.

"You've been the best friend, a daughter really, anyone could ever have," Emma said. "You've fought well for him."

Beautiful words, flooding over her. A tiny flutter in response. She rubbed her hands across her belly, wondering at it. Charlie had longed to meet this baby, and she'd so wanted to give him this gift. That and the gift of his family.

Addie settled her head back on her chair. "Didn't it seem strange that he never wanted to talk about the Tonquins?"

"Many people in my generation didn't want to speak about the past." Emma fixed the edge of his crumpled blanket. "I wish he would have told me about his family and his time in France, but I knew things had been hard for him. We were content to focus on the present and our calling as directors of Sale Creek. We've spent the past thirty-five years focused on how to support girls like . . ."

"Like me." Addie smiled. "You supported and encouraged and helped me find my way so I could help others."

"Not just others, Addie. It's okay to focus on yourself."

But she didn't want to focus on herself.

Emma studied the man in the bed, a deep love pouring out in her gaze. What would it be like to experience this kind of love for a lifetime? "I don't think he remembers everything from his younger years."

Addie closed her eyes, and her mind wandered to Oregon, to the beautiful lake and the men who oversaw the property, so different, the two of them. Yet they seemed to need each other. She could see Charlie with Caleb and Louis on a good day. Laughing even. Telling stories.

"You've done everything you could to locate a donor," Emma said. "It's time for us to let him go."

Addie shook her head. "He's not ready."

"We're not ready." Emma put her hand over Addie's. "You've already lost so much this year."

"It's not about me," she said quietly.

"What's it about?"

A pile of rocks, she thought, waiting to be thrown. "Righting a wrong."

A gentle smile warmed Emma's face. "Only Jesus can right a wrong."

"But I want to—"

"You've loved well, Addie, but no matter what you do, you cannot redeem the past. For Charlie or for yourself."

She closed her eyes for a moment, letting those words wash over her.

"It's a mess," she whispered.

"God often works miracles in the mess . . ."

"But who will lead at Sale Creek? He needs to be there."

Another smile on Emma's lips, a splinter of hope. "The board found a couple who are a perfect fit. They can start the first of the year."

Her mind spun, wanting to be happy and yet sorting out another change. Emma and Charlie . . . everything would be different soon for all of them when she still hadn't recovered from what had already changed. Would the spinning never end?

"It's a good thing," Emma said.

"I know."

"Charlie and I will stay in the guest cottage for as long as they need us."

"And then?"

Emma brushed her husband's hand. "A miracle, I hope."

"Adeline?"

She jumped, her gaze darting back to the bed. "Papa C!"

"You've returned."

She reached for the hand of this man she loved, his skin speckled and worn, but all she saw was the light radiating from within, illuminating the crevices deep inside, healing wounds. "I spent some time under your willow tree."

His lips pressed into a grin. "Bent but not broken."

"In its flexibility, the tree became stronger." She folded the edge of the blanket over his shoulders. "Just like you, Charlie. Whatever happened in the past, it made you strong."

He patted the sides of his pajamas. "Where's my wallet?"

Emma pulled it out of her purse, removing a wrinkled-up five-dollar bill. When he saw it, he settled back onto the pillows.

"I'll leave you two alone to talk," Emma said before kissing his head.

"You should . . ." Addie stopped before telling her dear friend to stay, seeing the tears in her eyes. "Get a bit of exercise. I'll call you if we need anything."

A brief nod, and Emma walked out the door.

"I've done terrible things, Adeline. Killed people . . ."

This man loved deeply, and he fought to protect those in his care. Whatever happened long ago, there was healing to be had.

"I never wanted to kill anyone," he said.

"I know."

"Jesus forgave my sin." His voice bent in the humility she'd come to admire. "I don't need to look back."

He was at peace with his past. Who was she to disturb it?

Then again, if he wasn't willing to fight for himself, perhaps he still needed her to fight for him. Was it wrong to keep hoping? She didn't know if it was better to keep fighting or say goodbye to her dear friend now, knowing he was forgiven.

"Looking back could heal your health and your heart." She tried to smile. "So you can hold your grandbaby."

"You'll have to show him or her pictures . . ."

"The girls at Sale Creek need you too. For one more day."

He seemed to contemplate her words.

"I met a man named Louis while I was in Oregon," she said softly, not wanting to startle him.

His eyes sparked. "Louis is still there?"

She thought of the man in the strange little hut, his mind roaming between the 1940s and 1960s, perhaps never fully present in 2003. "He watches over Ruby's house."

Charlie rested on his pillows again. "He will be loyal until the end."

"Is that admiration or an accusation?"

"Both, I suppose. It's good to be loyal to those you love. A calling for some. Obsession for others."

She thought of Louis cowering against the wall as she sorted through the papers, imposing on his space. "He has an entire archive about the Quakers' relief work in France. In it, there's paperwork about an Élias and Marguerite Dupont."

"My sister and me . . ."

She leaned closer. "Why won't you tell us about her?"

"It's not a story worth telling."

She sat back in the chair. "It's all so confusing, Charlie, and you are the only one who can sort it out."

When he mumbled something, she leaned closer to him.

"What did you say?"

"Marguerite's gone." His gaze traveled to the window, to the lights of the city beyond them. "The only person in this world who could possibly save me is no longer alive."

Her heart plummeted. She'd wanted so badly for Marguerite to help him find life. "Perhaps her children could donate."

"Adeline . . ."

She leaned forward, her resolve draining away. "What happened to her?"

"Long ago . . ." Tears fell down his face, his voice quieting as if he'd gone to another place. "I wasn't loyal like Louis."

"You hurt her?" Addie whispered, her mind wandering back to the gravestone in the trees.

"I snapped into pieces," he said. "Bent and then broken."

Chapter Thirty-One

Hatred rumbled in Charlie's gut like froth on the black seas. Tintin had been his hero for most of his childhood, but it was Captain Haddock that he understood. Haddock and his whiskey. Haddock and his failings. Haddock who could never seem to make things right.

Charlie licked his lips inside the moldy garage, his mouth dry, his forehead caked in sweat, as he waited for Kirk to retrieve something for them to drink in his shack of a house. Something that would erase the memories. The fear. The face of that coward in France who'd begged for his life before the Nazi blade that Charlie stole took one of its own.

His body rocked as if he were on Haddock's ship. *The Crab with the Golden Claws*—that had been his favorite Tintin story. The one about the opium smugglers.

"Scoundrels," he muttered to himself. "Slugs."

Roland and his sidekick, Loser Louis, were the slugs in his life. They'd thwarted him at every turn.

All he'd wanted was to live on his own. He'd already escaped the Nazis. Fended for himself and his sister in France. He and Marguerite had been just fine until Roland and Grace decided to march them off to Spain.

America wasn't anything like Tintin's adventure. He'd been kicked out of school, then he'd lost his paid work. Without money, he was stuck.

Why was it taking his friend so long?

If Kirk's old man found him in the garage, he'd make Charlie pay rent, and every penny that he'd earned at the farm was already gone. After the second fire, Roland had made his intentions quite clear.

Don't come back until you want to be part of the family.

What a sham. Grace and Roland weren't his parents and no matter what Grace said, her God was not his god. Only he and Marguerite were family.

Grace and her Bible, always quoting that fathead from the Psalms, the poet king who kept asking God to save him from the bad guys when he was messing around with his neighbor's wife. Like God would rescue David after what he did to the girl next door.

Grace's hero was the biggest sinner of all.

Charlie's laugh echoed across the Harley and rusty lawn mower, the jalopy up on bricks and a newly installed lock on the cabinet where Kirk's dad stored his alcohol.

Maybe he'd set a match to this place if the old man wouldn't cooperate. Maybe he'd stay and watch it burn from the inside. Then his head would stop pounding.

Kirk had started the fires around Tonquin Lake, after Ruby refused to give them any more of her pills. Not until they paid her.

Then she'd doubled her prices. Money and mushrooms. She wanted both in exchange for her drink and a few tablets from her bottle.

He had a whole bag of her stupid mushrooms ready—he and Kirk had picked them in the woods—but they wouldn't be enough to satisfy her. Not without some cash on the side.

He kicked the liquor cabinet, the pain shooting up his leg.

Neither fire had hurt anything except a few trees. Roland had doused the flames with a hose and a little help from Loser Louis. The boy had bragged incessantly about quenching the first fire after his great act of courage—turning on the spigot.

An idiot, that's what Louis was. Willing to do whatever the castle queen asked of him.

Kirk slogged back into the garage empty-handed. "He's onto us."

The old man was shouting from the shack. He didn't mind sharing a glass or two, he yelled, but he sure as heck wasn't going to let them guzzle all his liquor when a hardworking man needed a little something ready for him at the end of the day.

Charlie fingered the knife in his pocket. Liquor wasn't fun anymore; it barely even calmed the rage pent up inside him. It was a powerful need, though, and if he didn't get a drink soon, he'd get weird inside. Weepy. And then all that anger would explode.

"Nothing for us here," Kirk said after the door slammed. "We'll have to head back to Ruby's."

The quick shake of his head hurt. "She won't give us anything else without money."

"The witch ain't gonna know we're there."

Ruby didn't bother to lock up her vodka like Kirk's dad, but getting into the house would be tricky, especially at this late hour. She was a stickler about locks, always worried that someone was after her and her things. The last time he and Kirk had gone up to the castle, when Ruby was in town, they'd bribed Loser Louis with Peppermint Patties to unlock the door.

"We'll just borrow a little something from her." Kirk turned the gas knob on his motorcycle and lifted the choke. "Then maybe we'll stop by and visit that pretty sister of yours since your parents don't ever lock their doors."

Cement seemed to harden Charlie's spine. "You leave Marguerite alone."

Kirk grinned, his yellow teeth glowing in the moonlight. "Now why would I want to leave such a pretty girl alone?"

Charlie groped for the knife again, the one he'd carried all the way from France. "You touch her, and I'll kill you."

Kirk laughed, but Charlie was dead serious. Kirk might be older than him, stronger even, but Marguerite was only thirteen. Kirk wasn't touching her.

"I think she's a little sweet on me," his friend said before kick-starting the engine, and Charlie feared that much was true. Marguerite had been fixated when Kirk was still in school, as if she couldn't see his colors.

The motorcycle kicked up a storm cloud as they raced back toward the ridge. All the lights in Ruby's house were off except one that flickered behind curtains on the second floor. The bedroom of an eight-year-old loser.

Charlie peered into the garage window. "Her car's gone."

"She'll be out a few more hours," said Kirk, the prophet who didn't know much of anything. Then he threw a rock at Louis's window.

"Go away!" Louis shouted when he opened the window. Charlie could hear the disdain on his lips. As if the kid was judging them.

Ruby must have let him have it last week after he'd unlocked the door.

Kirk elbowed Charlie. "You talk to him."

Charlie rubbed his side. He would try, but he'd never be able to convince Louis to help them. "Just let us in one more time."

"Go home, Élias."

"Charlie!" he yelled back. That was his name now. Élias was a kid who'd been beat up by the Nazis. Who'd spent half his life on the lam. Charlie was the name of a man free to do as he pleased.

"Go home, whoever you are."

"Kirk brought you chocolates." As if Kirk would waste more money on candy.

"I don't want your chocolates."

"And we have a whole bag of mushrooms for Ruby," Charlie continued. "She's been asking us for them."

"She'll whip me if I let you in."

"Where exactly is your mommy tonight?" Kirk asked.

A sharp elbow back from Charlie, straight into Kirk's rib. "That's not helping."

Something fell from the sky, pinging Charlie's cheek. A jack, it seemed, hitting its target. Charlie rubbed his face. He thought Louis had closed the window until a squeak of a voice rained down.

"Paul took her to a party."

"So you can let us in," Kirk said. "Later, maybe, I'll take you for a ride."

One of Louis's weaknesses—he wanted to be just like the older boys. Like Charlie, he wanted to belong.

"Go away."

A handful of jacks pelted them like flak, and desperation raged in Kirk's eyes when he swore; Charlie could see it in the moonlight. He felt that same desperation. His mouth was desert dry, his mind dull. Another jack stung his forehead, and every muscle in his body ached.

They wouldn't hurt Louis. Just scare him enough to get a bottle from Ruby's liquor stash. And a couple pills.

The medicine made him feel like he was flying above the lake, above his life even, instead of trudging through it. The pills made him feel important.

"You don't have to unlock your back door after all." Kirk threw a rock up in the air and then caught it. "I'll just toss one of these through Ruby's window."

The threat worked. Louis leaned so far out that it looked as if he might fall. "You wouldn't—"

"I'll do whatever it takes to have some of her vodka. She shares it with everyone else. Why not us?"

"Because she didn't invite you here."

Charlie snickered until he saw Kirk's glare. Then he bit his lip.

"She ain't gonna be happy when she returns to find broken glass all over her floor, especially since you could have just opened the door. We're coming in either way, Frenchy. Up to you to decide how you want us to enter your castle."

A flash in his mind, and he was back in France, carrying Louis in the cold. Before they'd been rescued. Before Louis was a loser.

Charlie wouldn't let Kirk hurt the younger boy. All they needed was for him to open the door, then step away so they could trade a few sips of vodka and a couple white pills for the bag of foraged fungi. Ruby had plenty of dough, anyway, to build herself a castle and buy enough liquor to fill Tonquin Lake. It wouldn't hurt her to share a little with him and his friend.

They waited by the front door as if they were invited guests, escorted by a plump butler who stood no taller than Charlie's waist. Louis didn't bother to turn on the lights, but Charlie could see his scowl in the moonbeam that followed them, ricocheting off the papered walls.

It turned out that Ruby didn't have quite as much in her liquor cabinet as they'd hoped. Two bottles, almost empty. One of whiskey, one vodka.

Charlie dumped their bag of mushrooms on the dining room table before he and Kirk finished up both bottles, then began to search for Ruby's pills. Kirk trekked up to Ruby's bedroom, while Charlie turned back to the dining room, Louis trailing him like a flea.

The moonlight settled over all the faces on Marguerite's mural, familiar ones sneaking through the cold woods of France, searching for a place to sleep, something to stop the ache that had drilled so deep into their bellies they thought they'd never be rid of the hunger.

The cathedral. A wagon. Their escape across France. Marguerite hadn't forgotten any of it. His sister had captured their beginnings from the internment camp in Gurs to the bell tower in Saint-Lizier to a river below the Pyrénées. Soon an entire picture of their journey would spread across the wall, in colors that no one except the two of them would understand.

His brain muddled, he touched each face carefully, not wanting to ruin his sister's work. How were the others who'd crossed the mountains with them? Where had they settled after the war?

Questions raided his mind, ones rooted deep inside him, ones that he tried to keep underground.

What had happened to his mother and baby brother? They were dead, he knew this, but how?

His dad—he didn't care what happened to him. The man, he'd discovered, was a traitor like the shepherd in the mountains. He'd sold his soul long before the French were supposed to turn in their neighbors.

Sometimes, when he couldn't sleep, his mind leaned like the walls of that Spanish village along the border, thinking of all the ways he might have been able to rescue his mother and Olivier. In the camp or as they boarded a cattle car. Sometimes he liked to pretend they'd jumped off the train and he'd guided them across the border.

Why had his life been spared when so many had died? Thousands of children, he'd read. This question was one he'd never be able to answer, but here he was now, poisoning himself.

Loser Charlie. He'd been saved from Vichy France, but he wasn't free. He couldn't live without poison from a bottle.

The curtain started to lift as he rummaged through the cabinets, frantic for something that would help him forget. The vodka wasn't enough to still his racing mind, stop it from running away. He needed another drink. A pill. Needed something right now to yank the curtain back down, shove his memories into a welcome fog of nothingness to clear them away.

Dropping to his knees, he crawled under the table, pressing his hands into the rug, searching for a pill that might have dropped into this forest of yarn.

Louis looked under the table. "What are you doing?"

"Shut up."

"Ruby's going to kill you."

"I'm not afraid of her." Wasn't afraid of anyone except himself.

"Get off the floor." Kirk was in the room again, another bottle in his hands. "You trying to hide?"

Charlie stood up. "Did you find her pills?"

"The old bat." Kirk's laugh sent Louis cowering in the shadows. "She must have taken them out with her."

Kirk was as drunk as a skunk.

Drunk. Skunk. Charlie took the last swig of vodka, laughed at his rhyme. Then he tossed the empty bottle into the corner by Louis, the shattering of glass a dull thud in his head.

"Old bat, huh?"

A lamp switched on, and Charlie teetered as he turned, sea legs struggling on flat ground. Ruby was back in all her glory, fully jeweled with the tailwind of a pink Marlboro circling her head, just as drunk as them.

"You boys are back." Boredom dripped off her tongue at this news. "Miss me that much?"

Kirk wouldn't taunt her like he did with Louis, not as long as she baited them with a supply of liquor and pills.

She offered up one of her pink gems. Charlie declined—cigarettes did nothing to dull his mind—but Kirk took one for now and one for later.

"You'll have to buy me more vodka." She picked up the bottle on the table and glanced at the label. "And some whiskey too."

"We brought you mushrooms," Charlie said, trying not to slur his words.

Her laugh echoed across the room as she sifted through the pile. "These won't even cover what you already drank."

"We don't have any money left," Charlie said. Both of them were as broke as a—

Poke. Coke. He couldn't think of a rhyme.

"Then you'll have to borrow some."

Kirk cursed. "Cash don't grow on trees."

Ruby turned to the window, looking down at the lake. Two bullets honed in on the farmhouse.

Charlie shook his head. "They won't give me any more money."

"You're not going to ask."

Steal, that's what Ruby wanted them to do. Like they'd done to her and Kirk's dad except she wanted them to take money from the parents he was trying to disown.

And why not? Grace had taken him out of France when he wanted to stay, made him build huts on her farm. Then paid him pittance for his work. Why shouldn't he take what was rightfully his? They owed it to him.

He glanced up at a clock, trying to read the numbers, but they squiggled like newts on the shore.

"It's midnight," Ruby said. "They'll all be asleep."

"Roland never sleeps."

Ruby traced her Marlboro through the air as if she were seeing some sort of vision. "Itty-bitty fly on the wall told me he's spending the night down in Salem. Big meeting with bankers in the morning."

The fly must have been Marguerite, here to work on her mural. Who was milking the cows while he and Roland were gone?

"Go home," Louis spat as if he was personally kicking them out.

Kirk laughed as he turned toward the door. "Lock up after us, Frenchy."

"Actually." Ruby lifted the bag. "Let's fry these up tonight, Louis. We'll have a little celebration when the boys return."

Charlie's head was pounding again as they walked out the back door, stomping through the garden. If he didn't get another drink soon, it might explode.

The kitchen door to his home was unlocked. No reason to install locks, Grace once said, living so far out of town. Same reason she kept a wad of bills rolled up in a red Folger's can from the milk and vegetables they sold in Newberg, the can hidden back in the freezer compartment like no would ever find it there. Savings for the grocer or an unexpected bill or to pay those who labored with them at the farm.

Kirk stood by the sink, smoking his second cigarette as Charlie dug through foil-wrapped meat and aluminum ice cube trays that stung his hands. He didn't take all the money from the can. Only five bucks. Much less than they owed him.

His hand felt heavy as he pushed the refrigerator door closed, his legs dual anchors on a battered ship. The waves were almost too big for him to sail, the storm too strong.

"Let's go." He turned back to where Kirk had been standing, but his friend wasn't there.

"Kirk?" His shoulder banged into a wall, and he bit his lip to stay quiet. They couldn't wake anyone up. Even if Roland was gone, Grace would have his head for stealing. And he couldn't bear to see the disappointment in his sister's eyes if she saw him like this. A lousy drunk.

Black as night, that must be the color washing over his head right now. His mother would be ashamed. And his father too, traitor that he was.

Roland and Grace wouldn't understand his need for a drink, but he had to block out the demons. The face of the man he'd killed at the prison and the one in the mountains. Better those men than the children but still . . . those faces, the shock in their eyes, haunted him.

The man in the mountains was a rotten scoundrel, a turncoat, who didn't deserve to live.

Then again, neither did Charlie.

Roland was getting ready to meet with the banker, probably for a loan. He and Grace didn't have any income beyond this farm. Not like Ruby, who was rolling in cash.

The money burned in his pocket, begging for a return to the coffee can, but he had to have something else to drink. Roland and Grace wouldn't want him to steal Ruby's liquor.

He'd pay them back one day. It wasn't like they needed the cash to survive. He couldn't live without another drink.

"Kirk," he hissed again in the hall. If Grace heard them, she'd call the Lange family across the lake and then the police. Their flailing ship would be thoroughly sunk.

He rushed down the hallway, trying not to bang into the wall. Surely Kirk wouldn't pay a visit to Marguerite's bedroom when so much was at stake. Perhaps he'd stepped back outside.

But Charlie could smell the smoke before he ever got to Marguerite's room. His sister's door was closed, locked, and he heard something shuffle inside.

Dear God . . .

His first prayer in months. A desperate plea.

He'd break down the door if he had to . . . but how was he supposed to do that without waking Grace?

Marguerite screamed on the other side, and the demons from France scuffled inside him, forcing their way out.

"Open this door!" he shouted, twisting the knob.
Then the curtain in his mind parted, everything clear.
Another bang of his shoulder and the door went down.

Chapter Thirty-Two

Grace tried to pull Charlie off, but he'd cemented himself to Kirk's back.

"Stop it!" she shouted, but Charlie refused to let go. Kirk's hand was over Marguerite's mouth, stifling her screams, her very breath.

The girl had to breathe.

"Get off her," Grace yelled, trying to be strong, but she was nothing against this enemy. Only God could save her and Marguerite.

Charlie threw a punch, and Kirk fell off the bed, an ember dangling from his mouth.

If only she was stronger. She'd lift Kirk up by his collar and throw him out of this room. Out of her house. All she wanted was safety in this free world for her family, and this man was destroying it.

Another scream, but not from her lips. Or from Marguerite.

Charlie was screaming, one hand on his sister's chest, one on her arm, shaking her like a rag doll. Grace leapt forward and lifted the girl, shielding her daughter from both men.

Her feet stumbled as she backed toward the door, her heart shredding, and she could almost feel the river water on her toes, see the children who desperately needed help to climb the mountain. And the boy who'd stepped up to save them all.

The boy who could still save them.

"Stop it," she said again when Charlie pulled the knife from his pocket, but words, she knew, wouldn't deter him now. With Marguerite close to her chest, her whole body trembling, she prayed her psalm.

"The Lord is my light and my salvation; whom shall I fear?"

"You killed her." Charlie rammed headfirst into Kirk and the cigarette shot from Kirk's mouth, landing on the curtain.

Glass shattered—a lamp, the window, she didn't know. Then words shot out of Kirk's mouth like acid. Vile things about Charlie and Marguerite, about Grace and Ruby and Loser Louis on the hill.

A flame crawled up the curtain, igniting at the top. She had to get them out of the house.

"The fire extinguisher," she yelled, but Charlie still didn't look at her.

Kirk was on the floor now, something in his side, a curse fixed on his lips.

"Charlie," she whispered, trying to keep her voice steady. She couldn't do this alone. "I need your help."

Finally he looked at her, then down at Marguerite. But instead of helping, he fled into the hall, the front door crashing behind him.

She was on her own.

CHAPTER THIRTY-THREE

"He left all of us," Louis told Caleb from his armchair. "Didn't care one whit what anyone thought."

The boy crossed his arms, and Louis studied him for a moment, wondering if he was angry.

He should be angry. What Charlie did was unforgiveable.

"So you think he should die for leaving?" Caleb asked.

He hated it when the boy asked questions, especially ones that made him think. More than fifty years had passed now. He and Charlie—they'd both done things they weren't proud of.

"I suppose most boys do stupid things. They never care what others think."

Caleb inched forward. "Except you."

Louis wiped his arm over his mouth, craving a drink that Caleb wouldn't let him have. The boy had thrown away all his vodka, spilling it on the ground. And then Caleb planted himself by his recliner, watching him day and night like a staff sergeant.

No vodka. No coffee. Not even a Coca-Cola to be found.

A stockade in his own hut.

Outside the window was Caleb's dog, tied up to a post so he wouldn't chase the deer. Louis eyed him on the rope as he elbowed himself up on the chair. "It's time for me to break out of here."

He intended to find himself something decent to drink, even if he had to hitchhike into town, but all it took was one gust of Caleb's hand, pressed against his shoulder, and the sails collapsed.

He was nothing without the drink; the boy knew that. Couldn't do a blessed thing.

He puckered his lips together, and Caleb slipped a straw in between. Watered-down grape juice from the vineyard. He almost spat it out but opted to swallow instead. "I might just drop dead tonight if you don't get me something decent to drink."

"You can have all the fruit juice and smoothies you'd like."

"I hate fruit juice."

Caleb balanced the drink beside a stack of magazines. "You hate pretty much everything except your vodka."

"That's not true."

"Perhaps if you'd start searching for the good things in life, you might actually find them."

"Ruby was the only good thing that ever happened to me."

Caleb shook his head. "That's not true."

A helicopter swept in low, and he ducked, the noise stirring things up inside him. He didn't want to go back to Vietnam, not while Caleb was here. The boy shouldn't see him like that.

He clawed himself up on the chair, fighting the battalion of memories, the ones that made him sick. He needed to keep his focus on protecting Ruby's things, not on the memories trying to trap him. Poison him. Send him down into those black holes where a soldier never returned.

Darkness he didn't mind—the night kept them safe—but he wouldn't go back down into the tunnels. The fire.

A bomb exploded in his mind. A blaze of memories in the aftermath.

The night Charlie mocked him from below his window, told him he couldn't protect the castle when Ruby was gone. He'd never admit it now, but the older boys had scared him. He'd done his best to protect Ruby and her things, but then Ruby had come home and . . .

Everything had changed that night, he knew it, but still he struggled to remember.

"I don't think Ruby was really all that good," Caleb said. "To you or anyone else."

He blinked, pressing back into reality. "How would you know that?"

"You're not the only one who has talked about her. Before Grandma Lange died, she had a few things to say."

Mama Lange had raised Louis since he was eight, but she'd never understood Ruby.

"Grandma Lange said that Ruby was cruel to Grace."

Louis shook his head. "Grace never liked her much and Ruby never liked Grace either, but the woman invited me into her home. Then she asked me to watch over it. She wasn't supposed to be gone for long . . ."

Two weeks, at the most. That's what she had said. He and Paul were supposed to care for the house together.

Caleb's eyes flashed like he didn't believe him. "Why exactly did Ruby leave?"

"She . . ." His mind stretched like a ladder. Fragments—he could see more of them now. Ruby's finger on his nose when she told him she'd be leaving, her bright lipstick kissing his forehead, asking him—making him promise—to care for her things.

He squirmed in the chair, trying to leap into whatever alcove held that memory, dust it off after all these years. Only a little higher up, and he would remember.

A few days before the farmhouse burned, Ruby and Paul had been talking in the kitchen, whispering as Paul made their lunch. Usually Louis would have ignored them, his attention on the shiny jacks scattered on the rug, but the way they spoke, low and worried-like, he'd wondered if another crowd was about to invade their home.

He'd pressed his ear against the kitchen door, heard Ruby speaking. She wanted to take Marguerite on a trip to London soon, she said, and then she would travel to a festival in France, held in a town called Cannes. But it was a secret. Grace wasn't supposed to know, but Roland would thank her for it.

Paul had told her not to go—he remembered that now—told her that Roland would be angry.

A squeak on the floor, and Louis had leapt back to his squadron of jacks. Then Ruby had given him that last kiss before she spoke.

You'll watch over everything while I'm gone, won't you, Louis?

And he'd promised her right then that he would take care of the house. No one, he'd said, would bother her things. A promise that he'd broken days later when Charlie and his goon of a friend showed up with their motorcycle and mushrooms.

He closed his eyes and could see the blaze in the valley, the smoke that had flooded up from Grace's farmhouse, into their home. Ruby had been hysterical. Nothing would calm her, not even the mushrooms he'd managed to chop and fry on his own.

Roland, she'd said, was going to kill her.

Caleb interrupted the memory. "Did Roland kill her?"

He stared out the window at the pine trees, at the mutt looking back at him. Something bad had happened to Ruby that night, he could feel it in his gut, and he no longer wanted to dust it off. The memory needed to stay on the alcove forever, rotting away.

"Uncle Louis?"

"I need something else to drink besides this blasted water."

"It's grape juice."

"Give me some jungle juice already."

"I could add lemon."

When Louis groaned, Caleb leaned toward him. "You might be the only person who remembers what happened to Ruby."

His lips screamed for a drink, but his mind didn't return to Vietnam. It stayed on the farm, more than fifty years ago, the night he hurled his jacks at Charlie and Kirk.

Weeks after the fire, Louis had moved into the cottage with the Lange family. Eventually they adopted him, making him the older of their two sons. As long as the Tonquin family leased this land to the Langes, he'd been guaranteed a place to live in the shadow of Ruby's house, so he'd be here when she returned. Just like he had promised.

Except Ruby never came back.

Then he remembered the plate he'd found the next morning by Ruby's bed, some of the mushrooms he'd fried on the floor.

The plate that he'd spent a lifetime trying to forget.

"Caleb—" He felt sick. Charlie had done some stupid things when they were young, but Louis . . . he could never forgive himself.

The boy felt his forehead as if he had a fever, but the heat burned from deep within him. "What is it?"

"Ruby never left the castle."

Chapter Thirty-Four

A train chugged out of the station in Newberg, but Charlie didn't even look up from the bench. He still had four of the five dollars in his pocket, enough to get him to the other side of Oregon.

It wasn't far enough.

He'd have nothing left for food or board, but he didn't care about anything except traveling as far away as possible from the image of Marguerite hanging from Grace's arms, like Louis at the river.

He'd been so angry at Grace for leaving Louis behind and now . . .

He lay on the bench like a broken branch, no life left to course through his veins. What was he going to do without his sister?

Alone. The word rippled through him like an arctic blast to his hands, his feet. Limbs he could never seem to warm, not since he'd waded across that river and through the snow, carrying Marguerite on his back.

He'd traded everything good in his life for a drink that only made him more thirsty.

What was wrong with him?

He'd become just like his father, selling out those he loved.

He closed his eyes to block out the sunlight, block out the strangers shuffling across the platform. Nothing would take away the pain now. Nothing, not even Ruby's pills, could fill the crater inside his chest.

The bench shook again, the tracks rattling with the arrival of another train.

What if he wandered down the rails a half mile or so to lie down at the bend? The engineer would never see him as the train swept around the curve. He'd simply be gone.

Was he brave enough to leave this world?

He'd welcome the pain. The fade to black.

But what if there was life, like Grace said, after this one? A place to abide either in the heavens or below. Hell would be the worst kind of place for a sinner like him.

His sister and mother. Roland and Grace. His baby brother and even Louis. He'd never see any of them again.

His hand still trembled from the press of his blade into Kirk's belly. No chance now at redemption. Just like that, a blink of time, two people he'd once cared about were gone. One taken by Charlie's hand and the other . . . It was his fault that Marguerite was dead.

Sorrow, a monstrous wave of it, hit him solidly in the gut, tumbling and trembling, the current swallowing him. He didn't know for certain that his sister was gone, but he'd seen the despair on Grace's face. The agony. Then Grace . . .

He didn't know—didn't want to know—what happened to her.

Instead of helping, he'd stood like a coward on the hillside and watched the flames of his home funnel into the air. Two fire engines, their lights flashing, arrived much too late to save the farmhouse. They'd sprayed their hoses on burnt wood and charred stone, the heirlooms from Grace's grandparents and the hymnals that she'd collected over the years. And Charlie had done nothing. Hadn't even prayed like Grace would have done.

Traitor.

Like the man on the mountain. Like his father in Paris. Murdering people he loved for five bucks of poison.

The train tracks were where he should bed himself. It would be better for him and for Roland. The man who'd tried to step in as his father would kill him if Charlie didn't do it to himself.

Or . . .

He sat up.

Prison. In his muddled state, he hadn't even considered that. The police would find him soon and they'd put him behind bars. No one would come to rescue him there.

He searched for his knapsack, ready to escape again, but he'd taken nothing with him on this flight except for the money that burned through his pocket, scorching his skin. And a picture that he'd swiped from his sister's nightstand.

His head throbbed as he started to rise, but someone placed their hand on his shoulder, settling him back onto the bench. Only a few more seconds of freedom, then justice would be served.

He waited for handcuffs to clasp around his wrists. A short ride to the jail.

He should have made his bed on the tracks.

"I thought I might find you here."

He recognized the voice but didn't dare look up, didn't want to hear the truth from Roland's lips. It would be worse than jail.

"Where are you headed?"

There were no amends to be made for what he'd done unless Roland was going to take him to prison. What else would Roland want from him?

Charlie sat up straight, his gaze on the tracks. "I've got a plan."

"Do you have any money for your plan?"

"Four dollars, from the coffee can. I'll pay you back." Charlie finally looked up and saw the grief chiseled into Roland's face. The loss in his bloodshot eyes. He was too afraid to ask about Grace.

If Roland didn't drag him to jail, the tracks would be his penance.

Roland drew his wallet from his shirt pocket, the contents as lean as the man who carried it. They'd been happy at one time, the four of them, without much money. Then Charlie had gone and ruined it.

Opening the wallet slowly, Roland pulled out three bills. Twenty dollars each. A fortune for a farm family.

Last night, Charlie would have given anything for that, but now he shook his head. "I'm not taking your money."

"I wasn't planning to give it to you."

Charlie felt the slap of his words. Was Roland continuing to mock him? He deserved it, but still the words hurt.

Roland nodded toward the station door. "I'm going to buy you a train ticket."

Charlie closed his eyes again. "The house is gone . . ."

"It is."

"What about Marguerite?"

When he dared to look back at Roland, saw the shake of his head, Charlie felt any remnant of life drain out of him. He couldn't even walk down the tracks now.

"Where do you want to go?" Roland asked.

"As far away from here as possible."

Roland returned from the small depot with a copper-colored ticket. "I have enough money to get you to Tennessee."

When he held out the ticket, Charlie took it. "Please tell Grace I'm sorry . . ."

Surely she must have survived or Roland wouldn't be here.

"You'll find your way, Charlie." Roland clapped him on the back. "She's never going to stop praying."

"Tell her not to waste her time."

"Use the coffee can money to buy yourself some food."

He stared down at the ticket. "I don't deserve this."

"None of us deserve the good that comes to us," Roland said. "But this life is a gift."

Charlie didn't even say thank you. Years passed before he realized it.

After all Grace and Roland had done for him, he'd burned down their home. He'd killed Kirk and probably Marguerite and . . . he didn't know what else he'd done.

He'd go to Tennessee, wherever that was, and then . . .

He didn't have a clue what he would do next.

CHAPTER THIRTY-FIVE

"Is Papa C gonna die?"

A young woman sat beside Addie on the sunporch of the main cabin, a mug of hot chocolate in hand as they overlooked Sale Creek and Charlie's weeping willow. Norah was her name, from Knoxville. Their newest resident after she'd run away from a ring of teenagers who had come from hard places.

Beyond the tree and silver creek was the Tennessee River, a barge traversing its channel before sunset. Wind scaled the cliff at the water's edge, funneling up and then settling over the women. A glimpse of heaven—that had been Addie's first thought when she returned to Sale Creek as an adult. The house crowning a grassy hill, a strand of pearly-white cabins on both sides. At night the cabins lit up like a constellation across the ridge.

"Eventually," Addie said as the fading light pressed through the willow branches. "But I'm hoping he'll be with us a little longer."

Charlie was still in Atlanta, resting as his body tried to extract life from the latest transfusion, but she and Emma had returned to Sale Creek yesterday. Emma needed to pay their bills and meet with the houseparents before she drove back down to Georgia.

God had forgiven Charlie for that terrible night on the farm, but he'd told Addie in the hospital that the shame still plagued him at times. The weight of taking his sister's life.

The only family member who could save his earthly life was gone.

She and Emma had cried most of the drive home. For Charlie and Marguerite and the brokenness in their world.

With every new girl who came through Sale Creek, Charlie said, he saw his sister. A young woman who'd been uniquely and wonderfully made. Who had a gift to share.

Norah dug the heels of her cowboy boots into the floor, rocking back in her chair. "I heard you're preg."

"That's true."

"You got a boy or girl in that oven?"

Addie smiled. "I'm going to be surprised."

The girl looked horrified. "Why would you want to be surprised?"

She thought for a moment, wondering at the tangled emotions, the burdens, that Norah must carry. And she wanted this young woman to know the immense value of her life. "Because my baby—every baby—is a gift, and I don't want to unwrap my present early."

"You're strange, Miss Addie."

"Words that were never more true."

Norah studied her with bright-blue eyes that had been dull and drugged when she first came to Sale Creek. As the chains broke away, she countered quickly with her thoughts, a clearness and boldness that had endeared her to Emma and Addie alike.

"Someone said your husband killed himself."

Addie breathed deep of the river to calm her heart, twisting the band on her finger. "The police said it was an accident."

"But you don't know . . ."

"I don't think I'll ever know for sure."

"Why would he do that?"

She mulled over the question that had haunted her for months, wishing she had a better answer prepared. "Peter was successful, but he wasn't very happy. Sometimes he would be so angry . . . but I think he was mostly angry at himself."

She'd tried to fix the broken places, make it better for both of them. Tried to be the best wife, the best partner, the best chef so he would want to come home for dinner, but nothing she'd done was able to clean up the pieces.

Like Peter, Charlie said he'd tried a number of things in search of peace—happiness—for his shattered heart, but nothing had satisfied until he gave the brokenness over to God and asked Him to mend it. Then, years later, he'd boldly asked God to use his past to help others. Weave joy through the suffering in his story.

Shattered. Suffering. Surrender.

"How do you stop your anger?" Norah asked, her gaze on the river.

"Surrendering my future was the first step." With those words, the longing returned to Addie's heart to feel whole again. "We all make choices that damage our life and those around us, but God has given us the greatest gift in His Son to start again. All we have to do is ask forgiveness for what we've done in the past and choose to follow Jesus. Still people refuse this gift. They want happiness without humility. The gift without grace."

Norah sipped her hot chocolate. "It sounds much too simple."

"Simplicity is often where we find the greatest joy." When everything else was stripped away. "It's not the same as finding happiness in a person or thing. This sort of joy bubbles up from inside when you can't possibly explain it. Threads of hope in the midst of grief."

Someone shouted Norah's name from inside, and she groaned. "I'm supposed to be cleaning up the kitchen."

Addie smiled again, remembering how much she'd hated kitchen duty in her first months here. "I bet you can even find joy there."

"You're definitely crazy!"

"You can find joy wherever you go."

The ring of her cell phone made her jump, and her heart leapt on its own when she saw Caleb's number on the screen. He'd called several times since she'd returned, checking on her and Charlie after she'd told him that Marguerite died the night of the fire. He seemed to grieve this loss with her.

"Addie—"

Her heart skipped. "What is it?"

"Marguerite wasn't buried in the grove."

She leaned back against the chair. "What do you mean?"

"Louis says that he and Roland buried Ruby in the forest."

"Why didn't he tell you before?"

"He was confused."

Addie looked back at the creek and listened to the strange ending where Charlie's story had left off. The bag of mushrooms that Charlie and his friend brought, cut and fried by a boy who wouldn't know the difference between a poisonous mushroom and a perfectly good one.

Had Ruby meant to take her own life once her star had faded? Or had Charlie and his friend intentionally given them to her?

"If Ruby is buried there . . . where did Marguerite go?" she asked.

"The Tonquins moved soon after Ruby's death. We don't know where they went."

"If Marguerite is still alive, perhaps we can find her."

After she disconnected the call, she rushed back through the main house, into the office to search for Emma, but Emma wasn't there. A window stretched across one wall, overlooking the creek and willow. On the opposite wall was Charlie's gallery filled with paintings and professional photographs of resilient bent but unbroken willow trees. A collection of artwork he'd found and gifts from both donors and residents who'd been inspired by his passion.

A quick scan of the familiar pictures as she turned to find Emma. Then Addie stopped.

At the top corner of the wall was a new picture, an oil painting she'd never seen before. On the forefront was an iron gate with a silvery willow that bowed at the side. In the background, under the curved branches, was a stone house with a swirl of pink over it. A château that reminded her of the sketch that Caleb had found in Ruby's house.

Springing up on her toes, Addie lifted the painting off the nail and studied it closely through the glass. Hidden in a patch of wildflowers, at the base of the willow, was an *M*, painted yellow and blue.

The artist hadn't signed the front, so Addie turned it over to search for a signature, but brown paper was glued to the frame, protecting the print from damage.

She hurried out to the kitchen and found Emma at the sink, helping the girls with the dishes.

Emma eyed the painting in her hands. "Are you redecorating?"

"Where did you get this?"

"Leah sent it when she heard Charlie was sick." A former resident who had supported the home for years. "I was planning to surprise him when . . ."

He came home. The unspoken words hung between them, the hope that seemed to be crushed at every turn.

"Where did she get it?"

"I have no idea."

Addie turned over the frame again, and Emma studied the brown backing. "You want to cut it, don't you?"

"Yes, please." She'd retape the paper later, restore it to the best of her ability.

"There's an X-Acto knife locked in the pantry."

She rolled back the wrapping like it was parchment, bending but not breaking it.

And underneath . . .

A tiny hummingbird beside the neatly scripted letters. *M. Dupont.*

Addie looked up at Emma, and the wonder in the woman's eyes mirrored hers. Charlie's sister had survived the fire, it seemed.

She touched the yellow-and-blue hummingbird softly as if it might flutter away. As if this might all be a dream.

Emma's voice shook. "What if we can still find her?"

The very question stemmed from great courage, Addie thought, with the potential of another disappointment, another dead end on a very short road ahead.

"Not for the bone marrow," Emma said. "So Charlie can see her again."

"I'd like to try." Finding Marguerite would do his heart a world of good.

"Then you should. I'll call Leah right now to ask where she bought the painting." Emma rested her hand across the frame. "His sister . . ."

A flight of wonder in a single word.

Chapter Thirty-Six

LONDON
MARCH 1948

Grace slipped into the small Quaker meetinghouse in Westminster, not far from where George Fox and the first group of Friends met. Most London tourists visited the elaborate abbey nearby, but she found no solace in sculptures or stained glass. Here, in the simplicity of this space, she hoped to find peace. Shekinah for her soul.

No one else was in the room as she dropped to her knees, her elbows propped on one of the wooden chairs circled up for the next meeting. There she began to pour herself out, whispering the familiar psalm that had carried her across France and Spain and then back over the Atlantic, asking God for a way out of the darkness. Waiting for the voice she longed to hear. The breath of life in the stillness.

God was here in her brokenness, even if she didn't hear Him. She could feel His presence. The peace. God was everywhere, but He didn't seem to thrive in crafted monuments or gaudy cathedrals. He thrived in the quietness of a heart still enough to listen.

Roland had told her to take all the time she needed, hours if necessary. He and Marguerite were out exploring the streets familiar to him from his college years, perhaps as a balm to the heartbreaking months that preceded them here. Roland and Marguerite thrived in the chaos as much as the quiet.

Ruby had died the same night that Charlie ran away. Where she got the poisonous mushrooms, Grace didn't know, but her mother could tell the difference between a good mushroom and a bad one. With the fire raging downhill, it was almost as if she refused to be upstaged.

They buried her discreetly in the woods, no name to mark her grave. They didn't want throngs of movie fans on the property or those searching for retribution from broken promises that Ruby made. Even Paul, her closest associate, never returned to the castle.

Orange—that was the color Marguerite called Ruby. Hurt on the inside. Something had wounded her mother, perhaps when she was a girl, and Marguerite had grieved this loss for both of them. With the orange in mind, Grace was learning to forgive. She couldn't forget though, not entirely, all those years when Ruby refused to step into the role called motherhood.

After the fire, the injuries that Grace had sustained from carrying Marguerite and then dragging Kirk outside, Roland had nursed her back to health in Ruby's house. And she adored him for it. Kirk ultimately died of smoke inhalation, and in the first weeks, they thought they might lose Marguerite as well. Grace thanked God every day for sparing her daughter's life and the gift that must be shared with the world.

Then there was Charlie. Just thinking his name shot an arrow of sadness, despair even, straight through her heart. She didn't know where he went after the house fire or she would have gone after him.

Roland had reminded her—kept reminding both women—that his leaving was for the best. The boy who'd once protected his sister from harm was now a man who could harm her. Who could hurt them all.

Until Charlie was able to silence the wicked chorus inside him, listen to the one voice that would offer him life, he would destroy himself and everyone who loved him. She and Roland would do everything they could to protect Marguerite from the destruction.

If she'd returned Madame Dupont's letter right away, if she'd told Charlie about his mother, perhaps he wouldn't have run. Grace would never forget that either, the wrong she'd done in keeping that information from both kids.

She'd already begged God for forgiveness for waiting so long to respond. They were doing the right thing now in bringing Marguerite to London. She would be safe here with her mother.

Grace quieted her mind again, listening for the still voice. A car honked outside the windows. A child called out from the street for his father.

She was like this child, she thought, calling out to the Father above, asking for His attention once again. While she had no earthly father, other dads in this world, good ones who loved their children, would answer the call of their son or daughter in need.

And she was in desperate need.

What were she and Roland supposed to do now?

Quiet words wrapped themselves around her heart in that moment. And that lovely, warm voice, chilling the cold of her heart.

Live as I lived.

How do I do that? she begged. How could she live now with all the loss?

Love as I loved.

The arms of a cross spread across her mind, the brightest of yellows pouring over it. Even in the darkness, she could see the glimmer of His light.

Jesus had loved with His whole life. To His death. But death didn't stop it. His love spread like dandelions, she thought, the seeds scattering across grassy plains and forgotten weeds and rocky terrain, the healing blossoms growing in the hardest places. Like the winter roses in the mountains.

The losses behind her, the loss to come—it pierced like nails inside her—but she couldn't stop following His lead, spreading His love. No matter the outcome, she must continue laying down her life as a friend.

She rose from her knees to sit on one of the chairs, her hands folded together. The next step was a clear one, the way already paved, but she needed strength far beyond herself to take it.

Madame Dupont knew they were coming. It turned out that while Ruby's movie career was over, her investments had accumulated a small fortune. The castle was paid off, and without a will in place, Grace quietly inherited everything her mother had left behind.

Some of that money went to purchasing three airplane tickets to New York. Then they'd taken a ship across the ocean, cherishing every last moment with Marguerite, who lost herself again to her art, spending hours sketching and painting on the deck.

They'd wanted to bring Louis with them to London, welcome him into their family like they'd done with Charlie and Marguerite, but he refused to go. He was nine now, no longer a toddler to be carried, and he wouldn't survive this time, she feared, if they took him away from the land where he'd planted his roots.

The Lange family offered to give him a home in their cottage, make sure that he attended school, and Grace hoped they'd made the right choice to leave him in their care. As long as Louis lived on the land, the Lange family could stay in the lake cottage, but the castle would remain vacant for now. A local attorney, a fellow Quaker named Dawson, agreed to manage the details. The Lange family would pay Mr. Dawson a token rent for the cottage and surrounding property. One dollar a month until she and Roland returned.

Right now, she couldn't imagine ever going back. Only forward, no matter how difficult the climb.

The sun settled behind another building, her time here short. Another Friend would soon lock the door, and she didn't want to get lost in the maze of London's dark streets on her way to the hotel.

But she couldn't leave until God gifted her with courage, the very same courage that He'd given Jesus in the garden. She rubbed her wrists, asking for strength in what felt like a looming death.

Roland came to the door of the meetinghouse after night fell, Marguerite with him. And when she saw them together, her heart settled with the picture of God as Father watching over their beautiful girl. This picture, a glimpse of hope, was what she needed to travel through the darkest of valleys ahead.

Instead of returning to the hotel, Roland took them to Kensington, holding Grace's hand as they strolled among royal gardens, marveling at how the autumn flowers defied the cold. Then they ate bangers and mash in one of Roland's few stomping grounds that survived the war. In those last hours, they told Marguerite how much they loved her. How they would always be there, for the rest of her life, when she needed a friend.

Marguerite knew where they were going, but Grace still felt like a traitor when she guided them the next morning to a terraced home on Fournier Street. Madame Dupont was waiting at the door, although her surname, she quickly explained, was no longer Dupont. She'd married a British man who lost his wife in a bombing. It seemed the older woman had lost herself too as she stared at her daughter, too nervous to kiss her cheek.

Mr. Wilson seemed nice enough as he invited them into the home. They sat on a small patio, under the leaves of an elm tree, and sipped tea out of fine china, struggling for polite conversation when nothing about their history in the past six years was normal.

A young fellow stomped out the back door, and Grace stared. A miniature Charlie, it seemed, with wiry brown bangs that slipped over his forehead, patching his left eye.

The boy threw a rubber ball at the table and Roland caught it before it struck the teapot.

"I'm Oliver." The boy eyed the ball in Roland's hand. "Who are you?"

Marguerite turned toward her mother, her mouth wide. "I thought he—"

"He's your miracle brother. Hidden away during the last year of the war."

Grace thought the Dupont baby had surely perished in a concentration camp, if not on the transport east, but here he was, a hearty boy with the same flicker of boldness in his eyes as his older brother.

"I'm Marguerite." She leaned over, eye to eye like Grace had done with her when she was younger. "Your miracle sister."

Roland tossed the ball back, and Oliver grinned before tossing it to his sister. When Marguerite stepped away from the table to play, Mr. Wilson asked them about the farm, about their plans after they left London. Mrs. Wilson flinched when Roland explained that they had no plans. Everything since the war had been centered around providing for their children. *The Dupont children.*

He tried to correct himself, changing it again to *the Wilson kids*, but the damage had been done. Even though the tea was still warm, their departure was imminent.

"What about Élias?" Mrs. Wilson asked again, as if something might have changed since Grace told her that he'd run away. While she'd begged the woman for forgiveness for not writing sooner, Mrs. Wilson hadn't responded. Grace couldn't fault her for being angry—she had promised to care for both Élias and Marguerite from the moment she took them out of Gurs, but she'd lost this woman's son along the way.

She promised to let Mrs. Wilson know if she received any word.

"You're yellow and blue," Marguerite whispered at the doorstep. Love and sadness, entwined for a lifetime.

"Mostly yellow," Grace said. "I'll never stop loving you."

Roland was beside her. "*We'll* never stop loving you."

Mrs. Wilson shook her hand. "The Nazis stole my family, not you."

"I wish that I could have brought Élias . . ."

"Thank you for saving Marguerite." Mrs. Wilson reached down to pick up Oliver, the boy resting his head on her shoulder like his brother might have done. "And then bringing her back to me."

Marguerite kissed both Roland's and Grace's cheeks, and in her tears, Grace saw a bit of yellow and blue as well. Autumn leaves against the crisp sky.

Maybe one day Marguerite would return to them.

Maybe one day Charlie would as well.

She'd pray every day that they would seek the light, and she would follow as well in whatever direction that God led.

Resurrection was what they all needed now. Body, mind, and soul.

CHAPTER THIRTY-SEVEN

"I'm searching for information about the artist who painted this." Addie unwrapped the cloth and displayed Charlie's painting to a gallery owner in Nashville. "I believe her first name is Marguerite."

"Marguerite." The woman corrected Addie's pronunciation as she tapped a white fingernail on the side of the frame. "She prides herself on her French."

Addie's heart raced. "You know her?"

"I met her years ago at an exhibition. She has her studio in a French château. Perhaps this very one."

"Do you know the location of it?"

The woman lifted her nail, swirling it through the air like an ice dancer performing a figure eight. "Are you planning a trip to France?"

"No . . . well, perhaps." The owner's eyes narrowed when Addie tried to explain how Marguerite's brother needed a bone marrow transplant. Perhaps, like Norah said so boldly, she was a little crazy, but so was anyone who pursued a miracle.

Another customer came through the door, Addie dismissed, but she lingered in the shop where Leah had purchased this piece, studying the other paintings by Marguerite.

A stone hut, surrounded by sheep, was displayed on the gallery wall, and beside it was the painting of a shepherd boy in a long cape, his gaze captured by something in the distance, the clouds a swirl of color. The next piece was a girl on a riverbank, water streaming over her bare feet, then tumbling down a stretch of snowy rocks, the current turning into shards of glass below. Then a painting of a boy and girl together from the back, sitting on a dock, their toes in a pool of teal green.

Charlie would be captivated by his sister's art, the longing in these children's eyes, the startling beauty in the midst of pain. Good and bad fused together on canvas.

The last painting by Marguerite Dupont was quite different than the others, but Addie recognized the tree growing over the familiar lake. Except this willow was reflecting a flaming orange. The mirror to a fire that blazed in the distant pine trees.

Addie had no doubt now about Marguerite. She had only to find her, then she had to convince the woman that Charlie needed her forgiveness first before asking if Marguerite might have a child who, if matched, could share their stem cells.

After settling into a coffee shop, Addie began to search on her laptop. Samples of work from M. Dupont were aplenty but information about her personal life was scarce. Had she been hiding in France all these years? The fire in Oregon, the fear of her brother, must have rocked her young world. It seemed that she had run all the way back home.

Had Grace and Roland run with her?

Next she searched for Gurs—the camp where Marguerite and Charlie once lived—and then the town of Saint-Lizier and the village just south of it called Saint-Girons. Charlie didn't remember many of the names along their journey, including the château, one of a thousand at the feet of the Pyrénées—a mountain range that stretched almost three hundred miles across the base of France.

Some of the châteaus were private family dwellings, lodges for a weekend or summer retreat. Others were built as palaces for the aristocracy. None of those she'd found online looked like the picture she'd placed on the seat beside her. Even if she went to France, the likelihood of finding the château in Marguerite's painting was like finding a specific grape in Caleb's vineyard.

Then again, perhaps Caleb could help in the search. He had already combed through Louis's records until he found the Spanish town where Marguerite and Charlie had crossed the border. Tor was the name. A seemingly impossible climb from France, especially for a group of hungry and exhausted children.

But Addie knew a few things about the resilience of kids. The hike across the rugged mountains shaped Charlie into a man who wouldn't let the impossible stop him. Perhaps it shaped the tenacity of Marguerite and the others who crossed with them.

On her drive home, she dialed Caleb's number, and he answered on the second ring.

"Any luck at the gallery?"

"The artist is his sister," Addie confirmed. "Every painting has an identical *M* to the one on Ruby's mural."

"Amazing," Caleb replied. "Were you able to find out where she lives?"

"The gallery owner said Marguerite works in a château in France, and I'm wondering if she returned to the area where the children once stayed."

He reflected for a moment. "Finding her would be helpful for both of us."

A potential donor for Charlie, and Caleb could clear up the legalities for Louis and the Lange family.

"Can you ask Louis if there's a mention of a château in his paperwork?" she asked.

"He's not in the best of moods right now."

"He doesn't want to remember . . ."

"No," Caleb said. "But he can't escape it either."

"If Marguerite owns the Tonquin property, perhaps she will let him keep his home no matter what happens to the rest of the land."

An hour later Caleb called back. "Louis said the only château he knows about is Château Colibri. Roland's family owned the place."

"Colibri . . ."

"'Hummingbird Castle' in English."

The colorful hummingbird beside Marguerite's name.

Pieces fit together in her Tetris mind game, the bottom row filling up in an orderly fashion, sliding down. "So perhaps Grace and Roland took her there after the fire."

"Or maybe they visited and then moved someplace else."

"I have to go to France," Addie said. "Right away."

Perhaps it wasn't too late for restoration between Charlie and Marguerite. If she was alive, surely she'd want to know about her brother.

"I'm going with you," Caleb said.

She shook her head as if he could see her. "You don't need to do that."

"How much French do you speak?"

"Bonjour!"

"And . . ."

"Select words," she said as she exited up the ramp. "Plenty of people speak English there."

"Probably not where you're headed."

"And you know French?" she asked.

"Bonjour."

She sighed. "So you know as much as I do . . ."

"Pretty much, but after you tell them about Charlie, I'd sure like to talk to the Tonquins about their land." He paused. "Please, Addie. This means a lot to me as well. Until we find out their plans for the property, we don't know how long Louis will be able to stay here. He'd never make it as a guest in my home or at an assisted-living facility."

"I could meet you in Paris," she said. "We'd need to take the train down to a town called Pamiers and rent a car."

"If the translator gig doesn't work out, I could be the chauffeur."

She smiled at the excitement in his voice. "We may not find anything. A wasted trip."

"A trip to France is never wasted, especially . . ."

"Especially what?" she asked.

A cough. The awkward clearing of his throat. "Wallace is barking," he said. "I better go."

Classic evasion, but perhaps it was for the best.

There was no space left in her head for new pieces to fall.

Chapter Thirty-Eight

YAMHILL COUNTY
MARCH 1967

The forest was remarkably quiet, not a sound above the lake except the rustling of wind. After years of saving, Charlie finally had enough money to buy an airplane ticket from Chattanooga to Portland, and he'd arrived at Tonquin Lake with a crumpled five-dollar bill in his pocket, a duffel bag strapped over his shoulder. In his hands were a small bunch of flowers he'd purchased in Newberg.

Several uniformed men were also in the airport, returning from Vietnam, but instead of welcoming them home, a woman in the crowd spat on the soldiers. They'd silently wiped off the spit, ignored the jeers, but Charlie stepped between them and the angry woman. He was the one who should be ridiculed on his journey home.

When he arrived at Ruby's house, he threw the duffel bag on her porch and knocked on the door. He didn't know what he'd say, hadn't practiced a conversation with her like he had done a hundred times with Roland and Grace. He no longer wanted drugs or alcohol, hadn't touched either since he'd left Oregon, but he wanted to know what happened to Marguerite, clinging to the smallest of hopes that his sister had survived the fire.

It had taken years before he was finally ready to face the realities of what happened here. Years of repairing tracks for the Southern Railway while he completed night classes. After graduating from college, he'd dared to write Roland, but those letters had been promptly returned as undeliverable.

The man had made it quite clear that he'd wanted Charlie to stay as far away as possible from his family, but that was before Charlie had encountered God at a small church outside Chattanooga. He was sorry, so sorry for what had happened here—that's what he wanted to tell both Roland and Grace. How he wished a million times over that he had made different choices. Been honest about what he'd done instead of running away.

And he wanted to tell Kirk's father the same thing.

No more cowering in the shadows. Instead of running, he would make things right.

When no one answered his knock, Charlie glanced in the window, but all he saw was emptiness. Was Ruby hiding from him? He wasn't about to barge through the door like he'd done fifteen years ago. Patience was one thing he'd learned at the railroad company. Watching and waiting for the right time to repair the damage so one didn't get run over by a locomotive.

He picked up his duffel bag and hiked down through the trees, into the valley, memories both good and bad rushing over him. How he'd loved this place, the security of the farmhouse and barn, the care of Grace and respect of Roland and how Marguerite had thrived with her paints.

All had seemed perfect until he'd ruined it. By trying to forget the past, he'd destroyed the future for the only people who meant anything to him.

He wrapped his fist around the five-dollar bill that he'd carried around in his wallet for almost twenty years. One day, he'd promised himself, he would pay Roland and Grace back for what he'd stolen. Today he would deliver the money himself and hopefully find his sister.

"You there!"

He swiveled away from the water and faced a mountain of a man with a scrappy beard and hair growing like ferns over his ears, a bludgeon of wood in his hand. "Louis?"

"Go away, Élias." The boy had grown into a man, almost thirty now, shaking the tree branch when he spoke, but he reminded Charlie of the ailing toddler back in France. And later, the boy who'd crouched in the corner while he and Kirk wrecked his home. "This is no longer your land."

"I'm leaving," he said. "I just want to know where Roland and Grace went."

"They left after you did." Louis didn't move. "You burned down their house."

"I know—"

"And made fun of me."

"It was rotten, Louis. I'm sorry."

The man eyed his duffel bag. "You been in Vietnam?"

"I'm too old for the Army."

"Coward . . ."

"That much is probably true." The French had already been defeated at Dien Bien Phu. Even if he'd been old enough to volunteer, he didn't think he could stomach another war. "Have you been over there?"

"He's not going to Vietnam." A middle-aged woman stepped up beside Louis, untying the apron around her ample midsection. Mrs.

Lange—the woman who used to give him lemonade after he helped with chores.

"I hope not." He wanted to ask about Marguerite but stalled as the woman stared at him. He'd feared for so long that Marguerite had passed away in the farmhouse. Now he just wanted to know the truth. "Did she die?"

"The same night you left," Mrs. Lange said. "Buried up on the ridge."

Charlie gave a sharp nod, the hope of any reunion blown away. "Thank you."

Mrs. Lange glanced back at the cottage as if she was afraid that Charlie might burn it down. "I heard Louis tell you to leave."

The money stuffed back in his pocket, he hiked up the ridge and found the headstone in the trees, unmarked except for a Bible verse that he'd heard Grace repeat often in her prayers and the year he'd run away. He placed the tear-soaked blossoms by the stone and then he hiked down to Kirk's home.

Mr. Thomas was there, working on a motorcycle in the carport, beside the Harley-Davidson that looked as if it hadn't run in decades. Instead of telling Charlie to leave, the man gave him a hug.

"I'm going to the police next," Charlie explained. "Turn myself in."

"Why would you do that?"

"For killing your son."

Mr. Thomas shook his head. "Your knife didn't kill him. The smoke did."

He'd been drunk that night, the details fuzzy, but he was here to make amends. Restitution for what he'd done wrong.

But when he went to the police station, the chief sent him on his way. No unsolved cases, the man said, that involved him.

So he'd taken another airplane back to Tennessee, to a beautiful woman he'd met in church. One who'd been praying for him for years.

A new path, he'd told Emma on their wedding day. Across rugged mountains to find freedom. A life of redemption instead of regret.

He and Emma started climbing together as a couple, building Sale Creek Home for Girls along the way. A place for girls like Marguerite who'd been hurt in the past. A place for any young woman to heal.

Still, he wondered where Grace and Roland had gone.

Chapter Thirty-Nine

CHÂTEAU COLIBRI, FRANCE
NOVEMBER 1969

"'Tis the gift to be simple, 'tis the gift to be free, 'Tis the gift to come down where we ought to be . . ."

Grace sang the old song as she worked in the garden. Once dormant, the château's beds now sprang with life.

She pruned the dahlias, then braided together the soft branches of a ficus tree, potted in a ceramic jar once used for wine. Later, when the weather turned cold, she'd bring the jar inside. Just for the winter.

The song about simplicity continued in her mind, lyrics about bowing and bending, neither causing shame. Simplicity was often found in the bending, the bowing, of a place just right. The valley, according to the song, of love and delight.

The château and vineyard had found new life when she and Roland returned to France two decades ago. She'd taken Roland's

French name, becoming Grace Mercier. With that, she'd erased the Tonquin surname forever.

Hélène lived near the château until her death in 1955. The woman had asked regularly about Louis, and Grace read her the reports that Mrs. Lange sent through Mr. Dawson. After a difficult year serving in Vietnam, he had returned to live near Ruby's house. He was quite content, Mrs. Lange had said, to stay there.

While she and Roland still owned the Oregon property, Grace wanted nothing to do with the land and the destruction there. Mr. Dawson said the Lange family had cared well for the property and for Louis. Nothing else from that place mattered to her except the fact that Louis was safe.

The sweet memories of her grandparents, the hours they'd spent in the farmhouse, had burned with the fire. Whenever she thought about the lake and all its wonder, Charlie swept back into her mind like a locomotive, threatening to tear down what she'd built in France.

"Wait on the Lord: be of good courage, and he shall strengthen thine heart . . ."

Those were the words of King David, who, much later in life, had a son who tried to kill him. When Absalom finally died, in spite of all the destruction that he'd waged, David still mourned this loss.

Grace continued to pray daily for the boy who'd wounded their family. A boy who'd be a man now, almost forty, if he survived into adulthood. God knew where Charlie went, and He had strengthened Grace's heart as she waited for his return. Given her courage to continue living and then loving after everything fell apart.

Roland, she suspected, had an idea where Charlie fled after the fire. She'd asked him once, and the look on his face mirrored her pain. The worry that Charlie might still destroy all they'd built together.

She'd trusted Roland with her life when they crossed this countryside together in 1943, facing off the Nazis, and she trusted him even more now. He would do anything to protect her. And she would continue taking care of him for as long as God gave them.

When she wasn't tending her flowers, Grace was helping Roland in the vineyard or working at the hospital in Pamiers. It had taken her three more years to complete her nursing certification. Tante Grace, many of the children in her ward called her. An aunt if not a mother.

The gate squeaked open, and she turned to see the man who still made her heart flutter. Home, she'd discovered, was right by his side, wherever God took them. The Nazis had tried to steal away every ounce of hope with their threats, the nectar of their life, but hope swelled again in every flower that bloomed here, every new baby born, every child mended in the hospital ward.

"A letter for you," he said. "From London."

He lifted the envelope above his head, and she leapt up like a child to swipe it. While they'd had no biological children, God had given them back Marguerite and another son in Oliver, who'd visited every summer until he reached his college years. Mr. and Mrs. Wilson had relished a break to focus on their growing flock of children born without the sorrows of war.

Marguerite had since stepped into her thirties, married to her artwork even as she waited tables to pay bills. Oliver had graduated from the University of Nottingham and was on his way to becoming a very British barrister like his stepfather.

Roland and Oliver became chums during the summers, Oliver helping with the sheep that Roland accumulated faster than the bees that had colonized in their prized pear tree. In the evening hours, Oliver painted alongside his sister.

Grace tore open the letter, anxious to read every word.

A London art gallery had agreed to host Marguerite's first show. The owner had gushed, she said, about her vivid portrayal of color and shapes, the beauty of her summers in France juxtaposed with ruins from the war. The woman had offered her space to display her work in December. A full month exhibition.

Would Grace and Roland, she asked, cross the channel for opening night?

That question alone made Grace smile. She'd already crossed an icy river and the stormy Atlantic for Marguerite. She'd cross whatever necessary to celebrate the accomplishments of this beautiful woman who'd invited others to join her in seeing all the colors in her world.

Roland glanced over her shoulder, his touch warm against her skin. "How's Oliver?"

"He's been called up to the bar." Grace looked up. "But I don't have a clue what that means."

Roland grinned. "He's an official barrister now."

She couldn't have been prouder.

At the end of November, Roland and Grace spent the night in Paris and then boarded a ferry in their Peugeot, staying with one of Roland's university friends near Oxford. They spent an entire month in England, lunching with Oliver and visiting Marguerite's exhibit each night, secretly buying the few pieces that remained on New Year's Eve to display in the château.

The first of the year, the gallery owner asked Marguerite how long it would take to refill the empty wall. Two months, Marguerite had said, and then phoned Grace in tears. The prior exhibit had taken her more than two years to complete. She needed more space, she'd explained over the telephone, a whole studio to paint multiple pieces.

Grace knew with a simple glance from Roland that their hearts were braided together like the branches on her fig tree. Roland invited Marguerite to the château, to stay through the spring if needed, to complete enough artwork for several exhibits.

She transported her second exhibition up to London the first of March, and the owner wanted more. The colors on her canvases bloomed like the château flowers that spring. Wild and beautiful and sweet. The shapes and swirls in Marguerite's head, all the emotion stored inside her, spilled out in her rivers and gardens and the children who reminded her of all those who'd been lost during the war.

Wounds were restored with the oils, in the face of every boy and girl that she created. Colors washed over canvas like a shiver down one's spine. People often felt her paintings deep in their bones as if her paintbrush swept them into the fear or hope, deception or desire. And Grace marveled at it all, watching in wonder as Marguerite poured herself out again.

She'd trimmed her hours at the hospital. Instead of medicine, she delivered trays into the ballroom-turned-studio with fresh fruit and bread, endless pots of Darjeeling and Roland's Camembert.

None of them knew that this spring would be her last. At least, Roland and Marguerite didn't know, nor Oliver when he came for the week to help his sister transport another exhibition north.

But Grace had an idea as she turned the dirt in her garden on the days Marguerite was gone, pouring her heart onto the canvas of soil, thanking God for every blessing even as she prayed a blessing over those she would leave behind in God's hands.

Holding all of them up to His light.

CHAPTER FORTY

Caleb drove Addie to a remote iron gate with scrollwork like the one forged across Marguerite's canvas. A cavalry of trees flanked a long drive, uniformed branches mounted on their steady trunks. At the end was the gray stone of a château, standing proudly like a masterpiece from the Louvre.

The pieces were falling again in Addie's head, trying to find their place. This house, the person inside, she hoped, was the key.

"Come with me," she said. "I might need to borrow your French."

Caleb laughed. *"Bonjour?"*

"Exactly."

Friendship. Falling. Fitting pieces into place.

He hadn't volunteered to join her at the château, respecting the possibility that she might want to be alone, but she'd spent too much of her life alone. She wanted, needed even, Caleb's friendship to help her catch the pieces.

The gate was linked with a chain, blocking access for their car, but a door stood in the brick fence, draped with ivy. She brushed aside the ivy, relieved to find the clasp unlocked.

Turning, she motioned to Caleb. "You need to talk to them about the land."

"Today is for Charlie." He stepped out of the car. "Later we can sort out my family's business."

"Today is for all of us," she said.

He followed her onto the grounds, and they walked up the long drive, a vineyard sloping down the hill on one side. Sheep grazed in the field on the other side of the lane, idly watching the visitors.

"Lawn ornaments," she said.

"More like lawn mowers."

She eyed the farm animals, the craggy mountains behind them. "Or an artist who needs to eat."

They rang the bell at the front door, and a woman opened it right away as if she'd been watching them. Marguerite would be almost seventy now, but if she was healthy enough, strong, perhaps the doctors would make an exception to their age rule.

This woman in front of them was poised in a gray skirt and blazer that matched the stone walls. And a pale-blue blouse. She looked like she was closer to sixty than seventy.

"Miss Dupont?" Addie asked, hoping she knew English.

The woman shook her head as she pointed at the walkway. "Wait, please. In the garden."

They followed the aroma of autumn flowers to the right of the house, stepping into a manicured garden that reminded her of the grounds outside Ruby's castle, this one walled in by stone with a door at one side. The remaining blossoms in this place drooped toward the ground, tired after a long exhibition.

Addie smoothed her fingers over the leaf of a purple dahlia, speaking to Caleb. "The wind will steal these petals away any day."

"But the roses will come through soon enough."

Addie whirled around to see an enchanting older woman draped in a painter's smock. She was sitting in a wheelchair, pushed by the woman who'd answered the front door.

"The roses always return," she continued in perfect English, "like our hummingbirds."

"You're Marguerite?"

The woman studied both her and Caleb. "I am."

"We've come on behalf of your brother," Addie said.

A stroke of silence before Marguerite spoke again, her eyebrows furled. "Why didn't he come himself?"

"Because he's sick."

She shook her head. "I don't understand."

"Perhaps we should introduce ourselves," Caleb said, stepping forward.

Once again she'd rushed ahead without the proper protocol.

"Caleb Lange," he said, "from Oregon."

"Oregon . . ." Marguerite's voice drifted off as if captured by the breeze.

He kissed the woman's offered cheek, then stepped back.

"I'm Adeline Hoult," she said with a wave. Kissing, even on the cheek, was a boundary crossed. "Most people call me Addie."

Marguerite studied them closely. "Why have you come from Oregon?"

"It's a bit of a story," she said.

Marguerite glanced back at her attendant. "This calls for a glass of wine, I think."

The woman wheeled her up to a patio table, its iron legs matching the front gate.

"Would you like to sit?" Marguerite asked.

"Of course." Addie pulled out a chair beside her.

But Caleb didn't sit. "You have a beautiful vineyard."

Marguerite studied him. "You want to explore it, don't you?"

"I'd love to take a glance."

Marguerite shooed him away with her hand.

"Is that your husband?" she asked as Caleb walked toward the garden door.

"No, I'm a widow."

"He likes you. A lot."

Addie smiled. "It's impossible to know that."

Marguerite smoothed her hand over the long braid resting on her shoulder. "I know."

"I'm here because of Élias."

Marguerite's smile faded away. "I haven't heard that name in a long time."

"He goes by Charlie now."

The woman nodded. "He changed his name when we were children. I didn't think he would survive this long."

"He told me about the fire. Said he destroyed your family."

"He didn't destroy it," Marguerite said, her gaze resting on the ridge of mountains that crowned the garden wall. "The Nazis did."

"Charlie thinks you died that night."

"A piece of me did, perhaps. It was a difficult season for all of us."

The attendant brought a platter with sliced cheese and apples. Then she brought three glasses and a bottle of red wine. Local, Marguerite explained.

Addie placed a hand over her stomach. "I'll have to wait and drink it another day. For baby's sake."

"I don't know much about children, I'm afraid," Marguerite said.

Addie blinked quickly as if she could erase the disappointment over Marguerite never having kids, but Charlie needed the heart marrow of this reunion even more than bone marrow.

"Agnès will bring you Perrier to celebrate the upcoming birth."

"Thank you," Addie said. "Caleb will enjoy the wine when he returns."

"He has fled because of Charlie?"

Addie took a deep breath. "It's complicated."

"Nothing was ever simple for my brother." Marguerite took a long sip from her glass. "You said he's sick."

"He needs a bone marrow transplant, and a sibling is our best shot at finding a match. Or possibly a niece or nephew."

The liquid swirled in Marguerite's glass. A vortex of red. "And without this transplant?"

"He won't live much longer."

"I'm not angry at him for what happened. He loved me, I have no doubt, until he lost his mind."

"He found it again," Addie said. "Or at least he changed dramatically after wrestling with God for years. Eventually God captured his heart and completely redirected his life."

Addie told her about Charlie and the home that he'd helped start on Sale Creek. Then she glanced around at the vibrant color, so like the garden by Ruby's house. "You came back to the very place you ran from."

"Grace and Roland came first. They needed a place to recover after the fire."

"What happened to them?" Addie asked.

"Grace passed away in the fall of 1969. Her heart finally gave out."

"She was so young . . ."

"She loved well in her fifty years, hundreds of children during the war and then thousands later as a nurse. Whenever a child died in her care, a bit of her heart died with them, I think. She wanted to rescue every one of us, but sometimes she simply could not."

"Charlie will be happy to know that she helped so many."

"It was who God made her to be, and her legacy lives on. A new children's wing at the hospital has been named after her."

"Did you donate the money for it?"

Marguerite smiled. "A number of people donated in her memory."

That was a life well-lived, Addie thought. A woman who poured out good even when she bore the wounds of loss. Helped others even when the results weren't always what she'd hoped . . . or she didn't see firsthand the answers to her prayers.

"You're crying," Marguerite said softly.

"Grace will never know, but when she rescued Charlie, she helped save my life as well." God used this woman she never knew, a woman she longed to thank, to rescue her too.

Marguerite studied her again. "She knows, I think. Or she will one day."

Emma had said this journey to find the Tonquin family was for Addie as much as for Charlie. She hadn't believed her, but she saw it now. The redemption in her heart, the gift of a redeemed life for her baby. God was in the midst of it all. A light, a beacon, guiding her back to Him.

Marguerite tapped her nails on the table. "You said Charlie needs a sibling for a match."

Addie gave a sharp nod. "A potential match. There's only a 25 percent chance that it would work."

"I wish I could help."

"There are many factors," Addie explained. "Good health, age, a perfect HLA type."

"What is the age requirement?"

"Under sixty unless the donor is in excellent health but finding a match outside your family is impossible now."

"Between my age and my failing health . . . your doctors would never let me donate."

Addie nodded sadly. "I knew the transplant might not work, but in his last weeks, I was hoping Charlie could spend a little time with you."

Agnès poured sparkling water into Addie's wineglass and set the green bottle beside her. "Would you like anything else?"

Marguerite's gaze drifted back to the mountains, and Agnès didn't seem to be surprised at having to wait. The pace of life was different here, quiet moments built in to breathe the air that swept down from the Pyrénées, enjoy the flowers still in bloom.

"Ask Roland to join us please," Marguerite said. "He's in the barn."

Addie leaned forward. "Roland is still—" She stopped, the rudeness of her question echoing back before she finished the sentence.

"Yes, he's very much alive." Marguerite's laughter trilled like a songbird. "Years ago he stepped in to be my father, and I have simply refused to let him go."

Addie smiled. "I understand."

Marguerite glanced at the stone wall as if she could see Caleb on the other side. "Would your young man like to join us?"

"He's not mine . . ."

"You love deeply, Addie—I can see that in you—but there is much sorrow too."

"I've lost several people that I loved." Even as the words came out, Addie realized the irony. The woman before her had lost almost everyone she held dear when she was a child.

"How did you do it?" Addie asked.

"Do what?"

"Live with the loss."

"Living, I think, defies the loss. Loving well defies it too."

Addie rested one hand on her stomach again, her wedding band pressing against the fabric, a constant reminder of her loss. In spite of what happened with Peter, she had to figure out how to choose life for herself and her baby.

"There is a trail that runs through these mountains," Marguerite said. "Not the treacherous one that we took as children but a well-traveled path between the Atlantic Ocean and the Mediterranean Sea."

"The Camino de Santiago?"

"Exactly. Here we call it Pèlerinage de Saint-Jacques-de-Compostelle. The Way of St. James. One day, perhaps, you can take the pilgrimage. Listen as you walk."

"Perhaps one day I will."

A thin gentleman stepped out on the patio, his brown cap slightly askew, a limp balanced with a walking stick. He doffed his hat to Addie, and while he sat on the opposite side of the table, she could smell the barn on his chambray shirt, a neatly folded handkerchief peeking out of his front pocket along with a piece of straw. Marguerite reached over and removed a second piece of straw from his cap.

"If I'd known we were going to have guests, I would have put on my good suit."

"No reason to dress up for me," Addie said.

"I'm Roland, but I'm known around here as Grace's husband," he said, his words glazed with pride.

Marguerite patted his arm. "And the man who became my dad when I needed one most."

A slip of red threaded up his neck. Addie knew little of his story, but already she liked this man.

"This is Addie Hoult. She's here about Charlie."

Addie lifted her hand, and he shook it. "It's nice to meet you."

Roland sipped his wine. "How do you know Charlie?"

"He and his wife direct a home for young women outside Chattanooga. Most of us who lived there as teenagers know him as Papa C."

"Remarkable," Roland said, a slight shake in his hands as he lowered the glass. "I tried to find him years ago, but I figured he changed his name."

She shook her head. "He chose to keep Charlie Tonquin."

Roland took off his cap and ran a hand through his thick mop of hair. "Almost like he wanted to be found . . ."

"Tell us about him," Marguerite said.

And she told them what she knew about Charlie's earlier days in Tennessee, about his journey to find hope when he thought his life was through, returning to school when he was almost thirty and becoming a high school French teacher. About his marriage to Emma and their commitment to help young women who came from hard places. Give them an opportunity to thrive.

"What about young men?" Roland asked.

"They used to talk about opening a home for boys, but they couldn't finance both." Or lead both, she guessed.

Roland fidgeted with his gold watch. "You trust him?"

"With my life."

Then he smiled, his eyes gazing up at the blue sky. "Grace couldn't save him, but perhaps her prayers helped bring him home after all."

Caleb returned through the doorway and joined them at the table.

"This is my friend," Addie explained. "Caleb Lange."

"It's nice to meet you," Caleb said, offering his hand.

Roland didn't shake it. "Lange?"

Caleb nodded slowly. "The son of Jonathan Lange."

"You're not from Tennessee . . ."

"I've lived in Oregon for much of my life." Caleb glanced at her. "Addie found me when she was looking for Miss Dupont."

A burst of air, laughter, escaped from Marguerite's lips and she apologized for her faux pas.

Roland eyed her like she'd lost her mind, then he reached out to shake Caleb's hand. "Is the vineyard still there?"

"It is."

"Who's harvesting my grapes?"

Caleb smiled. "My family is preparing for it."

"What about the lake?"

"We don't have to talk about that now," Caleb said, trying to steer the conversation back to Charlie.

But the older man wanted to talk about the land. Grace's place, he called it, and he spent the next hour quizzing Caleb about everything from the management of the Dawson family to the state of the vineyard grown from his prized cuttings. And Louis—he wanted to know everything about the boy he'd taken to America with him.

Caleb told him that Louis was haunted by his time in Vietnam and perhaps his earliest years in France as well.

Roland nodded toward the window. "Charlie—he was called Élias back then—and my aunt carried him partway over the mountain pass until he was too ill to continue. He lost his parents in the Holocaust . . ."

Addie thought back to the stack of papers in Louis's hut. The collection of documents and names, evidence to prove his birth and then his journey to another land.

Had he felt rejected again in his later years from those who had rescued him?

She glanced at Caleb, searching for approval. He gave the slightest nod, permission to be honest about his uncle. "Louis is haunted by the war," she said, "and the memory of Ruby. For most of his life, he thought she was coming back home, but now he's realized she is gone for good. He thinks he killed her."

Roland drummed the edge of his walking stick against the table. "Why would he think that?"

Caleb told him the story. "Louis fed her mushrooms the night she died. He didn't know at the time they were poisonous."

"It wasn't his fault," Roland said. "He must know it wasn't his fault."

"Whose fault was it?" Caleb asked.

"Ruby's, I suppose. The investigator believed it was suicide, but out of respect for the family, he quietly closed the case. He recorded the cause of death as 'undetermined.'"

"Suicide . . ." Addie glanced out at the garden where Roland so carefully toiled to keep Grace's garden, her memory, alive. The man who had brought Louis to Oregon so he could thrive.

"Ruby grew up in Oregon," Roland explained. "She knew which mushrooms she could and couldn't eat."

"I will tell him," Caleb said.

A tear rolled down Roland's cheek. "I pray it will help set his mind free. So many need to be free . . ."

"It's my prayer as well."

"I'm not selling the land, if you're concerned about that," Roland said. "Grace and I wanted Louis to live there if he wants for the rest of his life."

"He may never say it, but in his heart, he would thank you for it."

"Does your family want to keep renting the property?" Roland asked.

"It's just me and Louis now," Caleb said. "I've purchased the parcel of land above the vineyard, but I'd like very much to continue renting the hut where he lives and the vineyard. Perhaps even buy it one day, if you decide to sell."

"You'll keep an eye on him?"

"As close of one as I can."

"I'll consider it," Roland said, and Caleb thanked him.

After moments of silence, processing it seemed, Marguerite clasped her hands together as if she'd examined all the evidence and made a decision.

Her gaze was on Roland when she spoke again. "Charlie needs a donor."

Roland shook his head. "The only money I have left is wrapped up in that land."

"Not money," Marguerite said slowly. "He needs a donor for a bone marrow transplant. Matching stem cells from a sibling."

Addie glanced at her. They'd already established, she thought, that Marguerite wouldn't be a candidate and she had no children.

"A sibling . . ."

"Can you return in the morning?" Marguerite asked. "After Roland and I have talked."

"Of course."

"There's a hummingbird," Addie said, watching it flitter around a bush.

"Hummingbirds always return home," Roland said, "unless their nectar is gone."

She glanced over at Caleb, wondering at these words, but he just shrugged.

Roland stepped around the table and kissed Addie's cheek. "Charlie is blessed to have you."

She cringed at first but didn't mind as much as she'd thought about this breach of personal space. "He's my only family."

When he looked at Marguerite, something passed between them that Addie didn't understand.

"One more day," Roland said.

And Addie smiled at the familiar phrase.

CHAPTER FORTY-ONE

The winding road led Caleb and Addie through the hills of Southern France, a formidable wall called Pic de Néouvielle ahead. When the road ended, Caleb parked beside an old pine tree and rounded the vehicle to help Addie out.

She didn't need his help, but he wasn't demanding her attention. Only offering, like he had with Roland. She finally took it and climbed outside, the mountain wind tangling her hair.

"How did the children do this?" She stared at the snowy mountain that rose ten thousand feet. The pilgrimage might be called the Way of St. James, but it seemed to her to be the way of everyone who climbed over the Pyrénées to find freedom or help others be free. "And the adults. How did they manage to hike over this range without packs of food or tents or gear?"

He scanned the range. "Where others saw impossible, they saw potential."

"Because they had no other choice . . ." Those not hunted would have taken a train or a car around to the other side.

"And yet thousands of people walk the path as a pilgrimage today," he said. "They are searching for something in the simplicity of this trail."

Just as she'd been searching this summer for answers in her heart. A pilgrimage in a sense. It was time for her to discover who she was without Peter or Charlie or even Emma. God had redeemed her for a purpose. A plan. It might not look like anyone else's plan, but it was okay. She only had to follow.

Addie zipped up her fleece and pulled a warm hat down over her ears. Even in September, it was cold at the base of this range.

She and Caleb would return to the States tomorrow, after breakfast with Roland and Marguerite. Both of them, she hoped, would be willing to travel to Atlanta soon. In helping right what Charlie had wronged, perhaps they could all find healing.

She glanced at the man hiking beside her and wondered at his journey before he'd purchased the vineyard. And at the question he'd asked her back at the gravestone. One she'd never answered.

"Peter," she said as they climbed toward a ridge. "That was the name of my husband."

"You don't have to tell me about him."

It had been easy to share her story with Norah, a girl who'd also been wounded by people she was supposed to trust, but not so simple with Caleb, an adult who could so easily judge when she'd already passed a verdict on herself.

She reached for a tree branch to use as leverage for her next steps.

"After I finished the program at Sale Creek, I received a scholarship to Bible college. Peter was a local pastor who spoke sometimes at the school. We began dating my junior year, and I thought we fell in love. It took six years of marriage before I realized that his love was a sham."

The story poured out of her, the years of uncertainty, questioning both herself and Peter, wanting to believe him when he said a parishioner needed help but doubting his word near the end. Her mind had tumbled last year as she tried to put things into place, understand what was happening on those nights he returned home long after dark.

A path wound up through the shelter of fir trees, barely wide enough for one of the shepherds in Marguerite's work. Then the trail dipped back down into a beautiful valley, the wind calming in the shelter between mountain and hill.

"It ended badly," she said as they crossed the valley. "He left me for another woman, and a car accident claimed both their lives. I'd worked hard to cover up my doubts about what he was doing. Refused to seek help because I didn't want to ruin his—our—reputation or God's work."

"Who would have been able to help you?"

She looked out at a flock of sheep grazing in the distance, a river beyond them. Would anyone have been able to stop Peter? She couldn't think of a single person, not his parents or brother, not the church elders or staff, who could deter her husband when he made up his mind.

A shadow swept across the edge of the valley, a cloud covering the sun, and the familiar shadow covered her heart. Fear no evil, that's what the Bible said, and yet some days it still felt like the shadow might swallow her.

"For a long time, I was the only one he'd listen to, but in the end, he wouldn't even listen to me."

"If you believe the Bible is God's Word—"

"I do," she said, no matter how difficult it was at times to understand.

"Then you know only Jesus has the power to truly save someone."

The words swirled around her like the colors on Marguerite's paintings, chasing away the shadows. She had loved Peter, cared for him, but only God could save him. In this life and the next one. She could speak God's truth, but she couldn't save someone's soul.

"Thank you," she said quietly. A gift, those words.

"I tried to save someone once," he said as they neared the river. "She made some tough choices, but I thought if I only loved her enough, she would change."

"Did she?"

"I don't know. She left me five years ago, and I haven't heard from her since."

Addie understood that desperation, the darkness when the light at the end of the tunnel seemed to flicker out.

"God brought me to a place," he continued, "where I knew I couldn't save her or myself, no matter what I did, just like you couldn't have saved Peter. And while Charlie may have saved your life, he can't save your soul."

He was right. When she was in a desperate place, God had used Charlie in his brokenness to show her the love of a father, give her a second chance. He'd used Charlie to help right what had been wronged in her childhood, but he couldn't save her for an eternity. She'd still had to accept this gift.

They reached the bank of a rocky river, about twenty feet across, and Caleb picked up a small stone and tossed it into the water with the others. Then Addie picked up a rock of her own and joined him.

The water splashed when her stone hit, triumphant as the river swallowed it up.

Was she going to allow her broken heart to destroy her life and the life of her baby? Was it worth it to continue carrying around the weight of Peter's wrongs?

She had to decide now. Had to let go of his deception, the darkness and wounds.

A second rock tossed into the water—this one for her husband who hadn't been delivered from evil. Then another one, heaved overhead, for the deception that broke them both, for the temptations in this fallen world that shattered their trust.

A fourth rock, a splash, for the baby who would never know its father. For all the girls at Sale Creek who didn't have a dad.

Another rock for the children here who'd lost their families. For the man back in Oregon who'd never fully recovered. For the man in Atlanta whose life was nearing the end.

She tossed rock after rock, wrong after wrong sinking into the water. Then she wiped her hands on her jeans and turned around.

Caleb was standing on the shore behind her. "Are you done?"

She glanced around her feet even as she searched her mind. "There aren't any other rocks to throw."

"I counted a solid dozen."

She smiled. Every single wrong was now on the bottom of the riverbed.

"Are you hungry?" he asked.

A flutter in her womb, laughter slipping from her lips. "Baby seems to be."

"Then let's go find something for all of us to eat."

They dined at a restaurant in a nearby vineyard, the sloped hills reminding her of Oregon. The antique furniture like the armoire inside Caleb's home, the scars of each piece fully exposed. For the slightest moment she missed the lake and its willow tree, the scent of honey and pine, the gray heron that swept over the water each evening, even the man who lived by the castle, trying to break free of his memories.

In the morning, she and Caleb returned to Château Colibri with *pains au chocolat* from a local patisserie. Marguerite gave them a tour of her studio and elegant gallery with her paintings and those of a dozen other artists who had synesthesia. Each artist, she explained, saw shapes and colors, the possibilities, where others saw only black and white.

Addie was mesmerized. With or without this gift, what if she could see things differently going forward? Potential in the plainness.

Her mind was ablaze as they joined Marguerite and Roland in the garden.

"We have an idea," Marguerite said over coffee and a pitcher of fresh cream. "To help Charlie."

"I'm afraid the only thing that can heal his body now is bone marrow."

And the doctors wouldn't let this lovely woman donate even if she was a perfect match.

Marguerite glanced across the table as if to ensure she and Roland were of the same mind. The older man nodded.

"I can't help him," Marguerite said, "but our younger brother is willing to try."

Liquid dripped out of Addie's cup, spotting the table, the words replaying in her mind as if she might have misunderstood them. "Younger brother?"

Marguerite dabbed the dark liquid with her napkin. "Oliver was only a baby when we left Gurs. Charlie doesn't know that he survived."

"He never mentioned a brother." Then again, he never spoke of his sister either. Did he think his entire family was gone? Perhaps he was too afraid to find out.

"Our mother survived the war, and I stayed with her and my stepfather until I finished university. Mum died fifteen years ago."

How might things have been different for Charlie if he'd known he had family? He and Emma might never have started Sale Creek. Addie and more than a thousand girls who'd gone through the program would never have known their care.

"Oliver would like to see if he's a match."

Addie couldn't speak, so Caleb closed the gap.

"Thank you," he said.

All Addie could think about were possibilities.

CHAPTER FORTY-TWO

"Marguerite is alive."

The words rolled around the hospital room like a crate on one of Captain Haddock's boats. And for a moment Charlie was a boy again, stomping through France, trying to stop the entire ship from sinking as he clung to his sister's hand.

Perhaps he had heard Adeline wrong. Perhaps he was dreaming in the haze of medication. Marguerite had trusted him with her life, and he had already squandered—crushed—her trust.

It wouldn't be long now before he crossed over the great divide between this life and the next. Before he summited the mountain one last time and was greeted at the border, perhaps, by a warrior angel. Or maybe his brother or mother or Jesus Himself.

What would it be like to see each of them?

Freedom was what he'd always wanted. Freedom, now, from this failing body. Freedom to be with Christ. Freedom to live forever without guilt or shame.

Warmth soaked through him as he lay in this narrow bed, all the way into toes that had frozen over long ago in the snow.

Warmth, freedom . . . for an eternity. He would laugh again with Marguerite. Sail across the heavenly seas together. Fly, even, without wings. Never again would he and his family have to face the tyranny of dictators or addiction. The evil that he and his father had succumbed to in this world. It had taken much of his life to forgive the man who'd fathered him . . . he was still working on forgiving himself.

"My sister is gone," he replied, his eyes closed as he rested. Soon, he prayed, he would see her. Soon he would ask her to forgive him for leaving. Wounding her. Stealing away her beautiful gift that was meant to be shared.

"No, sweetheart." Emma took her husband's hand. "Your sister didn't die that night."

His eyes opened slowly, as much energy as he could muster with his failing body. "But I returned to Oregon. Mrs. Lange said . . ."

Adeline's long hair slipped forward, the golden pieces framing her face like a halo. "Ruby Tonquin was buried in the woods. Not Marguerite."

His wife's lips pressed gently against his forehead, the healing balm of her words flooding through him.

But Roland—hadn't he said that Marguerite was gone?

His eyes closed, not to shut out these two women that he loved dearly, but to remember that night after the fire, the hours at the train station where he almost exited this life. Then Roland appeared—the man he'd looked up to as if he were a god in those early years. The man who'd given him the confidence he'd needed to defeat the enemy in his path. Who'd believed in him.

The man he'd failed.

Once Roland had wanted to father him . . . and then he'd given Charlie perhaps the last of his money to purchase a train ticket for him to travel as far away from Oregon as possible.

In hindsight Roland hadn't said precisely that Marguerite was dead, but he'd certainly implied it. And Charlie couldn't blame him. He was doing what he did best—protecting those he loved. Except this time, he was protecting them from the boy he'd once asked to be his son.

Charlie's eyes sprang open. "What about Grace?"

"She passed away," Adeline said softly.

He nodded, knowing that she was probably gone, but the grief surged again through his weary bones. "From the fire?"

"Oh no," Emma said, wanting to protect him like Roland had done with Marguerite. "Not until 1969."

"She worked as a nurse," Adeline explained. "She and Roland returned to France, and she continued to care for children there."

That news made him smile. Her faith had remained strong, he knew, until the end, clinging to the Psalms and the songs that God put on her heart. "Soon I will see her."

"But not yet," his sweet wife said.

"Emma . . ." He'd loved this woman since the moment that he'd met her, when he had dared step back into church long ago. They had been married more than thirty years now. He didn't want to leave her alone, but he could no longer fight this disease. "I can't stay here any longer."

A troubled look passed between the two women he loved. They might think him so sick that he wouldn't notice, but he saw much these days.

"What is it?" he asked.

The worry in Adeline's eyes faded into a smile. "We found a donor."

"But the doctor said it would be impossible now." He'd seen miracle after miracle in his life—but this time he thought God was calling him home. "One of Marguerite's children?"

"No—"

Emma interrupted her. "You'll meet the donor after you've recovered."

"But I'm ready . . ."

"For the transplant?" Adeline asked.

He shook his head. "To see our Savior."

Neither Adeline nor Emma spoke. They didn't try to convince him like they had before, saying he needed to meet Adeline's baby or spend more time with the girls at Sale Creek, but the sorrow returned to their eyes.

He wanted to spend time with Adeline's child, with all the girls in his care, but his body was ready to go home. It seemed frivolous to continue to fight, to extend his life just a few more years, when he'd tried to live fully these past four decades, serve God with the years that remained.

If God was calling him home, why should he continue to battle this disease?

Emma kissed his forehead. "Then you must go."

"Thank you both for finding Marguerite . . ."

"You have fought the good fight . . ."

He closed his eyes for a moment, whispered a prayer of thankfulness that the women couldn't hear. By releasing him, they'd given him a gift.

But his dreams didn't release him as easily. With prednisone coursing through his veins, he dreamed of the great chase—a recurring nightmare of men hunting him through the woods, a giant mountain ahead, the tall grass tangling, trapping his feet.

Then a shift in this dream, different than the others. The men disappeared and it was just him in a field. A valley like the one where he'd lived in Oregon. A small lake with a willow tree.

Instead of a farmhouse on the water's edge, an ornate gate stretched between two hills. Not white exactly, more like opal pooled with reflections of pink and the palest blue, scrollwork the finest of lace.

He couldn't see beyond the gate, and his heart longed for the beauty that awaited there. The peace inside. A fortress against evil and sickness, fear and shame.

He raced toward the gate, his legs as fit as they'd been when he used to run miles, racing toward the finish line, an eternity of wonder on the other side.

His hands on the gates, he tried to push them open, but they were soldered together. So he shook them, like he'd done in France, but they still wouldn't budge. And his heart began to plunge.

"For by grace you have been saved through faith, and that not of yourselves; it is the gift of God . . ."

Had his crimes been too great for this gift? He deserved being turned away, for the sins he'd committed in his youth. The lives he'd taken. Lies he'd told. Sins he continued to commit.

Like the king named David.

Despair swarmed around him, buzzing in his ears, and he didn't want to step into the next life now, not if he couldn't be with the Savior. He fell to his knees, knowing he was in a dream, yet the stones seemed to press into his skin as he begged for forgiveness. He wanted nothing of that old life.

He shook the opal gates again. It was unbearable, the barrier between him and the kingdom on the other side. He wanted only to be with his Savior.

A man appeared at the entrance. A gatekeeper, Charlie thought, checking to see who was rattling the lock. He wore a *bure* cape, a carved shepherd's staff resting over his shoulder.

Charlie fell back to his knees, all pride stripped away in the face of this humble man. "Please let me in," he begged.

The adventure of his life was finally over, he thought. The border crossing complete.

But the shepherd disagreed. "It's not time."

"I'm ready."

"But we're not ready for you."

Charlie's head rose in relief. He hadn't been barred from entering.

The man's smile was gentle, kind, but strength roared through every word. "You have been forgiven, but there is still work to be done."

Turning, Charlie saw the face of his sister in the meadow, playing in flowers that glowed with color, reflecting the light of this gate. He almost ran to her but stood mesmerized by the scene unfolding before him.

Another girl stepped out of the high grass, into the meadow. She looked like Adeline before she'd grown into an elegant young lady. Dozens of boys followed the girl into the meadow, then hundreds. Boys chucking clods of grass, blowing dandelion seeds, two of them throwing punches at the side. Ornery, like he'd once been.

"They need you," the shepherd whispered. "For just a little longer."

He was much too weak, he started to explain, too sick to care for another, but the shepherd was gone.

Reluctantly he turned toward the meadow. While he was ready to break down heaven's gates, cross over the border, it seemed he still had work waiting for him on this side. Children who needed hope for their future.

The boys surrounded him, and he felt the joy in their laughter, soothing the pain in his bones. God, perhaps, wanted to heal him in an unexpected way, but for what purpose, he didn't know.

He was loved, forgiven, and now he must be faithful, even if he didn't understand.

The children scattered back into the tall grass as his eyes opened, his chest aching. Emma was asleep in the chair beside him, and he found comfort in the sight of this beautiful woman who'd journeyed for more than three decades with him. Her cheeks were the softest ivory, no need of blush to color them, and her eyes a jade green that captured him still today. Refused to let him wander.

He'd never wanted to run again, not after God rescued him. Then he had proposed to Emma, and he'd been the happiest of men when she accepted, the honor of her *yes* replaying in his mind, that moment on the cliff, the sunset on Lookout Mountain where he'd dropped to one knee, and then five months later when she'd walked down the aisle in front of friends and her family to become his wife.

She had gently shepherded his wounded heart through the years, until he was able to give his fear to God. But sometimes in the night, when the old fears returned, he'd reach for her under the covers, pull her close. And she'd pray with the courage and strength of a warrior. Fight off demons with her words.

Emma finally woke in the chair and pushed back the strands of hair that had escaped her barrette. Leaning forward, she reached for his hand like she'd done so many times, except this time she wanted him to chase away the fears. "We thought we were going to lose you last night."

The shepherd's face swelled in his mind, the admonition to return to this world.

A shiver rippled through his body, but not from the cold. It was one stemmed in warmth. Awe. He'd glimpsed God, perhaps, in his dream.

"I thought I'd come to the end of my journey as well."

"One more day," Emma said softly, and he grinned before telling her about the gates and the hundreds of boys playing in the meadow.

She kissed his forehead. "It seems that God has something left for you on this earth."

"I don't know what it is."

"He'll guide your every last step."

Words spoken by one of the most faithful people he'd ever known.

Emma and Grace, both of them unbridled in their love for God, and Marguerite—had she been faithful with her life? Her gift? Perhaps that was what God wanted for him, to reconcile with the girl who'd been playing in the meadow.

"I'd like to see my sister," he said.

Emma tilted her head, a flash of surprise in her eyes. "We will ask her to come."

He shook his head. "I don't want her to see me like this."

She scanned the blanket over his body, the needles taped on his hand and arm, all of it keeping him alive. "How would you like to see her?"

He heard the caution in her tone, guarding herself against what she hoped.

"I want to see her when I'm well again."

Emma's hands flew together, two birds nesting against her chest. "You'll get the transplant."

"I don't believe I have much of a choice."

"I would never force you—"

"I know, Emma." He was supposed to try even if the transplant failed.

He had to trust the doctor and those who loved him. And most of all the Good Shepherd who wanted to provide for all of His sheep.

CHAPTER FORTY-THREE

Life-giving marrow from Oliver Dupont Wilson—a perfect match—was shipped on a direct flight from London to Atlanta. A week of chemotherapy led up to Charlie's transplant and then complete isolation as the drugs warred against his unhealthy bone marrow.

Oliver had asked to remain anonymous until after the transplant and Emma agreed. If Charlie knew about his brother, Emma worried that he'd refuse the treatment, afraid of endangering his brother in the process. And Oliver wanted to spend time, years even, getting to know Charlie after he'd recovered.

Emma wasn't allowed to be with Charlie for the infusion of stem cells, but she'd returned to Atlanta in October to be near him. Soon she would hand over the reins of Sale Creek to the new directors, but until then, Addie was staying in Tennessee to help.

Even though they had to step away from Sale Creek for now, Emma and Charlie had no intention of stepping away from their mission. The cells would settle, Addie prayed, deep into the marrow of his bones and then multiply, making healthy new blood cells on their own.

Marrow. Match. Mission.

Multiply.

The words fell into perfect place. Multiplication for Charlie would mean another opportunity to overcome the enemy, this one inside him. A refuge from MDS for his final years.

A full hundred days, the doctors had said, before they'd know if the cells had engrafted into the marrow. If the transplant was on track to cure the disease.

Until then, they would wait and pray and dream together.

Addie finished scrubbing the pot in which she'd attempted to make—and subsequently burned—oatmeal. She and her teenage helpers had salvaged enough of the crispy oats for breakfast, soaking them in milk and adding brown sugar and fruit to make it palatable.

Norah and the other girls were currently attending classes in the small schoolhouse that Charlie and several supporters had built using wood from this land, and their houseparents were resting and preparing for the long afternoon and evening ahead. Addie had taken over kitchen duty at the main lodge, the task of washing dishes a balm for her nervous hands, whispering prayers as she worked.

Caleb had flown straight back to Oregon last month to finish harvesting the vineyard. And she was alone again, awaiting news that the infusion was complete.

The doorbell rang, and she dried off her hands, rushing out to the family room. Addie glanced through the side window, expecting to see a delivery truck, but instead she saw Kirsten's familiar face. The professional attire of a teacher had been replaced by a sweatshirt and yoga pants and a messy pile of blonde on her head.

She flung open the door, and Kirsten embraced her. "I'm so glad to see you, Addie."

"I'm glad to see you too but—" Addie stepped back, worried. "Why are you here?"

"Thought you might need a friend today." She dropped her cell phone into her pocket. "Took the whole day off work."

Addie breathed deeply of the autumn air, calming her nerves. "Thank you."

"You want to get out of here?"

She eyed the worn path down to the willow tree, the footbridge across the creek that led to the forest and river. Then she reached for her sweatshirt hanging by the door. "Should we take a walk?"

Kirsten held up her keys. "How about ice cream?"

"Sounds good to me."

They drove into Chattanooga and ordered giant scoops of mint chocolate chip and fudge caramel. Then they crossed the Tennessee River on the pedestrian bridge, stopping in the middle to watch a sailboat.

"How is the church?" Addie asked, licking from her cone. The parishioners had been good to her, after they had recovered from their own shock, sending cards and emails and helping her secure the benefits from Peter's life insurance policy.

"We have an interim pastor now who has come out of retirement to help us get back on our feet."

"I'm glad."

"You should visit sometime."

"I don't know . . ."

"The women want to throw you a shower," Kirsten said. "After the baby is born."

"Really?"

"Of course. It will be the big event this winter." Kirsten pointed at Addie's cone. "You're going to have a giant mess if you don't eat faster."

Addie took a bite of the mint and chocolate. "That's awfully kind of them."

"They love you, Addie, and they hurt alongside you. Some of them understand what you are going through more than you know."

"I wouldn't wish it on anyone." When her baby moved, she took another lick.

Kirsten pointed at the golden band around Addie's finger. "Why are you still wearing your ring?"

"It doesn't feel right to remove it."

"Let me help you." Kirsten reached over and tugged it off. "What Peter did was wrong, to you and to all who trusted him. You cannot live the rest of your life bound to it."

Her mind flashed back to the hut in Oregon, the shrine on the wall to a woman who had both helped and harmed Louis Lange. Used him, it seemed, for her own gain. And still he'd been faithful to his promises.

She'd already thrown away almost all the wrongs that haunted her. Now she needed to throw away the last chain that bound her lest she get stuck circling for the rest of her life.

"God has big plans for you, Addie. You and your little one."

"I don't know what." Beyond helping Charlie, she had no plan. No possibilities for her own future.

"You wait and He'll show you the what," Kirsten said, opening up her palm.

Addie retrieved the ring. "I hope He will."

White-and-brown flashed in front of them, an osprey soaring by the bridge, returning to its nest on a platform built along the river's edge.

Kirsten nodded at the water far below them. "I think you should toss it."

"Seriously?" River rocks were one thing, but a gold ring?

"Forgive him, Addie. Remember the good, if possible, instead of the bad, but don't hang on."

She held up the ring, twisting it in the sunlight. It wasn't worth much in money but a fortune in memories. Or perhaps more like a debt. She thought she owed Peter in some strange way, that she was bound to his memory, but this was a shackle of her own making.

Addie tossed the ring up over the railing, caught it, and then she let it go, a hundred feet of falling before it disappeared.

Kirsten applauded. "You're free to dream again."

The void in her gut began to fill slowly. "Soon . . ."

"You're going to help kids, Addie, by sharing your life and your story. Kids who need a mom."

She shook her head. "They've already hired new directors at Sale Creek."

"Not in Tennessee," Kirsten said. "Although I will miss you terribly. Some place far from here. A place to start over."

Grace's Place.

The words flooded into her head, and she pushed them back out again. How was she supposed to help teenagers in Oregon? That was an impossibility.

"Your life isn't over," Kirsten said. "In fact, I think it just might be beginning. Charlie can run alongside you until he hands you the baton. Then it's your turn to run the next lap."

Addie covered her stomach with her hands. "I won't be running for at least four months."

"Perfect timing then."

Kirsten drove them back to Sale Creek and left her with a hug and a prayer for Charlie.

Emma phoned an hour later. "The transplant is finished."

"How is he?"

"Resting. He wanted me to tell you that no matter what happens, all is well with his heart and soul."

"I'm glad, Emma. When you talk to him again, please tell him that I love him."

"I will," she said. "We need more than one more good day this time. We need a hundred of them stacked up."

"A hundred more days then."

Multiply, she prayed as she returned to her work in the kitchen. In the multiplication, healing would be had.

CHAPTER FORTY-FOUR

January 2004

"He shouldn't come back to Oregon." Louis hacked away at a hydrangea bush even though he wasn't supposed to prune it until spring.

"Charlie is a good man," Caleb said, a plastic Target bag at his side. "Much different than the teenager who ran away."

"I don't believe it." Louis sat on the bench in the garden, shivering in the winter air. A New Year was upon them, but he wasn't one to make resolutions. Most of his life he'd spent following through with a resolution that he'd already made.

Except now he was no longer waiting for Ruby to return.

After Caleb had cleared out the vodka in his hut, banning Louis from even a sip of wine, the truth of what happened the night Ruby died finally chiseled itself back into his mind. That memory and many others had been restored to their proper place.

Some memories, ones from his childhood, he remembered with

clarity now while others, the hauntings he'd tried to drown with alcohol, had fallen into the background after many long nights, weeks even, with Caleb and his bottomless pitchers of grape juice.

Caleb called to his dog and Wallace ran to him. A glimpse—he saw it for just a moment—of how he'd been as a child, running like a hapless dog whenever Ruby called. He was always waiting, watching, listening for her voice.

When Caleb threw a stick, his dog rushed away. "How will you know about Charlie if you won't talk to him?"

But Charlie had been the one who'd mocked Louis long ago. Who'd hated him. Called Louis a loser.

Charlie wouldn't want to talk.

He looked out over the lake. So much was changing around him, he couldn't understand it all. Tara had stopped bringing him fudge soon after Pinky—Addie—left. Apparently her family was no longer needed to manage this property.

But Caleb was here almost every day with both food and company, and Jonathan visited over Thanksgiving when he was in town. The Lange boys hadn't forgotten him.

"Roland and Marguerite will arrive within the hour," Caleb said. "They want to see you."

"Why do they want to see me?" He remembered watching the Tonquin family as a child, wishing he could play with Marguerite and Charlie. Ruby never wanted him to play, and more than anything, he had wanted to please her, afraid that she would send him away.

Another memory crept into his brain, a vague one of Roland holding his hand as they boarded a ship, buying him a cherry soda in a place where everyone spoke a different language, taking him to a doctor when Louis was ill. And Grace, trying to help him with his schoolwork after Ruby died. He'd called her a mean name. Threw his pencil at her.

Caleb unknotted the ends of the plastic bag. "They said you're like family."

He batted those words away.

"Dinner's at six," Caleb said as if the deal was done. Then he handed Louis the bag.

Dinner would mean a bath. A shave. Stuff he didn't want to bother with, and yet . . .

Inside the bag were a new pair of trousers and a button-down shirt. Underwear and a pair of wool socks.

It had been years since he'd had new clothes.

"Six o'clock," Caleb repeated before he left. And Louis wandered back into the woods to tend the grave that was once overgrown.

He trimmed the grass with clippers, brought flowers from the garden even if Ruby didn't like them much. She would never return to Oregon, he knew that now, but she had cared well for him on her better days. Her motives for taking him in—he refused to question those. He had to look forward, not back, and Caleb promised that he wouldn't be doing it alone.

Family, that's what he had waiting for him across the garden. Family that had invited him to dine in Ruby's house.

Plastic crackled in his hand as he lifted the bag. A decent dinner wouldn't hurt him. Nor would a bath and fresh shave.

Perhaps he'd clean himself up and spend some time with Roland. He could ignore Charlie just fine.

Ruby he would admire for the rest of his life, but she'd no longer chain him here.

CHAPTER FORTY-FIVE

Twin pillars were mounted on each side of the airplane as it descended into Portland. Mount Hood pierced through a mantle of clouds on the left, the magma stewing deep inside its cinder cone. To their right was Mount St. Helens, a table-topped mountain with the height of its peak blown away by lava and smoke in 1980, the ash now resting in rivers and valleys across the Pacific Northwest.

Charlie had never imagined returning to Oregon, no reason for him to come back to the place where he'd almost drowned in his own shame. But they had flown in this morning, and now Adeline was driving him and Emma over the mountain pass and into the Chehalem Valley, past the train tracks where he'd almost taken his life. Soon they'd drive up Laurel Ridge so he could see his sister and Roland.

After all these years . . .

He never thought he would see his sister again.

The Hoult baby would come any day now, perhaps even before they left Oregon, but Adeline had been determined to accompany him and Emma on this trip. He'd never been able to stop her when her foot was down, ready to ford a new path, and he didn't want to stop her now.

God, it seemed, was giving him a little more time on this earth. He'd passed the hundred-day mark, and with every breath, he thanked God for the extra time with Emma and Adeline.

There was no guarantee of another day, but as long as his cells were being replenished, he would encourage the next generation to release the anger that stewed inside them in a healthy way. To acknowledge the wrongs—what had been done to them and what they had done to others—and then cast them all into a flood of living water that would carry them away.

Emma leaned forward from the back seat of their rental car, patting his shoulder. "Are you doing okay?"

"Haven't felt this good in years." While his body wasn't fully healed, the pain that once plagued his bones had subsided. And most of all, his heart was full.

Adeline drove them out of Newberg and into the hills where he and Kirk used to race like they were being pursued. In hindsight, he'd wanted to die on these roads. Penance for the lives he'd taken in France.

Perhaps Kirk had wanted the same thing.

Charlie had started the Sale Creek Home with young ladies like Marguerite in mind, thinking he would one day start a separate home for boys who'd once been like him and Kirk, but he'd realized early on that having both homes on the same property would brew a different kind of trouble. Yet as they drove through these hills, he saw the faces of the boys in that meadow, still vivid from his dream, getting ready to dive into the lake.

Perhaps it was still a possibility.

"Do you remember any of this?" Addie asked as they turned onto the lane that wove around Tonquin Lake.

"I'll never be able to forget this place."

"Caleb is excited to meet you."

Emma gently patted his shoulder again. Adeline understood in part why he was more nervous than excited, but Emma knew how complicated this day was for him. He'd already thrown his rocks into the river, but if all went well, it seemed God was giving a few of them back, polished into gems.

Adeline circled the lake so he could see it, past the foundation where the old farmhouse once stood, past the willow that he'd used as a refuge on those days he felt as if he might blow. Then she drove up the ridge to Ruby's castle.

More than fifty years had passed, but for a moment, he felt like that kid again who'd been scavenging on Ruby's floor, desperate for pills. Desperate to rid himself of the darkness, all the garbage, stuffed inside.

When Adeline stopped the car, he buttoned the tan overcoat he'd had for ages and dug in his pocket to make sure the five-dollar bill was still there.

Caleb Lange greeted him at the front door. He liked the fellow's strong handshake, the way he welcomed them inside, and how he smiled at Adeline as if she were a treasure. That's what he wanted for this woman who'd become like a daughter to him.

Emma held his hand when they entered the sitting room, all the furniture new. Roland stood first, embracing him in arms that once seemed to hold up an entire world, whispering an apology until Charlie stopped him. When Roland purchased the ticket to Chattanooga, he'd saved Charlie's life.

Roland hugged him again and gratefulness poured out of Charlie at the concern of this man who had desperately wanted to protect those he loved. Then Charlie dug into his pocket and removed the crumpled five-dollar bill that he'd kept for years.

"This is for you."

Roland looked down at the money, his face wavering between joy and something that looked like grief. "Keep your money, Charlie."

"I need to give it to you."

Still Roland didn't move.

"Please . . ."

Finally the man folded his fingers over the bill and swept it away, lifting a burden off Charlie's shoulders. A lifetime of shame vanishing with this seemingly small act.

Then he turned and saw a girl in a woman's body, wheeling up in a chair beside him. The eyes—curious and creative—he'd recognize them anywhere. Eyes that saw what others could not. Her braid was the same as she'd worn decades ago, the rest of her hair wrapped in a colorful scarf.

He'd drop to his knees beside her if he could, but someone pulled a chair out for him instead.

"Snowy?" he whispered.

"Blistering barnacles," Marguerite replied, laughter mixed with tears.

He reached for her hands. "I'm sorry." The only words he had.

She kissed his cheek. "You're a miserable wretch."

"I know—"

"What happened to Captain Haddock?" she asked.

"I tossed him overboard long ago."

"Maybe you could resurrect the good in him."

He smiled. "Blundering bazookas."

"Freshwater swabs," she said. "And you're not a miserable wretch anymore."

Could she see his color, a wellspring of golden light pouring out, all the love that he'd kept stored for her in his heart? This girl—a woman now—had inspired the direction of his life without even knowing it. God used the loss to renew his life.

He introduced Emma to his sister, and the two of them pooled the floor with their tears. How he loved them both. For this moment alone, he was glad for his extra hundred days of life.

Another man stepped forward. An athletic fellow in his middle years, warm brown eyes that seemed familiar.

"Thundering typhoons," the man said. "Ten thousand of them."

"Louis?" He didn't remember the boy quoting Captain Haddock, but perhaps he'd acquired a love for Tintin.

The man laughed with a shake of his head. "I'm Oliver."

Charlie's smile faded. It was the British name for his baby brother.

"Olivier," he whispered, knowing the truth even before the man acknowledged it with a nod. "You're not supposed to be—"

"A family near Gurs hid me for three years," he explained. "Mum found me after the war and then began to search for both of you."

Perhaps he should feel loss for the years gone between them, but all he felt was gain. His sister and brother, reunited with him in this life. Perhaps this was his vision in the meadow, the children playing together. God's original plan for the Dupont family before the enemy destroyed it.

Charlie studied his brother, remembering the newborn who rarely even stirred. "You were my donor."

"I've always been a bit out of sync in England," Oliver said, his hand on the back of Charlie's chair. "It was nice to finally be a match."

"Thank you—"

"Anything for my brother."

The word rolled over Charlie like a wave, the current pulling him back into this circle of family. They chatted together with Emma and Adeline and another girl, Caleb's sister, until Caleb announced that dinner was about to be served.

"They have a surprise for us," Marguerite whispered to him. "Wouldn't let any of us go into the dining room until you arrived."

"I'm glad to be here then."

An onslaught of memories accosted him as he followed Marguerite into the room, none that he wanted to relive. His sweet wife, holding his hand even now, would be appalled at what he had done.

She squeezed his hand, forging strength into him.

"Look at that," Marguerite whispered.

The mural had been finished, their arduous journey to the château and over the mountains and all the way to the weeping willow on Grace's land.

"It's beautiful," Adeline said.

Marguerite nodded. "Better than I could have done."

Caleb's sister, Reese, smiled. "I used the sketches you left behind."

"You captured the colors perfectly," Marguerite said. "Perhaps you could come to France one day. Spend some time with me."

He didn't need to have synesthesia to see the glow around Reese's head. Or the joy radiating in Adeline's smile. It was good for her to find these glimpses of happiness, good for the baby, good for the healing that still needed to take place after her baby was born.

On the table was a steaming bowl of beef stew and freshly made bread, seven of them gathered around to eat.

"Where's Louis?" he asked.

"I invited him to dinner." Caleb passed him a crock with salted butter. "But it seems that he had other plans."

Charlie understood why the man didn't want to come. No apology could reconcile all the history between them. He had to show Louis that he valued him as a man, a second brother.

He turned to his wife. "I need to visit Louis before we eat."

"In the dark?"

He nodded, an urgency growing inside him.

Caleb stood. "I'll go with you."

Emma began to stand, but he patted her hand. "Caleb and I will be fine."

"I want to go," Roland said, balancing himself on his cane.

But Caleb shook his head. "If he won't come back to the house with us, I'll take you to see him in the morning."

Charlie kissed his wife's cheek, buttoned up his old overcoat, and as the two men stepped outside, something dusted his hand, then his head.

Snow.

It whisked around them as they walked through the bedded flowers, the beam of Caleb's flashlight parting the flakes.

"Louis is not always well," Caleb said as they rounded the fountain.

"All of us who've lived through war carry a toll."

"Addie told me about Sale Creek," Caleb said as they neared the wall of pine trees. "I admire your work there."

"I think you might admire Adeline a little too."

Caleb stopped, the beam falling to their feet, shadows of snow circling it. "I didn't mean that."

"I know." Charlie clapped his shoulder. "But you are kind to her, and she needs kindness."

"Her heart is broken . . ."

"Peter broke it long before he died," Charlie said. "It's mending now."

Caleb lifted his flashlight again, the beam gliding over the hedge and bushes. And then it stopped on a blossom, pale-pink petals shimmering an opal white like the gates in his dream.

A winter rose.

Charlie stepped forward and brushed off the snow so the beauty, the strength, could thrive.

"I want to help her mend," Caleb said, "if she'll let me."

"Give it time."

Caleb nodded. "As much time as she needs."

"Who's there?" a voice called out from the trees.

Charlie glanced at Caleb before speaking. "Hello, Louis."

A man stepped out, dressed in black pants and a khaki-colored dress shirt, no coat to ward off the cold. Addie had told him about Louis's tangled beard, but the man's face was shaved, his long hair wet from the snow.

"We're getting ready to eat," Caleb said. "Thought you might have lost your way."

"Couldn't find my razor."

"Looks like you found it."

Louis didn't respond.

"You can come home with us now," Caleb continued. "There's plenty of food."

Louis eyed Charlie, and in the dim light, he could see the pain, the questions, that resided there. "That house is no place for me."

Caleb scanned the forest. "How long have you been out here?"

"An hour maybe. Or two."

Caleb took off his winter coat and draped it over Louis. The older man refused at first, but he didn't protest long.

Charlie swallowed hard before speaking. "I said some terrible things to you, Louis. A long time ago. Things that weren't true."

Louis shrugged his shoulders. "Water so far under the bridge there's no sense trying to draw it back up."

Caleb turned to Charlie. "Roland said you carried Louis through much of France."

Silence followed his words until a tuft of snow dropped from a pine bough, breaking the tension between them.

"That true?" Louis finally asked.

"Part of the way," Charlie said. "Others helped."

"Then Roland brought you here," Caleb continued. "But he never forgot you, Louis. He and Marguerite have a plan for you and this land."

"What sort of plan?" Louis asked.

"He'd like to tell you himself."

"Come with us," Charlie pleaded. "Up to the house."

Whether or not they discussed Roland's plan, they had to get Louis out of the snow.

Caleb pointed his flashlight beam back toward the forest's edge. "We have a hot bowl of stew waiting for you."

Louis ground his heel into the ground, then he stomped once on the mixture of snow and mud.

"What sort of plan?" he repeated.

"A refuge for boys," Caleb said. "Young men who need a home like you and Charlie did when you were kids."

Charlie smiled at this news. The boys in the meadow, he thought, who needed a family. He could see them here, swimming across the lake, building homes like he and Roland had once done. Boys like him and Kirk who'd needed to be redeemed.

Caleb continued talking to Louis. "Land for the boys to work and play and a permanent home for you, if you want it, in Ruby's house."

"I want to stay in my hut."

"Then a permanent home for you there."

Louis gave him a sharp nod, then buttoned Caleb's coat.

Charlie was in awe of it all—reuniting with the brother and sister he'd once thought lost, the possibilities—this dream—for the future, the joy in Adeline's heart, peace for Louis in his last years.

A glimmer of starlight slipped through the clouds as the three men trudged back through the garden. Snow had cloaked the rose again, but Charlie left the petals alone in their defiance of the cold.

The rose would survive the night, he had no doubt.

And it would grow again in the morning.

EPILOGUE

French Pyrénées
Nine years later

"I'm tired," Willow said, collapsing like spring rain into a puddle.

Addie nudged her. "Aunt Marguerite hiked this trail when she was nine."

"In a wheelchair?"

"Nope," Addie said. "But she carried a backpack."

"I can't do this on my own."

Addie took one of her hands, and Caleb reached for the other, lifting their daughter together like they'd done so often since they'd married, her laughter bridging the gap between them.

The smell of wild thyme swept in on the breeze, bolstering their climb up the stony shepherd's path. Agnès and Marguerite had driven them to the river yesterday where Roland's aunt had turned back long ago. They'd taken off their hiking boots and woolen socks and hopped stones across the cold water like the children before them. With the valley behind them, they began climbing in the sunshine, enjoying the beauty instead of worrying about what lay before—or behind—them.

Caleb winked at her, and she smiled back at the man who'd stolen her heart, helping her put all the pieces back together again. Seven years ago, Charlie had given Addie away by Tonquin Lake, Willow toddling up to her namesake tree with a bouquet of roses. At the water's edge, Caleb had promised to love both of them, cherish her and her daughter alike, for a lifetime.

Addie had given him her heart that day, and he'd cared well for it.

Not long after Charlie moved back to Oregon, the Tonquin and Lange families partnered together to start Charlie's Place, financed in part by churches across Oregon and one small church in Tennessee. Charlie had balked at the name, wanting to honor Grace instead, but he had no choice in the matter. Roland stepped in to manage the property, and he and Marguerite, along with Emma, decided that the boys at Tonquin Lake would be inspired most by Charlie's story.

A few months after Roland turned one hundred, he left the world to be with his Savior and his bride. Then Charlie followed him home last month.

What the families had started together was miraculous. Boys in their early teens came from troubled places across the Pacific Northwest. The ones with the hardest stories ended up chopping wood with Louis, learning how to overcome, and many had left the farm as men ready to conquer their world for good.

"Please, Daddy," Willow begged as they crested another ridge, her arms outstretched, blue eyes blinking as if she might cry.

Caleb leaned down and she hopped on his back for a ride.

Willow didn't remember the wedding by Tonquin Lake. All she'd known in her collection of memories was Caleb as her dad.

On their left was a stone cliff, and Marguerite had given precise instructions to circle around the back if they wanted to see the cave where she and Charlie hid.

They peeked solemnly into the cave opening, and Addie could almost feel the cold, the fear, for all who'd stopped here.

"I miss Papa C," Willow said as they turned back to the path.

"I miss him too."

They spent the night at a farmhouse not far from the trail—Agnès had arranged it all for them—and in the morning, after a hearty breakfast, they continued their climb.

Roland had been buried beside Grace in the village cemetery, but Charlie hadn't wanted a tombstone. He'd wanted his ashes to be carried away in the wind, at the place where he'd first found freedom. Emma asked them to scatter his ashes on the border between Spain and France.

When they were finished, they would return to Oregon with Marguerite. She and Emma had it all planned, with a little help from Reese. The older women would live out their years together on the hill. Painting and praying and grandmothering the boys who lived in A-frame homes around the lake.

A church bell rang out as they reached the summit, from the Spanish or French side, she didn't know. But this was the way of Charlie. The way of Marguerite and Grace. The way of all who'd crossed here in search of freedom.

Willow sat on a flat boulder, overlooking a valley in Spain, and Caleb slipped his arm around Addie as she opened the simple urn that Marguerite had painted gold.

Then she lifted it to the breeze.

Willow. Wind.

"Well done," Addie whispered.

Charlie wasn't in the ash that blew into Spain—he was in a world beyond borders—but his memory would linger, stirring in their hearts, multiplying through every girl and boy who heard his story.

The hope would scatter, she prayed, like the seeds of a willow, rooting itself in the damp soil. Bowing and bending in strength as it grew.

Bent but not broken.

MONTSÉGUR, FRANCE
SPRING 1940

Secret keepers—that was what Hanna Tillich called the sect of Cathars who once hid in this cavern. And she respected anyone who could keep a secret, especially one this big, to their death.

A breeze drummed against the rock walls, whispering stories from this old passage. Secrets that Hanna was determined to find.

If only she could decipher the cadence of the wind.

While her fellow archaeologists worked to excavate the cave's front room, she'd stolen back into this tunnel. Candlelight flickered across the wall, illuminating the charcoal etchings of three shields, each one marked by a rust-colored symbol that looked like an Iron Cross, the carvings well-preserved in the darkness of this grotto.

Hanna shivered in spite of the fur-lined jacket issued to her by Heinrich Himmler, the trowel in her other hand clanging against the metal lantern. Hundreds of Cathars had gathered in the ruined castle above this cavern in the thirteenth century, most of them killed by Catholic crusaders for refusing to renounce their faith.

Had some of the members been murdered inside this cave? Perhaps they'd left these symbols behind as a warning. Or a clue as to where they'd hidden their secrets.

She studied the crosses on the shields, so like the cross that had decorated her father's military coat when he fought against France. Like the cross the Führer awarded men today who were fighting for the *Vaterland*.

Hanna wasn't fighting, but her service for Germany, Reichsführer Himmler had said, was just as important as their soldiers. He'd hand-selected her and each archaeologist in his Ahnenerbe team to unearth evidence that would prove to the entire world that the German people had descended from the Aryan Nordic race. The Noble Ones.

But her team of archaeologists had traveled to Montségur for another reason. Seven hundred years had passed since the massacre here, but no one had discovered where the Cathars had hidden the Emerald Cup—the Holy Grail—that once pressed against Christ's lips at the Last Supper, later collecting drops of His blood. Three years ago, German explorer Otto Rahn had stolen secretly into this region and climbed the treacherous cliff up to this cavern, convinced that the Cathars had buried the jeweled cup in one of its passages.

Rahn had been the only German, to Hanna's knowledge, to ever excavate this cave, but no one knew exactly what he found. Rahn had died last year, taking yet another secret to the grave.

As strong as Himmler's drive was to unearth the Aryan roots of Germany, the man was also obsessed with finding this Holy Grail. A Christian artifact with mystical powers, he said, that could win the current war.

Hanna didn't obsess over power like Himmler and the Nazi leadership. Stories were her lifeblood, especially those from the past that could root a generation struggling to find its identity. After the devastation—the humiliation—of losing the *Weltkrieg* in 1918, the German people were desperate to pour a new foundation.

In the past months, Germany had finally begun to overcome the defeat of this World War by expanding their *Lebensraum*—living space—into France. Now Himmler had commissioned Hanna's team to find the Grail. They could search this entire region without government interference.

He'd promised to keep the Holy Grail safe under the mantle of the home forces and his SS officers so it wouldn't be destroyed like so many of the artifacts of Germanic roots, just like he'd promised to protect every German who'd rooted themselves in a Christian heritage. Their team still needed to keep the work quiet, though, as many who lived along the Pyrenees weren't fond of the new government or its interest in holy relics.

Another light bridged the chain of shields, and Hanna swiveled in her military boots, almost stabbing her superior, Kolman Strauss, with her trowel.

He knocked the blade away swiftly with the handle of his tripod as if it were a sword. She'd learned plenty in her four years at the University of Berlin, but fencing was not a required class for her studies in anthropology.

"These were carved by the Knights Templar," Kolman said, his easy smile excusing her ineptness.

She picked her trowel off the dirt floor and turned back to examine the sharp lines of each shield beside him. "One of the many mysteries in this place."

"She'll share her secrets with us."

The Brylcreem in Kolman's hair defied even the temperament of the wind, and his Aryan blue eyes had secured him a lifelong membership as regiment leader in Himmler's *Schutzstaffel.* His gray sleeves were rolled up to his elbows as if he were warm inside this frigid cavern, ready to capture on motion-picture film whatever this medieval religious sect had left behind.

Some historians thought the Knights Templar had collaborated with the Cathars to guard the holiest relics, but these etchings might not be artwork from the Cathars or Templars. It was quite possible that others, like Rahn and Hanna's team, had scaled the mountainside in recent years to seek treasure or simply to commemorate the six hundred thousand Cathars who'd been massacred during the Crusades.

"Kill them all for the Lord knows them that are His."

That's what the abbot supposedly said to validate the bloodshed of Cathars and Catholics alike in 1209. Let God sort it out in the end.

How exactly, she wondered, did God sort those who'd vowed to serve Him?

Despite Kolman's confidence about finding the Grail, the contents of this cavern were a mystery to all of them, shrouded in centuries of legend and literature. No amount of threatening or even coaxing would force her to give up her secrets if she wasn't willing to share.

But Hanna and Kolman and two other archaeologists could work here for days or weeks if necessary, however long it took to unearth any artifacts left by the Cathars. They would spend their nights at a vineyard, and each morning, they'd use ropes and the mountain's footholds to bring their gear up into the cavern while German soldiers guarded the cliffside entrance and waited in the surrounding forest below, in case the local residents decided to rebel.

Hanna prayed no one would threaten them or the soldiers. It would be senseless for any more blood to be shed here while she and her team were trying to protect the holy relics from harm.

She pointed with her lantern toward the narrow corridor. "I'm going farther in."

The feet on Kolman's tripod punctured the ground. "I'll retrieve my camera."

He had hauled his motion-picture camera up to this cavern with all of their supplies, just like he'd taken his camera with them to film their work across the continents, but she didn't want the camera peering over her shoulder this morning. The flood of Kolman's lights. He had plenty of earlier film to prove her worth, but if she didn't find anything today, all Himmler would see when they returned home was her failure.

"No," she insisted. "This is something I want to do alone."

A defiant strand of straw-blonde hair escaped from its prison of pins, and she set her lantern and trowel on the ground to remove a glove and return the strand to its messy chignon.

As her superior, Kolman could insist on accompanying her, but he stepped back. "You're a brave soul, Hanna."

"More curious than brave, I'm afraid."

"Both are important to the Ahnenerbe. It's unfortunate you're not a . . ." He stopped himself, but the unspoken word still dangled between them.

A man.

It truly was unfortunate. The few professional women in Germany were slowly being reassigned to other jobs. Hanna was the only female archaeologist still working in the field, but she suspected that would not last much longer. Himmler had recently moved the department of the Ahnenerbe under the umbrella of the powerful Schutzstaffel. As a woman, she would never qualify to become an SS officer.

But if the Holy Grail was hidden in this cave, if Hanna was the one to excavate it, surely Himmler would keep her employed. More than anything, she wanted to continue her work of preserving the history, the stories, of her people before their heritage was completely lost, but if she didn't prove her worth, her dedication, Himmler would reassign her to type, file, and transfer reports for one of his men.

"If I find it," she assured Kolman, "then I'll bury it again so you can film our discovery."

His sharp nod was one of respect for a colleague who was equally as focused on this task. "We're going to find it."

The other archaeologists had stopped in the front room to dig under a stalagmite, a fixture that French literature had deemed the Altar. A worthy location for a religious sect to bury their relics or bones, but it was too close to the entrance, she thought, for a powerful treasure like the Holy Grail. If the Cathars were willing to die for their secrets, they'd have taken great care about where they buried them.

Another gust shuddered through the entrance, loosened hair from her knot, and the strands folded themselves over her eyes, blinding her from the light. Kolman brushed the hair away from her eyes, and her skin flickered at his touch. Had he felt it too, the spark that passed between them?

"Hanna—"

"We have to find this cup," she said, hoping to dampen the flicker.

He smiled again. "I know."

"We can't lose our focus now."

He wrapped the hair over her ear, the flame sparking again.

Her first—her only—love now was digging for artifacts. She had to extinguish these schoolgirl notions before she made another choice she'd regret.

The trail of lamplight led her away from Kolman, into the unknown. A place where she thrived. She followed the wind and light through the narrow entrance, into a chamber with a ceiling that soared far beyond the range of her lantern. Like the nave of Lorenzkirche back home, the church she'd attended with Luisa each Sunday.

How she missed Luisa, her cousin who'd come to live with Hanna's family after she lost both parents in an accident. Only a few years older than Hanna, her cousin had become a tutor, sister, and friend, teaching her to search for answers to questions others didn't even know to ask.

Hanna smoothed her gloved hand over the ridges on the limestone wall, trekking over the hard-packed dirt embedded with stones, into an underground cathedral. Here the air was still and damp on her skin, the smell musty like the attic where she'd once played. Like the old graphite mine on her family's property.

The Cathars wouldn't have buried their treasure in a grand chamber like this, but they might have hidden it nearby.

The cave's ridges bowed into alcoves and tiny rooms notched into the sides. Cupboards, she thought, as she stepped into one. Or a cellar.

Hanna dropped her rucksack along a wall and then crawled with her lantern and steel trowel into a jug-sized room that spilled into an even smaller chamber. Lantern light danced across shells embedded in the walls and then something else—

The faintest sketching on *dem Stein*, a line—two lines—drawn in a white ochre faded with time, parallel in their fall to the ground.

She followed the stripes down to her knees and at the bottom of the wall was a triangular tip, stained a faint red like the Iron Crosses. A lance. Or a blood-tipped arrow.

Hanna swept her trowel across the surface as if it were a brush before edging out a neat square with the blade. This was what she lived for. The possibility of finding answers if only she chose the right place. Digging deep enough to locate whatever her team was searching for.

The utmost care was necessary when excavating, but she worked swiftly this morning, her heart pounding as she shaved away the dirt. When they were looking for remnants of Atlantis, the archaeologists used sifters so they wouldn't miss the smallest pieces that hinted toward the greater story. Here, though, they weren't looking for the pieces. Himmler wanted the entire cup. Intact. As if it were a white rabbit to pull out of their magician's hat.

He wanted the impossible really, but it was her job to either deliver it or produce enough evidence to continue their search.

Since receiving her degree in Berlin, Hanna had been trekking across Sweden and Tibet with the Ahnenerbe to discover where the Aryan people had originated and how Himmler could replicate their strength today. Power and proof of the Germanic heritage—the two things that Himmler seemed to crave more than anything.

They hadn't found conclusive evidence about Aryans in Tibet or Sweden, but they'd found dozens of shards in Sweden that pointed to an advanced civilization. Whatever Kolman reported back seemed to satisfy the Reichsführer.

In the light of a new candle, Hanna started to dig, willing the dirt to reveal its secrets. Square by square, meter by meter, she would search this room until she found either the cup or another clue.

An hour passed as she carved through the pressed soil, finding fragments of bone and pottery. Her trowel hit a stone, and she pushed her way around it, the rounded edges of this rock reminding her of home. The stones in the nearby labyrinth where her mother used to pray.

The steel blade clanked against something, and her heart lurched as the candlelight caught a glimmer of green.

She removed her pocketknife and had just begun to ease away the dirt when she heard Kolman's voice, shouting her name from another room.

Quickly she dumped the dirt back into the hole, smoothing it over, and then turned, lantern in hand, to crawl back into the chamber.

She wanted to film her discovery and then carry the treasured cup out in triumph so the entire team could see what she'd found hidden. So word would trickle back that Hanna Tillich had discovered this holy relic on her own.

If Kolman found it, he and his camera would take full credit.

Tossing her trowel beside her rucksack, she rushed back toward the cathedral chamber, the shadows from her lantern rocking across the walls.

"What is it?" she asked when she reemerged in the main hall.

Kolman grasped her wrist. "We have to leave."

"But—"

"Now," he said, his rank as an officer punctuating this word.

She shook off his hand. "I'll gather my things."

"We don't have time."

But her pocketknife and trowel, her pack with its notebook and pencils and extra candles were inside. She couldn't just leave them all behind.

"Time for wh—?"

A distant thunder echoed through the grotto, and she stared at the arc of light leading to the entrance, confused. The skies had been clear when they climbed to the cave.

"Someone doesn't want us in France." He was pulling her now into the passage, away from her things.

"I need my pack." And a glimpse at whatever was buried in the dirt.

"The others have already started down." It was his job to guide their team in and then out of this cave safely, but surely she had time to fetch her rucksack.

The sound of another explosion placed her firmly on Kolman's side.

She clipped into the mountainside hold before rappelling back into the forest.

In the morning, she'd retrieve her pack, after the soldiers had calmed this storm.

A NOTE FROM THE AUTHOR

This story stirred inside me as I rode the tumultuous wave of 2020. Then it poured out near the end of the year as a prayer of sorts, a deep desire for the balm of God's redemption in our broken world.

The courageous work of American and British Quakers in France was particularly inspiring to me in this season, including those staff members who were interned in Germany for helping Jewish children. The American Friends Service Committee and British Friends Service Council accepted the 1947 Nobel Peace Prize on behalf of Quakers worldwide in their effort to relieve suffering and bring peace between nations, loving their neighbors in a country ripped apart by war. Tens of thousands were fed through their work, and the AFSC helped create a child immigration bill in 1939 to bring twenty thousand refugee children into the United States. After that bill failed in Congress, according to Edward Stourton in *Cruel Crossing*, the AFSC staff secretly transported around eight hundred Jewish children out of France.

Herbert Hoover, a devout Quaker, spent part of his childhood in Newberg, Oregon, with his uncle and aunt who founded Friends Pacific Academy, the predecessor to George Fox University. After World War I, Hoover headed the American Relief Administration to aid starving children across Europe and made funding available for the AFSC to assist with this relief. Quakers continued their work in France through the 1950s, supporting more than twenty thousand refugees during and after the war.

The Winter Rose is not meant to be a reflection of modern-day Quakerism but a historical account of one woman who devoted her life to Christ and caring for His children. It is also a tribute to the men and women who sacrificed their lives to transport kids of all ages over the treacherous Pyrénées.

War destroys families, and as I researched the lives of refugee children who had been rescued during World War II, I discovered how their years in France, the loss of their family, affected each one profoundly. Some survivors began remembering the details in their later years, often after losing someone they loved. Some were able to find a measure of peace as they shared their experiences while others never talked about the war, the silent trauma of their memories often wounding both body and mind.

Denise Siekierski-Caraco, code-named Colibri, was a Jewish teenager who guided French refugees across the Spanish and Swiss borders. For forty years, she remained quiet about her work and story. "It was a much too difficult period, too painful," she later recounted, "and if after the war we had continued talking about it, I would not have been capable of going on with life or have the will to build something, to do something. . . . I would have continued to think about this all the time."

No one who has lived through a war remains untouched, but how does one find hope—redemption—after such a horrific experience? That is the question that drove me to write this book.

I am extremely grateful for the partnership of people from different faith backgrounds who contributed to this story. While I tried to be as accurate as possible with dates and major historical events, I changed some minor details to avoid confusion. For example, I used the recognized English versions of Tintin phrases and characters like Snowy, who is named Milou ("half-wolf") in French editions.

Thank you to the entire team at Tyndale House, including my editors, Stephanie Broene and Kathryn Olson, and my agent, Natasha Kern, for championing my work. I am blessed to partner with each of you and grateful for all your wisdom in helping me polish and share this novel.

To my brilliant critique partner Sandra Byrd, my dear friend and reader Michele Heath, and my personal Inklings: Dawn Shipman, Nicole Miller, Ann Menke, Tracie Heskett, and Julie Zanders. I am continually amazed by each of your talent and unique insight. My stories grow stronger each time you help me catch both big and little things.

Typically I travel to my main setting and hear stories in person, but COVID-19 put a damper on traveling and interviewing alike. The challenges of this year made me even more appreciative for all those who helped me virtually. A special thank-you to . . .

Don Davis at the AFSC Archives in Philadelphia for all of your support and reference information and permission to use the poem written by the refugee children of Gurs. Catriona Troth for your research and direction about Les Secours Quakers. Dr. Ronald Friend (Rene Freund) who spent several hours via Zoom sharing his remarkable story as a Jewish toddler rescued from a French camp by Mary Elmes, an Irishwoman employed by the AFSC before World War II and then the newly renamed Les Secours Quakers. Remarkably, his brother and mother also survived the war. Thank you, Dr. Friend, for gifting me with your story!

Tosha Williams, who dreamed about this story with me alongside a golden leaf–trimmed river in Oregon, for encouraging me to write about patina—the beauty of nicks and gashes that come with age—and *brocante*, the French concept of salvaging items that someone else trashed. Restoring and repurposing them, often in their brokenness, for a new life.

Carol Steen, a world-renowned artist, lecturer, writer, and both president and cofounder of the American Synesthesia Association. She opened my eyes to the wonder and variety of synesthesia and the many synesthete artists who see emotions, words, numbers, or music in patterns and color.

My local reference librarian, Adam Lewkowsky, who was able to secure a trove of historical resources in this trying year, and Julie Powers, the senior director of patient advocacy for the Aplastic Anemia and MDS International Foundation, for educating me on the history of MDS, the intricacies of a bone marrow transplant, and the recovery process. My aunt Janet died in 2018 from myelodysplastic syndrome that transitioned into acute myeloid leukemia, too late to find an HLA match. The availability of bone marrow transplants for seventy-year-old patients didn't become common until recently, so I had to change a few details about the treatment in 2003 for the sake of story. But this journey with my aunt makes me even more grateful for people like Ms. Powers who are educating and advocating for those diagnosed with MDS.

Those who serve at 5Rock Ranch and Camp Tilikum in Yamhill County: You are a blessing to me and the many who've found solace on your beautiful grounds.

Look up Château de Gudanes for the inspiration behind Roland's château. I think you'll lose yourself, as I did, in this old soul of a place. You can find more stories, links, and photos that influenced *The Winter Rose* at melaniedobson.com. As with all of my research, any errors are my fault.

Thank you to all those who held up my arms behind the scenes: My parents, Jim and Lyn Beroth, for your consistent love and prayer. My husband, Jon Dobson, who loves our family well and keeps me grounded on the most challenging of days while dreaming big when we feel called to step a new direction. My two courageous daughters, Karlyn and Kiki, who are growing into beautiful, thoughtful women. It delights my heart to see the joy and creativity you have embraced during what seemed impossible this year. Grateful for the peace that passes all understanding!

To our Lord, three in one, who creates, redeems, and promises eternal life for those who trust in Him. Any honor I lay right at Your feet.

DISCUSSION QUESTIONS

1. A winter rose blooms in the Pyrénées when the children near Spain and then again at the end of the story when Charlie comes home. What is the significance of this flower?

2. When Grace and the children finally reach safety, she reflects on the fact that all they have been through will shape the children for the rest of their lives. In what ways do we see these experiences shaping Charlie, Louis, and Marguerite? What childhood experiences—good or bad—have shaped your life?

3. In spite of Grace's desire to rescue children, she isn't able to save Louis or Charlie from the wounds of their past. Is there anything else she could have done as a foster parent and friend to love them more? What, if anything, would you have done?

4. Marguerite's gift of synesthesia gives her the ability to see emotion in color. How has God uniquely gifted you and how do you use this gift for His glory?

5. When Charlie is young, Grace praises him for his courage and his desire to fight injustice. Discuss Charlie's path from his difficult teen years to the maturity of adulthood. Why do you think he takes this detour before settling into a life of love

and service? If you are familiar with King David's story in the Bible, how would you compare and contrast his journey with Charlie's?

6. For much of her life, Grace clings to David's words in Psalm 27. Do you have a specific Bible passage or other writing that helps direct your path?

7. What is the significance of Addie throwing the rocks and later her wedding band into the water? Have you ever had to release a burden that you weren't meant to bear?

8. As a Quaker, Grace actively seeks God's peace in simplicity and quiet spaces. "Shekinah for her soul," she calls it. Do you have a quiet place where you can still your heart and listen?

9. Grace never realizes in her lifetime the results of her prayers for Charlie. How do you balance heartache and hope in your life?

10. From Caleb's furniture refinishing to Roland's renovations on the abandoned château, restoration is a key theme in *The Winter Rose*. While Charlie receives forgiveness in his younger years for what he did to the Tonquin family, he is given the opportunity much later in life for personal restoration. Do you have a story of redemption or restoration? Or is there a relationship that you still hope to restore?

ABOUT THE AUTHOR

Melanie Dobson is the award-winning author of more than twenty historical romance, suspense, and time-slip novels. Five of her novels have won Carol Awards; *Catching the Wind* and *Memories of Glass* were nominated for a Christy Award in the historical fiction category; and *Catching the Wind* won an Audie Award in the inspirational fiction category. *The Black Cloister*, her novel about a religious cult, won the *Foreword* magazine Religious Fiction Book of the Year.

Melanie is the previous corporate publicity manager at Focus on the Family, owner of the publicity firm Dobson Media Group, and a former adjunct professor at George Fox University. When she isn't writing, Melanie enjoys teaching a variety of workshops.

Melanie and her husband, Jon, have two daughters. After moving numerous times with work, the Dobson family has settled near Portland, Oregon, and they love to hike and camp in the mountains of the Pacific Northwest and along the Pacific Coast. Melanie also enjoys exploring ghost towns and abandoned homes, helping care for kids in her community, and creating stories with her girls.

Visit Melanie online at melaniedobson.com.

Connect with Melanie online at

MELANIEDOBSON.COM

OR FOLLOW HER ON

 facebook.com/MelanieDobsonFiction

 melbdobson

 @MelBDobson

CP1743

By purchasing this book from Tyndale, you have helped us meet the spiritual and physical needs of people all around the world.